BETTER THAN THIS

A NINE MINUTES SPIN-OFF NOVEL

BETH FLYNN

Better Than This

Edited by Amy Donnelly and Cheryl Desmidt

Cover Design by Jay Aheer at Simply Defined Art

Farmhouse Cover Photo by Scott Dry, Jr. @sadjrphotography on Instagram

Farmhouse Photo used with the permission of Carolyn West

Interior Formatting by Amy Donnelly at www.alchemyandwords.com

Proofreading by Judy Zweifel at Judy's Proofreading

ISBN: 9781078307062

Imprint: Independently Published

Better Than This is the third spin-off novel from The Nine Minutes Trilogy and can be read as a standalone. However, if you'd like to familiarize yourself with the rest of my books, I suggest you read them in the following order:

Nine Minutes
(Book One in the Nine Minutes Trilogy)
Out of Time
(Book Two in the Nine Minutes Trilogy)
A Gift of Time
(Book Three in the Nine Minutes Trilogy)
The Iron Tiara
(A Nine Minutes Spin-Off Novel)
Tethered Souls
(A Nine Minutes Spin-Off Novel)

Thank you for your support and readership!

For all my readers who are currently living in or approaching the fourth quarter. Newsflash: Your best is yet to come!

PROLOGUE

E veryone knows life can change in the blink of an eye, but what they don't know is if it will change for the better...or worse. A devastating car crash resulting from a blown tire. A winning lottery ticket bought with your last buck. A backyard pool without a childproof gate. Faulty house wiring that causes a fire erasing every tangible memory of your existence. Or in my case, catching my younger sister in bed with the man I'd given the best of my yesterdays and had promised all my tomorrows. All unforeseen circumstances we don't have control over. Or do we? Did the car owner know he had bald tires and drove on them anyway? Did they know the risk when they hired an unlicensed electrician to save a couple hundred dollars? Did I ignore the obvious signs that my marriage was deteriorating? Or did I see them and choose to pretend they didn't exist? So again, I ask, were these unforeseen circumstances? Or choices?

My story is as cliché as they come, and my experience couldn't add anything different or special to marriages across the world. Safe marriages, routine marriages, comfortable marriages. Even happy marriages.

I gave Richard what I believed were the best years of my life, accepting a childless union with the man who I thought could give me everything except children. It's not that Richard didn't want kids. It was that he couldn't have them. I knew that when we married, and it didn't matter. We were happy. At least I thought we were. Looking back now, I can see that it was an illusion we worked hard to create. We both needed something perfect to make up for our flawed and imperfect pasts. Doesn't everybody do that? Toward the end, we'd become nothing more than roommates. Talk about banal, right? Good friends who shared the morning paper over coffee and croissants and made it a point to play tennis at least two evenings a week. We shared household responsibilities, the remote, and little else. It was a business relationship, not a marriage. Our home, our routines, our lives were as sterile as his testicles.

Richard wasn't a bad guy. Unless you count sleeping with my sister as bad. It's strange how I've managed to forgive him. Once I forged through the grief, I was able to look back with more clarity. Richard had brought neatness and order to my life I thought I needed. And it worked. But only for a while. We knew something was missing and we both ignored it. Until she showed up.

My baby sister, Frenita, who at seventeen decided to call herself Fancy after the Reba McEntire song, had been down on her luck and asked to stay with Richard and me until she got back on her feet. Down on her luck, meaning her man of the hour, month, or year had dumped her. Fancy never worked a day in her life. She was a professional mistress who targeted men of financial means. At fifty-two years old, I considered myself an intelligent and savvy woman and never in a million years would've believed she'd target my husband. But she did. In the end, I'd wanted nothing more to do with her, but because she was my only living relative, I wouldn't allow myself to lash out. She was still my little sister, so I settled for distancing myself in place of vengeance.

Instead of staying in Greenville, South Carolina, and living with daily reminders of their betrayal, I went home. Pumpkin Rest was three hours away, where our elderly grandparents raised Fancy and me. A sleepy little hamlet in the northern end of South Carolina with one intersection and very few residents, it was a place where I wasn't reminded of the geometrically faultless straight lines of our luxury condominium in Greenville. Pumpkin Rest didn't have condos, car washes, cafés, or state-funded pristine parks. It couldn't boast of organic grocery stores, gyms, or fast food restaurants. The one intersection affectionately referred to as the crossroads, housed a small grocery store, gas station, diner, and pharmacy now turned hardware store.

I hadn't realized how much I'd missed it until I sought refuge in its quiet splendor. As badly as I'd wanted to escape the dusty and lonely roads of my youth, I'd never felt more alive than when I stepped on the porch of my childhood home for the first time in too many years to count. After not being able to keep up with the mortgage, the couple who'd purchased it after my grandmother's death eventually forfeited it to the bank. It remained abandoned and neglected until I bought it last year.

I glanced down at my hands. The age spots there were even more evident since I'd been working in my yard and kept forgetting to wear gloves. That wasn't entirely honest. I'd made a deliberate choice—there's that word again—not to wear gloves. I'd missed the feel of the rich, dark earth between my fingers and under my nails. Memories of Richard's soft and perfectly manicured hands dragged themselves up from the recesses of my brain. Hands that didn't like to get dirty. Hands that belonged to a man who insisted we buy a condominium so he wouldn't have to bother caring for a lawn or paying someone to care for a yard he didn't need.

I tossed a weed into the bucket beside me and stood up. After removing my floppy hat, I swiped my arm across my brow. It was a scorcher, and my back had started bothering me. I glanced over at the front porch and saw the dip in the roofline where a beam sagged. A gutter perilously dangled by a thread thanks to the previous night's rainfall. I cocked my head to the side and glanced at the siding that was so worn, the original wood peeked out at me like a forgotten friend. *It'll all get fixed in good time,* I told myself as I stretched while enjoying the melodic sounds of nature.

Other than my childhood best friend, Darlene, that's what I'd missed the most about Pumpkin Rest. The lack of human noise. The town was devoid of traffic, sirens, stores that blared music, and people talking loudly on their cell phones. I'd picked the perfect place to heal, to regroup, to rethink my life and my future. I was experiencing the epitome of contentment and couldn't fathom anything that could disrupt my retreat from the rat race.

I was about to resume my yard work when I stopped and looked around. I'd heard what I thought was a lawnmower. Impossible. Other than the Pritchard farm at the end of my dirt road, I had no neighbors. And the last of the Pritchards had died off, leaving no heirs. That wasn't entirely true. Two brothers were the rightful owners. The oldest, Kenny Pritchard, went to prison the same year their father died, leaving the youngest brother, Jonathan, a legal ward of the state. Kenny was killed years later in a prison fight, and the developmentally challenged Jonathan wasn't in a position to claim his property, leaving no one who wanted to assume responsibility for a dilapidated old farmhouse. I took a deep breath and shoved aside the grief that still rose in my chest when I let myself think about the Pritchard family. I'd considered buying the property to guarantee my solitude but saw no need as nobody in their right mind would want to live out there. The sound was getting louder when I realized that lawnmowers didn't rumble.

I turned around and watched as a motorcycle slowly made its way toward me. He must've missed or ignored the Private Road and Dead End signs. I walked to the edge of my yard to warn the solitary rider that the road didn't go through and that he should probably turn around in my gravel driveway. As he effortlessly glided past the front of my house, spewing dust behind him, I eyed his muscular and heavily tattooed arms. He was wearing a black do-rag on his head, and the sun bounced off an earring in his right ear. Dark glasses hid his eyes as he gave me a curt nod with a chin that boasted a neatly trimmed beard.

I raised my arm to motion him to stop when I saw his gas tank. My eyes widened as I recognized the image emblazoned there. That's not a…? Why yes, I think it is! *What a disgusting pig* I mouthed. It was obvious he'd caught me because I saw a hint of a smile before he continued his way down the road to nowhere.

"So, my disgust amuses you?" I said out loud as I watched his back, a thick braid swaying between his shoulder blades. I snorted and squatted to resume my gardening. I'll show him. When he finds out there's nothing at the end of the road except for a run-down farmhouse and neglected fields, he'll have to turn around. And when he does, I won't even bother looking up when he passes by. I smugly returned to my yard, concentrating on a patch that I intended to clear so I could plant vegetables.

After twenty minutes I had to use the bathroom and busted a move getting in and out of the house in two minutes. I didn't want to miss my chance to ignore him. The thought made me laugh at myself, and I returned to my weed pulling. Another twenty minutes passed, and I started to wonder if I'd missed him. I couldn't have because I'd watched from the bathroom window.

Two hours later (I know this because I kept checking my watch), I was forced inside by an afternoon rain shower, but I carefully kept an eye on the front of the house. I fell into bed that night exhausted and convinced myself that I'd somehow missed his return from the Pritchard farm. I didn't know if it was from the yard work under the relentless sun or my constant but obviously ineffective vigil that caused me to collapse into bed utterly spent. My last conscious thought before falling into a deep and dreamless sleep was, *what kind of man has a vulgar display of female genitalia painted on his motorcycle?*

CHAPTER 1

HE'S NOT MY BIKER

"A black do-rag and an X-rated gas tank? I'm impressed that you even know what a do-rag is, Barbie."

"Will you stop it, Darlene?" Ignoring my best friend's smirk, I added, "I saw my share of bloody do-rags in the ER. I can't believe our state doesn't enforce a motorcycle helmet law."

I was at Pumpkin Rest's only gas station inquiring about the previous day's mystery motorcycle rider. Darlene shook her head and replied in her smooth Southern drawl, "Nobody like that comes to mind. At least not while I've been on duty." She followed up with a feigned dreamy look and said, "I'd be hard-pressed not to remember a hottie like that passing through these parts."

Darlene's favorite country songs from the sixties and seventies floated through the speakers of the antiquated stereo system that was perched on a shelf behind her. We were being serenaded by Tammy Wynette who was telling us to "stand by your man."

I rolled my eyes at Darlene's comment and the song lyrics before saying, "I never said he was a hottie, Dar."

"You didn't have to," she laughed. "Perhaps he found his way off the Pritchard farm through some of the back roads."

The Pritchards had been notorious bootleggers and there were secret trails leading away from their property. It was possible, but not likely, that the biker had found one of those paths. However, if by some remote chance he had, he would've come out on the other side of their farm in a different county.

I shook my head in disagreement and stepped to the side while Mr. Shook came in to buy his daily newspaper and chewing tobacco. I watched as Darlene treated him like he was the most important human being on the planet. A wave of guilt blanketed me as I thought about all the years I'd lost with Darlene. We'd been best friends from the time I was thirteen right up until the day I left for college. Once I stepped over the threshold of my dorm room, I never looked back, not even coming home for my grandmother's funeral or the sale of her home. If it wasn't for Darlene, I wouldn't even have a box of the family keepsakes and mementos that she so lovingly packed and stored away so Fancy wouldn't sell or donate them. Or worse yet, throw them away.

"You okay, honey? I was only teasing, you know." Darlene's voice brought me out of my guilt-riddled memory.

"I was thinking…" I gulped. "Dar, I'm so sorry."

"Stop it. Stop it right now. We've been through this at least a dozen times since you moved back here. I've accepted your apology even though I didn't need one." She reached across the counter and took my hand. "I understand that you wanted more. I always knew you were destined for great things and I'm glad you followed your dream." With a sincere smile she added, "But I'm also glad you found your way back home."

This was the Darlene I remembered and missed. The friend who married Barry, her high school sweetheart, and was still over the moon in love after more than thirty years. The woman who raised five children, only one of them biological. The others belonged to her extended family who'd fallen on hard times. She was the friend who'd continued to send me Christmas and birthday cards every year since I moved away. The same person who welcomed me back with open arms and treated me like I'd never left. Darlene was a woman who loved unconditionally and forgave wholeheartedly. I couldn't think of anyone I admired more, and my eyes started to mist over with regret over the lost years I could've had with her.

I was saved from my remorseful thoughts when the chime alerting Darlene that someone had pulled up to the pumps echoed loudly. We both watched as a gray pickup truck towing a motorcycle parked, and a very tall, muscular man got out. He was obviously a Native American. And a handsome one at that.

"I haven't seen him before. Is he from around here?" I asked as I craned my neck to get a better look. She didn't answer as we spied an attractive woman emerging from the other side of the truck followed by a teenaged girl, and a boy of about five or six. The man opened the back door, unstrapped a baby from a car seat and handed him to the teen. "Looks like the dad has a lot of tattoos. Maybe he knows who the mystery biker is."

Darlene snorted. "So, because he has tattoos and is towing a motorcycle you assume he knows your biker?"

I ignored her question and continued to watch the family as the father reached into the bed of the truck and pulled out a container of juice. After handing it to his wife, he took the little boy with him to the other side and engaged the gas pump. In the meantime, the teenager rocked the baby on her hip while her mother wrestled with the bottle of juice and a sippy cup.

"First of all, he's not *my* biker," I grunted. "But yeah, maybe this guy, who I've never seen before, is friends with him and they ride together. He looks like he might know a thing or two about motorcycle gangs."

"Now your lone biker is in a motorcycle gang?" she squealed. "You have a vivid imagination, Barbie. And that's Christian and Mimi. They've been coming here for years. And they are as pure as the driven snow. There is no way that family knows anything about bikers, especially biker gangs." Darlene let out a bellowing laugh.

"Okay, okay," I conceded. I tore my eyes away from the family and gave her my full attention. "How do you know so much about them? Pure as the driven snow?"

Her eyes got bright. "It's a very romantic story. Christian and Mimi were childhood friends who lost touch, and eleven years ago they ran into each other in Pumpkin Rest of all places. Can you even imagine the chances of that? Right in front of the grocery." She proceeded to tell me a quick story about a makeshift marriage under the stars on the back deck of a vacation house he was renting from the Munro family.

I frowned. "The Munro family?"

"You wouldn't know them," she replied while shaking her head. "They were city-dwellers who bought up the Henderson parcel for next to nothing after Mr. Henderson passed away. They built a huge house on the lake."

I nodded my faint recollection of the last living Henderson as Darlene continued with her story.

"Talk about romantic," she sighed. "Christian and Mimi's parents bought the house for them as an anniversary gift several years back, and they've been coming here to celebrate ever since." Being directionally challenged since we were kids, Darlene waved her hand in the air motioning toward the east and said, "After they leave here, they head off to spend a little time with her family somewhere in Montana before heading home to Florida."

I smiled at the dreamy look in Darlene's eyes. It was quite a story and gave me a warm feeling. I squinted in concentration. "You said they ran into each other eleven years ago. Is the girl their daughter? Because she's no eleven-year-old."

Darlene nodded. "Yeah, Abby is Christian's daughter from a previous relationship. But, I'm pretty sure Mimi is the only mother she's ever known. The little boy, Tommy, is theirs together and they're in the process of adopting the baby, Micah."

We'd been so engrossed in our conversation, we jumped when the door opened and Mimi appeared.

"Hi, Darlene!" she called as she came in. "We're heading out and I wanted to say goodbye."

Darlene had just finished introducing me when the jingling of the door sounded again and Abby came in, still balancing the baby on her hip and trying to hold the hand of her little brother, who broke free and ran to his mother. He looked like a miniature version of his father, except his skin was a little lighter and his hair was shorter.

"Mommy, Mommy, I gotta pee," he shrieked. "Really bad. It's gonna come out all by itself!"

Darlene smiled and motioned toward the back. "Y'all know where the bathroom is."

Mimi reached for her son's hand and I could hear her as she headed to the back of the store. "Thomas Anthony, we left the house only twenty minutes ago and I told you to go before we got in the truck."

I chuckled to myself as I watched their retreating backs. Turning to the stunning teenager, I couldn't help but comment, "You have a beautiful family." The baby she was holding had a head of black curly hair, almond-shaped chocolate eyes, and dark-brown skin.

Abby broke out into a wide smile before sharing with us that they'd had the baby since he was three days old, and as soon as they arrived back in Florida, her parents would be signing the adoption papers that would make Micah Jamison legally theirs. And it would be just in time to celebrate his first birthday. This was all information Darlene had already known but was obviously new to me.

When Mimi and little Tommy reappeared, it was time for goodbyes, and less than five minutes later, the family was pulling out onto the main road. I turned back to my longtime friend and listened as Darlene speculated on how much the couple's parents had paid for the Munros' high-dollar vacation home. Apparently, the Munros had no intention of selling their home, until they were made an offer they couldn't refuse.

"Who knows," I replied nonchalantly. "They both might come from money. You seem to know everything about them. How come you don't know?"

"They don't share anything personal. I mean, I know how they bumped into each other and got married here." Darlene reached for a rag and dusted the counter and some of the displays. "I know they live in Florida, have three kids, and she has family somewhere in Montana, but other than that, they don't say much. Now that I think about it, he doesn't say anything at all."

After a bit more chitchat that concluded with Darlene inviting me to church, I skirted around the invitation by announcing, "I think I'm ready for stage two of my renovations. I've been putting it off but I have some gutter damage after that last storm. Can you think of anybody who's looking for work?"

After my initial move home last year, I'd spent as much time as I could in Pumpkin Rest having the electric, plumbing, and heating and air system modernized and brought up to code. I'd been a full-timer for almost a month now so it was time to dive into the structural and cosmetic part of updating my house.

"I can ask if one of the Shook boys is looking for extra money," she told me. She batted her eyelashes and I knew what was coming. "Or, you could ask Dustin. I know heating and air is his specialty, but I'm sure he'd give you a hand with some of the other stuff."

I let out a sigh. Dustin had installed my new heating and cooling system. He was a handsome thirty-year-old with his own business, who made it clear that he was interested in me. I blew him off. As a matter of fact, my new system was making some noises and I found the thought of calling him so unappealing, I lived with the racket instead. It occurred to me that the biker must have passed by my house and I hadn't heard him because of my louder-than-normal air-conditioning unit. Mystery solved.

"Dustin is the last person I want to call," I said matter-of-factly. I picked up a pack of gum and placed it on the counter with a couple of dollars.

"He likes you, Barbie. What's wrong with that?"

"Not interested, and you can keep the change," I said as I scooped up my gum and headed for the door. "And I have my bag with me so I'm going to stop at your granny's house and listen to her chest. If I even suspect her pneumonia is back, I'm going to drive her straight to the clinic."

"Good," Darlene agreed. "She is the most stubborn woman I know, but she'll listen to you. And, Barbie…"

I'd pushed open the door and looked back over my shoulder. Darlene was holding up a business card. "You forgot Dustin's number." She grinned.

"Bye, Dar. I have to come back for groceries and gas, so I'll see you in a little while." I headed for my Jeep Cherokee, hiding my smile from her.

I checked on Darlene's grandmother and headed back to the gas station and grocery store where I ran into a string of people I knew. Even though I'd left my job as a trauma surgeon in Greenville, I'd been working one or two days a week at the office of Dr. Charles Tucker which was about thirty minutes east of our little town and where the majority of Pumpkin Rest residents went for their medical care. It hadn't helped that our local family pharmacy had closed and was now a hardware store. The retired pharmacist had always gone out of his way to help the locals assess their ailments and determine if a trip to Dr. Tucker's was necessary. Apparently, I filled that void now. Almost two hours later, having discussed everything from arthritis and sinus infections to migraines and gout, I finished my grocery shopping, gassed up my Jeep, and headed for home.

The first thing I noticed when I pulled up to my house was that my dangling gutter had been put back in place.

I shook my head. Darlene must have called Dustin and he'd already come to the rescue. I breathed a sigh of relief, grateful that I'd missed him.

"Dar, you little stinker," I said, laughing as I carried my bags inside.

CHAPTER 2

BARBIE AND KEN

The next couple of weeks passed uneventfully and I stayed busy with my house projects, a few unavoidable trips to Greenville to wrap up some business with my attorney, and working at Dr. Tucker's clinic. I still hadn't called Dustin to thank him for the gutter repair. And since I no longer needed him to take a look at my loud air-conditioning unit because it stopped making the irritating noise, I saw no need to get in touch. Darlene continued to deny calling him about the gutter, but I chose not to believe her. After all, it was the only explanation, unless gutter fairies were roaming the area. I could've cleared up the mystery with a simple phone call, but I'd been avoiding Dustin.

Darlene had been right about one thing. Dustin had expressed an interest in me, but even after I'd turned down a few invitations, he still hadn't gotten the hint that I wasn't interested. Any reasonable woman might've jumped at the chance to be with a man like Dustin. He was smart, good-looking, hardworking, and kind. He was a lot younger than me, but that hadn't influenced my decision not to accept his invitation. I had no issues with younger men. The simple truth was that I wasn't attracted to him, nor was I looking for a relationship. Yes, he had the looks, the body, and everything else going for him, but there was no spark, no connection. No chemistry. And that was that.

It was a Monday morning and I'd volunteered to fill in for the resident doctor at the Hampton House, a privately owned assisted living facility about twenty-five miles north in the little township of Stillwell. She had a family emergency and asked if I wouldn't mind making a routine visit in her stead. Even though I was now a trauma surgeon, I'd started my career as a general practitioner. At some point I'd decided to challenge myself and went back to complete my residency in trauma. I now jumped at the chance to fill in at Hampton House as it gave me an opportunity to visit with some employees and possibly even some residents I'd known from my childhood, as well as put my GP skills to good use. I'd just pulled up and taken a final sip of my coffee before reaching for my purse, when I noticed something out of the corner of my eye. Stretching to get a better look, I almost spit out my coffee when my eyes zeroed in on the gas tank of a very familiar motorcycle. *What was the disgusting pig doing here?*

After signing in at the front desk, I scanned the halls as I made my way to the director's office. My high school friend, Sheila, hadn't changed a bit with the exception of some laugh lines around her eyes and a few extra pounds which only complemented her figure. After a warm greeting she offered her condolences for my situation. I wasn't surprised. Even though Sheila no longer lived in Pumpkin Rest, she was still privy to small-town chatter. She filled me in on details about her life. Two of her four children had moved away and her husband had retired. Based on what Darlene had shared with me, I knew better. Sheila's husband wasn't retired. He was a lazy bum who'd never held a job and regularly abused Sheila for years. It was obvious by the long-sleeved turtleneck she was wearing in this miserable heat that he was still doing it.

After walking me to the nurses' station, she asked if I would have time for lunch after my rounds. I apologized, telling her I wasn't able to stay and asked for a rain check. Perhaps Sheila would open up to me about her circumstances. I was in no position to be doling out marital advice, but I had seen my share of domestic violence in the ER. I must've looked distracted because she noticed my wandering eyes and asked, "Are you looking for someone, Dr. Anderson?"

I'd already told her to call me Barbie, but she insisted on being official. "Yes, I'm looking for someone who would probably garner some notice. He has long hair, wears it in a braid. He has a beard and is covered in tattoos."

She shook her head. "Some of our volunteers and caregivers have tattoos, but nobody fits that description. Unless he's a visitor."

I shrugged. If I made my rounds it would only be a matter of time before I ran into him. Unless he left before I was finished. After taking a few moments to familiarize myself with the list of residents I would need to see, I looked up, startled.

"Jonathan Pritchard is here?" I asked, my surprise obvious.

"Oh, yes," Sheila replied, clapping her hands together. "He came to live with us just last year. It's so good to have him back here. It's not

Pumpkin Rest, but it's also not the other side of the state. He gets regular visitors from some of the local people who knew his family."

Before I had the chance to inquire about his welfare, Sheila whispered, "People who knew his mother. It's no secret that nobody cared for his father."

That was an understatement. Kenny and Jonathan Pritchard's father had been a miserable excuse for a human being, and I'd hated him even more than I'd hated my grandmother. I wondered why Darlene hadn't told me about Jonathan being so close to Pumpkin Rest, but I immediately knew the answer. Darlene and I steered clear of any conversation that included the name Pritchard. I'd barely been able to say the name when I was telling Darlene about the disgusting pig who rode off toward their farm and never returned.

"How is Jonathan doing?" I asked Sheila, looking over his chart. Jonathan Pritchard was forty-seven, two years older than my sister, Fancy. He was developmentally challenged and would always function at a four- or five-year-old level. Before Sheila could answer, I added, "He still won't let any men near him?" It was no secret that his brother, Kenny, had suffered physical abuse from their father. Abuse that Jonathan had witnessed too many times to count. Everyone assumed it was the reason Kenny ran away from home when he was a young teen. My eyes glazed over as I continued to read Jonathan's chart which indicated female-only caregivers. I gritted my teeth in anger. *How could you have left your little brother?* I swallowed thickly. *How could you have left me?*

Sheila disrupted my thoughts when she excitedly said, "That seems to be changing. We have a new male caregiver who has been making serious progress with Jonathan. It's like a miracle."

I listened to her as I continued to scan his chart. We were interrupted when Sheila was told she had a phone call. Before going to her office, she informed me that Dolly would be assisting me on my rounds.

Dolly was an attractive and overly enthusiastic twenty-one-year-old with more pep and energy than a first grader. It was obvious after visiting the first two residents that she was well loved by those under her care. She handled them with kindness and patience, and I found myself admiring and respecting her. She wasn't trading hours for dollars. This woman loved her job.

Two hours flew by, and before I knew it, we'd come to the last resident. Jonathan Pritchard would be our final stop. I wondered if he would remember me. I hoped not. I hadn't seen him in years, and when I did, it hadn't gone so well. I'd left for college in 1984 and that was the same year his father died and he became a ward of the state. It was also the same year that Kenny had been sentenced to life without parole in a maximum-security prison in Florida. I would be giving Jonathan a routine checkup while Dolly administered his daily medication. As we approached his door, Dolly leaned into me and whispered above the noisy cart she was pushing, "I hope Jake is with him."

I knew immediately she must've been referring to the new caregiver Sheila had mentioned. Still, it prompted me to ask, "Why do you hope that?"

She gave me a sideways glance and said, "You'll see. He's old enough to be my daddy." A mischievous smile broke out on her face before she added, "And I'd let him spank my bottom any day. He is one fine-looking specimen." She waggled her eyebrows.

I had to bite the inside of my cheek to stifle a laugh.

I followed Dolly as she pushed the med cart inside Jonathan's room and announced us. "Jonathan, we have a special visitor today. Dr. Anderson is going to give you a little checkup while I get your medicine ready. Okay?"

Jonathan was sitting at a table facing the door. He was playing checkers with an opponent who had his back to us. I noticed that Jonathan's visitor had broad shoulders and was wearing a blue short-sleeved scrub shirt over a long-sleeved white tee. He had hair cropped close to his head with glints of silver. *Must be the older Jake that Dolly was hoping we'd run into,* I thought. I heard music, and out of the corner of my eye spotted an old boom box on the dresser. I didn't recognize the song or the man singing, but the beat was pleasant and the lyrics heartwarming.

It doesn't get better than this
For you and I on this drive is life and love
At its best
And it's all that I need

The man's voice reminded me of molasses—heavy and rich. My stomach grumbled and I immediately focused my attention on Jonathan who was wearing a Garth Brooks t-shirt. He jumped up, bumping the table and causing some of the checkers to scatter. An empty Dr. Pepper can hit the tile floor causing a loud ping to resonate off the walls. Clapping his hands, he quickly walked toward me repeating, "Barbie doll, Barbie doll, Barbie doll."

It was the nickname his brother had given me when I was nine. A lump formed in my throat as Jonathan threw his arms around me and hugged me so tightly, I couldn't breathe. He remembered me. Tears threatened as waves of grief and guilt washed over me. It wasn't until Dolly gently disengaged Jonathan's arms that I was able to focus on who could only have been Jake, the new orderly. He stood up and turned around to face me.

I took a step back as my mouth fell open. It was him—the disgusting pig. I could tell by the shape of his head, his jaw, his entire physique. He'd obviously cut off his braid and shaved his beard. He had a five-o'clock shadow laced with silver. I could see a hole in his right ear where an earring should've been. His arms were covered but I could see hints of the tattoos that were peeking out at the bands of his wrists and collar. And I couldn't miss the four-letter expletives that adorned his fingers right above the knuckles of both hands. But it wasn't any of those features that caused my heart to race in disbelief. It was his eyes. They were the same penetrating blue eyes that had held my nine-year-old heart captive and later caused it to stop beating and shrivel up in my chest.

Jonathan started to clap again, this time chanting, "Barbie and Ken, Barbie and Ken, Barbie and Ken."

I thought I heard Dolly giggle and say, "Barbie and Ken, just like the dolls. I loved playing with them."

It was obvious that I'd been misinformed. Kenny Pritchard hadn't died in prison. He couldn't have because he was standing right in front of me.

The disgusting pig extended his hand in friendship.

"I'm Jake Chambers. It's nice to meet you…" He paused and gave me a dazzling smile before adding, "Barbie doll, is it?"

For as long as I live, I will never be able to forgive myself for what happened next. It was unthinkable. It was inconceivable. It never should have happened.

The last thing I remembered was looking at his extended hand and back up to his eyes.

And then, I fainted.

CHAPTER 3

JAKE AND HIS MUSCLES

"I could've driven myself home," I snapped as Darlene did her best to fuss over me. "I don't know why Sheila called you."

It was hours later and I was sitting on my couch while Darlene hovered with another cup of hot tea. "And no, thanks. I'll be up all night peeing if I drink one more cup. Besides, it's too hot out for more tea. Menopause is still kicking my butt." I was alluding to the hot flashes that had recently started plaguing me again.

Darlene took the seat beside me and laid the cup on my scarred coffee table. "I think menopause is affecting you in more ways than one," she said with a half smile.

"I'm telling you, it is Kenny Pritchard, Dar. He's back and he's working at the assisted living facility." I waved my hand in the air. "He didn't die in prison and is now calling himself Jake something or another. You saw him when you came to pick me up."

"Chambers. Sheila told us his name is Jake Chambers. And I saw what you saw. A guy with blue eyes. He checks out, Barbie. Everything he put on his application is legit."

I harrumphed my disagreement. "The information and documents he provided could be fake."

"Except they're not. I stood right where you did when Sheila showed us his records and employment application. And Kenny's prison records too," Darlene reminded me. "For the second time I might add." After Darlene arrived to pick me up, I made Sheila show her the same information she'd already shared with me.

Darlene scooted closer to me and reached for my hand. "Look, sweetie.

I know the heart wants to believe what it wants to believe. But you are grasping at straws. Jake Chambers is not Kenny Pritchard."

"You saw the mug shots, Dar!" I fired back. "And my heart does not want Kenny Pritchard. We were children and I've been over him for a long time."

Darlene gave me a look that said she knew better. I blew out a frustrated breath and laid my head back on the worn couch. I stared at the ceiling and relived waking up on Jonathan's bed. Dolly was taking my pulse while the disgusting pig was holding a cold compress to my forehead. I heard whimpering and rose slightly. I could see Jonathan sitting in his chair, rocking back and forth. My fainting spell had frightened him.

I pushed the tattooed hand away from me and tossed the compress to the side. I sat up and jumped off the bed a little too quickly because I still felt slightly dizzy. I reached for something to steady myself and found that I was gripping a solid forearm. I yanked my hand away like I'd been scalded and approached Jonathan. He stood and I pulled him in for a hug while murmuring words of comfort that I was okay.

"Kenny saved you. Kenny saved you," he mumbled under his breath.

"Apparently, I remind him of his brother."

I knew the imposter had stepped over to us and I ignored him.

"I don't mind if he calls me Kenny." His voice was deep and warm, like homemade butter melting over blueberry pancakes. I despised blueberry pancakes.

Before I could reply, Sheila burst into the room. "Dr. Anderson, are you okay?"

"I'm fine, Sheila," I told her while softly rubbing Jonathan's back. I pulled away and looked up at him. He smiled and my heart melted. Jonathan had Kenny's dimple. The same dimple that adorned Jake's cheek.

Sheila insisted that I follow her back to her office. Dolly walked with us and wouldn't stop talking about Jake and his muscles.

"He caught you and laid you on Jonathan's bed like it was nothing," she said with a faraway look on her face.

I wanted to dig a hole and crawl into it.

After we got to Sheila's office and Dolly returned to her work, I almost had her convinced that I was okay until I mentioned that I thought her new orderly was Kenny Pritchard. That's when she insisted on calling Darlene to pick me up. "I'll make sure your car is brought to your house," she told me. She started to quiz me about my health when I cut her off and started asking questions about the new caregiver. I barely gave her time to answer before I fired off another one.

"He has an address over in Pickens County, and yes, I did a background check and a drug test on him, Barbie." I was obviously frustrating her because she dropped the formal name-calling.

"And?" I asked. "Does he have a record? Because he looks like he could be a criminal."

"Yes, he does, but because it was so long ago, and because he passed our drug screening and has excellent references, we hired him."

I quirked a brow. "What kind of record?"

Sheila went to a tall metal cabinet and pulled out a file. "It's all here." She laid it on her desk and rifled through it. "It says he was sentenced to prison in 1981 for three years but got out after only one." She looked up at me over the rim of her glasses. "That was over thirty years ago, Barbie."

I reached for his application and quickly scanned it. "His work history only goes back five years."

"That's all we require. He has glowing recommendations from two facilities like ours," she added.

"What did he do before that?" I wanted to know.

"I asked him the same thing." She hefted her left hip on the desk and gave me a sympathetic look. She thought I was losing my mind. "He's worked different kinds of jobs. Some construction, drove a delivery truck. He was remodeling a nursing home when he discovered he had a way with the patients and decided to give it a try. It worked out for him."

I circled back to his stint in jail. "What prison?" I huffed, raising my chin.

"It was in Texas." Her voice held a tone of sadness. "There is no way he could be Kenny Pritchard."

I watched as she moved to her chair and swung around to her computer and pulled up a page. She positioned the screen so I could see it from the far side of her desk. It was Kenny's mug shot from 1984. She pulled up one of Jake Chambers and split the screen. "Jake is a year older than Kenny. He went to prison in Texas and got out two years before Kenny went to prison in Florida. I agree that there's a resemblance, but that's all there is," she explained.

"Tattoos?" I asked, still not convinced.

She pointed to the screen. "You can see for yourself that Jake has several on his neck above his collar line. And the picture doesn't show anything below that. And Kenny's mug shot doesn't show any tattoos, but it mentions that he had one of a clock with a chain, possibly a stopwatch or pocket watch, on his right bicep."

I stiffened and asked, "Does Jake's mention a tattoo of a clock or a watch?"

She squinted at the screen and turned to me. "No, Barbie. No mention of any clock-like tattoos."

I shrugged my shoulders. I still wasn't convinced but knew I was grasping at straws.

"Okay, why does Jonathan call him Kenny?" I hovered over her desk, planting both hands on her blotter.

"I don't know, Barbie. Maybe because he has the same blue eyes as Kenny. Even in the mug shot Kenny's eyes are striking. You have to admit, so are Jake's. They stand out. It's probably why Jonathan, who was what, six or seven years old when Kenny ran away? It's probably why he's taken to Jake. It must be the eyes that are triggering Jonathan's memory." She gave me an exasperated glare. "Not to mention, Kenny Pritchard died in 2010."

"How can you deny their mug shots look identical?"

I could see Sheila trying not to roll her eyes. "Yes, they look alike, but you're missing an important fact, Barbie. Jake's mug shot with that scary-looking neck tattoo was taken in 1981. Kenny's was taken in 1984 and he doesn't have a tattoo on his neck. Now, unless Kenny had a tattoo with that kind of detail miraculously removed, they couldn't possibly be the same person. I'm sure their fingerprints would also prove it."

Of course what she said made perfect sense, but for reasons I couldn't identify, I felt the need to discredit Jake the caregiver. So I switched tactics.

I stood back from her desk and crossed my arms. Giving her the most disapproving expression I could muster, I asked, "Did you happen to see what Jake drives?"

"Yes. It's a motorcycle."

"Did you notice what is painted on the gas tank?"

I got a reaction from her, but not the one I'd wanted. Sheila's cheeks tugged upward in a wide grin as she brought her hands together in front of her. Assuming the posture of a studious student, she exclaimed, "Oh, yes! Isn't it beautiful?"

"Beautiful? You think it's beautiful?" I couldn't contain my shock.

"Of course!" She blushed a little when she added, "Orchids are my favorite flowers."

"You think that thing is an orchid?" My tone was mocking.

"You've never seen a radiant orchid before, Barbie?"

I threw my hands up in the air and spun around. There was no reasoning with her. I grabbed Jake Chambers' folder off her desk and sat down. She excused herself and left me alone. I combed through his file while I waited for Darlene since Sheila had refused to give me my car keys. I was determined to prove there was something wrong with Jake and his muscles. Not to mention his perverted fascination with radiant orchids.

CHAPTER 4

THE MEAN GIRL

Darlene released my hand and stood. Looking down at me with her hands on her hips, she said, "I still can't figure out what you're so mad about, Barbie. Are you upset that he's not Kenny? Because he has the same color eyes as Kenny? Or because he has an orchid painted on his motorcycle that you thought was something else? What has this guy done to disturb you so much?"

I looked away, embarrassed, and stared at an ancient picture on my living room wall. "I don't know, Dar. Seeing him has stirred something up inside of me. Something I thought I'd buried long ago." She didn't say anything and I looked up at her. Her expression told me she understood. I needed to lighten the mood so I gave her a goofy smile.

"You saw his bike when we left. Admit it. You can see how I thought it was female genitalia," I teased.

"You mean a vagina, Barbie? You are always so formal," she teased. "Let's just say I can see how he must be an admirer of Georgia O'Keefe's work, but that's all I'm admitting."

We were both laughing at how ridiculous I'd been when a knock interrupted us. I stood and Darlene followed me to the front door. A smiling Dolly was dangling the keys to my Jeep.

"I can't thank you enough!" she practically shouted as she thrust them into my hand.

"For what?" I asked, but I already knew the answer when I heard the familiar rumble of Harley-Davidson pipes making their way up my road.

"For fainting! I got to drive your car home and guess what?"

"You get a ride back to your car on Jake's motorcycle?" I replied blandly.

"It couldn't have worked out better if I'd planned it." Dolly's smile was so broad I thought her face would crack. Darlene started to say something but I interrupted her by thanking Dolly and shutting the door. I stepped over to the window and stood at an angle behind the curtain where I couldn't be seen. I knew the old drapes needed to be replaced but hadn't realized how badly until I was close enough to inhale their dank, musty aroma. I could feel Darlene's eyes boring into my back.

"Barbara Jean Anderson!" Her voice held a tone of authority.

"Not now, Dar!" I shot back as I spied on Jake and Dolly. I could practically feel a whoosh of air as she flounced toward my kitchen.

Three minutes later I found her washing my dishes. With her back to me she asked, "When did you become the mean girl at the eighth grade lunch table, Barbie?"

I let out a long sigh and she turned around to face me while holding a dishrag. "I didn't realize I had until just now," I admitted.

"Did it have the effect you intended? Will that poor girl ride all the way back to her car looking like a clown?"

I crossed my arms and leaned against the wide doorframe that separated the kitchen from the living room. When I'd answered the knock, I'd assumed Dolly had reapplied her bright red lipstick before she got out of my Jeep, and in her haste somehow managed to smear a streak of it up to the center of her right cheek. I should've mentioned it when she handed me my keys. Dar had tried to tell the woman and I'd cut her off. I didn't know why.

"Well?" she asked again.

"No, it didn't have the intended effect, and I don't know what came over me. You're right. I was never the mean girl." This was very true. I couldn't recall any past incident where I contributed to someone else's humiliation, let alone took satisfaction in it. Why now?

Darlene's face softened. Tossing the dishrag aside, she came toward me, wrapping me in a warm hug. "This past year has been more than tough on you, Barbie." She pulled back and held my hands tightly with both of hers. "Your move here wasn't actually a complete move with all the back and forth you had to do. You ended up staying in Greenville more than you stayed here."

I shook my head in disagreement.

"Barbie, you've been through a lot, and I think seeing this new employee at Hampton House has resurrected some very old hurts. And it's hard not to commingle them with the more recent pain you've been going through. Don't be so hard on yourself and do what you came here to do. Start over. Take care of yourself"—she smiled and gestured to my kitchen—"and this run-down old house. It definitely needs some TLC. Can you do that?"

"I dunno. Maybe. Yeah, probably."

"Good. And while you're at it, promise you'll start with the kitchen sink." Her eyes sparkled as she motioned toward it. "Your water bill must be through the roof with that incessant drip."

I laughed at her undeniable point. Even though I'd had all the internal plumbing gutted, I'd not gotten around to picking new fixtures and the original ones had seen better days.

"Flea market this weekend?" I asked. I was determined to restore the house to its original era which meant I wouldn't be using modern fixtures. It also meant that I'd be hunting local flea markets looking for older ones that were in good condition.

"It's a date," she told me as she reached for her keys.

That night as I sat at my makeup table and applied night cream to my face, I reflected on the young couple at Darlene's gas station and how their second-chance romance turned out so beautifully for them. I put the lid back on the jar and picked up my hairbrush. Staring into the mirror that sat atop my table, I thought about how I'd obviously missed out on the long-term wedded bless that Darlene shared with Barry. It was definitely too late for that.

"You're on your own, Barbara Jean," I said to my reflection.

I was a fifty-two-year-old single woman living in a town that was barely a dot on the map. Prospects for eternal companionship were slim, which was another reason I'd chosen to come home. I'd suffered more than one broken heart and wasn't about to allow it to happen again. I was an intelligent, educated woman who found immense satisfaction in my work and restoring my home. I didn't need a man in my life to mess with my peaceful existence. At least that's what I'd been telling myself.

Satisfied, I climbed into bed, but sleep wouldn't come. I couldn't erase what I'd seen while spying on Jake and Dolly. She'd run up to him waving her arms excitedly, trying to climb on the back of his bike. He'd been straddling it and stood up, grabbing her arm to stop her from swinging her leg around. He removed his do-rag and very gently steadied her chin by grasping it between his thumb and forefinger. He looked at her adoringly and had a barely perceptible smile on his face as he softly wiped her cheek.

But it wasn't the look he was giving her that was etched in my brain. It was the one he'd given me. It was almost as if he knew I was cowering behind the drapes spying on them. He knew what I'd done. He'd seen me shut the door before Dolly approached him so he knew I'd seen the ridiculous smear of lipstick on her cheek. It might as well have been a neon sign that said, "Barbie is a spiteful, small person."

I flipped over and buried my face in my pillow hoping it would help me forget. Jake's expression hadn't revealed judgment or distaste at my cattiness. He hadn't aimed a frown of disapproval or a smirk of reproof at my window. No, it was much worse than that. Once Dolly settled herself behind him, he paused before driving off and leveled a gaze my way. He appeared crestfallen, and I was horrified to realize that I could've handled any other expression than the one I saw on his face. It was a look of sheer and utter disappointment.

CHAPTER 5

A CHANCE TO MAKE AMENDS

I didn't know how I'd let the notion consume me that the new caregiver at the assisted living facility was the long-dead Kenny Pritchard. I apologized to Sheila when she called asking after my health. She readily accepted my request for forgiveness and didn't seem surprised when I asked which days Jake had off. I very much wanted to visit with Jonathan again, and it was obvious I didn't want to run into Jake while doing so. I also had another more personal matter I needed to address. She told me I should stop by the following Sunday or Wednesday.

Several days passed, during which time I kept myself busy with my part-time work at Dr. Tucker's clinic and concentrated on my many DIY home projects. It seemed that every time I repaired or updated one aspect of my place, something else broke. Darlene and I spent the weekend scouring flea markets for fixtures that suited my style. I hadn't yet found a decent kitchen faucet, but that was no longer an issue. The dripping had miraculously ceased. Darlene considered it Divine intervention. I figured I'd never tightened the levers sufficiently when turning it off. I did manage to find some perfect light fixtures and was going to make an appointment the following week for an electrician to install them.

After one of our excursions, I asked Dar if she wouldn't mind taking a longer drive. I had something on my heart and wanted to deal with it. Darlene readily agreed and gave me a curious look when we arrived at a Harley-Davidson dealership a few towns away.

"Are you getting something for your motorcycle man?" she asked.

"Just c'mon," was my reply as we exited the car.

The following Wednesday, I pulled into the Hampton House and breathed a sigh of relief when I didn't see a bike in the parking lot. Like

Sheila had told me, it was Jake's day off. I grabbed my purse and the item I'd purchased at the Harley dealership and made my way inside. I stopped at Sheila's office and apologized for a second time. Her eyes were warm when she assured me an apology wasn't necessary. She told me she understood the stress I'd been under and how stress manifests itself in unusual ways. I agreed.

My second stop was Jonathan's room to say hello. He wasn't there, so I set out to track him down. I was told by one of the resident volunteers that Wednesday was bingo day and I would find him in the game room. I stood in the doorway unnoticed and watched him. He was sitting at a table with a young lady who had Down syndrome. Every time she or Jonathan heard a number that matched their cards they squealed and high-fived each other. I couldn't contain my smile at seeing him so happy.

"Her name is Cindy and she's Jonathan's best friend. And other than checkers with Jake, bingo is his favorite game."

I hadn't heard her come up behind me, but I was glad she did. I turned around to face Dolly. Before I could say anything, she smiled warmly and said, "I'm glad you're okay, Dr. Anderson. You scared us last week."

"Thank you, Dolly. I'm fine. I don't know what came over me."

She giggled and said, "A couple of us speculated that you got a case of the Jakes. You almost hit the floor right after he tried to shake your hand."

I gave her a sheepish grin and asked, "Is that what the women around here get when he shows up? A case of the Jakes?"

"Oh yeah. Not only is he handsome, but he is such a gentleman. He's always going out of his way to open doors and carry stuff. If he's sitting at a table in the cafeteria and a woman walks over to him, he stands before offering her a seat at his table. My momma instilled manners in my older brother, but I never remember her teaching him to do that. Heck, Jake even pulls out chairs!"

I hadn't been around Jake enough to comment, and didn't reply as I shifted the bulky parcel I was carrying, balancing it on my hip. She noticed and gave me a curious look and I remembered why I'd brought it.

"Oh, I have something for you." I held out the package and indicated for her to take it from me. She hesitated at first, but then extended her hands.

"For me?" Her eyes were wide.

When I smiled she walked over to a table and set it down. I watched as she noisily removed the box from the loud, crinkly plastic bag. Her eyes lit up when she realized what it was and thanked me profusely as she removed the item from the box.

"If it doesn't feel like a good fit, the store will take it back," I informed her.

"I just can't thank you enough. I've been meaning to get one." Her eyes were warm. "I don't know why you bought this for me, but I appreciate it."

"No thanks are necessary, Dolly. Just promise me you'll wear it."

She started to answer when we were interrupted by a loud scuttlebutt in the bingo room. She gave me an apologetic smile and I nodded understandingly before taking my leave. I was almost out the door when I remembered what I had in my purse. I was going to leave it with Sheila when I first arrived but changed my mind. After seeing Dolly had no hard feelings I was feeling a bit better about it and started to do an about-face when the sliding doors opened, and Jake appeared.

I must've looked startled because he said, "I didn't mean to scare you."

"I thought you were off today," I replied a little too quickly and instantly regretted it.

"How did you know I was off? Were you looking for me?" He gave me a brilliant smile that made his dimple appear almost bottomless.

Crap.

I didn't want to admit that I'd specifically asked when he wouldn't be there. I also didn't want him to know that I'd delivered a small gift for Dolly and had something for him as well. I planned on leaving it with Sheila and limiting my future visits with Jonathan to Wednesdays or Sundays. I tried not to stammer a response and quickly collected myself. I was a mature, successful woman. An exceptional trauma surgeon who dealt with life-threatening situations without warning. I could handle an ex-con with a showstopping smile.

"Actually, I was going to leave something for you with Sheila," I admitted. He raised a brow and watched me reach into my handbag.

"I saw this, and since you're the only person I know who wears them, I bought it."

I couldn't read the expression on his face as I placed the do-rag in his hand. It was wonder mixed with gratitude, and something else I couldn't read. The smile disappeared and he looked almost flustered. I couldn't imagine someone like Jake being tongue-tied, but he appeared to be at a loss for words. I almost wished he'd stayed that way.

"Let me take you to dinner?" he asked.

Now it was my turn to be flustered. Dinner? With the man I referred to as the disgusting pig just days ago? He must've felt he'd overstepped because he immediately followed up with, "Or how about coffee? To thank you for this." He held up the gift.

What could it hurt? I'd obviously gotten off on the wrong foot with Jake and it was a chance to make amends. It was an opportunity to show him that I wasn't a small and catty person. It might also prevent future visits from feeling awkward were we to run into each other. I must've been tense because I felt my shoulders relax. I was getting ready to accept his invitation to coffee when a loud shout interrupted our conversation.

"Jake!"

We both turned to find Dolly heading our way carrying the gift I'd delivered. "Look what Dr. Anderson gave me." She didn't give him a chance to reply when she came to a stop and looked at me. "It fits perfectly. Thank you again."

I could feel Jake's eyes on me. I avoided looking at him as Dolly rambled on about how she would always wear it and was glad she didn't have poufy hair because a helmet would flatten it out.

"You bought a helmet for Dolly?" Jake asked, his voice soft.

I chanced a glance at him and warmth invaded my veins due to the adoration written all over his face. I nodded. I couldn't see her but could tell through my peripheral vision that Dolly looked at him, then at me, and back at him. She interrupted the moment saying, "Dr. Anderson, my mother wanted me to tell you hello."

Jake and I turned to her, giving her our attention, but she wasn't looking at me. She was looking at him. "Dr. Anderson went to school with my mother."

Jake acknowledged her comment with a smile.

"But they weren't in the same grade." She put her finger to her chin like she was thinking. "Dr. Anderson is older than my mom. By about two years, right?" she asked, giving me a sideways glance.

And there it was. The claws were out. I hadn't misjudged Dolly's work ethic, but I had miscalculated her prowess as a woman. A woman who saw me as a potential rival. She was making sure Jake knew I was old enough to be her mother. I could almost hear her thoughts, *what man in his right mind would choose a fifty-two-year-old divorcee over an attractive and vibrant twenty-one-year-old?*

She didn't wait for me to respond but jumped to the next topic that was meant to discourage any romantic notions she'd imagined were brewing between me and Jake Chambers.

"I can't wait to wear this on our date tonight," she said while holding up the helmet.

Jake shifted and I thought I saw his jaw go rigid.

"It's not a date, Dolly."

"When a man goes to a woman's house to pick her up, it's a date,

Jake," she replied with a laugh. She turned to me. "Right, Dr. Anderson? Wouldn't you call that a date?"

I adjusted my purse on my shoulder and smiled at her. I stepped in between them as I headed for the sliding door and called over my shoulder, "Give my best to your mother, Dolly."

It wasn't until I pulled into my driveway that it occurred to me that Jake had shown up on his day off. I couldn't help but wonder why, but immediately dismissed it. I fell asleep that night telling myself I was grateful I'd never accepted his invitation to have coffee.

CHAPTER 6

THE ORIGINAL BRANGELINA

D ays later, I stood on my front porch, hands on hips, and watched the electrician I'd hired drive away. He'd just finished installing a new light fixture over my dining room table and wall sconces on each side of my front door.

Before going back inside, I took a moment to appreciate my view. Directly in front of me, on the other side of the dirt road, were fields as far as the eye could see. Andersons had owned this property since before the Civil War. My ancestors were cotton farmers who worked their land and paid for outside labor during harvest. Staunch abolitionists of slavery, my relatives paid dearly for their refusal to support the South. It cost some their lives. The home I was living in and restoring was the third one on this site. The first two had been burned down by angry town folk.

To my right was a huge wall of forest that separated our fields from the Pritchards. It was a good thing I couldn't see their home from here. If I could, I would've bought their land and leveled the old farmhouse.

Movement to my left interrupted my musings and I sighed inwardly when I recognized the fiery red Mercedes XL 550 creeping its way up my road. I knew where it would stop and I cringed at the thought of spending even one minute with Frenita Anderson.

"I see you've done wonders with Grandma's place." Fancy's tone was filled with sarcasm as she wobbled on high heels toward my front porch carrying a plastic red bin that matched the color of her car. The overwhelming scent of her perfume reached me before she did as an unexpected breeze lifted up her skirt.

"What are you doing here, Frenita?" I asked. She hated when anyone called her Frenita.

"Uh!" She rolled her eyes as she stepped up, thrusting the red box in my hands. After glancing around my front porch with disapproval, she said, "I cannot imagine what prompted our mother to insist on naming me that awful name."

"You know exactly why she named you that. She was trying to earn a tiny bit of approval from Dad's mother. Grandma hated Mom. Remember? All we ever heard was how our mother stole her only son away."

The name Frenita was a combination of our paternal grandparents' names, Fred and Juanita Anderson. I guess they could've been considered the original Brangelina of the seventies. Our mother had been a trend-setter when she named my sister Frenita, but she would never live long enough to know it.

Fancy rolled her eyes and said, "You've always made our grandmother out to be a horrible woman, Barbie."

"She was a horrible woman, Fancy." I set the box down on a battered Adirondack chair and crossed my arms. "She made my life miserable when we moved here."

"You've always had a chip on your shoulder because she liked me more than she liked you. I don't see what the big deal is. I didn't get all bent out of shape because you were Granddaddy's favorite." She held her left hand out and concentrated on her manicure.

I couldn't believe we were having this conversation again, and like all the others before it, she was in complete denial. "There's a big difference between favoring one child over another versus treating one like pure garbage. Granddaddy loved you just as much as he loved me, Fancy. He spent more time with me because he felt sorry for me. He knew Grandma couldn't bear to look at me."

It was true and my sister knew it. I was the spitting image of our mother—the woman who our father fell in love with and married after a three-day whirlwind romance. They settled in the seaside town of Cape May, New Jersey. It hadn't mattered that Dad had left Pumpkin Rest a couple years earlier. Our grandmother always had high hopes of him returning. When he married, she saw those hopes dashed. And she never forgave our mother for it. When our parents died in a fire, and Fancy and I were forced on our only living relatives, that lack of forgiveness was trans-ferred to me and eventually manifested into pure and unadulterated hatred. Juanita Anderson was a witch.

"She wasn't always good to me, Barbie. She had her mean moments."

Fancy was probably remembering the one time she'd gotten in trouble for playing with matches and almost burned the house down. Our grandmother had tanned her bottom good. Considering the home's history and that our father had perished in a fire made it almost understandable.

"I remember one time she took a switch to you, and other than that one time, she doted on you. You were two years old when we moved here and she took pleasure in spoiling you rotten." I couldn't bring myself to repeat that she found most of her pleasure, not in spoiling my sister, but in watching me suffer as I stood on the sidelines and observed it. My grandmother was a bitter and evil woman.

"Fine, fine. You win, Barbie. Again. Okay? Grandma loved me and hated you." She shifted and adjusted the bodice of her sundress. "You're coming up on the fourth quarter, Sister. Maybe it's time you moved past it."

I didn't see how I'd won, but I wasn't in the mood to tangle with her again. I tilted my head to one side. "The fourth quarter?"

"Yes, darling sister. The fourth quarter. You're pushing sixty," she said matter-of-factly.

"I am not pushing sixty, Fancy. I'm fifty-two. And if you're referring to the fourth quarter as my life span, I've got a long way before I hit seventy-five."

"I guess you'd think that if you thought you would live to be a hundred. But, for argument's sake, let's say the average lifespan of a woman is eighty. Then from sixty to eighty is the fourth quarter and you'll be there before you know it."

She was right about that and I'd known it. I just hadn't assumed she was smart enough to know it. I wasn't sure what irritated me more—that she'd made an intelligent observation or that I'd dumbed down for her sake and was the one who sounded stupid. Or worse yet, the nagging thought that she was right.

I was approaching the fourth quarter. That thought stuck in my craw as I rolled my eyes and asked, "Why are you here, Fancy?"

She let out a dramatic sigh and said, "It's hotter than a blister bug in a pepper patch. Can you at least invite me in? I assume you have air-conditioning."

I reluctantly turned, opened the door, and waved her inside. As she walked past me she said, "You might want to grab that bin. It's for you."

She headed for the kitchen, but I didn't miss the arrogant shake of her head as she walked through the living room, dismissing my taste in furniture. I'd bought just enough for comfort until I finished the renovations and decorated it more to my taste. It was used, but in good shape and sturdy.

She sat in a kitchen chair and asked, "Do you have any sweet tea?"

I plopped the box down on the table and made my way to the fridge. After filling a glass with ice cubes and tea, I asked, "Do you want a straw?"

She scoffed and her accent became exaggerated when she said, "No self-respecting Southern woman sips iced tea from a straw."

"Hmm. I suppose if we leave the self-respecting part out you might be right. Do you want a straw or not, Fancy?"

"You are such a snob, Barbara Jean!" she spat, while straightening up in her chair.

I ignored her and handed her the glass. I took the lid off the plastic red container and my breath caught. "Why did you bring this stuff?"

"Because it's rightfully yours," she said, her tone calm.

"I don't want it, Fancy. None of it." I sat in the chair across from her and pulled my hair into a ponytail, but without a band to hold it, I let it fall.

"I don't want it either, Barbie. It just feels." She paused and shook like she'd gotten a chill. "Wrong."

"This," I spat while waving my hand toward the bin, "feels wrong, but seducing Richard away from our marriage didn't?" I was making a serious effort to prevent my voice from rising an octave.

"Hmph! You didn't have a marriage. I lived with you, remember? I saw what you had, and it definitely wasn't a marriage."

I'd had enough. I couldn't do this again. "What my marriage was or wasn't is none of your business, Fancy." I stood up abruptly and said, "It's time for you to go. Take the glass with you." She didn't stand up, but instead set her drink on the table and started drumming the wood with her pointy pink nails.

"Barbara Jean, since I returned what is rightfully yours, I think you should do the same."

I shook my head, wondering what nonsense she was going to vomit out next. "Do the same with what?"

She stood up and looked around the kitchen, and it occurred to me what she wanted.

I shot up out of my chair. "Oh no! You have some nerve coming here thinking you're entitled to this house. You're the one who insisted we sell it when Grandma died. You got half the profit from that, Fancy. I bought this house back from the bank after they repossessed it from the new owners. You aren't entitled to it."

She laughed. "I don't want this house, Barbie. Of course not. I know it's yours." Her smile looked sincere. "I'm here for some of the things that were in it before it got sold. I never got around to getting everything."

She was lying. It had taken her less than two days to get home after our grandmother passed, but once here, she wasted no time tearing through our grandparents' personal belongings to see what was of value.

"You got everything, Fancy," I told her.

"Not everything, Barbie. I know Darlene got here before me and packed some things up for you. Some of Granddaddy's things." She paused. "Some of Dad's things."

I frowned. "You already know what Dar saved for me. I told you when you came to live with Richard and me. I even showed you the note from Darlene that listed it all out."

"I don't think she told you about everything," she said.

Exasperated, I looked at the ceiling. "Why don't you just say it, Fancy. What do you want?"

"Fine!" she shouted. "I want Daddy's Civil War coin collection. Half of it belongs to me."

"Fancy, I haven't seen that collection in years. It was here when I left for college and I can assure you it's not in the box Darlene gave to me when I moved here."

"I don't believe you." She thrust her chin in the air.

"I don't care if you don't believe me. You can see for yourself."

I stalked toward the living room and opened a tiny door beneath the stairway. I retrieved a brown cardboard box that was smaller than the one Fancy had brought. I held it out to her and said, "I looked through it when I moved back, but haven't unpacked it yet. Everything Darlene took for me is in here. Look for yourself."

She yanked it from my hands, swiftly walked to the couch, and sat down. She set the box on the coffee table and opened it. I watched as she rifled through it. "There is nothing but junk in here," she complained.

"It's not junk, Fancy. Those are things that belonged to Dad and Granddaddy. They may not have any monetary value, but they're important."

She smoothed her dress. "I don't see how an old leather wallet that doesn't have any cash in it"—her tone seethed with condescension—"holds any importance."

"Ah…I think I'm beginning to see what's going on." I walked toward her, and bending over, closed the box. Picking it up I returned it to its spot underneath the stairs. After shutting the tiny door, I faced my sister. "The Richard well is almost dry. You're looking for money. That's why you came here. You think I have Dad's coin collection. Well, I don't have it, Fancy. And I never did. I can only surmise that Grandma sold it before she died. You can spend the rest of the day looking through every corner of this house if you want to. I'm not holding out on you."

I watched her stiffen and her shoulders slumped. For a split second I thought she looked older than me.

"Why do you hate me so much, Barbie?" she asked, her mouth drooping.

"I don't hate you, Fancy. I love you. I've always loved you." I crossed my arms and looked away. My next admission would be painful, but true. "I didn't even hate you when Grandma was so mean to me."

"I don't believe you," she replied.

I gave her a level look. "If I hated you, you wouldn't be living in my condo."

"Then what is it?"

I waffled for a moment but decided she deserved the truth. "I have a difficult time respecting you, Fancy. I'm sorry, but I can't respect someone who doesn't respect themselves. You are a bright and beautiful woman. But, instead of relying on your intelligence and opting for an education, you've only ever relied on men. You see your value based on the material things men can provide. You're worth so much more than the balance in some man's bank account. Can't you see that?"

I'd obviously struck a nerve because her back snapped into perfect posture again, and she jutted out her chin along with her oversized implants. She looked me up and down. "This is about respect?" she asked in a mocking tone. "You've always thought you were so much better than everyone else, haven't you, Barbie?" I didn't flinch as she scrutinized my stained t-shirt, tattered work jeans, and scuffed sneakers. Her eyes rested on my face, and she smirked at the lack of makeup. She took her time glancing around my living room.

"Your education and self-respect have done wonders for you, Sister. You live by yourself in the middle of nowhere in a house that smells like someone's week-old laundry. You drive an old Jeep and you dress like a homeless person."

I watched her swallow and wait for my retort. When I didn't give one she huffed her way past me and charged out the front door, not bothering to close it behind her. She jumped into her car and peeled out, scattering dust and rocks all over my new garden.

I retrieved the box she'd delivered from the kitchen table and walked with it to the closet beneath the stairs. After opening the door, I crouched. Before closing the lid, I sifted through the contents again. A wave of sadness descended.

"I'm not sure what to do with you," I sadly confessed to the red plastic bin that was filled with items nobody wanted.

I made room for it next to the cardboard box Darlene had saved for me, popped the plastic lid back in place, shut the door, and headed out to my garden to undo any damage Fancy's dramatic retreat may have caused.

CHAPTER 7

DELIBERATE CHOICES

I t was days later and I'd wandered into the only diner in Pumpkin Rest so I could have the place mostly to myself before the regular breakfast crowd showed up. After turning on my laptop and praying the Wi-Fi would be in a good mood, I balanced my checkbook online.

The diner hadn't changed much in almost thirty years. The linoleum floor was cracked and yellowed, but spotless. The walls were freshly painted a bright sky blue to match the weathered vinyl booth and counter seats. Some sported duct tape where the vinyl was worn and starting to rip. The yellow and blue calico curtains at each window were faded, but clean. I kept an eye out for Darlene who was working the early shift at the gas station. I knew when she saw my Jeep she'd stop in before she had to clock in at six.

"Fancy meeting you here, darling," she said as she approached me.

"Uh, that name!" I teased. She scooted into the booth and signaled the only waitress, Judy, for a cup of coffee while I briefly filled her in on my sister's recent visit.

"Just promise me you're not letting her get to you, Barbie. The last thing you needed was a visit from Frenita Anderson!"

"You know I never let Fancy get to me. I'm more put out that she would think I'd deliberately withhold Dad's coin collection from her. Not to mention that her only concern was for its value. She doesn't have a sentimental bone in her body."

"So, what exactly did you tell her?" She didn't meet my eyes but seemed intently focused on putting cream in her recently delivered coffee.

"I told Fancy the truth. I remember when Grandma died, you sent me that letter and told me that you went to the house and boxed up some personal things you thought I'd want. You even listed them out for me. And how you stuck the box on a shelf in your pantry and it's been there ever since until you gave it to me when I moved back here. When Fancy came to live with me and Richard she asked about that box and I pulled out the letter and showed it to her."

"You kept my letter?" Darlene asked, her smile sweet.

"I kept all your letters, Dar. I wasn't very good at reciprocating, but I couldn't let myself part with them." I swallowed my guilt and added, "And when she showed up the other day, I pulled the box out and showed her what was in it."

I slowly shook my head. "I just realized something, Dar."

"What?" She grasped her coffee cup with both hands and slouched forward. "That if you'd had that Civil War coin collection when she first moved in with you and Richard that she might not have made a move on your husband and ripped apart your marriage?" She raised a knowing brow.

"Yes," I said in stunned wonder.

I watched Darlene swallow and look away.

"What is it, Dar? What aren't you telling me?" I slowly closed my laptop and waited for her response.

Her eyes got misty. "Do you regret it? If you'd had a choice, would you have rather given her those coins and kept your marriage intact?"

Her question caught me off guard, but it didn't take me long to come up with a truthful answer. I'd been giving a lot of thought concerning deliberate choices over the past several weeks. "No, Darlene. I don't regret it. Fancy talked a lot of trash yesterday, but she did get one thing right. Richard and I didn't have a healthy marriage. It was a façade." I cocked my head to the side. "Why?"

She let out an audible breath and smiled. "Whew! I guess I did the right thing then. I knew it would be important to you and I promise it's been in a safe place." She took a sip of coffee and said, "I took that coin collection and it's been tucked away in my bedroom closet ever since."

"Darlene!" I practically yelled. But I wasn't angry. I was relieved.

"I remembered that time I was at your house and your grandma had taken Fancy out shopping for a new dress. It was a month before our senior prom and she knew it and had no intention of getting you a dress." Darlene's face turned into an angry grimace. "She was always doing something like that on purpose. Fancy was about eleven and wasn't in need of anything new to wear. We snooped that day. Do you remember?"

I nodded. "We found my father's coin collection." It was in a wooden box with layered trays. We'd just lifted the one tray out when we heard my grandmother's car coming up the road. We put it away and I never got another chance to look through it again before I left for college.

"I remembered where we found it and I made sure I got it for you." She bit her bottom lip before asking, "Are you mad at me?"

"Mad? I could kiss you!!" I whisper-yelled.

"I'm sorry I haven't gotten around to telling you about it. Something told me to wait, and now I know why. You wouldn't have deliberately lied to Fancy when she asked about it." She tucked a piece of hair behind her ear. "Do you want me to bring it over to your place?"

I took a minute to answer. Half of that coin collection did belong to Fancy, but I wasn't in the frame of mind to figure out how to manage it. It had stayed safely in Darlene's closet for all these years. A few more weeks or months wouldn't be a problem. "Can you hold on to it for now?" I asked.

"Of course I can, Barbie." She looked at her watch. "I've gotta run."

Before I could say goodbye, she peered over my shoulder, and with a blush creeping its way up her neck, said, "This seat is warm and I'm sure Barbie wouldn't mind the company."

Before I could object to finishing my coffee with who could only be Dustin, I inhaled a whoosh of intoxicating air as Jake Chambers took Darlene's seat and said, "I never got to buy you that cup of coffee." He eyed my half-filled cup and said, "I hope you'll let me pay for that one."

CHAPTER 8

A BASEBALL BAT AND BLUEBERRY PANCAKES

I was too caught off guard to object so I conceded. "Yeah, sure," I told him followed by a quick, "I don't know how much longer I'll be here though."

"No problem. I'm used to eating here alone." He was wearing a black tight-fitting t-shirt and the earring was back. I didn't know what kind of pants he was wearing because he'd slid into the booth so fast, but I assumed they were jeans.

I heard Judy ask from behind me, "The usual, Jake?"

He gave a thumbs-up and said, "Yes, please," with a pleasant smile.

"You come here a lot?" I asked as I removed my laptop from the table and set it next to me.

He gave me a lazy grin. "Isn't that a pickup line?"

"If we were in a bar, I'd say yes. But considering we're in a sixty-year-old diner in the middle of nowhere, I'm going to go with no. Just an honest inquiry."

He chuckled and thanked Judy when she refilled my coffee and brought him a fresh cup.

"I come in about twice a week." I pushed the cream and sugar closer but he politely shook his head. He took a sip of his coffee and asked, "Am I interrupting something important? Like work?"

"No," I assured him. "I was balancing my checking account. Wi-Fi at my house is sporadic, but mostly nonexistent. It's a tad better here so I like to come in once in a while when it's not so busy and log on." I didn't mention that I was going to get an internet booster that would rectify the situation.

I must've frowned because he followed up with, "Was there a problem? With your account?"

"No, nothing's wrong. I'll just have to admit to Darlene that she was right about something." I lifted my mug to my lips and, after swallowing, explained. "I don't pay much attention to my water bill, but Darlene had gotten on me about a leaky faucet. And she was right. There's been a small spike in my payments for the last couple months. It's nothing really. But I also noticed a pretty decent sized increase in my electric bill too. Makes me wonder if something is off there as well."

"I'm sure if you call them they can straighten it out," he said.

"Like I said, it's nothing. The faucet isn't leaking anymore. I'll just wait and see what next month's bill looks like."

Was I actually discussing my utility bills with Jake Chambers?

After a few more minutes of idle pleasantries he must've noticed Judy bringing his food because he straightened up and moved his mug out of the way. She set his plate in front of him, along with pancake syrup. I saw what he was eating and my distaste must've been obvious.

"You don't like pancakes?" he asked after thanking Judy.

"I love pancakes. I just don't like blueberry pancakes," I admitted.

"Why not?" he asked while pouring a healthy amount of syrup on them. "Allergic to them or just don't like blueberries?"

I didn't answer and he looked up. Shaking my head I told him, "No. I like blueberries and I'm not allergic to them."

His face registered curiosity and I shrugged my shoulders. "I've never eaten blueberry pancakes before." I knew my reply sounded lame, but I didn't owe Jake Chambers an explanation.

"Then how do you know you don't like them?" he questioned.

"I just know," I barked a little more briskly than I intended.

He didn't seem offended and instead of prying further he started cutting up his breakfast into man-sized bites. I changed the subject.

"I didn't hear your motorcycle when you pulled up."

His fork was full, and before putting it in his mouth, he said, "I drove my truck today."

"I didn't know you drove a truck."

I heard someone say, "Good morning, Doc," and I turned to say hello. It was a local man I'd recently treated at the clinic and I was worried that he might start providing details of his latest ailment which included an itchy scrotum, but he tipped his cowboy hat and kept walking.

Jake had taken a bite of his breakfast and, after swallowing, said, "I love my bike, but it's not very practical on some of these roads. I picked up a used F250 truck." He pointed his fork toward the man's retreating form. "You get that a lot?"

"Yeah, it's one reason I like to come here super early." I cocked my head to one side. "You're not wearing your scrubs. Are you off today or working a later shift?"

He reached for his coffee. "I'm off. One of the guys had some personal business and asked me to trade with him. I have errands to run and planned on heading over to the Harley dealership for a bike part. Heard it might rain so I thought it better to take my truck."

He must've been going to the same dealership where I'd bought the helmet for Dolly and the do-rag for him. "Thank you again for the do-rag. It was kind of you."

I lowered my eyes to the mug tightly clasped between both of my hands. I didn't want to talk about that day. I didn't want to ask how his date went with Dolly. After all, I didn't care. Right? I looked back at him and gave him a bright smile. "You're more than welcome. I would've bought you a helmet too if I thought you'd wear it."

He laughed and I started to fidget in my seat. He took notice of it and changed the subject.

"Your house is off the beaten path. Aren't you ever afraid of being out there all alone? I'm not asking because you're a woman. I have no doubt you can take care of yourself."

I wondered how he knew I was alone, but quickly dismissed it. Everyone in Pumpkin Rest knew I lived by myself. It was an accurate assumption on his part. I thought about his observation before answering. "When you put it like that, I guess I should be, but I've always felt safe in Pumpkin Rest. Nothing bad ever happens here."

"Said the person being interviewed on the evening news when something bad and unexpected happens in small towns across the country." He paused and scratched his jaw. He needed a shave and the sound his fingers made against his five-o'clock shadow sounded oddly appealing. I wondered for a split second if I could replicate the sound with my nails. "Do you know how to shoot a gun?" he asked.

"No. Well, kind of, but not really. I used to shoot my grandfather's old shotgun at coffee cans when I was a kid." The memory rushed over me and I smiled wistfully. "He used to have to stand behind me so I didn't get knocked on my butt."

"Do you still have the gun?"

I shook my head. "I don't need it. I keep a baseball bat the previous owners left behind the front door," I informed him as I reached for a napkin and wiped a spot on the table where my cup had left a ring.

"An aluminum bat isn't going to provide the kind of protection you'd need if someone invaded your home." He sounded almost aggravated. "Why don't you let me teach you how to shoot? I have a handgun you could practice with. You can even keep it."

His offer surprised me. I hadn't thought about learning to use a gun. Richard had been vehemently opposed to guns and I always thought I was too. Until now.

"Can I think about it?" I asked, while checking my watch. I was due at Dr. Tucker's clinic soon and I didn't think it was the kind of decision I wanted to make on the spot.

Jake gave me a brisk nod before lifting his coffee cup to his lips. As I watched him take a healthy swig, my eyes wandered to his neck.

"That's an interesting place to get a tattoo," I remarked.

He laughed. "Yeah, I didn't always make the best decisions when I was a kid."

"Why wasn't it a good decision?" I asked. I was curious what he had to say about it.

"It's kind of hard to impress a potential employer with a scary-looking skull staring at them over your collar. And since I'm not into turtle-necks…" He sniffed and added, "Well, like I said, it wasn't the best decision I made when I was younger."

"I guess if you were going to use a tattoo to cover something up, it would've been understandable." I reached for my cup and brought it to my mouth. Before taking a drink, I tilted my head sideways and observed the flames that came out from each side of the skull and made their way up the side of his neck.

His expression registered mild surprise. He sat back against the booth and scrubbed his hand down his face. Taking a deep breath he pitched forward, placing his elbows on the table. "I can see why you thought I was Kenny Pritchard. I saw his mug shot and I know why you might think my tattoo is covering something."

"I—"

He lifted his right hand, interrupting me. "I was curious about him after I started working at the assisted living facility. Especially after Jonathan kept calling me Kenny. I looked him up and I agree with you, Barbie." He quickly interjected, "Is it okay if I call you Barbie? I won't do it at work, but it feels weird calling you Dr. Anderson right now."

"Barbie is fine. And I'm not the one who insists on being called Dr. Anderson at Hampton House. That's Sheila's rule. Not mine."

His expression was one of empathy when he said, "What I'm trying to say is I get it."

"Well, you're the only one who gets it," I snorted.

"Our eyes, facial features, and jawlines are somewhat alike." He gave what appeared to be a thoughtful pause. "I saw the similarities in his mug shot to my younger self. We were close to the same age too."

"I appreciate you telling me that." I meant it. I knew for certain he wasn't Kenny Pritchard and something inside me felt a sliver of satisfaction knowing he didn't think I was completely ridiculous for assuming he was when I'd first met him.

"Besides, if I wasn't convinced of it before, I am after having breakfast with you," I said with an awkward grin. I looked at my watch again. "I'm not trying to be rude, but I have to get to work." I grabbed my laptop and purse and scooted out of the booth.

For someone so tall and wide he moved with a swiftness that surprised me. He was on his feet before I was and offered me his hand. I took it without thinking and thanked him for the coffee. I didn't reply when he said he'd like to do it again.

As I walked away he asked, "What did I say that convinced you I'm not Kenny?" I turned around to face him. His eyes were sincere and warm and I almost considered not telling him for fear of sounding stupid.

"It wasn't anything you said," I replied as I used my free hand to dig in my purse for my keys.

"Okay, what was it?" he asked as I once again turned to the door to leave.

I slowly shook my head and told him, "The real Kenny Pritchard would never have ordered and eaten blueberry pancakes in front of me."

Hours later I was stitching up a construction worker who'd sliced his hand open when something occurred to me. All morning I'd been mentally wading through the sea of dialogue I'd had with Jake at the diner. And no matter how many times I'd recalled our conversation, I couldn't for the life of me remember telling him that the baseball bat I kept behind my front door was aluminum.

CHAPTER 9

THE EXTRAORDINARY INTERPRETER OF
SECRET GLANCES

L ittle by little my house started to feel like home. I had to admit there was a smug satisfaction in turning Juanita Anderson's run-down farmhouse into the place I intended to permanently call home. But, if I was honest, I wasn't doing it to spite the grandmother who'd made my life miserable. I was doing it for myself. And since I didn't plan on or foresee having a man in my future, I felt I was restoring the place as a tribute to the only two men in my life who'd honestly loved me. My father and grandfather.

It was the little things in the renovation that brought me joy. Like making sure the painter clear-sealed the closet doorjamb where the markings of my father's growth spurts had been recorded. I'd discovered them when I was measuring the interior of the closet in his former bedroom. I couldn't bring myself to have the painter erase that small piece of my dad's childhood, so when he suggested covering it with a sealant to preserve it, I quickly agreed.

I'd decided to turn that room into a combination office and guest room. Too bad I couldn't think of one person who might ever stay in it. Before I let that thought bring me down, I quickly rinsed out my coffee cup and dashed out the front door. It was Sunday morning, and after my weekly visit with Jonathan, Darlene and I were going to hit a few flea markets further west. I jumped in my Jeep and headed for the assisted living facility.

I was in Jonathan's room finishing up our fifteenth game of checkers when I heard, "I thought that was your car outside. Nice to see you, Dr. Anderson."

As I turned to greet the familiar voice, Jonathan started clapping and chanting, "Barbie and Ken. Barbie and Ken."

I stood and began to collect the checkers. "I didn't think you worked on Sundays."

He walked toward us and high-fived Jonathan before answering. "Normally I don't, but today was a special case."

"Oh?"

"One of our residents is a retired fireman who's been confined to his bed for a few years now. You probably remember him from when you covered rounds that day," he added. "He didn't like me at first because of...you know, how I look." He laughed before saying, "But, he came around and we've been buddies ever since. Anyway, his normal bath day is Thursday, and I'm the only one who can lift him using the sling without hurting him." I nodded and he continued. "For whatever reason, they had to reschedule his bath to today and I knew he wasn't going to like it. He can be feisty and I knew he'd be trouble if anyone else tried to lift him. I dropped in to help out."

"That's so nice of you to come in on your day off." I tried not to show how impressed I was with his kindness toward one of the residents, and an ornery one at that. He was right, I did remember the man and he had given me a hard time. Apparently, Jake had managed to soften him. That was admirable.

I finished putting the checkers away and addressed Jonathan. "You know Darlene will be here soon so I have to go. But I promise to come back on Wednesday for bingo with you and Cindy." His answer was a big smile and a tight hug.

"I'm going to walk Dr. Anderson out, big guy," Jake told him. "I'll be back to see you."

We left Jonathan's room and headed down the hallway side by side. I hadn't seen Jake in two weeks—since we'd had coffee at the diner.

I blurted out the first thing that popped into my head. "How did you know my baseball bat was aluminum?" I looked sideways at him, but my question hadn't phased him.

He shrugged nonchalantly and said, "The bat you told me you keep behind your front door?" Without waiting for me to reply he casually answered, "I didn't think about it. I figured it would be wooden or aluminum. I had an aluminum one when I was a kid."

It was as good an answer as any. "You play baseball?"

"Played," he said with emphasis. "Little League was a way of life for me growing up."

"Did you grow up in Texas?" It was an assumption I'd made based on his prison record.

He stopped and turned to me with an expression I couldn't decipher. Had I crossed a line? Did he have something to hide?

"Let's do coffee again and I'll tell you about my childhood and you can tell me about yours. No blueberry pancakes this time. I promise." His eyes seemed to be filled with regret. He was remembering my feelings toward my least favorite breakfast without even knowing the reason behind it. He wasn't making fun of my disdain for blueberry pancakes. He was respecting it. I felt a warmth in my belly. Perhaps Jake Chambers with his scary prison tattoos and offensive gas tank wasn't such a bad guy. I wanted to accept his invitation but wasn't sure how much I cared to share about my miserable upbringing.

In the end, my hesitation to answer may have saved me some embarrassment. I was a millisecond away from asking what morning he wanted to meet when something caught his eye and he looked away. I followed his gaze and it landed on one of the LPNs on duty. It looked like she'd been trying to get his attention. Her name was Yvonne. She was probably in her mid-forties, and an attractive brunette with the whitest teeth I'd ever seen. She had a shapely figure and I was certain her oversized chest wasn't a result of surgery. However, it was obvious that her tan was store-bought.

She looked at Jake with an apologetic smile. "They asked me to stay a little longer. Do you mind waiting for me?"

He shook his head and said, "No, I'm in no hurry. We can leave as soon as you're ready."

My disappointment was staggering. *Well, at least he graduated from liking giggly girls to women,* I thought as I tried to grapple with my feelings. I was wondering what Dolly thought of the competition when Yvonne said, "I made your favorite dinner. It's in the Crock-Pot and I can't be sure, but I think it's going to turn out pretty good."

Just then, a familiar voice asked, "Why aren't you answering your texts?"

I looked past Jake and saw Darlene bounding toward me with a smile. "I've been standing out front waiting for you." She'd attended her regular Sunday morning church service in Pumpkin Rest and had her oldest son drop her at the assisted living facility so we could drive together.

"I didn't get a text," I answered honestly, secretly grateful that she'd rescued me from having to turn down Jake's invitation to coffee. I pasted on a smile and said, "It looks like I'm out of here. Have a great day." I took off without giving him a chance to reply.

As we drove to Pickens County, Darlene interrogated me about my visits to Hampton House, but she was mostly interested in Jake. I told her why he was there on his day off and she was just as impressed as I'd been.

"And you haven't seen Jake before today?" she inquired. "Not since the diner?"

"Nope. Haven't seen him since." I adjusted the air-conditioning vent away from my face. "And before you get any grand ideas about playing matchmaker, I'm pretty certain he's seeing someone."

"Me? Matchmaker?" She placed her hand against her chest dramatically. I couldn't help but laugh.

I filled her in on the interaction I'd witnessed between Jake and Yvonne.

She slapped her thigh and said, "That means nothing. He could've been giving her a ride home, Barbie, and she's repaying the favor with a meal. You've already told me he's a nice guy. I just don't see him asking you to coffee one minute and turning around to spend the afternoon and have dinner with a woman he's seeing the next. He doesn't strike me as the type. And he's never mentioned a girlfriend to me."

I knew Darlene had occasional interaction with Jake at the gas station, but it was obvious she'd been reading him all wrong.

"There's something else." I turned on my left blinker and waited for a car to pass.

"What? What else is there?" She sat up straighter and turned in her seat to face me.

"Before Yvonne asked if he wouldn't mind waiting a little longer for her, they exchanged a glance."

"What kind of a glance?" Darlene leaned toward me. I had her attention.

"The kind of glance you don't want others to see. A secret glance," I whispered for emphasis.

"Oh, well, if there was a secret glance, I can certainly see why you've written him off." There was no missing the sarcasm in her tone. She followed up with, "I forgot that you aren't only a gifted surgeon, but you're also an extraordinary interpreter of secret glances."

Her description was ridiculous and we both started laughing.

"Fine. I'll give him the benefit of the doubt," I told her. "Maybe, and I'm only saying maybe, if he asks me to coffee again, I just might accept."

An hour later, disappointed that I couldn't find any suitable fixtures for my renovation, we made our way through the throng of sellers and buyers when I stopped short and stared ahead. Darlene had continued walking and talking. When she realized I was no longer next to her she stopped and walked back to me. Following my gaze she let out a loud sigh, and I didn't have to see them to know her shoulders sagged.

"Dirty darn it," she said in a low voice. "I had such high hopes for the two of you."

"I know you did, Dar, but it's fine. Better to know now, right?"

It turned out that Jake Chambers was the type of person to ask a woman out for coffee moments before spending the afternoon with his girlfriend. I watched as he stood about three booths ahead of us, holding hands with Yvonne. They looked like they were haggling with a man who was selling furniture. When Jake wrapped his arm around her waist and pulled her to him, I turned around.

"There has to be another way out of here," I told Darlene as I did my best not to stomp my way to the nearest exit.

CHAPTER 10

YEAH, I'LL BE YOUR FUN BUDDY

I'd turned into a grump and Darlene called me out on it more than once. I blamed it on hormones and she called me a liar. She was right. I was angry. Not at Jake but at myself for letting in a smidgen of hope that there might be something more to him. I'd been letting men disappoint me and break my heart since 1975, the year my father died. I was more determined than ever to break the cycle. I just didn't know how.

I would see an opportunity a week later when I pulled into my driveway after an extremely long day and saw the familiar pickup truck that boasted the name of the town's only HVAC company parked in front of my house.

Dustin was sitting on my porch in the old Adirondack chair I'd recently painted fire-engine red. He stood and walked down the steps. I turned off the ignition and got out of my Jeep.

He greeted me with an embarrassed smile and said, "I knew if I waited long enough you'd eventually come home."

I'd seen Dustin in town a few times over the past few weeks. He was always friendly but had stopped asking me out. Seeing him at my house reminded me that I'd never thanked him for repairing the loose gutter. It would seem rude to continue avoiding an expression of appreciation. I walked toward him and said, "I've been meaning to thank you for forever, and I keep forgetting." I pointed to the right side of my house where the gutter had been dangling.

He followed my gaze, then stuck his hands in his pockets and rolled back on his heels. He looked momentarily confused so I quickly added, "You know, for repairing my gutter. I never thanked you."

He pasted on a dazzling smile before saying, "I'll accept your belated thank-you if you'll have dinner with me."

"Is that why you drove all the way out here?" I asked, stopping to shift the grocery bag I was carrying to the other arm. "To ask me to dinner?"

He grinned. "I thought playing hard to get and leaving you alone would make you change your mind. It hasn't worked, so I came out here to ask again. And since you reminded me you owe me a thank-you, I'm gonna take advantage of it."

He took the bag out of my arms. "Unless there's something in here I can cook for you."

"Now you want to cook for me?" I laughed. He was cute, and even though I didn't find myself attracted to him, I couldn't deny the small thrill that came with knowing he was interested in me.

"Sure, I'll cook for you," he countered with confidence.

That's when I made up my mind to accept his invitation. I didn't have any intention of using Dustin. I would make it clear to him up front that I wasn't interested in him romantically. But if he wanted to pursue a strictly platonic relationship, I wouldn't mind spending time with him. As Darlene had ranted at me more than once, "You're only fifty-two, Barbie. You don't have to date, but you do need to have some fun." She was right.

"Unless you can whip us up something from two cans of green beans, coffee creamer, toilet paper, cotton balls, and laundry detergent, we might need to head into town for dinner." I unlocked the front door and he followed me inside.

"I'll take you anywhere you want to go, Barbie." He said it with such sincerity, I almost felt bad that I didn't see him the way he saw me. He carried my groceries to the kitchen and I followed him. When he set the bag down on the counter, I took the opportunity to lay my cards on the table. His face registered disappointment, but he recovered and smiled at me.

"Yeah, I'll be your fu—"

"My fun buddy," I interrupted.

He laughed and said, "That's exactly what I was going to say. Not the other thing. I respect you too much, Barbie. I won't be inappropriate, but I'm not going to lie to you. I'm going to do what I can to change your mind."

"I need twenty minutes to take a quick shower and get ready."

Forty-five minutes later, we were walking to his truck when I heard the familiar rumble coming up my street. The timing couldn't have been worse. Another woman might've seen this as an opportunity to show Jake she'd caught the eye of a much younger man. I wasn't that woman. I'd never played games, and I didn't intend to start now. I was wondering if I would have to introduce them. I cringed inwardly when I remembered that I'd gone to school with Dustin's father. *You need to make sure Dustin has thought this through,* I reminded myself.

I busted out with, "You know I'm old enough to be your mother?"

Dustin looked away from the biker who was slowly coming toward us and said, "You don't look like any mother I know, Barbie." The compliment provided the reassurance I was seeking, and I walked to the edge of the yard as Jake brought his bike to a stop.

I gave him a sincere smile and said, "I thought you already figured out this road doesn't go anywhere."

He didn't return my smile, but instead looked at me, then Dustin, then back at me. I felt his eyes rake over my body as he took in my loose, flowing skirt, strappy sandals, and tight-fitting tank top. I had a light sweater slung over my arm. The tank top didn't show too much cleavage, but enough to hint at what was beneath.

His jaw appeared tense when he said, "I did some exploring that first day. It actually comes out in Pickens County if you know which trail to follow." His voice betrayed no emotion. It was so even I could've placed a level on it.

"Oh, I didn't realize you knew about those roads." I paused and asked, "How often do you use my road to cut through?"

His answer was curt. "Once in a while."

I didn't know if the heat I was feeling was from Jake or the setting sun at my back.

There was a long, awkward moment that Dustin interrupted by walking up next to me and lightly grabbed my elbow with his left hand. "We better get going, Barbie." He extended his right hand to Jake and introduced himself. Jake took it but his expression never changed. His blue eyes were sharp and intent as he gave an abrupt nod. He turned his attention to me and I almost shrank under his gaze. But my momentary weakness turned to shock when he said, "You need to change your skirt or keep your legs closer together when the sun is behind you. I'm pretty sure I can see the outline of your radiant orchid." Without giving me a chance to reply, he revved his bike and sped off.

Dustin took me to a quaint Italian restaurant about thirty miles west of Pumpkin Rest. I spent the entire drive trying to convince him that Jake was a good guy, and that he only appeared menacing and rude. I spent the rest of the evening trying to convince myself that I believed it.

CHAPTER 11

FIREFLIES AND FLASHLIGHTS

D inner with Dustin was more than pleasant, but if I was honest, I'd rather have spent my evening with a sandwich, a glass of milk, and an old movie. The conversation started out normal enough. He seemed genuinely interested in me and my work, and he asked about and made several good suggestions concerning my home renovation. I was grateful he never touched on my divorce or reason for moving back to Pumpkin Rest.

I learned that his original dreams were dashed when he suffered an injury on the football field and forfeited his college scholarship. He could've pursued another career, but football had been his life and he didn't have a backup plan. So he decided to stay in Pumpkin Rest and help his father with their family-owned HVAC company. The couple of years he'd given himself to rethink his future turned into more than a decade, and at thirty years old he appeared happy with his decision to stay close to home. He didn't seem bitter about it, and I admired his positive attitude. He'd expanded the family business and now had a fleet of trucks that serviced several surrounding counties. When I asked him why he wasn't married, his answer was simple. He'd never found the right woman.

I remembered squirming in my seat at his last comment and changing the subject. It wasn't until our small talk circled back to my early years growing up in Pumpkin Rest that I started longing for the comfort of my bed and DVD remote. Dustin seemed curious about the Pritchard farm. He'd grown up hearing tales from his grandfather about the best moonshine east of the Mississippi coming from their illegal, hidden stills. I'd told him it was true, but those stills had long since dried up and the family's secret recipe had died with Kenny Pritchard.

"My high school buddies and I spent every spare moment we could combing that abandoned farmhouse and looking for hidden underground bunkers and still sites," he'd confessed.

I'd sipped my wine and listened. I was certain Dustin and his friends hadn't been the only ones to hope something had been left behind that would give up the Pritchards' secrets.

A blanket of melancholy washed over me, and I ordered a second glass of wine, hoping it would dull the memories that threatened to steal my buzz along with my peace.

Hours later, the moon was hiding behind heavy storm clouds as we drove down my pitch-dark road. I blinked my eyes a few times. "Isn't it late for lightning bugs?" I asked as the gravel crunched beneath the tires of his truck.

"I guess a new batch showed up 'cause it's so warm. You didn't even need your sweater," he reminded me.

We eventually rounded a curve and I could see the flicker of my front porch lights in the distance. By the time he delivered me to my front door, I was certain we'd said everything we had to say, and I wouldn't be receiving a second invitation from Dustin. I was wrong. He'd walked me to my door and lightly held my hand in both of his. He said he'd like to take me someplace a little more fun next time. He told me about a restaurant that served the best wings in the South, and he'd recently learned from some friends that the second Saturday of every month was country music night. They brought in local talent and did live performances.

"You like country music, don't you?" he asked. I didn't want to admit that I'd almost forgotten how much I loved it. It was one of those things I'd left behind when I moved away to college. It wasn't popular at school and I ended up listening to what everyone else listened to. I'd poked fun at Darlene's choice of music at the gas station, but truth be told, I loved it. I'd just forgotten I loved it. Without warning, the song I'd heard my first day at Hampton House popped into my head and I found myself swaying to a beat I was shocked I remembered. I couldn't recall what I wore yesterday, but I remembered the deep timber of the artist's voice from several weeks back.

"Yeah," I told Dustin as I tried not to sound too enthusiastic and stilled my swaying. When he didn't say anything I looked past him, distracted by the fireflies.

"Fun buddies, Barbie. That's all," he told me. "Good food, good music. A fun crowd. I probably should've waited until Saturday and taken you there first. I enjoyed tonight, but I think we took an unexpected U-turn somewhere along the way. Will you give me another chance? Please?"

I nibbled on my bottom lip, contemplating my answer. I'd enjoyed Dustin's company until he'd brought up the Pritchard farm. And there was nothing unusual about that. The Pritchards had been well-known and their escapades had been part of the local folklore going back to before the Civil War. It probably would've been more unusual if their name hadn't been brought up in a conversation about growing up in Pumpkin Rest.

I accepted his invitation, and before I could explain why I wasn't going to invite him inside, he brought my hand to his lips and kissed it lightly.

"I'll wait until you're inside and hear you lock the door before I leave," he informed me.

I watched from the window as his taillights disappeared from view. I headed for the bathroom and washed my face and brushed my teeth. I removed the night shirt and robe I kept on a hook behind the door and changed into them. Since the house only had one bathroom on the first floor, I usually took care of my ablutions before heading upstairs for the night. I snickered to myself when I thought about how many times I'd recently had to head downstairs in the middle of the night to relieve myself. "You need to get yourself a chamber pot or have your old bedroom turned into a master bath sooner than later," I said out loud. Stupid menopause. Even though I was on the back side of it, as a physician I should've been more prepared for the inconvenient symptoms that sometimes hung around for longer than they were welcome.

I harrumphed when I reached the top of the stairs and instead of heading for my bedroom, I walked past it. Without turning on any lights, I crept through the dark to the little room just beyond. I felt the weight of memories envelop me like the heavy storm clouds that were threatening outside. When Fancy and I had first moved to Pumpkin Rest, I could've shared my father's old bedroom with her, but I'd desperately wanted my space. I was nine at the time and remembered worrying that hearing me cry into my pillow every night would eventually have a negative effect on my baby sister. My grandmother was against the idea at first, but she changed her tune when she realized the only space available to me could best be described as a storage closet. It was probably the beginning of the malicious mind games she would take pleasure in playing. It was ironic that I'd given her the first batch of ammunition.

My grandfather spent an entire morning hauling away an antiquated sewing machine, stacks of outdated newspapers and magazines, boxes of canning jars, a broken ironing board, and a plethora of junk just so I could have my own room. The tiny area had probably served another purpose in the past because there was one window facing the west. There was enough space for a twin bed, a nightstand, and a dresser. My clothes that needed to be hung went on hooks that my grandfather installed behind the door. As a teen, I became creative and constructed something along the lines of a clothesline that took up one corner.

I now stood in front of the door and slowly opened it. It would be the first time I'd looked in this room since I bought the house. The previous owners had left a pile of unwanted possessions, and after hiring a local kid to empty it for me, I'd shut the door and not opened it since. The creaking should've sounded eerie, but this room brought back a few warm and happy memories I'd wanted to ignore but couldn't. Just for tonight I craved to feel what I felt back then. I needed to resurrect that sense of connection to someone who'd cared. At least I'd thought he'd cared.

There was no light from the moon and I didn't want to flip on the bright overhead bulb so I took out my phone and used the flashlight app to scan the small space. Too little for a bedroom but definitely big enough for a good-sized bathroom, I'd already had Dustin, the plumber, and the electrician rough out the room. I looked at the markings and noticed where they'd installed pipes in the walls and vents and drains in the floor according to the drawing I'd given them. I aimed my phone at an untouched area of hardwood floor by the window and felt a lump form in my throat. *I wonder if it's still there.*

I made my way to the window and sank down next to the spot. I softly caressed the ancient wood, finding the place where it could be lifted to reveal what lay beneath. I tried to use my nails to dig into the crevices, but ended up getting a splinter instead. If I'd been able to pry up the board I knew I would've found a flashlight that had been resting in secret slumber for almost forty years. A flashlight that boasted the initials K.P. scrawled in Kenny's careless handwriting. We didn't have permanent markers back then. *I wonder if his initials have faded away. Erased by time, like our love for each other.*

I felt the tickling of a solitary tear as it made its way down my cheek. But I didn't swipe it away. I let it fall. I let the next one caress my heated skin. Before I knew it, water was leaking from both eyes, but I didn't care. Since I'd heard the news that Kenny Pritchard had run away, I'd kept every tear walled behind my eyes. I now let them rise in an explosion of emotion that I'd been unable to allow before.

I wasn't being entirely truthful with myself. I hadn't cried when I'd heard Kenny had run away. I'd cried when I realized he wasn't coming back.

I turned off my flashlight app and slowly went from sitting to lying on the floor in a room so dark I couldn't see my hand in front of me. I felt a rush of emotion as I remembered the summer when I was thirteen. My grandfather had insisted that I be allowed to go away to a girl's camp for a week. My grandmother had fought him on it, but he was adamant. I think he may have been concerned that Kenny and I were becoming too close and that I needed to spend some time with other girls my age. This was before I'd become close to Darlene, and he thought it would do me good to get away from Pumpkin Rest for a little while. After all, it was only for a week.

At first, I didn't want to go but had to admit the idea of being away from my grandmother, and the extra summer chores she gave me, was appealing. Kenny wholeheartedly agreed. I wrote to him every day for the first seven days. Then something unexpected happened.

A girl I'd met at camp was staying an extra week, and her parents offered to pay my tuition if I agreed to stay. I hadn't realized then that this girl was having a difficult time making friends and when we clicked, her parents, who'd been desperate for her to interact, saw it as an extended opportunity for their daughter to fit in. I missed Kenny and Jonathan, who'd followed us practically everywhere. I'd even started to miss my bratty sister, Frenita, but I was enjoying myself and didn't think another week away from Pumpkin Rest would be the end of the world. I told her parents they would have to call my grandparents at a certain time when my grandfather would be sure to answer the phone. Otherwise, they would've gotten a resounding no from my grandmother.

After fourteen days at camp I could tell by the look on my grandfather's face when he picked me up at the bus station that he had bad news. We stopped on the way home at a Dairy Queen where we took our food to an outside picnic table that was covered by the dappled shade of a stately old oak tree. It was there over my uneaten cheeseburger and melted vanilla shake that he told me how Kenny had run away days after I'd left for camp.

"I don't believe you!" I screamed. "Kenny wouldn't run away without telling me."

My grandfather's eyes were sad when he told me that our next stop before we got home would be the police station. "I told them I would bring you in to tell them what you know, if anything. They seem to think he's not a runaway and said that kids who leave home usually show back up in less than a couple weeks anyway, so they didn't feel the need to make the long trip out to camp to talk to you." I didn't ask him why the police didn't call the camp to speak with me.

I told the authorities what I'd told my grandfather. Kenny had not shared with me any plans to leave town. My grandfather tried to stop me from spouting off that, more than likely, Mr. Pritchard had done something to scare Kenny away. I told them about the abuse. They pretended to be sympathetic and said not to worry. He would get tired of living on the road and be back before school started.

The distant hoot of an owl broke the dark, still silence as I rolled onto my back and blinked into the pitch-black abyss of my future bathroom. Determined to stamp down the sadness, I used the sleeve of my robe to wipe away the tears and let a smile tug at the corner of my mouth when I remembered why the flashlight was hidden beneath my bedroom floor. This was the happy memory I'd been searching for. The one that made my heart swell. Soon after I moved to Pumpkin Rest and we became friends, Kenny and I set up a secret code to communicate after dark. The Pritchard farm was separated from ours by a wall of forest that included a couple covert tree houses that were used by lookouts back when they ran moonshine during Prohibition. After everyone was asleep, Kenny would sneak out to the one that faced my bedroom window and send me messages using a flashlight. Our code was silly and rudimentary, but it was ours and we eventually perfected it. Our friendship grew along with our private messages we shared at night.

My grandmother caught us one evening when she went outside after she'd heard thunder and remembered she'd left clothes on the line. Kenny had signaled me it was starting to rain and he was going in for the night. If I hadn't signaled back we might not have been caught. She marched up to my room, flung open my door and grabbed the flashlight from me, saying if she ever saw it missing from the pantry again, she'd hit me with it. I knew she'd make good on the threat and I told Kenny about it the next morning at the bus stop. A few days later he gave me his old flashlight and told me to find a good hiding spot. I'd used an old-fashioned metal nail file to jimmy up the floorboard closest to my window. My hidden flashlight was my secret and I reveled in having pulled one over on Juanita Anderson.

I sighed and my smile evaporated when I remembered driving home from the police station. I was still in denial that Kenny had run away. It was well after dark by the time we got home, and without even saying hello to my grandmother or Frenita, I dashed up the stairs to my bedroom. I frantically searched for the nail file. I needed to pry up the board and send him a message. I knew he'd been hiding in the tree house for more than a week and was waiting for me to get back from camp so he could tell me what was happening.

"Frenita!" I screamed at the top of my lungs. "Do you have my nail file?" I knew she'd taken it. She was about six years old by then and had already started with her prissy ways. Not caring whether or not my grandmother would follow through on the beating she'd promised a few years earlier, I marched down to the pantry and swiped the flashlight from the shelf. I ran back up the stairs and had reached the top step when I heard my grandmother's voice float up behind me. It held a tone of malice laced with smug satisfaction.

"You can keep that one, Barbara Jean, but you're wasting your time. That Pritchard boy has up and left and he ain't coming back."

I didn't have to turn around to know she was sneering. Later, I'd resolved never to let her see my heartache and pain when I'd realized she was right. I'd spent the next few weeks scouring the Pritchard farm, checking the tree houses, the secret bunkers that contained the stashes of moonshine that Mr. Pritchard still made, as well as our favorite hiding spots. It became my obsession, and I even made it a point to recheck certain places, as well as keep up my flashlight vigil. Our favorite spot was a hollowed-out tree on our property. Kenny and I used it to hide the occasional Mason jar of moonshine that he stole from his father. If he was going to leave me a message, that was our hiding place. I finally stopped checking. I never returned the family flashlight to the pantry and I never asked for my nail file back to lift up the board. I knew what was beneath it. A flashlight without a message to send.

I let out a deep breath and realized I'd let the joyful memories of secret messages and hiding places be extinguished by the anguish of him leaving without so much as a goodbye. I wasn't a drinker, and the two glasses of wine I'd had at dinner started to make me feel queasy. Or maybe it wasn't the wine. Maybe it was the memory.

I sat up, faced the window, and rested my elbows on the low casement sill. I reached for the lock above my head, and after unlatching it, opened the window about two inches. I leaned onto the small ledge and rested my chin on my forearms. My lids started to droop and eventually close as I inhaled the fresh country air.

I didn't know how much time had passed when I opened my eyes and sat straight up. I tried to fathom what had startled me. It was an eerie feeling. Like I was being watched. I was sitting in the dark and no one could see me. Outside, the sky was black as tar. I'd turned off my front porch lights so there wasn't even any light sneaking around the side of the house. Staring out the window was like looking at a black wall. And then I saw it.

I gasped when I caught sight of a flicker of light from afar. My brain desperately scrambled around for the memory of our secret code. My breathing was coming in shallow gasps as I felt around the floor for the board desperately trying to get to the long-forgotten flashlight. It had never occurred to me that by now the battery would've eroded and a forty-year-old flashlight was useless. In my haste, my hand knocked my phone and I heard it skitter across the hardwood and stop with a thud against the opposite baseboard. The noise shook me out of my panic, and I circled back to the window.

The lightning bugs. I wasn't seeing flashlight signals from the distant tree line. It had been a lone firefly. Taking a calming breath, I brushed my hand through my hair and resumed my original position with my chin pressed against my forearms which were again resting on the low windowsill. I waited for the lightning bug to serenade me with its sparkle. Nothing. I stared into the moonless night and willed the firefly to resume its dance. Still nothing. It was obvious this hadn't been a good idea. The familiar ache of my thirteen-year-old heart pressed down on my chest like an anvil. *Stop torturing yourself, Barbie. Let him go.*

I slunk back to the floor and didn't fight the sleep that was beckoning. I drifted off with the sound of Darlene's voice echoing in the back of my mind as I mentally conceded that she'd been right. I'd never gotten over Kenny Pritchard.

CHAPTER 12

MOONSHINE ISN'T THE BEST MEDICINE

"You need to snap out of whatever this is, Barbie," Darlene said, giving me a firm but understanding look. "So you had a couple of glasses of wine the other night and thought you saw Kenny signaling you from one of the tree houses. So what?"

It was two days after I'd fallen asleep in my old bedroom. We were sitting on my back-porch steps taking modest sips out of a Mason jar. Ignoring her comment, I passed the jar back to her and watched her take another shallow taste. I shrugged my shoulders, feigning nonchalance.

"You were tipsy and figured out it was the lightning bugs getting the best of you, so what's the big deal? It's not like you're in denial. You owned up to your mistake that Jake isn't Kenny. How is this any different?"

"It just is, Dar. I should know better. I've been making ridiculous assumptions. It's not like me and I'm tired of feeling stupid. And I'm even more tired of being haunted by why Kenny left without a word. It's been almost forty years. Why haven't I gotten over it?" I sat with both elbows resting on my knees and looked out over the acres of barren fields behind my house. Storm clouds were rolling in from the north and there was a chill in the air. I welcomed the bite of autumn that had blown in overnight and left goose bumps on my arms and neck.

"Because he hurt you, Barbie. What he did was unfair and heartbreaking, nobody would argue that. But Kenny is gone, and can't come back. You may not have forgotten him or the pain he left behind, but you've moved on from the little girl whose heart was crushed."

"Have I?" I asked with a cynical laugh.

"Yes, you have. You've made a good life for yourself. You've always been a fighter, a survivor." She rested a hand on my thigh.

"I didn't fight for my marriage," I said flatly.

"I think we both know it wouldn't have changed the ending," she quietly answered. "And as far as Kenny is concerned, you have no choice but to move on. You can stay in this funk of always wondering or you can put it behind you and see what God has planned for you. Besides, you are way too hard on yourself, and even more than that, I don't think you're being honest with yourself."

"I already admitted that you were right, Dar. I told you before that I agreed with you—I'm not over Kenny Pritchard." I absently twirled the Mason jar in my hands. "I'm over the love part. I'm no longer in love with him. Haven't been for a long time. But I'm not over the abandonment. I still can't get past the fact that he left without a word. And after you told me he was in prison, how he never once replied to any of my letters."

"He didn't reply to most of mine either, Barbie."

I twisted my head around to face her. "Most of yours? Does that mean he replied to at least one of them?"

She nodded. "The first one was to thank me for visiting Jonathan when he was sent to a home on the other side of the state following their father's death. And a few more after that. They stopped after a while."

My eyes burned with the sting of unshed tears. After the breakdown in my old bedroom, I didn't think I had any left. I'd visited Jonathan, too, but it hadn't gone well. He'd seen me and his brother together so often that I couldn't go near him after Kenny ran away. His mind couldn't imagine one of us without the other and when I showed up without Kenny, it only upset him. Even after Kenny left and years before I'd headed for college, I'd tried to take Jonathan fishing, or hiking in the woods like we'd done with Kenny. But he would see me and start crying uncontrollably. I had no doubt that if Jake hadn't been in Jonathan's room at Hampton House on my first day there, it would've played out like it had the last time I saw him. I'd been a college student and happened to be attending a lecture near Jonathan's group home when I stopped in unannounced. My visit without his older brother in tow upset him so badly they asked me not to come back.

I felt Darlene's hand gently rubbing my back. I stifled a sniffle and asked, "Did Kenny ever mention me in his letters?"

I wouldn't look at her. I didn't want to see pity in her eyes. I took another swallow of the fiery liquid and concentrated on my grandfather's old woodshed. It looked like it was ready to fall down.

"Only once," she practically whispered. "After I'd written that you'd gotten married."

This time I did look at her.

"He wrote back that he was happy for you. That you deserved to be in love. To have a happy life."

"That was all?" My voice was hoarse. It was clogged with thousands of words that would be left unsaid.

"Yes, that was all."

I sat up straight and put the lid back on the Mason jar. "I guess there's nothing left to say then. It's a mystery that will never be solved, and like you said, I have to put it behind me." I started to wilt again and heard myself say, "Maybe coming back here wasn't such a good idea after all."

"Stop talking nonsense, Barbie! Whether you want to admit it or not, this is your home." She pointed back over her shoulder and said, "*Your* home. It no longer belongs to Juanita Anderson and her miserable self. You were loved and are still loved by more people than just me. Look how happy you make Jonathan. And the town folk are so glad to have a doctor in their midst. You must be the last doctor on earth who actually carries a medical bag in case of an emergency. And that comes with a responsibility and expense that you incur without complaint. And think about it, how many doctors nowadays get paid in hugs, fresh eggs, buttermilk pies, and promises to flush out your septic when it's time?"

Her last comment made me laugh.

"You belong here, Barbara Jean Anderson. I just wish the real Barbie would show herself."

Her last comment startled me. "What do you mean by that, Darlene? I'm the real Barbie. I haven't changed."

"Oh, please. The real Barbie wouldn't have turned in her track sneakers for a tennis racket. Or convinced herself she likes classical music instead of country."

"Tennis was something Richard and I could do together at his club," I said somewhat defensively.

"And let me guess? They didn't play country music at the club?" she argued using air quotes to drive home her point. "I think you stopped being who you were because of Richard. You already told me how he insisted on that fancy and ridiculously expensive condo because he didn't want to hassle with a yard. He was an attorney and you're a doctor for goodness' sake. Ever heard of a lawn service? I find it hard to believe that you agreed since you grew up getting your hands dirty."

Is that what I'd done? Traded in my true self for the life that Richard had meticulously mapped out for us? Dar was right. I was a runner. Had always been a runner until Richard convinced me to take up tennis so we could do something together. I'd gotten tired of asking him to run with me and eventually those solitary jogs in the park turned into tennis matches with him at the club. And as far as the country music was concerned, I'd started listening to it again after college, but Richard insisted on classical when we were together. Whether we were at home or in the car, he'd turn into The Music Nazi. And he always had a good reason why. After all, that's what he did for a living. He was a litigator. He could convince a squirrel that it was a zebra. Classical music was good for the soul, it smoothed out the rough edges of our stressful days, he'd told me. Eventually, I'd believed it.

"We didn't need a yard because we couldn't have children," I countered, feeling the need to defend myself.

"Bull," she tossed back at me. "You could've adopted children."

I felt lightheaded and couldn't decipher if it was from what we were drinking or the slow dawning that her accusations were true. Darlene had come dangerously close to a truth I'd not allowed to surface since the day I said my wedding vows. Richard had been a white-collar bully, and worse yet, I'd enabled him. He'd completely orchestrated almost every aspect of our marriage. And I'd been so absorbed in my work and being the perfect spouse, I'd allowed it. I was mortified at the realization. I jumped up and started pacing.

"You're right, Dar. Everything you said is right." I stopped and gave her a hard stare. "Richard never abused me. Richard was a good guy. I need to be clear about that."

"I never thought Richard wasn't a good guy, Barbie. He had to be good or you wouldn't have married him. I'm only saying that in the little time we've gotten to know each other again, and the stories you've shared about him, it seems that you lost your way. He led and you followed."

I plopped back down next to her and ran my hands through my hair. "Is it possible I subconsciously allowed it because I needed someone to be in charge? I'd worked so hard to become a doctor; I think I was exhausted with responsibility. Like I needed someone else to take the reins for a while. I never realized I'd never taken them back or asked to share them."

"I think it's very possible. Maybe it's why you've been fighting so hard to prove yourself capable since you've been home. You have an air about you now that says you don't need anybody. It's not a weakness to need or count on others. Look at how many people here rely on you. Do you see them as weak?"

"Not at all," I stated. I looked over and smiled. "Why do I feel like a weight has been lifted? I guess I should be angrier with myself, but I'm not. I feel." I paused, searching for the right word. "Relieved. I feel relieved and lighter for some reason."

She reached for the Mason jar and, holding it up, asked, "Because moonshine is the best medicine?"

"Not bad for forty-year-old hooch, is it?" I teasingly elbowed her in the side.

"This goes down so smoothly. After all these years and it still packs a punch. No wonder the Pritchards' moonshine had a good reputation." She giggled, followed by a belch.

"You remember what it tasted like?" I questioned.

She shook her head, unscrewed the lid, and took another sip. "No, I'd never tried it before today, but I'd heard about it." She delicately wiped her mouth. "I can't believe you found four jars still intact."

"Me either." Before Darlene showed up, I'd grabbed a basket and trudged out to the woods searching out every secret hiding place that Kenny and I had stashed moonshine. These were all places that I'd checked after he'd run away, but had never revisited to collect the liquor. Some places were vacant. It was possible I hadn't remembered correctly or my grandmother had found them. She knew that Kenny and I used to steal the whiskey and bury it. It's why we had more than one hiding place, and how I managed to find four jars. There were probably more if I could remember where they were.

After taking another swig, Darlene passed the jar back to me and held up her hand indicating she was done. I looked at the vessel that we'd barely put a dent in and had to agree. This stuff was potent.

We spent the rest of the morning scraping wallpaper off the dining room walls while she continued to dish out words of wisdom that soothed my spirit. It wasn't until hours after lunch that Darlene insisted the moonshine had worn off and she could drive home. I busied myself with chores and was so tired I skipped dinner. I showered and headed straight for bed. Even though I was no longer feeling the effects of the alcohol, I took two aspirin before heading upstairs. I had another busy day tomorrow and didn't want to wake up with a moonshine headache. They were the worst.

I crawled into bed and thought about Richard and how a lot of the things Darlene touched on had been true. But I found myself unable to dig up any anger toward him. I'd already forgiven him for leaving me for Fancy. As far as our marriage was concerned, Richard had grown up in an uncontrolled and chaotic environment, so he was doing what he thought necessary. He managed every aspect of our lives for us. It was my fault for getting caught in his net. If I'd resisted, he would've conceded, but I'd been happy to let him take the lead while I concentrated on my career.

"I guess we were both a little at fault, Richard," I whispered into the dark. As I drifted off into what would be a dreamless night without any bathroom interruptions, I realized that moonshine wasn't the best medicine. Letting go of the past and forgiving yourself was.

CHAPTER 13

WHAT'S FOR DINNER, DARLING?

I didn't want to get out of bed. The wind was blowing so hard the house was creaking. It appeared that autumn skipped her subtle shift into winter, which seemingly appeared about eight weeks early. It was freezing and I'd gone to bed the night before without turning on the heat. I shivered as I made my way downstairs to the bathroom and thermostat. Sitting on the cold toilet seat I mumbled, "Sure could use a hot flash about now." My hormones refused to answer, choosing instead to lie in wait to ambush me at a more inconvenient time.

I poured myself a cup of coffee and headed for the couch. I turned on the television and checked the local news for the weather report. I was right about it feeling like winter. It was the coldest day in late September since 1905. The silver lining was, they were predicting a return to average temperatures by tomorrow and a heat wave next week. Sounded to me like Mother Nature had gotten into my moonshine because she was acting crazy.

I peeked outside and saw a gray and murky sky. It was a day that screamed for scarves and soup. Better yet, stew. For once, I had everything I needed, and before I knew it, I had all the fixings for Brunswick stew filling up my Crock-Pot.

I looked at my watch. I had plenty of time to drive to Greenville for my appointments and make a couple of stops to do some shopping. It was time to buy a good pair of running shoes. I arrived at my doctor's appointment ten minutes early and was ushered in immediately. Dr. Natalie Hoskins was a lovely woman about my age. I'd been seeing her for the past fifteen years. After we exchanged pleasantries, I updated her on my current health status. All was good except for the occasional night sweats and hot flashes.

After handing off my pap smear to her nurse who left the room, she said, "I see you're using your maiden name, Barbie. I like it. Barbara Jean Anderson has a nice ring to it and is a lot easier to pronounce than Poznanski."

I laughed and told her I agreed. She excused herself while I got dressed. I was gathering my things when there was a light knock at the door and she returned with a pained expression on her face.

"Is something wrong?" I questioned, feeling the slight head rush of someone who's about to get bad news. The last time I felt like this was when Richard sat me down for "the talk."

"Yes and no. It's your sister, Frenita. I hadn't realized that she was here being seen by my associate. She left about five minutes ago."

I wasn't surprised that Fancy was here even though it was highly coincidental that we showed up on the same day. More than a year ago, I'd recommended this practice and insisted she visit a doctor when she first moved in with Richard and me. I'd been appalled when she admitted to not having regular gynecological checkups.

"Is she okay? Is something wrong with her?" My heart skipped a beat. I may have had issues with my younger sister, but I didn't want anything bad to happen to her.

"No, Barbie, nothing is wrong with her. I'm afraid she pulled a bit of a scam on the new girl we have in reception."

I raised an eyebrow and pulled my purse tightly against my body. It was an automatic reaction when it came to Fancy. Protect what's yours, or she'll wrestle it away from you.

"Apparently, she called the office a few weeks back and asked when your next appointment was. She sweet-talked the girl into telling her, and she made an appointment for a half an hour earlier than you."

"Okay, well, I can see why the girl told her. Frenita can be very persuasive. But you said she left five minutes ago. I don't have the best relationship with her, but no harm done since I've obviously missed her."

Natalie's expression told me she knew why I had an issue with Fancy and that she didn't blame me. It also told me she had more to say.

"I'm sorry, Barbie. She skipped out on the payment, telling our billing clerk that it was on your tab."

I almost laughed. Of course she did. I didn't even have the wherewithal to be embarrassed. It was typical Fancy. I told Dr. Hoskins not to worry and that I would cover the office visit.

"No, we don't expect you to pay for it. We're going to write it off. I'm letting you know that we won't see her again. She's banned from the office. I feel bad doing this since you're a colleague, but…"

I held up my hand. "Don't feel bad. If anything I should be apologizing to you for recommending this office to her in the first place. I'm sorry, Natalie."

A few minutes later, I made my way out of the medical complex and started walking toward my car. I stopped short when I saw a familiar face. It was Jake. He was casually leaning against the hood of a car that was backed in next to my Jeep. As I got closer, I noticed he was wearing scrubs. *He must be here in some official capacity*, I thought. I know my face registered concern because, as I got closer, he pushed off the car and said, "Nothing's wrong. I'm here with the Leavitts." He gestured toward the building I'd just exited. Stan Leavitt was a resident at the Hampton House. Instead of taking the facility's official van for his cardiologist appointments, Mrs. Leavitt insisted that someone trustworthy drive her and Stan down to Greenville in their car. I'd never ridden in one but figured a Jaguar was a lot more comfortable than the van.

I nodded my understanding when he asked, "Are you okay?" He motioned toward the building that had offices for a multitude of medical professionals.

"Oh yeah, just a yearly checkup." I realized that I hadn't seen or spoken to him for a few days, and the last time was when he commented on my skirt. He'd been right, and after he rode off on his bike, I'd left Dustin waiting in his truck while I ran back into the house to change into jeans.

"How was your date?" As he walked toward me, I thought I detected a change in his attitude. It was like the air between us crackled with tension. I was getting ready to tell him it wasn't a date or any of his business when a vehicle drove up behind us. Not caring that she wasn't in a parking spot, Fancy got out of her car and approached us.

"I thought that was your car, Barbara Jean," she said with an exaggerated Southern drawl. As she got closer, I noticed her pupils were dilated. She was poised to jump into full-blown seduction mode. She was practically licking her lips as she sauntered toward Jake. "I was getting into my car across the way when I saw this handsome doctor changing the tire on your Jeep."

"I'm not a—" Jake started to say when I interrupted him.

"My car had a flat?" I looked from Fancy to Jake.

She didn't give him a chance to answer when she said, "Yes, it did. And he was flinging your tire around like it was a powder puff. You never told me you knew such a strong, successful doctor."

She walked toward the car and started touching the Jaguar emblem. I couldn't believe it. She was actually stroking the hood ornament. *Oh, Fancy.*

I rolled my eyes and looked back at Jake. "Is it true? My car had a flat and you changed it for me?"

He shrugged. "Didn't take me long. It was nothing."

She turned around and pressed her backside up against the front of the car. I recognized the same posture she'd used to steal my husband and it included the lowered chin and the subtle chewing of her bottom lip. Her forced puppy dog eyes were batting ridiculously huge lash extensions when she triumphantly announced, "I'm glad you aren't completely devoid of decent taste in clothes. I see you're wearing the scarf I gave you, Barbie."

Fancy acted like I selected my wardrobe from a dumpster. Just because I didn't drop twelve hundred dollars on a designer blouse didn't mean I didn't have nice clothes. I'd had enough of my sister, and decided to thank Jake and be on my way when Fancy cooed, "Since my sister is so rude, let me introduce myself. I'm Fancy, Barbie's much younger sister, and you are?"

"Jake Chambers," he stated, as he discreetly stepped to my side. He didn't extend a hand in friendship or say it was nice to meet her. He barely acknowledged her as he stood next to me and told me he would stop by my house later to retrieve the flat tire from my trunk and pick me up a new one.

I knew the instant Fancy realized she was being dismissed. She tossed her hair and narrowed her eyes at me. With a menacing upward tilt of her chin, she stood up straighter and asked, "So, Barbie, are your lady parts all in working order? I'm sure you had more *mature* things to discuss with your gyno than I did."

I was getting ready to blast her about running out on the payment when she looked at Jake and said, "You know, the things that are a concern for women Barbie's age. I've got it right, don't I?" She cocked her head to one side. "The dreaded menopausal symptoms that make you miserable. Or are you already past that?"

Were we really doing this? Was she so outraged that Jake wasn't falling at her feet that she had to stoop as low as slinging insults about menopause? Before I could share that if she hadn't already she was getting ready to turn that same corner, Jake wrapped his arm around my waist and pulled me toward him. Without looking at my sister, he tugged the scarf down and buried his face in my neck. "I don't care what your older sister thinks, Barbie." I knew he was deliberately goading her with the older sister comment. I heard her gasp and knew he saw it as an opportunity to lay it on thicker. "Mmm…you smell delicious, baby. I can never get enough of you." I felt the scratch of his whiskers on my neck and had to stop myself from closing my eyes. "What's for dinner tonight, darling?" he teased.

I don't know who was more stunned, Fancy or me. She was used to getting all of the attention and Jake was completely snubbing her. I was ignoring her too, but not deliberately. I practically melted against him. His mouth was warm against my neck, his body hard against my side. And his smell. If sizzling whiskey poured over ice gave off an aroma, that's how Jake smelled. Hot and masculine, but sharp and clean. I was close to losing myself in the fictional encounter when Fancy's voice broke the spell.

"And everybody knows that no periods mean no children. Then again, that was never in the cards for you anyway, was it, Sister?"

"Frenita, this is not the time or the place," I growled as I reluctantly disengaged myself from Jake and walked toward her. "You have some nerve…"

"I have some nerve for what? For telling your boyfriend"—she paused for dramatic effect and fluttered her eyelashes one more time—"the pathetic details about your doctor visit, or how I rescued Richard from a dull and sexless marriage?"

I couldn't believe she was doing this, but I knew why. What I didn't know was why he felt the need to let her think we were a couple, but I'd be lying if I didn't admit it gave me satisfaction to watch her get shut down. That's when it occurred to me why he'd done it. He wasn't interested in her and thought it would be easier to pretend we were together than to have to turn her down. All of a sudden, I felt very sorry for my sister.

"Look, Fancy. I know things are probably hard for you right now, so why don't we—"

"Hard for me? Things aren't hard for me, Barbara Jean. Things couldn't be better." She motioned to the car behind her. It wasn't the fire-engine red Mercedes she'd shown up with several weeks ago, but what looked like a brand-new white BMW. "I don't need your pity, *big* sister. If anything, you're the one to be pitied."

She was visibly upset and talking nonsense. Where had pity introduced itself into the conversation? "Fancy, you're not making sense. Let's not do this now, okay?"

"Do what? Talk about who deserves pity? That's you, Barbie." She tilted her head to one side, and with a malevolent gleam in her eyes, she seethed, "You know Richard could've had children?"

I didn't know where she was going with this, but I did know she was wrong about that. "No, he couldn't, Fancy."

She laughed. "Right. He told you about how he'd contracted mumps when he was a boy and it made him sterile."

"Yes, that's exactly right. It's rare, but it does happen." I brushed my hand through my hair and returned it to the pocket of my jacket.

"Richard lied to you. He'd had a vasectomy before he met you. He never wanted kids. I believed him too until I found the scar. But I guess you were never down there enough to notice it." She produced a winning smile that conveyed she thought she'd hit the lottery.

It was as if she'd pulled a rug out from under me. She started going on about how he'd planned to have it reversed for her, but I barely heard her. There was a freight train pounding through my head, muting her voice. I knew Jake exchanged some words with her, but I didn't even hear them. It wasn't until she got in her car and left that I heard Jake ask, "Are you okay, Barbie?"

I shook it off and turned to face him. "Of course. I'm fine. That's my sister doing what she does best."

"Being a total shrew?" he asked.

"Yeah. That and more," I said with a heavy sigh.

He looked at his watch. "I need to go inside and get the Leavitts."

"Of course, go, go," I said, shooing him away with my hands in the direction of the building.

"What time should I come by?" he asked.

"Come by for what?" I started walking toward my car.

"To get your flat tire. And dinner."

"You were serious about dinner?" I spun around and stared, slack-jawed.

"You weren't?" he countered.

I didn't answer, and he headed for the building, calling over his shoulder, "I'll see you at seven, Barbie doll."

CHAPTER 14

WOULD YOU LIKE TO MEET MY EX-
HUSBAND?

I drove home in a confused haze of emotions. After getting in the car, I tore off my scarf and shoved it inside one of my shopping bags. What had gotten into my sister? Why was she so hateful all of a sudden? We'd never been close, but her behavior was beyond anything I'd faced before. Yes, she'd stolen my husband, but I didn't remember experiencing a victorious evil from her. It had been the opposite. She'd gone out of her way to be nice back then because she'd felt guilty. I gave a sidelong glance at the bag that was perched on the passenger seat, remembering the day she took the scarf off her neck and wrapped it around mine, telling me it went better with my coloring. How ironic that today was the first day I'd worn it since that encounter over a year ago.

And Richard. I banged my hand hard against the steering wheel. I thought we'd said everything we needed to say to each other. It was why I harbored no bad feelings toward him. He'd come clean, confessed his guilt and remorse at having hurt me. But he'd never owned up to a vasectomy. Perhaps it wasn't true. And even if it was, at this point, did I even care? What would it matter?

I got home in record time and checked on my stew—perfection. I cleaned up the mess I'd left in the sink, and wondered if Jake liked wine. I hadn't realized he was serious about dinner, but since it was already made, I didn't see the harm in sharing a meal. Besides, I reminded myself, I owed him for fixing my tire.

I stayed busy for the next couple of hours, and at six thirty, thinking he was late, decided that Jake was a no-show. As I washed my face and changed into my Wonder Woman pajamas—a gift from Darlene—I didn't want to admit that I was disappointed. And I was also no longer in the mood for Brunswick stew. I turned off the slow cooker, poured myself a glass of wine, and headed for the couch. At seven o'clock there was loud banging on my door. Between my closed drapes, the brutal wind outside, and the blare of my TV, I hadn't been aware that someone was at my house. Clutching my glass, I jumped up and peeked out the curtain. Jake was standing on my porch, albeit an hour late. He saw me and smiled.

I didn't have time to change back into my clothes, so I did the next best thing. I drained the rest of my wine in one long gulp, hoping the buzz would erase my self-consciousness at getting caught in my PJs. I opened the door and teasingly waved the empty glass in front of my pajamas. "This is what you get when you're an hour late."

He gave me a heart-stopping smile and said, "I'm right on time, Barbie doll."

I stood aside, motioned him past me and told him, "You said six o'clock."

"I said seven o'clock but I don't want to waste the night arguing, so if we can agree to disagree, I think it'll make for a more pleasant evening. What smells so good?"

I knew I should've been embarrassed by the earlier over-the-top soap opera performance by Fancy, and my current Wonder Woman display, but for some reason I wasn't. Jake had seen me without makeup and sweaty the first day he drove down my street. He'd seen me faint at Hampton House. And as he'd pointed out a very short time ago, he could see the outline of my radiant orchid through my sheer skirt. I giggled at the memory and hiccupped. Too much wine a little too quickly. I looked heavenward and silently pleaded to the God I'd lost touch with so many years ago, *please don't let me make a fool of myself.*

It was like Jake read my mind and didn't want me to worry. Taking the glass from my hand he pulled me toward the kitchen asking, "Is there anything I can do to help with dinner?"

"It's already made. I turned off the Crock-Pot earlier, but it should still be hot." He parked me in a kitchen chair, threw his jacket on a hook by the kitchen door, and went to work.

I couldn't help but admire the view. I'd not had an opportunity to really observe Jake, and I'd be lying if I didn't admit to myself that he was an impressive specimen, and the total opposite of every man I'd ever been attracted to. I guessed him to be about six foot one, with broad shoulders that showcased a wide but solid upper body. He wore a red flannel shirt over a white tee which stretched taut against his back. He'd rolled up his sleeves exposing heavily tattooed and muscled forearms. He wore dark blue jeans that hugged his rear and thick thighs, and tapered down to dark boots with laces. His close-cropped hair revealed the same streaks of silver that were evident in his beard which was starting to grow in. And his eyes. I had to make an effort not to sigh out loud. They were brighter than the sky on a cloudless summer day.

I gulped as I watched him rummage through my refrigerator and cabinets, and before too long he'd put together a salad, set the table, and was slicing up and getting ready to toast a stale loaf of ciabatta bread. We made small talk as he effortlessly glided through each task. He seemed to know his way around a kitchen.

It prompted me to ask, "How long have you been a bachelor?"

He stopped and looked up like he was giving it serious thought. Then finally answered with a laugh, "Fifty-five years."

"You've never been married?"

"Nope," was his casual reply.

"How long has it been since you've been in a serious relationship?" I pushed.

Ignoring my question, he asked one of his own. "How long were you married?"

"Too long." I let out a breath and drummed my fingers on the table.

"Why too long?" I didn't get the feeling he was being nosy. He seemed genuinely interested. I didn't know how I'd surmised that from only three words.

I was literally saved by the bell when the oven timer went off. "Bread's done," he announced to my relief.

My appetite returned and I felt the slight wine buzz retreating from my brain. We spent the next forty-five minutes enjoying the meal and discussing everything from my Brunswick stew recipe, to Jonathan's sweet professions of undying love for Cindy, and finally my confession to harboring some hooch from the Pritchard stills.

He didn't ask, but as we cleaned up the dishes together, I offered to let him try the famous Pritchard moonshine. A few minutes later we were sitting on my couch passing the Mason jar just like I'd done with Darlene only yesterday.

"It's definitely potent," he remarked after a healthy swallow. "I've heard about this stuff. It's legendary around here. They say the recipe died with Kenny."

I told him he was right and found myself sharing some details about the Pritchards, even going so far as to tell him about the tree houses that had been built during Prohibition. He listened with what appeared to be sincere interest, and I found that talking with Jake felt natural. I wasn't feeling defensive like I had that night when Dustin mentioned the

Pritchard farm. It's probably what prompted me to open up about my relationship with Kenny Pritchard, and as we passed the Mason jar, I told Jake about Kenny's abrupt and unexpected disappearance from my life. And for the very first time, it didn't pain me to talk about it.

He listened without interrupting me and never once made me feel ridiculous for my obvious obsession over Kenny's abandonment. It was actually the opposite. He asked questions about my true relationship with Kenny, and urged me to think of any possible way Kenny might've left me a message.

I shook my head. "That hope died long before Kenny did. I searched every place he could've left me a note," I admitted.

"When you said you were looking for these"—he paused and lifted up the jar—"you said you couldn't be sure that you got them all."

"I suppose it's possible there's a message out there somewhere." I used my right hand to sweep the room with a grand gesture. "But I highly doubt it. Kenny wouldn't have left a note in a random hiding spot. He would've used one of our regular places. He wouldn't have risked me not finding it," I explained.

He appeared to briefly ponder it and changed the subject.

"I've heard rumors about you." His voice was soft.

I braced myself and swallowed. Turning slightly to face him, I prompted, "Let's hear them."

"I've heard you referred to as the Monster of Monteith Medical."

"Guilty!" Raising my hand, I took the moonshine from him and laughed. He was alluding to my reputation in the emergency room at the hospital in Greenville where I used to be on staff. I'd earned the nickname years ago after going head-to-head with another physician who, in my opinion, wasn't as interested in quality healthcare as he was in his retirement. The nickname stuck. I was actually proud of it. I thought the conversation would lean toward my career, so Jake caught me by surprise with his next comment.

"You're obviously a tough chick. Why didn't you stand up for yourself with Francine this morning?"

"Fancy." I corrected, and took another sip. "My sister's name is Fancy. It's actually Frenita, but that's a story for another day."

"I can see why she prefers Fancy," he said with a grin. "But seriously"—he frowned—"why didn't you let her have it today?"

I looked at the ceiling and, clutching the jar with both hands, tried to gather my thoughts concerning Fancy. Jake was right about my nickname. I was a hard person to work for in the emergency room and never had any qualms about putting someone in their place when it came to the welfare of our patients. But I appeared like a total pushover when it came to my sister. It wasn't like I didn't want to blast her. Somehow, I always managed to bite my tongue with Fancy.

"Because she's my little sister," I blurted out with an apologetic sigh. "She was very young when our parents died. She doesn't remember them. I've always felt protective toward her. And I know she gets her mean streak from my grandmother, but I don't blame Fancy for that. It's not her fault she was influenced by a witch of a woman."

"What if it wasn't your grandmother's influence? What if your sister is just a rotten person? How far does she have to go before you tell her to get lost?"

There wasn't an easy answer to that. Fancy had already ruined my marriage and was living in my home in Greenville. She'd made it clear she wanted Dad's Civil War coins so she could pawn them. And just today she'd tried to humiliate me in the worst way possible to get Jake's attention.

"I'm not sure there's anything else she could do. And since I haven't lost my temper with her yet, I doubt there are too many buttons left she could push."

He looked like he didn't believe me, and his next comment proved it.

"You're wrong. It'll happen when you least expect it. And it'll be something small that will set you over the edge."

I shrugged and said, "Maybe. Maybe not. Time will tell."

"I can't believe your husband would leave you for someone like her. I'm not trying to knock your sister, Barbie, but she doesn't even hold a candle to you."

I was afraid I might blush, so I made light of his compliment by saying, "As she pointed out, she is my *younger* sister."

"Whose gray roots were showing." He snickered and added, "Yeah, I might be a guy, but I noticed them. And the inch of makeup on her face. It's covering up something she doesn't want anybody to see." He reached out and lightly brushed the side of my face with the back of his hand. "You're a natural beauty, Barbie. I like that you don't feel the need to hide from your true self."

I didn't know how to react to what he'd said or how the warmth from his knuckles on my cheek made it tingle. So I did the stupidest thing ever.

I lifted up my hair and showed him the gray that was starting to show. I may have been seven years older than Fancy, but I'd inherited somebody's good genes. My gray hadn't revealed itself until last year, and so far, it was only coming out on the underside of my locks. I silently thanked whatever distant relative had passed down that trait.

He didn't say anything and I was horrified to realize that he might've been thinking I was exposing my neck for another reason. I tried not to swallow as I indulged myself in the memory of what his breath felt like there only a few hours ago.

He reached for my hand and pulled it away, allowing my hair to fall back into place. "I like your new haircut. Did you get that done in Greenville today?"

I turned to face him. "Yeah. Do you really like it? I wasn't sure because it's shorter than I'm used to. My stylist suggested it. She called it a choppy bob."

"It suits you." His voice sounded hoarse and I found myself unable to meet his eyes. "I would've told you how pretty it looked earlier but your sister kind of ruined the moment." He gently removed the Mason jar from my other hand and took another long swallow. He held it up to me and I followed suit. "I still think your ex is a fool," he muttered.

"Was a fool," I corrected before swiping my arm across my mouth. *How ladylike, Barbie. Why don't you try picking your nose for the kill?*

"Was?" He raised a brow.

"Would you like to meet my ex-husband?" I didn't wait for an answer as I stood up and walked toward the small closet beneath the stairs. I opened the door and bent down to retrieve something out of the red plastic bin Fancy had delivered weeks earlier. I walked back toward Jake and laid the heavy object on the coffee table with a thud.

"Jake, meet my ex," I said as I motioned toward the urn filled with Richard Poznanski's ashes.

CHAPTER 15

MIDDLE-AGED CARELESSNESS (MAC)

J ake was genuinely shocked. He'd had no idea that Richard had died a few months earlier. Then again, the only person I'd told was Darlene and she would never reveal that detail of my life. I suspected that Sheila might've known because she would have occasion to speak with some of my colleagues in the medical community, but she was too much of a professional to gossip. I remembered her offering her condolences my first day at Hampton House. Then again, she could've been offering her sympathies for my failed marriage, which was obvious since I'd returned to Pumpkin Rest sans husband a year earlier.

"I don't think anybody knows he's dead," Jake surmised as he set the Mason jar on my coffee table and turned to face me. He casually rested his right arm across the back of my couch, dangerously close to my neck. "Are you okay?"

I explained it was highly unlikely that anybody would know about Richard's death. Greenville was hours away from Pumpkin Rest, and it wasn't like Richard's obituary would've run in our local paper. It was printed every Wednesday and was less than ten pages.

"But are you okay, Barbie?" His concern produced a few lines across his forehead.

"I'm fine. I really am. I was shocked by Fancy's little revelation earlier today, but other than that, I'd made my peace with Richard before he died. I moved here over a year ago, and when he was diagnosed with a rare and aggressive form of cancer, I went back to Greenville to manage his treatments. He may have dumped me for my sister, but I couldn't bring myself to turn my back on him." I looked at my lap and waited for Jake to say something. I felt his fingers lightly brushing the back of my hair. I fought the urge to press my head back against his hand.

"How did Fancy handle all this?"

I looked up at him. "Fancy never loved Richard, and I felt bad that he realized it before he died. She was living in the same house with him and moved into a guest room when he got sick and could barely bring herself to visit him in the room they'd shared. She tried to act like she cared, but her real concern was his will."

I filled Jake in on the pathetic details of Richard's estate. Or rather lack of one. Even I hadn't known he'd developed a serious gambling addiction two years before he left me for my sister. And it was nothing short of a miracle, for reasons I could no longer remember, that we'd taken the advice of a financial consultant early in our marriage and put the deed of our home in my name. If not for that advice, I was certain Richard would've gambled away our condo.

"So, he divorced you, died broke, and left an empty pot?"

"Yeah, kind of." Before he could ask, I explained, "He died before the divorce was finalized. In the end, he refused to sign the papers for the divorce he'd asked for. I'm technically a widow, not a divorcee."

"And it's why you told your sister today that you knew things were hard for her. She's broke." It was a statement, not a question.

I absentmindedly fiddled with my earring. "Yes. But it's obvious I was wrong. When Richard still had some money, he bought her a brand-new Mercedes. I saw the title to it and it was in her name. But she was driving a new car today, and I know Richard didn't leave her the means to pay for it, so she must've found a new man. I'm sure she'll be moving out of my condo soon, if she hasn't already."

"After all of that, you still let her live in your home?" He shook his head in disbelief.

"I didn't have the heart to throw her out," I confessed.

"If she's found a new man, he's downgraded her."

Jake's comment was unexpected. "Why do you say that?"

"You told me earlier how she ran out on her doctor bill." He paused and scratched his jaw. "And that Beamer wasn't new. It looked like it was in excellent condition, but it was at least nine years old. There's a lot I don't know, but I do know a little something about cars. I guess most guys do." He shrugged nonchalantly. "She's driving an old BMW. She must've sold the Mercedes, used the cash to buy the used Beamer, and kept whatever was left over to live on."

After describing Fancy's modus operandi, Jake and I surmised that she'd most likely upped her attack against me out of sheer desperation.

She thought Jake was a doctor and saw him as her next potential source of income. When she thought he was my man, it only fueled her desire to snatch him up, resulting in an uncalled-for personal attack on me.

"I don't care what her reason may have been, she had no right to treat you like she did, Barbie. If she were a man, any man," he quickly clarified, "I'd have laid her out in a heartbeat."

I tried not to bristle at his comment. I was in the business of saving lives and had sewn up my fair share of people who'd been on the losing end of a fight. I focused on Jake's left hand, which was casually resting on his knee. I had no doubt it could do serious damage.

"What are you thinking?" he softly prodded.

"That there are other ways to settle differences," I replied.

He looked unconvinced. "Yeah, I'm sure there are. I also know that not everybody can be reasoned with."

"I can see how Fancy might fall into that category," I sadly admitted. I wasn't certain, but I thought I might've slurred my last sentence. I looked at the jar and was surprised to see it was almost empty. Concerned that I might embarrass myself, I decided to shut up and let Jake do the talking. I started by asking him if he'd grown up in Texas. I was surprised to hear that he'd only been in Texas long enough to get arrested and thrown in jail for a year.

It turned out that Jake Chambers was raised in Florida. South Miami to be exact. The only child of older parents, his nickname as a child had been Mac.

"That's a cute nickname. Where did it come from?"

"My uncle gave it to me. Said I was the result of middle-aged carelessness. Hence, Mac."

"Oh, how mean!" I shouted but had a hard time suppressing a laugh. "Your parents were older when they had you?"

He smiled. "A lot older. And let's say I was a huge surprise, but they handled it well. I had a very happy childhood. My parents had their own business. Tropical Landscapes and Nursery."

"The orchid on your bike?" My eyes were wide.

"Yeah, the orchid on my bike. I grew up surrounded by flowers."

I told him that I'd looked at his file at Hampton House and hadn't noticed he was from Florida. He explained how at eighteen, he'd broken his parents' hearts when he took off with a buddy to make some quick cash in Texas.

"We got out there, got some stupid, scary-looking tattoos." He stopped and gestured to the hollowed-out skeleton eyes that were peering over the collar of his shirt. "Found an apartment, got a job to make us look legit. I even got a Texas driver's license."

"And?"

"Started stealing cars and lots of other things when we weren't at work." He gave me a mischievous smile and said, "It's how I got your tire out of your trunk."

I formed a silent "oh" with my mouth. I hadn't even thought to ask how Jake had managed to get into my locked Jeep. Could I have subconsciously remembered seeing auto theft on his rap sheet?

"Made a lot of dough, " he continued. "Got caught. Did some time in a Texas prison. Went back to Miami only to find both of my parents were in poor health."

I got the distinct impression he felt his stint in jail might have had a direct correlation to the decline in his parents' well-being. "When I looked at your prison file and work history, which only went back five years, I didn't see that you lived in Miami," I told him.

"I guess it wouldn't have been there. My arrest and the subsequent record would've listed my Texas address. And five years ago I moved out of Florida, so my work history starts in Georgia."

"And all the years in between?"

"I floated from town to town in Florida. I've lived in Fort Lauderdale, Jacksonville, Tampa. And before you ask, sometimes I was on good behavior, sometimes not. I've done everything from long-haul trucking to construction to HVAC work. I took anything I could get when I first got out of prison."

"You didn't have any interest in furthering your education? I'm assuming you graduated from high school?"

"Yeah, and managed to get a college degree along the way. Unfortunately, I could never find something I was passionate about."

I was drunk, but fighting it because I found his story so interesting. "Sheila told me you were remodeling a nursing home when you found you had a knack for caring for the elderly and people with special needs. Perhaps having older parents somehow influenced that."

"It was a big influence." He shifted uncomfortably before looking away. He stood abruptly and excused himself to use the bathroom. During the three minutes he was gone, I developed a pounding headache and felt like the room was starting to spin. I'd over drank my limit and was going to pay sorely for it in the morning.

We talked a little more. About what exactly, I had no idea. At some point, I remembered lecturing him about the dangers of drinking and driving. I think he laughed and warned me about the perils of drinking and walking. I remembered him asking me out for Saturday night, and I told him I had plans. I didn't tell him what they were, because I couldn't remember.

I also didn't remember saying goodbye to him. I didn't remember walking him to the door, locking it, or making my way upstairs. I didn't remember what could've been the last hour, thirty minutes, or two minutes of our time together. It was a total blank. The only thing I could remember was the sinking disappointment when I finally remembered why I couldn't see him on Saturday night. It was because I'd already made plans with Dustin.

CHAPTER 16

THE BEST DREAM EVER

I was dreaming and I didn't want to wake up. I was wrapped in strong arms and pressed tight against a hard chest. I opened my eyes and saw the underside of Jake's jaw. I inhaled his scent and sighed. He chuckled and I burrowed in closer, not wanting the dream to end. His movements felt solid and effortless as he navigated the stairs. He softly kicked open the door to my bedroom and turned on the light with his elbow. He walked to my bed, bent low, and with the hand that was under my legs, managed to pull my comforter down. After gently laying my head against the pillow and pulling the comforter up to my chin, he must've sat down because I felt myself roll toward him. My dreams were always detailed, but this one felt so real I didn't want to lose it.

"I have a feeling the Monster of Monteith Medical may need a doctor tomorrow. I shouldn't have let you drink so much, Barbie." His voice was teasing but concerned.

I thought about opening my eyes, but was afraid it would signal the end of my dream. So I didn't reply and smiled in my sleep. I sensed him leaning over me and felt something hot on my neck. And unlike the parking lot in Greenville, it wasn't just his breath. I felt his lips making their way up to my ear where they gave a gentle tug on my lobe.

"It's probably not a bad thing you won't remember this tomorrow. I know you don't trust me, Barbie doll, and I'm sorry for that." More kisses on my neck, my cheeks, my eyelids.

I groaned and reached for him. Wrapping my arms around his neck, I grabbed the back of his head and guided his mouth until it found mine. His kisses were soft and exploring at first, and as they became more urgent, I started running my hands up and down his arms. His muscles responded to my touch, and I marveled at their hardness. I felt him shift on the bed, and I tried to maneuver beneath him, but I couldn't because he wasn't lying next to me, but still sitting, his hip hard against mine. His tongue tasted like moonshine, and I mourned its loss when he stopped kissing me to nip at my lips. I was determined to take this dream as far as it would let me. I wrapped my arms tightly around his back and pulled him closer. A moan escaped on his breath as he removed his mouth from mine and started kissing my neck again. His whiskers were scratching against my skin as his lips explored every inch of available flesh below my chin.

And then he stopped. I wanted to know why and to read his expression, but my eyelids weren't cooperating. I felt him pull back and heard him say, "No. Not like this, sweetheart. If we ever make love, it's going to be perfect, and you're going to remember it." I almost didn't recognize his voice. It was gravelly like laryngitis was sneaking up on him. There was one last soft kiss at the base of my ear, followed by, "I've loved you for as long as I can remember, Barbie doll. And I should stay away from you, but I don't know if I can." And then he was gone.

I mourned the loss of his heat, his scent, the loss of him. And before I knew it, I was running through the woods. The trees had long arms, and their hands were tearing at my new Wonder Woman pajamas. They were trying to tell me something, but I couldn't hear them. Fireflies chased me, and even though fireflies are silent, these were shrieking. As they got closer, they emitted a loud shrill that hurt my head. As I continued to run, I realized that Mason jars were dropping from the sky and hitting the ground all around me, their contents splattering against the forest floor. The treetops offered no protection, as I continued to run with heaving breaths. I didn't know where I was going, but there was a terror and desperation to protect my heart from the Mason jars. Even in my dream, I knew that was ridiculous. How could a Mason jar hurt my heart? It was my head that worried me. And immediately after having that thought, and before I could raise my arms to shield my head, one hit me and I felt an explosion of pain.

I opened my eyes and immediately shut them as I blindly grappled around for my alarm clock. It explained the shrieking fireflies from my dream. My brain felt like it was trying to squeeze itself out through my eyes. My tongue was stuck to the roof of my mouth, and my bladder was threatening to explode. I couldn't remember the last time I'd had a hangover this bad. Probably never.

"What have you done to yourself, Barbie?" I croaked.

I hobbled downstairs to the bathroom. After relieving myself, washing my face, and brushing my teeth, I took a good look at myself in the mirror.

"You look like crap," I said to the haggard creature that was staring back at me. I had dark circles under my eyes, and my neck looked red and blotchy. I inched closer to the mirror for a better look as I ran my hands over my neck. The dream. I dreamed Jake—at least I thought it was Jake—had kissed me. It seemed so real. I even felt his short beard as it grazed my skin. I put my fingers to my lips and tried to remember. Had Jake carried me upstairs and put me to bed? Had he stayed around long enough to kiss me?

I shook my head and immediately regretted it. I practically staggered to the kitchen for water and the extra-strength aspirin I kept in the cabinet. I took two pills and downed the entire glass of liquid. I flipped on the coffeepot and tried to make sense of my dream.

If it had happened, why would Jake say he'd loved me for as long as he could remember? Or was I remembering it wrong? What if it didn't happen? I jumped up and ran to the front door. It was locked from the inside. I walked back to the kitchen and saw the back door was also secured. And he wouldn't have climbed out a window. I puzzled over it for a few more seconds when it occurred to me that he'd admitted to being a thief. He might know how to leave a locked house undetected. *Nah, you're only wishing it wasn't a dream,* I told myself.

But, my neck. I touched my hand to it and smiled. My neck is tender. It was beard burn. He'd carried me upstairs, tucked me in and kissed me. I didn't have an explanation for the things I thought he'd said, but it didn't matter. I couldn't stop thinking about what it felt like to kiss him. Or what it would've felt like if we'd taken it further.

The rest of my morning went by achingly slow, but I was okay with it. I was a creature of habit, and shouldn't have set my alarm yesterday for this morning, especially since I didn't have anywhere to be today and could've slept in. Instead of going back to bed, I lazed around in my pajamas, drank my coffee, watched the news, and tried to recall as much of my evening with Jake as I could. I was reveling in the realization that the kiss had been real and I had the red neck to prove it. I felt much better after a mid-morning shower, and I headed upstairs to get dressed. I'd just tossed my robe on the bed when something caught my eye. It was the scarf I'd worn yesterday. The one that had been a gift from my sister over a year ago. I don't know what inner nudge caused me to pick it up and look at the tag. I felt heat slither up my spine as an inner rage started to build.

I was allergic to the exact scarf fabric. It wasn't a life or death allergy, but an irritating one that would cause me to break out in a burning red rash and Fancy knew that. She'd deliberately wrapped that scarf around my neck a year ago knowing it would cause a reaction. I must've been wearing a turtleneck then because I didn't remember it bothering me.

Before I'd gotten too wasted last night, I distinctly remembered Jake telling me that Fancy would do something to put me over the edge when I least expected it. And it would be something small that would set me off. He was absolutely right.

"I'm done with you, Frenita!" I screamed.

I didn't know what hurt more. Knowing that my sister had deliberately given me a gift that she knew would cause an allergic reaction, or that the redness on my neck wasn't from Jake's kisses. It had only been a dream.

CHAPTER 17

THE LONESOME KEG

I couldn't determine what made me crankier. The realization that my encounter with Jake had only been a dream or the relentless yearning for it to be real.

"I don't know what I'm doing, Darlene," I confessed one afternoon. "I thought I came here for solitude and introspection. Instead, I've found…" I paused, wondering exactly what it was I'd found.

"Love?" Dar interrupted.

I rolled my eyes and stepped back while she waited on a customer. It had been four days since my encounter with Fancy, and my impromptu dinner date with Jake. I hadn't seen or heard from him since but did notice the spare tire on my Jeep was replaced with a new one. A flat tire he must've retrieved from my trunk without me knowing.

Darlene thanked her customer and said, "Just because he did the tire switcheroo without you knowing doesn't mean anything. It's likely he didn't want to bother you. Or maybe he's embarrassed that he opened up to you that night."

"He hardly seems like the type to be embarrassed." I fiddled with a pair of eyeglass chains that were dangling from a display on the counter.

Darlene started laughing.

"What is so dang funny?"

"You. You're funny, Barbie. You're thinking about him. You like him. Admit it!"

I was going to deny it when I recognized a song that had come on. "I know this song. It was playing in Jonathan's room my first day at Hampton House."

"Jake gave it to me," Darlene said as she motioned to the stereo on the shelf behind her. "He said he heard this guy when he played a small club down in Georgia. He bought a couple of the man's CDs and gave me one. I don't plan on giving up Loretta Lynn or Conway Twitty anytime soon, but I love this guy's sound."

I inclined my head as I let the lyrics wash over me:

Cuddled up tight got my arm around
The radio is crankin' up a Southern sound
Brown hair's blowin'
Anywhere we're goin' is fine with me
She gives me that look in the rearview
We don't say much 'cause we don't need to
As long as we're together I'll drive forever as far
as I can see
It doesn't get better than this

"I didn't know you and Jake were getting so chummy he managed to talk you into changing up your music repertoire. What else do you talk about?" I wouldn't look at her as I feigned interest in straightening a rack of chewing tobacco.

"If you're trying to find out whether or not he told me anything about his relationship with Dolly or Yvonne, you'll have to ask him yourself, Barbie."

"He may have told me the other night, and I might not remember," I huffed.

"Then you'll have to ask him again," she countered with a snicker.

"You're enjoying this way too much." My words were accusing, but my voice was gentle. I loved this woman more than anybody in the world.

"Forget Jake." Putting the subject to bed, she asked, "Tell me what you're going to do about Fancy."

"I've given it a lot of serious thought. I love my sister, but can't bring myself to like her. I need to remove myself from her life."

Darlene's eyes flickered with empathy. I described how I planned on taking my father's coin collection to get three honest appraisals. I would buy out Fancy for her half of the average fair market value.

"And?" she urged.

"I'm going to meet with a realtor in Greenville next week. I'll be putting the condo up for sale and will make it a point to visit Fancy and tell her what I'm doing. That will be her warning to find a new place. She can stay there until it sells, but if she doesn't leave before then, she'll have to take it up with the new owners." I stood up straighter and gave Dar a serious look. "I'm done with Frenita Anderson. For good this time. She is poison, and I've been more than generous. She saw me wearing the scarf Tuesday, and still couldn't bring herself to do the right thing by telling me I would have a scratchy red neck before the day was over." I paused and felt my shoulders slump. "I feel like I've given her so many chances, Dar."

She gave me an understanding look. "You're the queen of second chances, Barbie. Don't ever let yourself feel like you haven't done enough." Changing the subject, she asked, "So, you're still on with Dustin tonight?"

"Yeah." I couldn't muster any enthusiasm. "We're going to some country music joint that supposedly has the best wings around. Not that I'm a fan of wings, but I wouldn't mind listening to some good music." I stepped aside as Earl Adams came in and bought a pack of cigarettes. He looked at me sheepishly. "Caught."

"I don't need to tell you those aren't helping your cough, Earl."

"I know, Doc. And I'm trying to cut back." He thanked Darlene, and had almost made it out the door when she yelled after him, "Be sure to remind your missus that she's in charge of coffee and donuts after tomorrow's service."

"Yes, ma'am," he told her as he tipped his hat and left the gas station.

"Dustin must be taking you to The Lonesome Keg."

"Never heard of it," I said with a shrug.

"It's about an hour northeast of here. It used to be called Chicky's," she told me.

"Never heard of that either," I admitted.

"You probably wouldn't have." Darlene looked thoughtful for a moment before adding, "Chicky's might've opened around the time you left for college. The new owners bought it a few years back and changed the name to The Lonesome Keg."

After a little more chitchat with Darlene, I gassed up my Jeep, grabbed some groceries, and headed for home. Hours later, Dustin picked me up, and after giving me a peck on the cheek and admiring my outfit and new haircut, ushered me out to his truck. The drive to The Lonesome Keg was pleasant enough. Dustin truly was a nice guy. He was a gentleman and had a fun, quick wit that made me laugh a few times. After arriving at our destination, he came around to open my door and escorted me inside.

I immediately noticed a band setting up on a stage on the opposite side of the room. A long bar was situated on one side, and booths and tables took up the rest of the space. Alabama's

"She Ain't Your Ordinary Girl" was drifting from the jukebox.

"Ah, there they are," Dustin blurted out while pointing to a table. One man, who appeared to be about Dustin's age, was waving us over.

After being introduced to Dustin's friends, I was happy to see they seemed like a friendly group and hoped we'd find something in common. Sadly, Dan, a web designer who stood and plastered his wet mouth all over my cheek, was already drunk. His date, Marcy, who couldn't have been more than twenty, spent the next fifteen minutes telling the table in excruciatingly painful detail how all of her psychic's predictions had come true. The other couple was married and looked closer to Dustin's age. William was one of Dustin's HVAC technicians, and Connie was a full-time student who was working on her second master's degree. Dustin had already shared that I was a physician. After Marcy's lengthy psychic discourse they all took turns telling me about their ailments, their misdiagnoses by quacks and their crappy insurance. After fielding as many questions as I could, I excused myself to use the restroom. Before returning to the table I made a beeline for the jukebox. I was glad to see it had a wide variety of artists spanning the past four decades. While selecting some songs, I struck up a conversation with a silver-haired man in a wheelchair who introduced himself as Mike, the former owner of the establishment. He told me that back when he'd owned the bar, and before he'd been confined to a wheelchair, the place was a biker bar.

"It's a more mellow crowd now," Mike explained.

"No more bikers?" I asked with a smile before choosing "Good Hearted Woman" by Waylon Jennings.

"Eh, a few show up now and then. Might get some tonight since we'll have live music. Hopefully, they'll be on good behavior."

"And if they're not?" I gave him a quick glance before selecting "This Kiss" by Faith Hill.

"That's why I'm here. I'm good at keeping the peace." He winked and politely excused himself before he rolled over to the stage.

After selecting a few more songs, I headed back to my table. When I took my seat Dustin said, "I think the music is going to start soon." Our waitress showed up and I ordered another soda while the rest of the group asked for another round of alcohol. They teased me about being a lightweight. I didn't care and definitely didn't feel the need to explain that I'd drunk more in the last week than I had in the last year. *Who's supposed to be the designated driver?* I silently wondered. William was starting to get loud, and when Connie tried to shush him, she only ended up aggravating him instead.

"Well, I don't know why we can't just ask her," he shouted, sending a spray of spittle.

I felt five pairs of eyes land on me. I looked to Dustin and he said, "Everybody knows you were raised in Pumpkin Rest."

"And that your farm was near the Pritchards'," Dan, the drunk wet kisser, added.

I wasn't sure what they were trying to say, but I didn't have to wait long for an answer.

"Everybody thinks you know how to make the Pritch guy's moonshine." This from Marcy who must've been feeling a little buzzed herself.

I twisted sideways in my seat so I could face Dustin. His expression seemed hopeful and, at the same time, apologetic. All of a sudden, I felt very out of place. Truth be told, I'd felt out of place after first meeting Dustin's friends. They were all very nice, but I'd spent the last hour trying to find one common thread with any of them, and came up blank. I let out a long sigh. *I don't belong here,* I told myself. I looked around the table and tried not to shake my head. Another woman might be perfectly comfortable in this scenario. Not me. And I realized that it wasn't because of our age differences or because I didn't have anything to talk about with them. It was because I was pretty much a loner. And I already had a best friend. I didn't need a fun buddy.

I was deliberating on whether or not Dustin was sober enough to drive me home when the band started playing. I recognized the voice immediately. It was the same one I'd heard coming out of Jonathan's boom box, the same one I'd heard this afternoon at Darlene's gas station. The deep timbre of the lead singer's voice catapulted me back to the first time I'd locked eyes with Jake Chambers. And that's when I felt him. I didn't have to turn around to know he was in The Lonesome Keg. I didn't have to turn around to know that he was looking at me. But I would have to turn around to know whether or not he was there with another woman.

CHAPTER 18

YOU MUST BE QUITE THE CHARMER

"Some bad-looking dude is staring at you," William stated very loudly. Marcy quickly added, "You mean that good-looking bad dude." Her eyes were wide.

"Oh please tell me he's not one of the bikers you picked a fight with last time," Connie whined to her husband. I barely heard her over the band.

Dustin leaned over and whispered in my ear, "It's your friend, Jake," at the same time, William slurred, "Nah, he's not one of 'em."

I slowly turned around and met Jake's level gaze. He was about three tables away, casually leaning back in a booth. He was alone. He raised his can of Dr. Pepper to me. I smiled and waved. "I'm going to go say hello. Do you want to come with me?" I shouted over the music to Dustin. Without waiting for him to answer, I stood, hefted my purse on my shoulder, and scooted in my chair.

"Maybe later," he shouted back. "You go ahead. I'll get us another round."

Jake stood as I approached. He motioned to the seat across from him and waited for me to sit before he sat back down. The band was now playing a slow song and couples were making their way to the dance floor. I wanted to ask him if this was where he'd wanted to take me when he asked me out last Tuesday. I also wanted to thank him for changing my tire and ask how much I owed him. I wanted to grill him on how friendly he'd become with Darlene, and ask what his connection was, if any, to the band that was playing. All those questions were tripping over each other in my head and couldn't find their way to my mouth. So I blurted out the thing I wanted to know the most.

"Did you come here alone?"

He gave me a knowing grin, and I could only hope I wasn't turning red.

He took a sip of his drink before answering. "Yeah, I came alone. The lady I wanted to bring already had plans." He motioned with a sideways tilt of his head toward Dustin's table.

Before I could comment, he added, "Can I get you something to drink?"

I peered over at Dustin and his friends. "I probably should head back. It feels rude to have come here with him and have a drink with you." I barely got the words out when I saw a tall brunette, who was probably close to my age, making her way toward my vacated seat. Dustin seemed to know her, and before offering her my chair, turned my way as if to ask permission. I smiled and gave a quick nod of assent. I felt a little less guilty about wanting to say hello to Jake who'd been watching the scene play out.

"Well?"

"I'll have what you're having," I laughed. I was feeling something I hadn't felt in a very long time. I was feeling as giddy as a schoolgirl.

He waved a waitress over, ordered two more Dr. Peppers and a couple of appetizers.

While we waited for her to return, I asked him about the band and how often he frequented The Lonesome Keg.

"This is my first time." He casually waved toward the stage before adding, "And I'm only here because I heard they were playing." He told me the same story Darlene had shared. How after hearing them play down in Georgia, he'd liked them so much he grabbed a couple of their CDs.

"You must be quite the charmer," I told him. "She's still stuck on her country oldies. I know she likes you merely because she's playing the CD you gave her."

He told me how much he liked Darlene, and after agreeing how special she was, I asked what I owed him for my tire. He brushed me off and said I didn't owe him anything. After some back-and-forth, I finally conceded with a sincere, "Thank you. I owe you one."

"Doc? Is that you?"

We both turned our heads at the same time as Mike rolled to the end of our booth in his wheelchair. I hadn't recalled telling him I was a physician, but I realized he wasn't talking to me. He was smiling at Jake and asked, "How many years has it been?"

Jake looked at me, and back at Mike. "Too many to count," he replied with a broad smile that deepened the dimple on his cheek. He exited the booth and bent over to hug Mike. It looked like they might've exchanged words, but it was hard to tell because they were turned away from me. There was a lot of laughter, handshakes, and comments about how many years it'd been and what were the chances they'd run into each other. But I wasn't thinking about any of those things. I wanted to know why Mike had called Jake *Doc*.

CHAPTER 19

TWO SCARY-LOOKING BIKERS

I waited until Jake sat down again and after he formally introduced me to Mike before I asked, "Why did he call you Doc?"

Jake hesitated. Before he could answer, Mike piped up, "Jake was the Dr. Pepper guy." We both looked at Mike at the same time, and he motioned with his hand toward our drinks. "You know, Doc for Dr. Pepper?" He broke into a wide grin before adding, "Not to mention I'd recognize that tattoo anywhere." He pointed at Jake's neck.

Mike told me how back in the 1980s he used to bartend at a place called The Red Crab in Fort Lauderdale, Florida. "Jake was the soda delivery guy. And every single day he'd hit the Crab around lunchtime. Always ordered a burger and a Dr. Pepper." Mike sat back in his wheelchair beaming, proud of himself that he'd remembered such a detail.

Jake looked at me and said, "I told you how I took any job I could get back then. Driving a soda delivery truck was one of them." He inclined his head toward Mike and said, "He started calling me Doc, and eventually the regulars did too."

"Was The Red Crab a biker bar?" I asked. "Like this used to be when you owned it?"

When Mike told me that it was, I looked at Jake. "Were you a biker? Did you belong to a gang or something?"

"I've ridden a motorcycle for as long as I can remember, but I never formally joined the gang that frequented the bars where I delivered. They tried to recruit me, but I never bit. I knew them, I hung with some of them, but I never rode with them."

Mike nodded his agreement. He slapped Jake on the shoulder, "You always seemed like a good kid, Doc."

There was some laughter at Mike's use of the word kid to describe a fifty-five-year-old adult. He went on to share with us how he'd lost the use of his legs and couldn't seem to find a doctor who could tell him why. I referred him to a phenomenal neurologist.

There was good-natured conversation, and we laughed and ate while Mike filled Jake in on some of the people they used to know. By this time, I wasn't worried about Dustin or his friends missing me. It wasn't too long after I'd sat down with Jake that Dustin began to look very cozy with my replacement. It was also evident that the whole table was getting seriously wasted. How was I going to make sure they all got home safely? For that matter, how was I going to get home? *I'll probably have to drive Dustin home and get his truck back to him tomorrow.* I sighed and felt my shoulders sag.

The band had taken a break, so I excused myself to make another visit to the jukebox. When I returned to Jake's table, there was a loud skirmish, and I realized with horror it was coming from Dustin's crowd. A very drunk William was staggering toward two very scary-looking men. Dustin had followed him, and was trying to pull him back to their table.

"Ah, heck. Here we go again," Mike said with a roll of his eyes. "You'd think that youngster would've learned his lesson last time. He's gonna get the tar kicked out of him again. And his friends will too. The new owner should've banned him from coming back."

From what I could surmise, the two men William was mouthing off to were bikers who'd exchanged words and punches with him on a previous occasion. "That kid started with them last time, and I've no doubt they'll finish him and his friends this time. I need to call the law." Mike's tone held an edge of irritation.

I was horrified to think that Dustin was going to be involved in a brawl that he didn't start. And worse yet, he didn't stand a chance against the two threats who stood with clenched fists at their sides.

"Can't you do something?" I pleaded to Mike. When Jake started to get up, I said, "No. Not you. I don't want you involved in anything."

"Dustin's friend is an idiot. And there's no time to wait for the law," Jake said while looking down at Mike. Ignoring me, he continued, "I might need a quick escape."

"You got it," Mike said before pulling out a sawed-off shotgun discreetly tucked in the side of his wheelchair.

"Barbie," Jake turned to look at me. There was a fire in his eyes that brooked no argument. "Take these," he said, handing me his keys. "My truck is parked right under the sign, and it's facing the road. You get in it. You start it up, and you lock the doors. Move over to the passenger seat and watch for me to come outside. When I do, unlock the doors. You got it?" His tone was one of authority.

I wanted to argue with him, to talk him down, to tell him that I didn't want him involved. But I also knew Dustin and his irresponsible drunk friend didn't stand a chance. Those two bikers would do a lot of damage before the police arrived. Something told me Jake knew what he was doing, and just like I never wanted anyone telling me how to run my operating room, I wouldn't be telling Jake how to handle this situation, especially since I felt responsible for him being in it. By now, I could hear Connie screaming, and people were backing away from a scene that couldn't possibly end well. A look of mutual respect passed between us. I gave him a reassuring nod and grabbed my purse. As I took off, I thought I heard Mike say, "Looks like you got yourself a real keeper," to which Jake responded, "Yeah, I think so too."

CHAPTER 20

MEN AND WOMEN CAN'T BE FRIENDS

I'd only slid to my side of the truck minutes earlier when I turned and saw Jake approaching. That was fast. I unlocked the door and he jumped in. We sped off into the night, leaving a spray of gravel as he gunned the motor and we peeled out of the parking lot.

"What happened?" My hands were shaking. I could handle being up to my elbows in blood and bowels during surgery, but the thought of what might've gone down after I'd left the bar made my pulse race.

"Not too much." He glanced over. "You okay, baby?"

I was still too shaken to let the endearment wash over me, and with a quivering voice, asked him to tell me the details. He described how he got between William and the two men and tried to make peace. "I told the two bikers that he was a punk and to ignore him. Mike came over and said he'd called the police and they would be coming to escort William out of the establishment. Then I offered to buy them a few rounds."

"And they were okay with that?"

"No," he laughed. "The big one told me to mind my own business." Jake paused and shot me a look. "He used more colorful language though," he said with a laugh before adding, "We had some words, and the other one took a swing at me."

Before I could comment, he added, "He missed. I laid him out with one hit to the side of his face. Mike handed me his shotgun…"

I must've gasped because he said, "And I used it to smack the other guy across the head. They're both out cold, but they'll be okay."

"Should we have stayed to give our statements to the police?"

"Mike didn't call the police. But he let the troublemakers think he had. They'll wake up with sore heads, and he'll smooth it over with some free drinks. The new owner likes having Mike around because he knows how to deal with rough customers."

"And what about William and Dustin?"

"Mike said he'd make sure they all get home safely."

I turned to face him, leaning back against the truck door fully. Swiping a hand through my hair, I stared at his profile and said, "You seemed to handle this well. Like you knew what you were doing."

"I've been in my fair share of unpleasant situations," he offered. "And before you get your doctor hackles up, nobody got seriously hurt."

I must've bristled at the comment because he went on to explain. "I know you're sensitive to people getting hurt, especially when it's a preventable injury."

I reached across the truck and lightly touched his right bicep. "The only person who could've prevented this was William. Thank you for stepping in when you didn't have to. And I'm kind of glad those two bikers will wake up with headaches. I'd have felt horrible if they'd hurt you."

"And I thought it was Dustin you were worried about this whole time." He glanced my way with a stern expression.

"Dustin and I are friends," I said with a wave of my hand.

"Men and women can't be friends." His words left no room for argument.

"Ah, you must be a fan of *When Harry Met Sally*."

"Never met 'em," he stated.

I waited for him to follow up with a punchline from the movie, and when he didn't, I realized he thought I was talking about real people.

"Harry and Sally are from a movie," I explained. He didn't respond. "You've never seen the movie *When Harry Met Sally*?"

He shook his head. "Never seen it. Never even heard of it. But if Harry is telling Sally that men and women can't be friends, he's right."

"How could you have never heard of this movie?" I slapped my hand against my thigh and teased, "You must've been living under a rock for the past thirty years."

I spent almost the entire drive home quizzing him on movies and pop culture, and instead of being appalled over how few movies he'd seen, I was secretly excited at his suggestion that we should watch some of them together.

There was a lull in the conversation, and for the first time, I noticed the truck radio must've been on the entire time. I heard a familiar tune and felt myself stiffen. Dolly Parton sang "I Will Always Love You" with her beautifully unique voice.

"Do you mind if I change the station?" I asked.

"You don't care for Dolly?"

"I love Dolly. Just not this particular song," I wouldn't meet his eyes.

"Does your dislike of the song have something to do with Kenny?" he asked.

"I guess so," I replied while nonchalantly fiddling with the radio. I would never admit it was the song that had been playing when I lost my virginity to Kenny so many years ago.

He remained silent while I found another station that played country oldies. I'd been reacquainting myself with all the songs I'd missed over the years. I smiled when "Check Yes or No" by George Strait came on.

He started to quiz me again on my supposed friendship with Dustin, so I took the opportunity to ask him about Dolly and Yvonne.

He gave a hearty laugh before telling me that he could see why I might've thought there was something between them. "You must not engage with the employees when you're at Hampton House. If you'd chatted up any of the other women there, you'd know that Dolly isn't interested in the man. She's only interested in being the first to get the man. I guess she has something to prove. Poor kid."

"Poor kid?" I humphed. "That poor kid did her best to humiliate me the day I bought her a helmet. And she was quick to make sure I knew you had a date that night."

"I'm glad you don't humiliate easy, Barbie." His voice was filled with admiration. "And as for our date, she needed someone to give her a ride that night. I was only being nice."

"She gave me the distinct impression you two had a thing."

"Yeah, she gave a lot of people that impression, but it wasn't true. If anything, that girl was like gum on my shoe. I couldn't get rid of her."

I laughed at his description and he told me that Dolly had finally given up and set her sights on the new respiratory therapist that visited Hampton House twice a week. "And Yvonne? I couldn't help but overhear that she was making you dinner that day I ran into you." There was no way I was going to mention that I'd spied him with her later that day at the flea market.

I saw him wince and scrub his hand down his face. "Yeah, Yvonne." He turned to look at me, and if I hadn't known better, I would've thought he was in pain. "I'm surprised you haven't heard about that one, but I know you don't hang around Hampton House to listen to gossip."

I shook my head. "Nope, I haven't heard anything about you and Yvonne," I confessed.

"She told me there was a guy at a flea market that she'd bought a dresser from and that she had no way to get it home. The man kept offering to deliver it, but she felt uncomfortable telling him her address. She said that he seemed interested in her and she wanted to discourage him, so she asked if I wouldn't mind taking her there and helping her load it in my truck. She wanted to pay me, and when I said I wouldn't take her money, she offered to make me dinner."

"Makes sense," I admitted.

"Yeah, except that wasn't her real intention." He gave me a sidelong scowl before continuing. "When we got there she asked if I wouldn't mind making it look like we were a couple so he would get the hint and leave her alone. Turns out, it was a guy she'd been out with a couple of times, and he'd dumped her. She kept showing up at his booth and did buy a dresser from him." He rolled his eyes and let out a sigh. "She was using me to make him jealous."

I stifled a smile. "Did it work?"

He shook his head and laughed. "I don't think so. I'd never seen a guy look so relieved in his life."

We finally turned onto my road and I was immediately on alert. I sat up, looking around the truck. "Do you smell that?"

"Smell what?"

"That metallic smell. I smell blood. Do you smell blood?"

He didn't answer and, horrified, I undid my seat belt and slid over to him. He objected as I ran my fingers cautiously over his stomach and chest. They finally found their way to his lower left side right above the hip bone. He had a jacket bunched up and pressed between himself and the truck door. How hadn't I noticed? He barely made a sound when I pulled the jacket away and realized it was soaked in blood. The look of pain he'd given me when I mentioned Yvonne didn't have anything to do with her. Jake had been stabbed.

CHAPTER 21

IT'S A BALL AND CHAIN

"I can't believe you didn't tell me. We should've gone straight to the hospital," I practically screamed.

"No hospital," was all he said as we rolled up to my house. "And it's nothing."

"This much blood isn't nothing, Jake. And neither is a stab wound." I'd been enjoying his company so much that almost an entire hour went by without me noticing he had a severe bleeding wound. At this point, I didn't know if I was mad at him or myself. He walked into the house without my assistance, and I directed him to a kitchen chair. I flipped on all the lights and grabbed my medical bag. I had what I needed to clean the wound and stitch it up.

"I wasn't stabbed." His voice was hoarse. He lifted his shirt, and I knelt next to him to inspect it. "It's a cut from a beer bottle," he corrected.

I looked closer at the jagged edges of the cut as well as the blood smeared on his skin and was hit with an overwhelming sense of nausea. *How strange. This never happens to me.* I stood up and felt a wave of dizziness.

Jake reached for my arm and grabbed it to steady me. "Are you okay, sweetheart?" he asked, his eyes darting up. "You're looking pale."

Ignoring his question, I ran to the bathroom. I didn't even get a chance to close the door behind me. Before I knew it, I was on my knees emptying my stomach. I felt a warm hand on my back and turned to look at him. "I'm okay. Must've been something I ate," I lied. "You need to sit down. I'll wash up and be out in a second."

When I returned to the kitchen, Jake told me, "It was an accident. If we go to the hospital, they might ask for an incident report."

"Accident?"

"Dustin's drunk friend thought he was helping me out when he started swinging blindly with a broken bottle. He probably doesn't even know he hit me. The guy may be stupid, but I don't want him getting into trouble."

Since his shirt was already torn I used my scissors to cut it off of him so he wouldn't need to lift his hands above his head. I rolled up my sleeves, washed again, and put on my gloves. I knelt down next to him and did what I do best. Refusing something for pain, he didn't flinch when I shot the wound with lidocaine for numbing. I went to work sanitizing it and then suturing it closed.

"You should sleep here tonight," I told him as I tossed my disposable suture kit and the used vial of lidocaine in the trash can and walked to the sink to clean up. "You've lost a decent amount of blood, but nothing life-threatening. Still, I don't think you should be driving. You can have my bed since I don't have one for my guest room yet." I could tell that he was going to object so I kept on talking. "Besides, the couch is too small for you to be comfortable. I have a big t-shirt you can wear." I went to the bathroom and returned with clean towels. I was standing at the sink running one of them under warm water so I could wash his torso and arms. He wasn't saying much so I assumed the numbing was wearing off and the deep cut was starting to hurt. "I can give you something for pain and an antibiotic," I called over my shoulder.

After wringing the water out of the towels, I turned to him and stopped cold in my tracks. I'd been so focused on his wound, I hadn't noticed it before, but now it stood out like a neon sign.

On his right bicep was a tattoo of a black ball with a chain. I shook my head to clear it as I walked closer. He followed my gaze, and after looking at me, then his arm and back at me, he asked, "Are you okay?"

There was a hushed moment before I asked while pointing at his tattoo, "What is that?"

"A ball and chain," came his casual reply. "You know, to remind me of what it was like behind bars."

I got closer and lowered my face. "It looks like it could've been something else."

"Like what?" His eyes were starting to get heavy. He'd had a long night.

"Like a pocket watch with a chain." I stood up and took a step back. "Kenny's rap sheet said he had a pocket watch tattoo on his right bicep. Your tattoo reminded me of it."

"If you're still thinking that I'm Kenny Pritchard, you're wrong, Barbie doll. I swear—"

I stopped him. "No, I don't think you're Kenny Pritchard. I only said the shape reminded me of a tattoo described on his arrest report. That's all. The pocket watch was actually something important to me. I didn't tell you about it the other night, but maybe I'll fill you in tomorrow." I pulled him to his feet and guided him upstairs to my room.

That night as I lay in the dark staring at my living room ceiling, it wasn't the harsh events of the evening that kept me awake. It wasn't even the tattoo that reminded me of Kenny or the memory of the pocket watch that had meant so much. I recalled a story a friend had told me. He was a talented cardiothoracic surgeon, the best in his field. He shared that he and his dad had been working under the kitchen sink to repair a leak when his father complained that his left arm had gone numb. In a panic, my friend stood up to check his dad's symptoms and promptly fainted. He explained how he was in the heart business, but when it came to his father, fear of losing him was so overwhelming he passed out in the old man's arms. Thank goodness it turned out to be nothing, but I remembered hearing that story and thinking how that could never happen to me. After all, trauma was practically my middle name. I'd dealt with some of the most gruesome medical emergencies anyone could imagine.

I shifted uncomfortably on the couch and pulled the blanket up to my chin. I thought about the man resting right above my head. In my bed. I hadn't vomited up my Dr. Pepper and appetizers because they didn't agree with me. There was a deeper reason. For the first time in my career, I saw the blood of someone I cared about and it scared me to death. And worse yet, I didn't know which revelation I found more frightening. The fact that I cared about Jake Chambers. Or knowing that if anything happened to him, I'd be devastated.

CHAPTER 22

MY LONELY ADIRONDACK CHAIR

I groaned as I stretched and tried to get my bearings. Like a flood, memories of the previous evening washed over me, and I quickly sat up. The sun was streaming around the edges of the curtains. I jumped up and ran to the window. Jake's truck was still parked in the front driveway. I hurried upstairs and peeked in my bedroom. I remembered waiting for him to use the bathroom before I'd ushered him upstairs last night. After determining that my largest t-shirt was too small for him, he'd kicked off his boots and socks, unbuckled his belt and loosened his jeans, and climbed beneath my heavy quilt without saying a word. I'd started to tell him he could give a shout and I'd come upstairs if he needed anything, but was interrupted by his soft snores. It made me smile before I left the room.

I now stood in the doorway and couldn't tear my eyes away from him. He was sprawled on his back, and the covers were only pulled up to just below his belly button. He had one bare leg stretched out. The other one was hidden beneath my quilt. I noticed his jeans were on the floor. The waistband of his underwear was visible from the folds of his pants. Which meant he was sleeping in my bed, totally nude.

I felt a wave of heat rush up my spine as I allowed myself the luxury of watching him sleep. And I'd thought he looked magnificent while making a salad in my kitchen the other night? I inwardly scoffed and silently inhaled while I soaked in every visible inch of him. My eyes traveled from his slightly mussed hair to his short silver-streaked beard that camouflaged a strong jaw. Then down his neck to the scary skull that had become so familiar. I walked closer and tilted my head as I observed some of his tattoos. I'd been in physician mode, and other than the ball and chain, hadn't given them much notice last night. One caused my heart to lurch. Ignoring the uncomfortable sensation, I admired his other tattoos. Their colors and designs danced across a broad, muscular chest and tapered down to a highly defined abdomen. *I guess I know what he does in his spare time,* I mused.

I walked around the other side of the bed and saw that the bandage wasn't stained. *Good. No leakage and the stitches held.* I was going to check him for fever but didn't want to wake him. I carefully pulled open a drawer and took out some clothes. I spotted my new and unused running shoes I'd left on the dresser and quietly slid them out of the box. I closed the door behind me and headed downstairs to use the bathroom.

After washing my face, brushing my teeth, changing my clothes, and putting on my new shoes, I started the coffeepot and walked out to the front porch. I slowly stretched as I looked at the vast expanse of fields and pondered what, if anything, I should do with them. I wasn't a farmer but knew my property boasted fertile soil. Enjoying the brisk, but not too cool air, I sauntered down to where my gravel driveway met the dirt road and asked myself if I was ready. The answer was yes, so I took a right and headed toward the Pritchard farm.

I wasn't in as good cardiovascular health as I'd hoped and realized I was starting to wear thin as I approached the first line of trees that separated our farm from the Pritchards'. I slowed to a walk as I tried to catch my breath. I stopped when I got to the trees and wondered if I should veer off the path and see if I could find the tree houses. I decided against the idea and with caution kept walking. I'd told myself I would be able to gaze upon the Pritchards' old homestead and feel nothing. Now I wasn't so sure that I wholly believed it. I didn't stop, and after getting a second wind, I was able to pick up the pace again. I could see the curve in the road ahead and knew that, once I followed it, I would come face-to-face with my past. I was feeling empowered when something stopped me. I'd come to a small sign in the road. One that had never been there before. It looked like one of those official-looking county markers. It had a number that was attached to a long, steel rod that had been set in the ground just to the right of the road. I found this curious. *Why was the county placing markers on a private road?* I wondered. And how long had the post been there? It looked fairly new, but what would I know? I hadn't wandered this street since before I graduated high school, and that was over thirty years ago.

I looked at my watch and realized I'd run long enough. *I need to be there when Jake wakes up,* I told myself. The Pritchard farm had waited for this reunion for more than three decades. It could certainly wait another day. I didn't know if it was the second wind or knowing who would be waiting for me when I got home, but I found a burst of energy as I headed back toward my place. I could see him standing on my front porch, and I waved as I got closer. When I ran up my driveway, he walked toward me. He was wearing a clean shirt and offered, "I had a spare in my truck. I was too tired to mention it last night."

I was huffing by this time and could only nod. I was going to ask him how he was feeling when he started peppering me with questions about where I'd gone. I waved my arm toward the Pritchards' as I bent over and placed both hands on my knees. "Whew," I barely got out. "I'm not in as good a shape as I thought."

"You went to the Pritchard farm?" he shot back. "You were there?"

I stood up and smiled. He was frowning and I surmised that his side was hurting. "No." I shook my head. "I almost got there but turned around at a marker in the road I don't remember ever seeing before." I took in a deep breath. He seemed almost relieved which was understandable. Exploring an abandoned house alone wouldn't have been a wise choice.

"Why do you only have one chair on your porch?"

We both looked over at the red Adirondack chair that graced the front of my house. It stood in stark contrast to the faded siding that was badly in need of a new coat of paint.

I shrugged and said, "I don't know. I guess because it's just me. Why would I need another one?"

"So, if I want to enjoy my coffee on the front porch with you, you'll have to sit on my lap?" he teased.

"Is that an offer?" I laughed.

"A standing one," he replied, his face more serious.

"If I wasn't in desperate need of a shower or concerned about tearing your stitches, I might've taken you up on it."

He started to say something when we both heard the crunching of gravel and turned at the same time. I recognized the midnight blue pickup truck that was making its way toward us. It belonged to Darlene's oldest child, Matthew. I knew parents weren't supposed to have a favorite child, and Darlene was no exception. But I knew Matthew was very special to her for many reasons. The one that stood out the most was because he'd chosen his family and Pumpkin Rest over the lures of the big city. Most kids, myself included, took one look at the outside world and couldn't wait to escape small-town life. Matthew had done the opposite. After getting his degree in psychology at Arkansas State University, he chose to come back home, marry his high school sweetheart, and give Darlene and her husband three grandchildren. He commuted to his job as a counselor for underprivileged adults who were battling drug and alcohol addiction, while his stay-at-home wife homeschooled their children. And it didn't hurt that he'd named his oldest daughter after Darlene.

I smiled as I walked toward the truck that had pulled up behind Jake's. Darlene jumped out, and after slamming the door, stuck her head back inside the open window. "Tell your father he doesn't need to come get me. I'll get a ride." She blew her son a kiss. Matthew waved at me and gave Jake a gentleman's nod before he backed out and drove away.

Darlene stood with hands on hips and looked from me to Jake, then back at me. "I heard over coffee and donuts at church this morning that there was an incident at The Lonesome Keg last night that involved you two."

Without missing a beat I piped up, "And you had to have poor Matthew drive you all the way out here to find out? You couldn't have just called?"

"I did call and you didn't answer," she shot back. "Which only upped my sense of concern." She busted out laughing. I laughed too because I knew Darlene had been rooting for me and Jake to get together and she had to see if her subtle cheerleading had paid off.

As the three of us made our way into the house, I shared the details of the previous night's events. She showed concern when I told her that Jake had suffered a serious cut by a jagged bottle. "And how in the world has the gossip made its way back to your church's coffee and donut hour?" I wanted to know.

She sat at my kitchen table and shook her head at my offer of coffee. "Oh, you know small towns. I think someone's cousin, who happens to be best friends with someone else's sister-in-law, who works with the guy at the feed store, whose wife teaches the second grade Sunday school class, who—"

I held up my hand to interrupt. "I get it." I took a deep breath and told her, "I'm pretty sure nobody knows that Jake got hurt. He'd like to keep it that way." I looked to Jake for confirmation and he dipped his chin in agreement.

Darlene made breakfast while I changed Jake's bandage, checked him for a fever, and wrote a prescription for antibiotics. He shook his head at my offer to give him something for pain. I don't remember how the conversation veered toward Jake's old nickname, and I watched as Darlene appeared puzzled but seemed to shake it off.

"I just had a tiddlywink," she offered.

Jake looked confused so I explained, "It's Darlene's description for déjà vu." He laughed at my clarification and took a sip of his coffee.

"So, Doc, huh?" Her wheels were spinning at top speed. "Are you a doctor?"

Here it comes, I thought. *The inquisition.* Darlene was very detail oriented and I knew she'd be grilling him for the next hour so I decided to rescue Jake by quickly explaining the Dr. Pepper reference.

She laughed at the explanation and stood. Scooting in her chair, she directed at me, "Barbie, I hope you don't mind if I leave you with the dirty dishes, but I need to get home." Before I could reply she turned to Jake and said, "If Barbie gives you the all clear, could you drive me home?"

Jake and I stood at the same time, and if I hadn't known better, I'd have thought he seemed nervous. It was probably the pain and he might've been second-guessing his decision to turn down a prescription. I was on the verge of telling Jake that I needed to take a look at his stitches in a few days, but Darlene was already herding him out to his truck. He climbed in and gave me a wave. By the look on his face, one could've sworn he was heading to the guillotine. I had to laugh as I watched my best friend climb in next to him. I could tell by the stern expression she wore that she would be reading him the riot act about the dangers of bar fights. She would then proceed to lecture him on not overexerting himself and tearing his stitches. And I was certain she would follow it up with a lesson on making sure he took all the antibiotics I prescribed.

I watched them drive off and walked back up the steps to my front porch. I stopped and looked at my lonely Adirondack chair. *I could buy another one,* I speculated, but decided against it. The thought of sitting on Jake's lap was too darn appealing.

CHAPTER 23

CONSIDER YOURSELF OFFICIALLY EVICTED

"Only one coin was missing?" Darlene frowned as she gazed at me over her reading glasses. Taking them off, she set them on the counter, leaned her elbows on the countertop next to them, and propped her chin in her hands. "That seems weird, Barbie."

"I totally agree. Was it missing when you took the collection?" I glanced around the gas station and waved to a local man who was filling up his half-gallon drink cup with Dr. Pepper. I tried not to sigh when I thought of Jake. I'd only seen him twice since the bar fight, and that was only to quickly assess his wound. It was healing nicely, and the stitches could be removed soon.

She straightened up and slowly shook her head. "I never looked. It was the same day I boxed up a few personal items for you. I stuck that box in my pantry and hid the coin collection in my bedroom closet. I never took the time to open it before I tucked it away."

We recalled the last time either of us had seen what was in the antique wooden storage box. It was when we were teenagers and snooping. We'd found the hidden treasure and only removed one or two trays before we heard my grandmother's car. Neither of us had looked inside the box since. For all we knew, the lower part of the box could've been stuffed with newspapers. But it wasn't. When I'd taken it to the first appraiser, his eyes went wide as he carefully removed five trays filled with Civil War coins in pristine condition.

"Based on the order the coins were stored, the appraiser is guessing at what the missing one might be. And if that's the case, it's the most valuable coin out of all of them." I stepped aside while the customer paid for his drink.

"Does he think it's possible your father never acquired that coin and left the spot open hoping to find it one day and add it to his collection?"

I scratched the side of my nose. "The appraiser said it was a possibility." I paused and thought for a moment. "My father left his collection at the house when he moved away and married my mother. It's possible he took the one coin with him to sell." Since we had no way of ever finding out, I continued, "Regardless, I have two appraisals now, and because they're so close I'm not going to bother getting a third."

I was satisfied that I was finally in a position to confront my sister, share half of what was rightfully hers, and move on with a life that didn't include Frenita Anderson. Leaning over the counter, I hugged Darlene and told her I would text her when I got back to town. I was on my way to a three-day medical conference in New York. I'd daydreamed more than once about asking Jake to join me, but an overnight trip would come with complications. Most particularly, the sleeping arrangements. I may have been more than a little aroused by seeing his naked body in my bed, but that didn't mean I was emotionally ready to jump into the sack with him.

I wasn't surprised that I found myself fantasizing about Jake on the three-hour drive to the airport in Greenville. But what I did find astonishing was that my musings weren't about sex. I pictured myself walking hand in hand with him through Times Square, sharing a cappuccino while visiting the Museum of Natural History in Manhattan. Or laughing over a joke while we ate at a restaurant that only served macaroni and cheese concocted a hundred different ways. I discovered that I liked being around Jake, and wondered if he enjoyed my company as well.

When I landed at LaGuardia, I got a text from him saying he knew it was short notice, but would I be interested in having dinner tonight at his place? I couldn't contain my smile at the invitation and noted that I found a smidgen of satisfaction in being justifiably unavailable. I caught a cab and reflected on my way to the hotel how I'd hardly seen him since that Sunday morning. And when I had seen him, he'd seemed preoccupied. I was going to ask Darlene exactly how much of a scolding she'd given him the day they'd driven off together, but whenever I tried to bring it up, she shrewdly skirted around it.

I texted back that I was out of town, but that I would've said yes. And seeing how I was in New York City for three days, I would have to decline politely. Those days flew by with a frenzy of conferences, catching up with old friends and making a few new ones. The last evening I found myself having dinner with six colleagues. Slowly, the dinner guests politely excused themselves until I found myself alone with Dr. Gil Saunders, a neurology professor at a prestigious New

England university. He'd been one of the guest speakers at the conference, and I didn't think it was a coincidence that he kept showing up in
my small circle. My suspicions were confirmed when he reached for my
hand and told me he'd like to pursue our friendship, offering to travel
south as often as possible to see me. I gazed into his intelligent and
hopeful eyes, and willed myself to say yes. After all, he was a smart,
attractive widower with no children. We had a lot in common, but I
couldn't.

He saw my hesitation and told me that if I changed my mind, I knew
where to find him. When I got back to my hotel room, I wondered if my
judgment had been clouded by thoughts of Jake. It's not like we'd
communicated all weekend. He wasn't a texter. He still used an old flip
phone, so I knew texting with his meaty fingers was difficult. Regardless
of the reason, I couldn't seem to drum up any enthusiasm for Gil Saunders
and that was that.

My flight landed in Greenville without incident. I took a deep, calming
breath when I saw Fancy's white BMW parked in one of the two allotted
spots for my condominium. I had a key but didn't want to barge in unannounced, so I knocked. I was surprised when Fancy opened the door,
looking haggard. It was the first time I could ever remember seeing her
without makeup since she discovered mascara when she was eleven. She
had her long hair pulled back in a sloppy ponytail, the gray roots Jake had
noticed weeks earlier screaming for attention. She was wearing a bathrobe
that was two sizes too big and her bare toes boasted chipped pink polish.

"To what do I owe the pleasure, big sister?" came her sarcastic drawl.
She stepped aside and I walked past her into the bare and expansive foyer
that overlooked a huge formal living and dining room, my eyes widening
as I went.

I spun around and asked her incredulously, "Where is everything?
Where's all my furniture?"

She closed the door and sauntered toward me. With a casual shrug, she
offered, "Needed some cash."

I didn't care about the furniture. There wasn't anything in the house
that I'd wanted anyway. Perhaps my offer was going to make this easier
than I thought. "I've got something for you." I reached into my pocket and
took out an envelope. "This is for your fair half of Dad's Civil War coin
collection. Darlene has been holding on to it since Grandma died. I've had
it appraised." I gestured toward the envelope she held and continued,
"Two independent appraisals are in there. I could've bought you out for
the average, but I'm giving you half of the highest appraisal." When she
didn't respond, I promptly added, "And I'm meeting with a realtor in

thirty minutes. I'm putting the condo up for sale. You have until they sell it to find a new place to live."

She leaned back against a wall and did a slow clap. "I guess this is you being holier than thou? Tossing your sister a bone so you don't have to feel guilty for kicking me out of my house?"

"*My* house," I interrupted. "It wasn't my fault Richard didn't leave a provision for you in his will. Not that he had anything left to leave. I've been more than generous by letting you live here, Fancy. And you should consider yourself lucky that I don't deduct the cost of the things you've sold out of that check." I pointed to the envelope she was still clutching.

She rolled her eyes and tore into the envelope. I watched as her expression changed from one of disinterest to one of excitement. She hadn't estimated the collection's worth, and I could envision her licking her lips in anticipation of where she would spend the money. I didn't know what I expected, but it certainly wasn't her next comment.

With feigned concern, she let out a long sigh and asked, "You're certain I can't stay here?"

"Yes, I'm certain," I said with a smirk. "It's time for us to part ways, Fancy. I don't want any ties to you or Richard. This condo is a reminder of a past I'd like to forget. I'm sure you'll be fine."

She stood up a little straighter and walked toward me as she returned the check to the envelope. "Of course I'll be fine, Barbie. After you give me the rest of what is rightfully mine and mine alone." She looked up at the ceiling, and with a tone dripping with mock sympathy, said, "I'd hoped it wouldn't come to this, but it's your fault. Believe me when I tell you, I never wanted to play this card, Barbie. But you've given me no choice."

I couldn't even begin to fathom what she was talking about, but found myself getting lightheaded when Frenita Anderson dropped a bombshell I hadn't seen coming. Never in a million years would I have believed it if she hadn't sashayed off to another part of the house and returned with the offensive proof.

I read the document, and with a shaky voice said, "This means nothing. So Dad married Mom when she was pregnant with me. So what?" I'd always been told my parents' anniversary was in June. Their original marriage certificate had been lost in the blaze that took their lives. Apparently, Fancy had sent away for a copy that listed the actual date in September.

"It's true, Barbie, and we can prove it with DNA testing. You're not an Anderson. Dad married Mom when she was pregnant with another man's baby. That other man being your real father." She reached out and gave a disgusted flip of my hair before adding, "The man whose anti-aging genes you so obviously inherited."

Shaking my head I spat back, "No. No way. There is no way that our hateful grandmother wouldn't have thrown this in my face for all those years."

"For someone so smart you really are dumb," she countered. "Why do you think Granddaddy had the deed to the farm put in your name? Because he knew. And it was the only way he could keep our grandmother from telling you." She cocked a hip and said with a droll laugh, "Think about it. You were blackmailing Juanita Anderson and didn't even know it. If she'd so much as spouted off one word of this to you, you could've sold that farm right out from under her and she'd have had no place to go." She looked at her fingertips that were in dire need of a manicure and added, "I wouldn't have even known if she hadn't started calling me before she died, ranting about how mad she was at Granddaddy for giving you the house." She waved her unmanicured hand in the air before adding, "How he threatened to kick her out when he was still alive, and still lording it over her after his death by making sure you got the farm and all the property."

I'd always figured my grandfather deeded the farm to me before his death to ensure I'd always have a home, not because he was blackmailing my grandmother into keeping her mouth shut about my paternity. I was too shocked to remind her that I didn't have to split the profit with her after the farm sold, but apparently she was thinking the same thing.

"I could've probably taken you to court for the whole return on the farm after she died. You know, since you weren't a *rightful* heir." She blew out a breath and said, "But I wasn't hard up for money then." Her eyes turned menacing and she added, "Poor Barbie. I remember you proudly telling your stupid friends that our mother told you how Dad fell in love with her after a three-day whirlwind romance. Guess she left out the part that she was pregnant with another man's illegitimate child."

If it were true, it would explain a lot. My parents' need to distance themselves from my grandparents. Juanita Anderson's disdain for my mother and more than instant hatred for me. Her favoritism toward Fancy, her grandchild by blood. My thoughts drifted to my sweet granddaddy, who, if what Fancy was telling me was true, wasn't even my real grandfather. He knew, and he protected me before and after his death. First by forbidding Juanita Anderson to tell me, and later by transferring the farm into my name. A guarantee that his hateful wife wouldn't risk having me sell the property right out from under her. She probably could've legally challenged it, but didn't want to chance it not going in her favor. I could've rightfully evicted her and a then eleven-year-old Fancy from their home. Too bad the miserable old crone never knew me well enough to know that I would never have done that.

"Like I said, I'll be needing the other half of that stupid coin collection's value." She crossed her arms and smiled like a Cheshire cat. "You scraped together the first half so I'm sure you won't have any trouble coming up with the rest." She leaned back against the wall and tilted her head to the side, her evil grin revealing the empty space in her chest where a heart should have been.

I sucked up my obvious discomfort and looked Fancy in the eyes. I wasn't in the mood to be bullied. "If what you say is true, I'll take it to my attorney to sort it out. In the meantime, I've decided to rescind my offer to pay you for even half of the coin collection. It was left in the house when Grandma died, and since the house was in my name, it belongs to me." I had no idea if this was true, but it hit the target. Fancy looked like a deer caught in the headlights. A very bewildered deer. "And you sold *my* furniture." I swept my hand over the room. "That's stealing, and I'll have to think about whether or not I'm going to press charges." I snatched the envelope out of her hand.

I walked to the door, and after opening it, I turned to her and said, "As far as letting you stay here until it sells, as of this moment, consider yourself officially evicted." I strutted out of my condo without bothering to close the door behind me.

CHAPTER 24

ANDERSONS ARE CONNECTED BY THEIR
HEARTS

I barely remembered my conversation with the realtor as I sped back to Pumpkin Rest. I'd signed the appropriate paperwork, permitted them to do whatever was needed if Fancy didn't cooperate when they need to show the condo, and sought the refuge of my car in a trancelike state. I called Darlene from the road and breathed a sigh of relief when I found out she was home and not at work. I wanted her to be with me when I talked to the one person who could confirm what Fancy had told me. I wouldn't need a DNA test, as I trusted this person wholeheartedly.

I realized on the long drive home that I wasn't as upset about Fancy's revelation as I should've been. I didn't care if I wasn't an Anderson by blood. I bathed in the warm remembrance of my parents' and grandfather's love, and that was enough for me. And if there had been even a smidgen of guilt about removing Fancy from my life, I could honestly say it was gone. But still, something deep inside me needed to know the truth.

I picked up Darlene and shared the details of my conversation with Fancy. I could tell she didn't believe me when I told her I was okay and was afraid I might have a breakdown once I knew the truth. She gave me a doubtful and worried glance.

"You're sure you want to know?" she asked as she got out of my Jeep and slammed the door.

"Absolutely," I assured her. And I meant it.

We found Darlene's granny on the back porch snapping green beans. Granny "Dicey" Zachary was born and raised in Pumpkin Rest, and considering she'd be celebrating her one-hundredth birthday next year, it was probably safe to assume she'd spend the last of her days here as well. She'd raised seven sons, the youngest being Darlene's father. Dicey still lived with her oldest child in the home where her husband had been born. Darlene's bachelor uncle had never married. He was now of an age that they both needed help from the family, and Darlene's plethora of cousins always pitched in to take care of their personal needs and their home.

"Granny," Darlene said, before parking herself on a sturdy crate across from her grandmother, "Barbie wants to ask you something. It's very important to her. Something she heard from Frenita."

Dicey set her bowl of green beans on the table next to her rocker and reached for her pipe. After tamping down the tobacco and lighting it up, she took a long, slow draw before blowing the match out with an exhale.

"Is that okay with you?" Darlene prodded.

"If it's what I think it is"—she looked up at me through wizened eyes—"she needs to be sure she's prepared to hear the answer." Her voice was husky. Exactly what you'd expect from someone who'd been smoking tobacco since she was ten years old. When I nodded, she pointed with her pipe to another crate. I took a seat next to Darlene and rested my elbows on my knees.

"I'm not afraid of the truth," I confessed.

"Good," she said before taking another puff. "I take it the apple didn't fall far from the evil witch's tree?" I smiled at her Snow White reference. "That little shrew of a sister told you, didn't she? I had a feeling Juanita didn't take that tidbit to the grave with her."

"So it's true?" I confirmed. "My mother was pregnant with me by another man when she married my father." Darlene reached for my hand and grabbed it tightly. "I'm not an Anderson, am I?"

"Your granddaddy knew this day might come. I've always wondered why the good Lord kept me around longer than a person has a right to walk this earth. Now I know why. It was so I could be a voice for Fred Anderson. To tell you the truth, and more importantly," she added with a cackle while aiming her pipe at me, "to make sure you know that you are more Anderson than your sister and wicked grandmother could ever hope to be."

I didn't know what she meant but knew not to interrupt.

"You're right. Your mother had unmarried relations before she met and fell in love with your father. Your granddaddy, Fred, didn't get many details about who your blood father might be, but I got the impression it wasn't a good story. One that was best left alone." She gazed out over her back yard and took another draw from her pipe before continuing. "But who sired you didn't matter to your daddy or granddaddy. They both loved you with their whole hearts and then some. But that evil Juanita wouldn't have it. She not only resented your mother for keeping your father away from Pumpkin Rest, but she saw her sin, her secret, and it ate her alive. Eventually churning out hatred toward an innocent."

"Her sin? Her secret?" I heard Darlene's voice asking the question that had been ready to explode from my lips.

Dicey scoffed, and then proceeded to tell a story about the most beautiful woman in the county. Juanita had been a real stunner back in the day. Unfortunately, the only man she wanted didn't want her. And when she found herself unmarried and pregnant with that man's child, she did what any desperate woman would do back in those days.

"She pulled a Scarlett O'Hara," Dicey stated. "Just like in the movie with that handsome Rhett Butler, Juanita went after her sister's intended. Fred Anderson was engaged to Juanita's younger sister until she swooped in while her sister was away at nursing school. She turned on the charm and wooed your granddaddy like there was no tomorrow. Made him believe she was in love with him. Got him to marry her." There was a dramatic pause, and I wondered if there was more to the story. Taking a deep breath, she looked thoughtful for a moment. "Fred Anderson never forgave himself for falling for her and breaking his intended's heart. But, back in those days, you lay in the bed you made for yourself."

I was certain my jaw hit the floor. "Are you telling me my father wasn't even an Anderson? That my grandmother was pregnant with him when Granddaddy married her?"

Dicey bobbed her head with a solid, "Yes," and followed it up with, "Juanita Anderson was nothing but a hypocrite!"

"Did my grandfather know?"

She gave me a knowing look. "Since the beginning of time, women have been covering up illicit pregnancies with accidental falls causing them to go into early labor. In Juanita's case, she hid the pregnancy well, eventually telling everybody her water broke when she fell off a stool while retrieving a jar of pickled okra off the top pantry shelf. She proceeded to give birth to a healthy ten-pound baby boy almost two months before her due date." She scoffed. "He was no preemie, and your granddaddy was no fool. She came clean with him and begged his forgiveness."

She looked at me with sympathy lodged in her soulful eyes that were set back in the deep crevices of her lined face. "Your granddaddy and I were best friends. Much like you and that Pritchard boy. We had tough upbringings and found comfort in our mutual misery. It never got romantic-like with us, but we were there for each other. That's how I know so much about him. But those stories are for another day," she added wistfully. "If the good Lord sees fit to keep me around." She shifted in the rocking chair. "What you came here to find out is true. But I needed to tell you the whole truth. And now you know it. Your father wasn't an Anderson and neither is that gnat you call a sister."

"I had no clue," I said, stunned beyond belief. "I don't have a lot of memories of my grandfather and father interacting, but the ones I do have were always heartwarming."

"Fred Anderson loved that boy as his own," Dicey said, her hardened vocal cords taking on a dreamlike quality. "He never once treated him like anything other than his blood kin. Even loved him more than I see some fathers love their sons if you ask me." She raised her chin higher. "And Fred told me that should there ever come a day when you asked, I needed to tell you the truth. He managed to keep that witch's pie hole closed while he was alive. He never laid a hand on her but she afeard him all the same. Your granddaddy could be a formidable man. Stern, but always fair. I guess you already figured out that he put the deed to the property in your name as a secondary means to scare her into keeping the truth hidden. He never wanted you hurt and never wanted you to think you weren't wanted or loved."

I smiled, letting warm memories of my grandfather wash over me. "He was my hero. Even more so after Kenny ran away. He died right before I graduated high school. Almost like he knew it was okay to leave me after I'd earned my scholarships and was accepted to college."

Dicey grunted in agreement before continuing. "Fred always said that you and your daddy were more Anderson than Juanita and Fancy could ever hope to be." She thumped her heart with a gnarled hand. "Andersons are connected by the heart, not the blood. And I ain't seen anybody with more heart than your granddaddy. He even let himself love that shrew of a woman until she started showing her hateful self at your daddy's new wife and then at you."

After thanking Granny Dicey and promising to come back for a visit without my medical bag in tow, I kissed her forehead and walked out to the car with Darlene. Her uncle passed us in his rickety old truck as we pulled away. "Anna Claire is bringing your supper over tonight!" Darlene yelled out my window as she leaned over me. He replied with a thumbs-up.

We'd turned onto the main road when I felt Darlene's hand lightly caress my shoulder. "Barbie?"

I looked over at her and smiled. "I'm okay, Darlene. I promise. And before you ask me, the answer is no. I don't want to know who my biological father is. As misguided as it was, at least I know why my grandmother despised me. And whether you choose to believe me or not, I'm telling you there is peace in knowing the truth. I believe what Granny Dicey said about my grandfather telling her I was more Anderson than my grandmother and Fancy could ever hope to be."

"I'm so glad to hear that, Barbara Jean." Her use of my full name told me she was serious.

"And I'm going to fight Fancy, Darlene. I'm not giving her a dime."

"Good girl!" came her exuberant reply.

"And it's not about the money, Dar."

"I know it's not, Barbie."

Darlene turned on my radio and found her favorite station. Waylon Jennings was warning mothers everywhere not to let their babies grow up to be cowboys. Darlene and I sang at the tops of our lungs along with him. To my disappointment, she turned down a Trisha Yearwood classic to ask me about Jake.

"He texted me when I was in New York and asked if he could make me dinner at his place. Of course I had to tell him no because I wasn't here."

She gave a small nod of assent, and a glimmer of approval was in her eyes.

"It's almost time for my shift. You can drop me at the gas station on your way home," she informed me.

I recognized Jake's truck at the pumps. He'd left it unattended and was coming out of the station carrying a fountain drink. I knew it was a Dr. Pepper and felt a tug of satisfaction in knowing a silly but intimate detail about him. After parking and getting out of the car, Darlene and I met up with him at his truck.

We made some small talk where Darlene subtly alluded to me having a bit of a bad day. I told her she was making a bigger deal out of it than was necessary. I couldn't explain why, but I had a feeling of peace that I'd never had before. If anything, there was a sense of relief in knowing why I'd always been on the receiving end of my grandmother's nasty stick.

"It's probably not a good time to ask for a favor." Jake had finished putting on his gas cap as he leaned up against the truck.

"I'm fine. What do you need?" I asked with a smile.

"Think if I stopped by your place later you could take out my stitches?"

"Absolutely. It's time for them to come out anyway."

We picked a convenient time, said our goodbyes, and I hopped into my Jeep. Who'd have believed with the day I'd had that the prospect of removing Jake's sutures would make me smile the entire drive home.

CHAPTER 25

RELAX AND LET YOURSELF ENJOY THE RIDE,
SWEETHEART

O nce home, I unpacked my bag, changed into a pair of jeans and a comfy blouse, and took my mail out to the front porch. I made some calls and arranged to meet with a couple of subcontractors about my renovation. I must've lost track of time because before I knew it, the familiar rumble of a motorcycle caught my attention. Jake pulled up to my house, parked, and made his way up the porch steps.

"C'mon inside," I told him as I jumped up from my chair. "My bag is in the kitchen." I walked toward the front door. Before I could reach for the doorknob, he grabbed my hand and gently yanked me to him. I looked up into his eyes and noticed a glint of mischief in their depths. I felt a jolt of adrenaline when I thought he was going to kiss me. I tried to play it cool and tilted my head slightly to the side. When he didn't make a move, I shifted uncomfortably and asked, "What?"

He started to raise his shirt and said, "You might want to take a look first."

I cast my eyes downward and frowned. "Where are your stitches?"

"I took them out yesterday," he admitted with a sheepish grin.

I placed my hands on my hips. "Then why did you ask me to take them out when I saw you at the gas station?"

"I wanted an excuse to see you."

A breeze wafted up onto the porch, bringing with it his sharp, masculine scent. I bit my lip to hide my smile. "I'm glad," I admitted.

He walked down the steps to his bike and bent low to retrieve something from one of his leather saddle bags. I followed him, and he handed me a helmet I recognized. My mouth must've been hanging open because he said, "Let's go for a ride before the weather gets too cold."

I shook my head. "I can't get on the back of a motorcycle."

"Yes, you can, Barbie. I won't take you far. I'll drive slow and promise I'll be more than careful."

My brain said not to do it, but my heart wanted to give it a try. I grabbed Dolly's helmet out of his hands and asked, "I guess she gave this to you when you made it clear you weren't interested?"

He pointed to a scuff mark on the left side and said, "She threw it at my head and missed."

I was still hesitant so he offered, "We'll make it a short ride. Wanna grab some supper at Crossroads Diner?"

After changing my shirt and shoes, I carefully climbed on the back of his bike. "I can't believe I'm doing this," I grumbled as I tightly clutched him from behind.

He wrestled my right hand from the death grip that was fastened to his shirt. Bringing it to his mouth, he lightly kissed the inside of my wrist and said, "Relax and let yourself enjoy the ride, sweetheart."

I didn't release my vise-grip hold until we'd left my dirt road behind and were riding on smooth pavement. I found myself relaxing then, enjoying the warm breeze, the solid form I was nestled against, and the momentary freedom from responsibility. Jake was true to his word. He didn't drive too fast, was cautious around cars and trucks, and didn't try to show off or impress me with unnecessary antics. I rested my chin on his shoulder and shouted, "You should be wearing a helmet!"

I saw his left cheek tug upward in a grin as we pulled into the diner. Darlene waved from her perch behind the gas station counter, a mile-long grin spreading across her face.

He helped me off the bike. "That wasn't so bad, was it?"

"It was kind of fun," I reluctantly admitted as I stretched my legs.

We took a booth in the back and ordered two blue plate specials. I asked for a sweet tea, and he ordered water. We spent the next ten minutes talking about my reservations concerning motorcycles. I told him about some of the injuries I'd treated as a result of careless drivers. He agreed and thanked me for giving him a chance to prove himself a responsible one. We both concurred that it was only as safe as other drivers allowed. "Not everyone respects a motorcycle," he told me. "It's up to me to have my guard up when sharing the road."

He asked me about my trip to New York. I told him the boring details, leaving out my short time with Dr. Gil Saunders. He asked if I wanted to talk more about Fancy's revelation, as well as Granny Dicey's confirmation that I wasn't an Anderson. He remained quiet when I told him I was fine, and I liked that he believed me and didn't push it. Our conversation circled back to my trip, and I had him laughing so hard I thought he might tear his newly closed wound. We'd been talking about airline travel, and he'd asked me the worst part of the trip. I told him it was the hour I spent on the tarmac listening to the ninety-eight-year-old gentleman next to me give a dissertation on the emotional and physical benefits of making love with an up-and-coming centenarian.

"Why didn't you put your headphones on or pick up a magazine?" he asked me, his face red from laughing.

"I didn't want to be rude. Besides, he wouldn't stop talking. Never even took a breath." I took a sip of my tea and set my glass down.

"Did you eventually blow him off?"

"I didn't have to." I rolled my eyes. "He finally excused himself so he could go to the restroom and empty his catheter bag."

Jake spit his water across the table following my last comment. "Sounds like a real Casanova," he managed to say while wiping his chin.

The rest of our time together passed quickly. We laughed, we shared stories from Hampton House, he told me a little more about his childhood, and I shared a little more about mine.

"The pocket watch," he said after he'd signaled the waitress for our check. "You told me there was a pocket watch that was important to you. What did you mean?"

I exhaled slowly. "It was something my grandfather gave me. It was a broken old watch handed down by generations of Andersons. It was battered and probably not worth much. But it was special. It was permanently stopped on nine nineteen." I was staring at my empty plate and raised my eyes to meet his.

"Granddaddy always said it was a lucky watch. Every Anderson that carried it managed to avert some disaster. He'd regretted that he'd never gotten around to giving it to my father. I guess he felt it had some kind of magical powers that could've saved his life. It's why he gave it to me when I was just twelve." I swallowed and sat up. "Anyway, I gave it to Kenny right before I left for summer camp. We'd shared what I guess you would call a special moment the night before—at least it was special to me. I gave him the watch for safekeeping. Proof of my love. Proof that I would come back from camp and we would pick up where we'd left off." I looked away shyly.

"You gave him your virginity that night." Jake's voice was barely a whisper.

My eyes darted back to his. "Yes, and it's not easy for me to admit considering how young and irresponsible I was back then. We didn't use protection." I took a big breath. "It was a big moment for both of us. Anyway, I thought it was."

"Being irresponsible is understandable. Like you said, you were both young. Vulnerable."

I sat facing him, shoulders hunched. "That's when I gave him my most valued possession to validate my love for him. My granddaddy's watch." I paused. "I thought he would've left it for me before he ran away. When I saw on Kenny's rap sheet that he had a tattoo of one on his right arm..." My voice faded as I tried to gather my thoughts.

Sensing my sadness, Jake asked, "How did it end that night?"

"Not good." I looked up at him and could feel the heat making its way up my neck. "The worst possible thing happened."

Jake didn't say anything as I took another swallow of tea. "His father caught us right in the middle of round two. Jonathan was asleep in the bedroom they'd shared, and we were buck naked on the living room floor. It was his father's regular drinking night with his buddies, but he got home early and caught us. We never heard him drive up."

Jake sat back and scrubbed his hand down his face. "Whew. What did he do? Rough him up? Threaten to tell your grandparents?"

"No," I replied, my voice monotone and lifeless. "It was worse than that."

Jake raised an eyebrow.

"He stood over us with his hands on his hips while we scrambled for our clothes."

"And?"

"He just laughed. Not a funny 'ha, I caught you' laugh. Not even an embarrassed laugh."

I shivered when I remembered the humiliation of that night almost forty years earlier. And how I couldn't even begin to describe to Jake or erase from my memory the most evil, maniacal, bellowing laugh I'd ever heard.

CHAPTER 26

HE'S NOT WORTH IT

The sun was setting, and Jake insisted on having me home before it got dark. I appreciated the gesture but couldn't help but wonder the entire ride home if he was ever going to ask me again to dinner at his place like he had when I was in New York. We dismounted from his bike, I took off the helmet and started to hand it to him when he waved it off and said, "You keep it. I don't plan on having anybody else on the back of my bike that'll need it." I tucked it under my arm and headed for my porch, not wanting him to see the smile that was causing my cheeks to burn.

I could feel his presence behind me as I marched up the steps. He exuded raw masculinity that was intoxicating, and I had to remind myself that we weren't exactly a couple. I was pondering the exact nomenclature that might describe our relationship when I felt his warm hand pressed against my back. I'd been getting ready to retrieve my keys from my front pocket but stopped and slowly turned to him. He brought both hands up to my face and softly pressed his forehead to mine. "I know it went against everything you believe in, but thank you for riding with me tonight." His voice was deep and raspy.

"Thank you for respecting that and being super careful. And thank you for dinn—" The words died on my lips as his found mine. My arms had their own plans as they wrapped around his back and pulled him closer. His kiss was soft at first, gentle and cautious. When I moaned, he deepened it, only stopping to tease my lips with soft nips. I was a fifty-two-year-old woman who'd experienced too many kisses to count, but this one undid me and was better than I could've imagined. It was like nothing I'd ever known or felt before. There wasn't just physical heat radiating from Jake, but a spiritual one that was targeting my soul. This was the moment I realized I might have started falling in love with Jake Chambers. The revelation and 'danger ahead' warning blaring in my head were almost as alarming as the loud shrill coming from my back pocket.

He reluctantly broke our kiss and said, "You might need to answer it." He shifted uncomfortably and took a step back. I reached in my pocket and pulled out my phone. I looked at the number and didn't recognize it. Normally, I wouldn't take a call from an unrecognizable number, but since returning to Pumpkin Rest and not knowing who might need me in an emergency, I answered it and immediately put it on speaker. Thank goodness I did.

I didn't recognize the voice at first. It was familiar but it sounded like the person was speaking through a clamped jaw. It was a woman and she was whispering, "Please come."

I shook my head and said, "I'm sorry. I don't know who this is."

"Please come to my house."

"It's Sheila," Jake said before snatching the phone out of my hand. He took it off speaker and put it to his ear. I watched his expression change from one of concern to anger as he questioned her. He hung up and said, "Please grab your bag, Barbie. I know where she lives. I can drive us there in your car."

I retrieved my house and car keys from my other pocket, and after letting myself in, handed them to Jake so he could start my Jeep. I quickly gathered my medical bag, some extra supplies, and flipped on a few lights before shutting the door behind me. I used a key I had hidden on the front porch to lock it.

Jake was frowning when I got in the car. "That is the worst place to hide a key."

"How would you know?" I asked as I buckled my seat belt.

"Because if I was going to break in it's the first place I would've looked."

The thirty-minute drive to Sheila's house was filled with tension as Jake explained that he'd known about the beatings doled out by Sheila's abusive spouse. "She tries to hide it, but everyone knows what's going on at her house."

"Her voice sounded funny," I interjected. I didn't want to say what my suspicions were about a possible injury she may have sustained. "Why doesn't she call the police?"

"She has in the past." Jake glanced over at me before returning his eyes to the road. "Reported it and pressed charges. She did what she was supposed to do. Didn't even back down from his threats and had a restraining order issued. He was fined and had to do community service and take anger management or domestic abuse classes." He shook his head as if he couldn't remember for sure. "He was on good behavior for a couple of years and she took him back, convinced that he'd changed."

"She told you all this?" I asked his strong profile.

He gritted his teeth and replied, "I confronted her when I noticed the bruises. She tries to hide them, but she's not always successful. She's too afraid of him this time. He said that if she ever called the police like she did last time no restraining order would stop him from killing her."

"Oh, poor Sheila," I cried as we sped through the twilight dusk. By the time we pulled up to Sheila's remote home on the backside of several acres, the sun had completely concealed itself behind the distant mountains and darkness blanketed the sky.

One car was parked in front and a front porch light was on, the only signs that someone might be home. We ran up the steps and Jake cautiously opened the unlocked front door and yelled, "Sheila, it's Jake and I have Barbie with me."

We heard crying and I sensed him feeling around for a light switch. Once he found it and the living room lit up, I suppressed a gasp at the sight before us. I ran to the unrecognizable woman sprawled out on a plush brown recliner. I looked back at Jake who said, "I only saw Sheila's car out front, but I want to make sure he's still not hanging around."

"No…" came a small whimper. "No, please, Jake." She coughed and blood spewed out of her mouth. She was in a lot of pain and her teeth were tightly clenched when she said, "He's not worth it."

"It's okay, Sheila," I said as I segued into trauma mode. "Jake is a smart guy. If he finds him, he'll know what to do." Switching tactics, I started checking her vitals and said, "We need to get you to a hospital."

"No, pleeeeaaaase…"

I gently swabbed her face, gritting my teeth at her eyes that were swollen shut, a nose that had been flattened, and a bottom lip that was hanging off. "Your jaw is broken, Sheila. You have to go to the hospital."

Jake returned and informed me that he was certain her husband was long gone. I told him that she needed to be seen at the hospital. Ignoring her feeble objections, he wasted no time in carrying her out to my Jeep where he gently laid her across the back seat, her head resting on my lap. We drove in silence as Sheila regained and lost consciousness several times.

The sun was almost up by the time Jake and I headed for my house. We'd stayed at the hospital all night and explained the situation when Sheila's oldest son and daughter arrived. The hospital called the police and her children assured us they would make sure their mother pressed charges.

The drive home was a very solemn one. I broke the silence by saying, "I can't believe Sheila thought to call me instead of an ambulance. She had some serious injuries. I can't imagine the pain she was in when we got to her."

I watched as Jake gripped the steering wheel, his knuckles whitening. "A man who abuses a woman is the lowest form of a coward. Did you see a lot of it in the ER?"

"More than I care to admit." I let out a long sigh. "I'm against violence. You know that," I qualified.

Jake's response was a grunt.

"But I can't help but wonder, if a man who does this to a woman felt for one second the kind of pain he was inflicting, would it make him think twice about doing it? I've heard her husband is a mountain of a man. She didn't stand a chance against him. She has a broken jaw, a broken nose, an insane amount of stitches in her lip and chin, a torn retina, a punctured lung, and a broken wrist." I twisted hands in my lap. "He probably broke that when she was defending herself." A tear dripped down my cheek as I tried to stifle a sob. Jake immediately pulled to the side of the road, and in one swift move reached across the front of me, unfastened my seat belt, and pulled me against him.

"It's okay, Barbie, let it out," he whispered into my hair.

I pulled my legs up so that I was sitting on them, tucked my face into his shoulder, and sobbed. Not just for Sheila, but for every woman who'd suffered abuse and lived in fear of the men to whom they'd once promised all their tomorrows.

CHAPTER 27

WOULD YOU LIKE SOME COMPANY ON
SUNDAY?

The next couple of weeks felt like they were going to explode with unwanted anxiety and unexpected activity. The anxiety came from Sheila being released from the hospital and refusing to press charges. The police were forced to make an arrest because of the severe beating she received, and the court issued a no-contact order against her husband. But with the state's cases on backlog, there was a good chance it would get dropped. Especially with her refusing to prosecute.

Since only two of Sheila's children lived in the area, and they both worked full-time, her friends at Hampton House and her church organized meal delivery and helped with chores. I did my part by bringing over a few dinners. During those visits, I tried to offer words of encouragement and comfort concerning the situation with her husband. It was a difficult fence for me to straddle. As much as I wanted to see him prosecuted to the full extent of the law, I'd never lived in fear of my life and therefore was out of my element in the advice department. I did offer my spare room, telling her I'd have a bed delivered immediately if she would accept. Just like she refused to stay with her children, she turned down my offer with a grateful but firm no. I also volunteered to cover for the resident doctor at Hampton House, who'd agreed to handle all of Sheila's responsibilities while she was recuperating.

I didn't mind working at Hampton House. It gave me more time with Jonathan and, of course, I got to see Jake. We shared a few meals together in the cafeteria, had breakfast at the diner, and he managed to tag along for a grocery store run with me. He spent his only days off managing all the workmen who'd suddenly decided to grace my house with their presence before the weather turned frigid. In less than two weeks, I had my roof and exterior siding replaced, and they were supposed to start painting the house, inside and out, in a few days.

I was now on my way home after an exhausting day at Hampton House and decided to stop in and see Darlene at the gas station. She saw me pull in and waved me inside.

"Where have you been hiding, Barbie?" She ran around to my side of the counter and squeezed me. "Yep," she teased while pulling back to look at me, "you definitely look like a woman in love."

"Oh, stop it," I smirked. But she was more spot-on than I cared to admit. I spent the next twenty minutes filling her in on the time Jake and I had shared since that first kiss on my porch. I told her how busy we'd been, and about a make-out session in his truck that made my lower abdomen ache for more.

"And he hasn't tried any more than that?" she asked, her eyes wide.

I shook my head. "Nope. He wants to." I waggled my eyebrows. "I can feel that he wants to, you know?"

Her reply was a small giggle.

"But he stops right before we get there. I've spent more time with Jake at Hampton House in the last two weeks than I have since that first day he drove down my road. I see how he operates and he's a take-charge type of man. But he's reserved with me." I brushed my hand through my hair and blew out a breath. "I'm at an impasse. On one hand, I'm still not ready to commit to being a bed buddy with him." I paused and gave Darlene a direct look. "Before you ask, I don't know how he feels because we haven't talked about our feelings. So I'm still not sure how to define our relationship." I picked at a piece of lint on my jacket. "And on the other hand, I wonder if there's something about me that's turning him off."

She rolled her eyes and said, "I've been married since two weeks after my eighteenth birthday so I don't know how all of this works. What I do know is that you're not turning him off. I bet he reads you better than you think, Barbie." She walked around to her side of the counter and leaned across it. "What if he's not pushing because he senses you're not ready? Or even better yet, what if he cares about you and this isn't a casual bed buddy thing to him? Maybe it's too important to him to mess up."

I didn't want her to see that her comments made me hopeful, so I casually shrugged before adding, "And he still hasn't asked me over to his place."

"I'm sure the invitation is coming," she said while smiling past me at two teens who'd walked in. As was my custom, I stepped aside while the boys paid for their gas and made small talk with Darlene about an upcoming sports event. I recognized one from the clinic and asked how his shoulder was feeling.

"Healed up real nice, ma'am. Thank you," he said with a respectful tilt of his chin.

Immediately after they left, my phone rang. It looked like a number from Hampton House but I didn't know who it was. After a thirty-second conversation, I hung up and told Darlene, "That was one of the nurses from Hampton House. She thought I'd want to know that everyone there is a mess over what they heard."

Darlene tilted her head and asked with concern in her eyes, "What did they hear?"

"Due to a huge backlog, the state decided not to press charges against Sheila's husband and he's back home."

Darlene's hand flew to her mouth as she slowly shook her head. "That is awful news."

I told her I concurred, and after a few more minutes of conversation, I stretched over the counter to hug her goodbye. "Jake is coming over tomorrow night for dinner and I need to grab some groceries. He mentioned how much he likes Italian so I'm going to try to whip up something special from scratch."

"Your place for dinner? That sounds like it could turn into an interesting evening," she teased.

"It's only dinner. One of the reasons we haven't seen each other that much is because he's been covering for one of the night shift orderlies. He has to be at work by eleven. Between working full-time, picking up a couple of all-nighters, and trying to manage some of my renovation on his days off, he's running ragged." I laid a twenty on the counter. "I'm gonna use pump two." Afterwards, I headed over to the grocery store, got my supplies, and drove home.

The next night, Jake showed up on time with a bottle of wine and a big brown grocery bag.

"What's in the bag?" I asked after he gave me a sound kiss on the lips before making his way to the kitchen.

"Stuff," he called over his shoulder. "And what smells so good?"

After describing my homemade Italian cuisine, he told me, "Perfect. I knew you'd make something good. That's why I stopped off for fresh cheese." I walked up behind him as he was taking something else out of the bag. He held it up and said, "I didn't know if you had a cheese grater, so I brought my own."

Just like I felt during that first dinner of Brunswick stew that we shared so many weeks ago, Jake looked like he belonged in my kitchen. I set the table while he poured the wine. I fiddled with the flowers that he snuck in without me noticing while he messed around with one of my kitchen chairs that was wobbly. At one point, he stopped what he was doing, stood, and pulled me into his arms. Resting his chin on my head, he said, "I love how you smell, Barbie."

I buried my nose in his neck. "You smell pretty good too." I kissed him right below his left ear. I thought I felt his body stiffen as he cleared his throat and said, "I need to get that cheese grated."

He grabbed a bowl and headed to the sink with the block of cheese and his grater. I went back to arranging the flowers in an old vase I'd found in the pantry.

"Would you like some company on Sunday?" he asked without turning around.

"Sure. I guess. Who?"

"It's supposed to be the last warm day in fall. Jonathan always talks about a fishing hole somewhere in the back of your property. I'll borrow the van and bring him and Cindy for a picnic and some fishing." He stopped and turned around to look at me. "Only if you want to, though."

I was stunned to hear that Jonathan remembered the lake. The last time I'd been fishing was with him and Kenny almost forty years ago. The freshwater lake on my property was where I'd met Kenny the first time. I smiled as I remembered crouching down in the mud while I attempted to set a broken leg on a frog. The frog's leg wasn't broken, but I thought it was. He was too slippery for me to get a popsicle stick to stay in place with tape, and instead of making fun of the misguided efforts of a nine-year-old girl, eleven-year-old Kenny grinned and offered to help me.

"Yes, that sounds like fun. It's about a mile hike though. Do you think Jonathan and Cindy will be up for it?"

"Yeah, they can handle a hike." I could hear the happiness in his voice as he added, "And one of the guys I work with said he'd loan us all the gear."

"I'll make lunch," I offered. "Are peanut butter and banana sand-wiches still Jonathan's favorite?"

He didn't answer, and I thought I heard him grunt and say something under his breath. Before I could ask what was wrong, he said, "I think I may have ruined the cheese."

I walked over to the sink and peered around him. "What happened?"

"I wasn't paying attention, and I used the grater to take the skin off my knuckles."

"Ouch!" I replied before retreating to get some disinfectant. He told me he didn't need a bandage, but I convinced him it was the only way to control the bleeding.

After I cleaned and wrapped his hand, he insisted on wiping up the mess in my sink. He carefully grated more cheese, teasing that he felt obligated since it was his blood and skin that ruined the last batch. Our time together flew by, and before I knew it, I was on the front porch kissing him goodbye. He seemed reluctant to leave me but said he had to stop at home and change before heading to work.

"Speaking of home," I pressed, "where exactly do you live?"

He rattled off an address from the next county over that I didn't recognize. I tried to remember if it was the same one from when I looked at his employment application so many months ago. It wouldn't surface and there was an awkward silence as I held my breath in anticipation of an invite. When it didn't come, I must've looked crestfallen because he took my hand in his and hesitantly asked, "Would you like to come over sometime? I asked you when you were out of town if I could make you dinner. The offer still stands."

"Are you sure?" I asked, somewhat skeptically. "Because I'd be lying if I didn't admit to being a little curious about where you live."

"We'll pick a night when I bring Jonathan and Cindy over on Sunday." He gave me another lingering kiss that made my heart flutter. I stood in the soft glow of my porch lights until his truck disappeared.

CHAPTER 28

IRONIC COINCIDENCE INDEED

I t was Saturday morning, a couple of days after I'd made Jake dinner. I was handling rounds at Hampton House when I received a page. As I approached the nurses' station, I spotted Jake talking to two men. I got closer and recognized the badges around their necks, indicating they were with law enforcement.

"Dr. Anderson," the younger of the two said, extending his hand. "Is there somewhere we can talk privately?"

I ushered us all into a conference room. After a round of introductions, the detectives explained that Sheila's husband was in the hospital. He'd sustained a severe beating after leaving The Mangy Mutt Pub on Thursday night.

"A severe beating?" I asked.

The older detective, who reminded me of Richard Nixon, nodded his head and explained. "The Mangy Mutt is his regular Thursday night haunt. A couple of other patrons heard him bragging about how the day before he'd learned all charges were dropped against him. He was out celebrating. Buying everybody drinks."

"We know what he did to his wife," the younger one interjected, a tone of sympathy attached to his comment. "We have witnesses that said he left the bar alone at exactly eight o'clock. People that left after him said they remembered seeing his car in the parking lot much later than that, but he wasn't around. They assumed he'd called someone to pick him up."

"I'm not sure I'm following you." I glanced over at Jake, who was sitting at the end of the conference table with his left ankle crossed over his right knee. He was casually leaning back in the leather chair, focusing on what the younger man was saying.

"Someone grabbed him, dragged him around behind the bar, and beat him pretty severely." He stopped and looked over at Jake before returning his attention to me. "The bartender found him at two a.m. when he was closing up and taking the garbage out back."

"Why are you telling us this?" I wanted to know.

Richard Nixon's twin straightened up in his chair and said, "We hear from the interviews we've conducted that the general consensus says this man deserved every bit of what he got. Especially after what he did to his wife. It's possible there are people who might want to serve up their own form of justice." He rolled his eyes Jake's way and I felt my posture stiffen.

"If you're hinting that Jake may have had something to do with this, you're wrong," I stated emphatically.

"We know you two were the ones who brought Sheila Dunn to the hospital. We know you're close to her. And with Mr. Chambers' past criminal record—"

I cut him off. "You can stop right there." I scooted my chair closer to the conference table and leaned over it to get up close to the two detectives seated opposite me. "I can assure you that Mr. Chambers couldn't have committed this crime. Would he have wanted to? The answer is probably yes, along with more than half the people in this town. But it's impossible. I will swear to anyone that asks that he was with me that night. He arrived at my house a little before seven and he left right around ten so he could go home and change his clothes before going to work."

"And you have my timecard that confirms I clocked in here an hour later at eleven o'clock," Jake added.

"Mr. Chambers, are you right or left-handed?" one of them asked.

"I already told you I'm right-handed."

Both detectives gave me a hard look when the younger one asked, "Can you confirm how Mr. Chambers sustained the injury to the knuckles on his right hand?"

This told me they'd already asked Jake and were now asking me to verify his answer. "He was grating cheese at my house the night you say Mr. Dunn was attacked. The grater slipped and shredded his knuckles. I patched Jake up myself." My voice had taken on the tone of authority I'd used at Monteith Medical.

Dolly knocked and peeked her head in. "I'm sorry to interrupt but Jake is needed."

"We're done here," Richard Nixon said.

Jake stood and excused himself. The detectives asked him to give them a call if he thought of anything that might help their case. When Jake closed the door behind him, I asked them why they were even bothering with trying to find the person who committed the attack. They politely explained that it was procedure and that the investigation would more than likely lead nowhere. Since the bar didn't have surveillance cameras and without any credible witnesses, including the victim who claimed not to remember anything, they were coming to the end of their interview process.

They thanked me for my time and as they were walking away I couldn't help but ask, "Detective?"

The younger one turned around. "Yes, ma'am?"

"What kind of injuries did Sheila's husband sustain?"

He put his hands in his pockets. "A broken jaw, torn retina, unrecognizable face, punctured lung, and a broken wrist. The same injuries he inflicted on his wife." He shook his head and said with a sardonic grin, "An ironic coincidence, don't you think?" Without waiting for me to answer, he walked out the door to catch up with his partner.

I felt a chill as I stood alone in the abandoned conference room trying to gather my thoughts when, without warning, one of them bumped into a memory. It was the conversation Jake and I had the night we took Sheila to the hospital. I'd commented on the way home how I wondered if feeling the same pain they'd inflicted on their victims would deter an abuser. I shivered and whispered to the empty room, "Ironic coincidence indeed."

CHAPTER 29

Jake and I trailed behind Jonathan and Cindy as we made our way to the lake that was hidden from the world on the back side of my property. I couldn't help but smile as I watched Jonathan carry a blanket tucked up under his left arm while tightly clutching Cindy's hand with his free one. She was adorable in her hiking boots, sweatpants, and long-sleeved Dr. Who shirt. She carried the picnic basket in the crook of her right arm.

"She adores the tenth doctor," Jake told me as we marched behind them. "Whatever the heck that means."

"I've never seen the show. I'm just as stumped as you are," I assured him.

"Kids." Jake chuckled under his breath.

I hadn't given any consideration to how Jonathan would act when they arrived at my house. Would he look down the road and remember his old life? And worse yet, what would we do if bad memories from his childhood had resurfaced? I'd expressed my concern when they'd first arrived, but the issue never arose.

"He still calls me Kenny, so this is a happy memory for him," Jake reassured me. He was astounded that Jonathan recalled the way to the lake. He led our little procession without once getting lost or confused.

"Like you said," I reminded him, "a happy memory."

Once we arrived, I had Cindy help me spread out the blanket under a shade tree while Jonathan and Jake got the fishing poles ready. After the four of us did a little fishing, Jake and I got comfortable on the blanket and watched as Jonathan and Cindy enjoyed themselves.

"I can't believe they were trying to tie you to the crime because of your injured hand and a thirty-year-old prison record," I told Jake as I leaned back against the tree and sipped on water. He was sitting next to me with his hands on his knees, clutching a cold Dr. Pepper.

"Don't be surprised. I was a viable suspect. It's how it is, Barbie." He looked over at me before adding, "It's how it always will be. A record doesn't go away."

"Really?" I tilted my head. "Would you believe I got an email less than a month ago where some stranger offered all kinds of professional hacking services?" I shared with him that for a ridiculous fee the email outlined how they could erase any criminal record, increase a credit score, make credit card debt disappear, remove unwanted content on websites, and a myriad of other services that sent a streak of fear down my spine. "It's downright scary how vulnerable we are."

He took a hearty swig of his soda and without looking over at me said, "I still use a flip phone that's on its last breath, so it's all beyond me. But I'm not surprised. Even I've heard of the dark web, and I'm sure any decent hacker knows how to scrub the internet."

We jumped up when Jonathan and Cindy both hooked a fish at the same time. Their excitement was palpable, and after helping Cindy reel in and unhook her fish, which she insisted be returned to the lake so it could have a happy life, Jake and I wandered back to the blanket. I reached into the cooler that he'd lugged the whole mile and pulled out a plastic container of fruit. I yelled to Jonathan and Cindy, offering a snack. Both declined my offer. I couldn't even entice them away with their favorite snacks that I'd packed—applesauce with cinnamon for Jonathan, and chocolate pudding cups for Cindy. I reminded them that it was almost time to reapply their sunscreen and held up the container of fruit to Jake. He shook his head and asked, "Why no blueberry pancakes?"

His question took me by surprise. I didn't answer right away. He didn't push as I slowly chewed a piece of melon and let the lonely buzz of a solo bee, and the smell of lake water mingling with fresh air, take me back to my childhood.

"It's stupid," I admitted.

"Probably not, but I'd like to know if you'd care to share."

I snapped the lid back on the container and returned it to the cooler. "It was after I first moved in with my grandparents. Blueberries were in season and my grandmother told me that if I picked them, she would make me and Fancy homemade blueberry pancakes."

I must have had a dreamy look on my face because Jake asked me, "What are you remembering right now?"

"I thought Frenita was the prettiest baby I'd ever seen. She was a toddler, but it was right after we moved here. She still looked at me like I'd slid down off a rainbow wearing a gown made of gold with a crown of jewels on my head. I was her hero back then."

I shook it off and swallowed my discomfort at how quickly that had changed. "Anyway, I spent an entire afternoon picking blueberries. The next morning I headed downstairs to the kitchen. My grandmother had a stack of pancakes sitting in the middle of the table. It was as high as the milk pitcher. My granddaddy had already headed out back to work on his tractor, and Fancy was sitting at the table on a stack of pillows stuffing her little face."

"And?"

"My grandmother told me that I was a lazy slob. I didn't come down early enough to help her in the kitchen so I wouldn't be getting any pancakes. She plopped a bowl of cold oatmeal in front of me and told me to eat up." I met his eyes briefly and looked away. "I swore I would never give her the satisfaction of thinking she'd hurt me. I turned up my nose and pretended they didn't interest me." I gave a cynical laugh. "I can't tell you how many times after that she made blueberry pancakes and piled them up in front of me almost daring me to eat them. To fall in love with them so she could revel in the memory of her cruelty that day. I was obstinate and refused to give her the satisfaction." I turned to him. "See, I told you it was stupid."

He shook his head. "No, it wasn't stupid, but it does give me an idea of how stubborn you can be. She's been dead for a long time, and you've honestly never tried blueberry pancakes?" He gave me a doubtful glance.

"Not once," I replied with an indignant tilt of my chin. "I guess I won't let her win. Even from beyond the grave." I adjusted myself on the blanket and blurted out, "Your turn. Who is Emmy?"

I knew I caught him off guard when his brow crinkled and he gave an absentminded tug of his beard.

"How do you know about Emmy?"

"I *don't* know about Emmy. That's why I'm asking." He still looked confused. "I saw her name on your chest." I was not only curious about the name but its placement. I wouldn't ask, but secretly wondered why her name was displayed above his heart, and yet, the space over his heart was oddly devoid of ink. It was the only place on his chest and arms that didn't have a tattoo.

"Ah," he answered. "The tattoo. Of course."

"And?" He didn't answer right away so I prodded. "I know you said you've never been married, but did you love her? I mean, her name is permanently on your body."

"Yeah, I loved Emmy." He smiled wistfully. "It was Emmaline, but I was the only one who got away with calling her Emmy."

Like an old beach ball with an unseen leak, I felt myself slowly deflating. I don't know why, but the thought of Jake loving Emmy bothered me. And I had no right to be bothered. He knew how much I'd loved Kenny. And of course, I was in love with Richard when I married him. I shirked off the exasperating thought. "Tell me about her." I reached over and plucked a flower, feigning interest in the petals.

"Emmy was different. So very different. She was extremely old-fashioned." The corner of his mouth tugged up in a grin that told me he was enjoying a secret memory. I felt my back involuntarily tighten. "She could be a little snooty, but she had a heart of gold. She came from money, and when her fortune dwindled away because of poor management by an accountant, she had a hard time adjusting. But she did. She was resilient."

"She sounds pretty amazing." The comment was sincere, but it was laced with a tad of jealousy that I didn't want to admit.

He looked over at me and smiled. "She taught me a lot, but more than that she believed in me. She's the one that encouraged me to take the road less traveled. It's why I'm in Pumpkin Rest."

I laughed and told him, "I can assure you any road that leads here is definitely the one less traveled." He gave me a heart-melting smile and I asked, "So what happened? Where is she now?" I wanted to know. Had to know.

"She died."

"Oh, Jake!" I cried. "When?"

He gave a thoughtful pause and looked up at the sky. "It'll be two years next month."

"I'm so sorry." My deflated ego could pound sand. I was genuinely sad for him. I reached out and softly stroked the side of his arm. He grabbed my hand and held it tightly for a few quiet moments.

"I am too," he admitted while releasing my hand. "You two would have liked each other. You have a lot in common believe it or not. I think you both have experienced the same kind of pain." He thumped his chest over his heart. "And she was as stubborn as you are."

The sun decided to hide behind a dark gray cloud at the same time the flowers that were still in bloom tossed their bright heads in a gust of wind that surprised us.

Jake jumped up and said, "I didn't see any rain in the forecast, but looks like it's time to start packing it up."

I agreed and said we could eat lunch back at the house.

After we made our way home and unpacked and devoured our meal, I could see that Cindy and Jonathan were getting tired. The long walk and fresh air must've made them sleepy and I knew they were ready to head home. Jake loaded them and the borrowed fishing gear in the van and ran back up the porch to kiss me goodbye.

"Friday night at my place?"

"I'll be there. What time?" I tried not to let my smile get too wide.

"I'll pick you up at six. Is that too early?"

"Pick me up?" I laughed. "You don't need to pick me up. I can drive myself. I don't remember what you told me the other night so text me the address and I'll put it in my GPS."

He gave me a quick kiss and walked down the steps toward the van. "I invited you to my house. I'm coming to pick you up. And that's final."

I put my hands on my hips. "Seriously? What is this, 1950? You sound so old-fashioned, Jake. Where did you get the idea you need to pick me up?"

He was gripping the van door handle and gave me a serious look. "Emmy was a lady and showed me how to treat one. And you're my lady, so I'm picking you up, Barbie." He didn't give me a chance to reply as he climbed into the van and backed out of my driveway. I waved to the three of them as he drove off.

I was listless that night. I couldn't stop thinking about the woman he'd loved. The one whose name was memorialized on his chest forever. The one who taught him values and how to treat a lady. How could I ever hope to compete with someone who died and left an imprint not only on his chest but on his soul as well?

CHAPTER 30

I'M HERE TO PAY A TAX BILL

"You told him the blueberry pancake story, huh?" Darlene asked while we stood in the cabinet and counter section of a large home improvement store that was an hour outside of Pumpkin Rest. It was Thursday and Darlene and I had planned a girls' day out. We'd managed to spend the entire morning making some selections, and as soon as I set up a delivery time and gave them a deposit, we were going to have lunch and visit a salon.

"Yeah, and he didn't say much. Only that he understood and that I was stubborn."

"And he's right," she scoffed. "I've always said you were the queen of second chances. Why you can't find it in your ornery self to give a couple of blueberry pancakes another chance, I'll never know!"

"I'm stubborn, not ornery," I reminded her.

"You're both," she admonished with a laugh.

At Darlene's request, we ate lunch at a vegan bistro. "It's all the craze now, and I'm glad to say I've tried it, but it's not for me." Darlene delicately wiped her mouth with a cloth napkin.

"For someone who insisted on trying it and cleaned your plate, are you sure about that?" I teased as I pulled out my credit card. Today was my treat. My way of thanking Darlene for all the free time she'd given up to help me with my renovation selections.

We walked to a quaint coffee shop/bookstore and settled in a cozy corner with our drinks. We had an hour before our salon appointment for mani/pedis, waxing for me, and a facial for Darlene. I spent the next hour filling her in on Sunday's fishing excursion. It took me a while before I told her about Emmy.

"And this bothers you why?" She quirked an eyebrow.

"Who said it bothers me?"

"It would be rude to roll my eyes, but they're aching to move." She brought her cup to her lips, and before taking a sip, said, "I know you too well, Barbie. It bothers you that he loved someone."

"Ugh," I groaned. "I know. I don't know what's wrong with me. It's not like I've never dated or wasn't in relationships with people who'd cared for others before I came along. I feel like I'm in middle school again. Jake makes me feel things I haven't felt in decades, Dar. You're right." I looked up and begged God, "Please help me to stop acting and feeling like an idiot."

"There's nothing wrong with you, and you're not an idiot." She reached over and playfully slapped my knee. "I can see how it would be hard to measure up to a woman who's no longer around to make mistakes. But that's not where you should focus. You need to see, really see who's looking back at you from the mirror. You are an amazing woman, and just like you faulted Fancy for only seeing her worth in what a man could give her, you need to stop defining yours by what men have taken from you."

"That stings, Dar."

"Good," she flung back at me. "Sometimes a little tough love can go a long way. And if I have to nip at you once in a while to let you see the light, then so be it."

I gave her a sincere grin. "Promise you'll always set me straight."

"You can count on it."

On the drive home, I told Darlene about my decision to have a whirlpool tub installed in my new bathroom.

"I thought you were going to add a claw-foot bathtub like the one downstairs." I glanced over and watched her admiring her fingernails. She must've felt my stare because she looked up and asked, "Why did you change your mind?"

"Jake changed my mind. When I told him what my plans were for the bathroom, he asked why I needed another old tub and shower since I already had one downstairs. And when I explained that I was trying to restore the house to its original era, he asked me if I was going to find a refrigerator from the 1940s."

Darlene scrunched up her nose. "Ew. You didn't tell me you were buying old retro appliances."

"I'm not, Darlene," I replied with a tad of impatience. "That was his point. I'm restoring the kitchen and using cabinets and flooring from that era, but of course I'm going to put in new appliances. He said one claw-foot tub was enough and I should have a nice big tub and a separate shower in the master bath. And I'll be using retro tile and accessories that will still give me the same effect I'm aiming for."

"It makes sense," she agreed. "When is your contractor going to start?"

"He can't start for a few weeks, but Jake insisted on prepping the room for me."

"What kind of prepping?" she wanted to know.

"I don't want a tub I have to climb over the side to get in. I want to step down into it, so the floor needs to come up by the window, and he needs to reinforce beneath it to support the weight. He offered to manage the subcontractor for me, and I jumped at the chance. I offered to pay him, and he got offended."

Darlene was digging in her purse and mumbled, "Yeah, sounds like a guy thing." She offered me a piece of gum while asking, "Have you heard anything from your realtor?"

I popped the treat in my mouth. "No, and I haven't called her. Things have been so hectic lately. Hey! Did that guy give me the finger?"

"I believe he did!"

"What'd I do?" I frowned and looked in my rearview mirror.

"Forget him. Tell me what you're wearing tomorrow night."

I woke up the next morning with a smile on my face and wondered whose bed I would be waking up in tomorrow morning. As Darlene had reminded me more than once, I was overthinking. But I couldn't help myself. I felt that having dinner at his place might propel us to another level of our physical relationship and I still wasn't sure how I felt about it. Every part of my body ached for Jake, but the sensible side of my brain had erected an impenetrable wall. "I can't believe you're worried about coming off as a prude," I said to my ceiling. Frustrated, I grabbed my pillow and pulled it over my face. "You haven't been on a date in decades. Decades!" I screamed into it. *Just enjoy yourself and see how it goes,* I told myself.

Tossing the pillow aside, I jumped out of bed and raced downstairs to use the bathroom and start the coffeepot. I headed back up to my room to change into my running attire. I'd still not had the opportunity to jog back over to the Pritchard farm, and I was happily stunned to realize I didn't care. I'd been running in the opposite direction a couple of times a week to retrieve my mail from the post box at the other end of my road. I still wasn't back in the cardiovascular shape I'd been in over a year ago, but I was getting there and was enjoying the physical as well as mental benefits of exercise.

I was home sooner than expected, and after a cup of coffee and a simple breakfast, I spent the morning and most of the afternoon working around my house. The painting contractor knocked on the door to ask me a few questions and double check my color selections. He was confident his men could knock out the dining room and upstairs guest bedroom in a few hours. I'd gone to school with him and had no problem being alone in the house with him and his two grown sons. They left around two o'clock, and after locking the door behind them, I showered and headed upstairs to get ready for my dinner date.

You're being ridiculous. He won't be here for four hours. I spent the next hour sitting at my dressing table in my robe, experimenting with makeup. Taking a closer look at my face, I saw the crow's feet on each side of my eyes and hoped they looked more like laugh lines. I played around with my face, using my fingers to pull my skin taut in certain places. I could certainly use a minor lift in a few spots, but nothing earth-shattering. At least not yet. After applying only light makeup, I stood, threw off my robe, and looked at my nude body in the full-length mirror on the back of my bedroom door.

I turned around and peered back over my shoulder to size up my butt. The old gray mare wasn't what she used to be, but all those years of running and tennis had been good to me. I wished it was a tad higher and firmer, but it wasn't an awful butt. I turned around and stared at my chest. If only my girls were a little perkier too. I looked down and pinched my right thigh. The cellulite was there, just hiding. I stood sideways and grabbed my stomach. I didn't see how it could ever be flat again. I might get it to look a tad less bloated if I changed my diet and did some sit-ups, but I liked to eat and hated sit-ups.

For one split second I let the discouraging image of what Dolly probably looked like nude sneak up on me, but immediately squelched the thought. Very few fifty-two-year-old women could've competed with my body when I was twenty-one. It was asinine for me to do it now. "I've taken care of myself, this is the normal process of aging, and Jake likes me. And if he sees me naked and runs, then it's his loss. I'm sure he has a few hidden age secrets of his own," I said to my reflection. After giving myself a good talking to, I got dressed and realized I still had a little over two hours to kill.

I'd meant to take care of a tax bill and hadn't been able to pay online so I grabbed my purse, locked my house, and climbed into my Jeep.

There was a small satellite county office in the same building where I worked at Dr. Tucker's practice. I noticed his parking lot only had a few cars and two belonged to employees. It must be a slow day. The county tax office was at the opposite end and only one vehicle was parked in front. I pulled up next to it and went inside.

A pleasant-looking elderly woman with outdated bouffant hair and overstated lipstick asked, "How can I help you, young lady?"

Her compliment made my day. I quickly introduced myself.

"Are you the doctor who works part-time at the clinic next door?" she wondered aloud. When I told her I was, she thanked me for sewing up her great-grandson who'd had a playground incident a month or so earlier that required a few stitches in his chin. After some chitchat, I explained why I was there.

"I need to pay a tax bill for a piece of property." I rattled off the name and address.

"Do you have the bill with you?" she kindly asked.

"I don't own the property so I've never received one. I've managed to keep up with the payments by checking online when I know it's due, but I couldn't find it this year."

"Let me see what I can find." She adjusted her glasses and turned to her computer screen. I glanced around the small office while I pondered the reason behind my visit.

When Mr. Pritchard passed away, he'd left a sizable life insurance policy in Jonathan's name. And because they had no living relatives, except for Kenny who was in prison, Jonathan became his sole heir and a ward of the state. Even with all his rottenness, I was grateful that Mr. Pritchard had provided for Jonathan. The money that was left to him was absorbed by the state to pay for his medical and living expenses. The Pritchard farm was to be sold and the proceeds would also be used for Jonathan's lifetime of care.

I think I was in my third year of college when I became overly curious and started snooping to find out if anybody had purchased the farm. I was shocked to find out that even though it was owned by the state, the property was still in Mr. Pritchard's name and it showed there were three years of property taxes owed. I wasn't sure if it had slipped through the cracks, was a glitch in the system, or if there was a backlog and it hadn't been taken care of yet. Even with my hurt and anger still simmering toward him, I must've been hopeful of a less-than-slim chance that Kenny's sentence would be shortened or revoked. And something in me was petrified at the thought of him getting out of prison, retrieving Jonathan from his group home, and having no place to go.

So I scrounged, borrowed, worked extra shifts, and paid off that past due tax bill. As the years passed, I continued to check, and every year, a new bill was due, and I managed to pay it. I never inquired about the supposed glitch. Almost seventeen years ago, I gave the responsibility to Richard's administrative assistant who handled our joint household checking account. She would look the same time every year and pay the bill out of that joint account. With Richard gone, I'd assumed the task again. I was able to pay it online last year, but couldn't find a record of it recently.

"I'm sorry it's taking so long but I can't find it in my system," the sweet clerk told me with a puzzled expression.

"Is it possible the property was sold?" I was more than a little shaken at the idea. I didn't know why, but couldn't fathom the thought of anyone other than a Pritchard living on their property. Knowing that was impossible, I braced myself for her answer.

"No. If it was sold, I'd still be able to find the address." She looked thoughtful. "Unless…"

She started typing frantically and I tried to lean over the counter to see if I might catch a glimpse of her screen.

"Bingo!" she shouted. "It wasn't sold. It was part of a rezoning project last year between our county and Pickens County. It's why you didn't see a tax assessment on our website. It's migrated over to *their* website." She sat up and smiled.

This might explain the strange marker I'd come upon the day I jogged toward the Pritchards' farm. The property was now in another county and they'd marked the new zone.

"Would you happen to have access to the Pickens County computer system?" I hoped my voice didn't sound desperate.

"No," she told me. "But anybody can look up land records. Let me get on their website and do a little investigating for you. It might take me a few minutes. And if I can't find it, my niece works over there. I can always call her. Is there something you can do while you wait?"

I told her I would run over to the clinic and ask about my schedule. When I returned twenty minutes later, she greeted me with a smile.

"This is the new address assigned by Pickens County. You can pay online at their website." She handed me a small piece of paper, and as I read it, I had to blink my eyes to make sure I was seeing it correctly. I barely remembered thanking her and leaving the office as I walked in a zombie-like trance to my car. The man I was certain I was in love with had been keeping a huge secret from me.

CHAPTER 31

IT DIDN'T SEEM LIKE A GOOD TIME

I warred with myself the entire drive home. My first instinct was to show up on Jake's doorstep and demand his reason for not telling me he'd purchased the Pritchard farm. For not telling me he was my neighbor. I certainly wasn't the real estate police, but it seemed like a pretty big detail to leave out of our conversations. *It sure does explain his concern about my jogging adventure to the Pritchard property the morning he woke up at my house.*

By the time I arrived home, I only had thirty minutes before Jake was supposed to show up. I passed the time by checking my makeup, making a grocery list, and folding some towels. After I put away the last towel, I retired to the only chair on my front porch and waited.

I watched as his truck slowly made its way up my road. *Should I be thinking of it as our road now?* I wondered. When he pulled into my drive-way, he gave me a hesitant smile. I realized that he was nervous and this was probably a big deal for him. I found my earlier anger fizzling as he got out of the truck and greeted me with a kiss on my cheek. He took me by the elbow and escorted me to the passenger side, and after closing the door behind me, trotted around to his side and jumped into the driver's seat. He started to back up and stopped where my gravel driveway met the dirt road. He took a deep breath and, taking his foot off the brake, began to turn the wheel of the truck so he could leave the same way he'd come.

"It's okay, Jake. You don't have to take the long way around. I'm assuming that's why you wanted to pick me up? To give you some time to explain."

He jammed on the brake and looked over at me. "How long have you known?"

I looked at my watch and then at him. "Almost an hour and a half."

"Barbie, I should've told you. I was going to tell you more than once, but—"

I cut him off. "It's okay. But what I don't understand is why you felt you needed to keep it a secret for so long."

He put the truck in park and turned off the ignition. After casually leaning against the door so he could face me, he enlightened me about his arrival in South Carolina several months prior.

"I was taking the road less traveled, falling in love with small-town America when I drove through the one intersection at Pumpkin Rest and ended up in Stillwell. I stayed in a motel for a few days and heard that they were looking for help at Hampton House. Sheila gave me a job, and I worked it out with the motel's owner to let me rent for the month. I didn't know if I'd be staying or for how long." He raked his hand through his short, cropped hair. "Jonathan immediately took to me, and I started hearing stories about his family and the farm where he'd grown up. I went looking for it on my day off, and I found it."

"Were you already living there that first day I saw you?"

"Yeah, I'd been living there for a few weeks before you moved back here permanently. I'd heard about the lady doc who'd bought her childhood home, but I'd never seen you. I guess you were coming and going at random when you were trying to be there for Richard in Greenville."

He was right.

"Anyway, you didn't look happy the first time you saw me, so I stopped using the road. When the county rezoned the property, and that was months before I moved here," he quickly clarified, "they must've widened one of the old Pritchard trails and connected it to the other county. It's the same amount of time to get to Hampton House from my side of the road as it is if I passed by your house."

"That would explain why Darlene had never seen you before that," I surmised. "I guess I wasn't very welcoming back then, was I?"

"I'm not sure if it was that or your sensitivity to the Pritchard name."

I couldn't argue that one.

"So, I waited until I got to know you better. I should've told you sooner because I never knew if you'd show up there one day. Like the morning you went for a jog." He paused and tugged at his short beard. "I waited a little longer and finally decided to go for it. I invited you to my place for dinner, but you were in New York."

"Yeah," I interrupted. "But that was almost a month ago. Why have you waited so long before extending a second invitation?"

"Barbie, do you remember what you found out the day you got back from New York?" He reached for my hand and held it. "The day you told your sister you were evicting her?"

"Of course I remember. I found out about my family roots. Or rather lack of them."

"Right. It didn't seem like a good time to dump another surprise on you. And that was followed up by that dirtbag beating the crap out of Sheila." He shook his head. "Like I said, it just didn't seem like a good time."

His voice matched his eyes. Both were thick with emotion and regret. I smiled and gave his hand a tight squeeze. "I can't believe I'm saying this, but I'm kind of curious to see what you've done with the place."

CHAPTER 32

IN HIS YOUNGER DAYS HE HELPED LAW
ENFORCEMENT FIND DEAD BODIES

W e slowly made our way down our shared dirt road to the Pritchard property. When we passed the county marker, I couldn't help but ask, "I wonder why they didn't mark the road correctly?"

"What do you mean?"

"The first set of trees that divide our farm from the Pritchards' is on their property but we already passed them. The marker should be a few hundred yards behind us." I looked over at him. He was shaking his head.

"No. The stakes aren't wrong."

"Yes, they are. There are at least two hidden tree houses in that first row and they belong to the Pritchards." A thought occurred to me and I snapped my head around to look at him.

He must've sensed it because he peered over at me before returning his eyes to the road. "What?"

"Have you ever been in those tree houses?" I inquired through narrowed eyes. "With a flashlight?"

"Are you nuts?" he shot back. "I found those tree houses and they're barely staying up there. The wood is so rotten only a fool would try to climb up to them. Why?"

"Oh, nothing." I shifted in the seat, secretly embarrassed that I was subconsciously accusing Jake of sending me flashlight signals a few months back.

"Back to the property marker, Barbie. Those trees are on your property."

"Jake, I grew up here." I pointed back over my shoulder toward my house that was no longer visible. "I think I would know my property."

"Well, you don't," he said as we rounded a curve and the old Pritchard farm came into view.

Instead of the dilapidated farmhouse I remembered from my youth, I was surprised to see a well-cared-for home. It was the same small one-story structure, but it was neat and orderly. Something it had never been before.

"I still have a lot of repairs, but I took care of the important ones," Jake told me. "The roof needs replacing, but I've stopped it from leaking until I get that done. It had some busted windows but I replaced the glass panes instead of the whole window units. That'll have to be done eventually though. And you can see it needs a coat of paint, but it can wait. I'm concentrating on replacing rotten wood siding and this summer it'll be ready for paint."

"Kind of like what I'm doing," I added breathlessly, unable to tear my eyes away from the front of the house. "Except that you're doing it all yourself?"

"Yeah, just me."

He threw the truck in park, turned it off, and came around to open the door for me. I was speechless as I walked up a small stone path with neatly trimmed grass on each side. I could see where Jake had cleaned up the yard. Off to the right was a dumpster.

He answered my unspoken question. "It's a rental for whenever I find something that needs to go. I've already filled it up twice. That's how much junk and trash I've had hauled away. It's easier than making dump runs with my truck."

"I can't believe what you've done with this place by yourself in the short time you've been here," I marveled.

"I still have a lot to do, Barbie. The inside is clean but still pretty raw. I bought a new fridge and stove, and the plumbing and electricity work, but I haven't replaced their guts like you did. I'll need to hire people to do that. I have a lot of time on my hands so it'll eventually get done."

"You work all the time, even on your days off. When would you have time to do anything?" I asked incredulously.

"I'm an insomniac. I don't sleep." He opened the front door and waved me inside. "The night you stitched me up was the best night's sleep I've had in years."

I hesitated at first, unsure if I was ready to take this stroll down memory lane. In my shock at finding out where he lived and subsequent curiosity, I'd forgotten to consider how I would feel after stepping in Kenny and Jonathan's childhood home. A home I knew intimately. The small living room with a fireplace would be on my left. A wall would separate it from a tiny kitchen that faced the back of the house. Directly in front of me would be a small dining area off the kitchen. To my right, there would be two bedrooms separated by a solitary bathroom.

I stepped over the threshold and was immediately greeted by a huge German shepherd.

"Out of the way, Henry," Jake commanded the dog. "Let the lady through."

Henry whined and took a few steps back.

"You have a dog?" I squatted down and started scratching his ears. "When did you get him or have you always had him?"

Jake tossed his keys on a table to the left of the front door. "Henry is old and his bones hurt, but he is the most loyal and well-behaved animal I've ever come across. He's retired from the K-9 unit a few towns over."

"K-9 unit?" I abruptly stood. "Is he one of those dogs that chases down suspects and attacks them on command?"

Jake bent down and stroked Henry's soft, thick coat. "Nope. He's a cadaver dog. In his younger days he helped law enforcement find dead bodies."

I grimaced and looked at Henry. "Well, this is a good place for him to enjoy his retirement because he's not going to find any dead bodies way out here. And with all the acreage that comes with this house, he'll have a lot of room to run. He can even come visit me when he feels like it."

Jake gave me an odd look. "Do you want to see the rest of the house?" he asked cautiously.

"Yes, I'd like that," I answered as I eyeballed the small living room. There was a comfortable-looking couch against the wall that separated it from the kitchen. It had one side table that was home to an unremarkable lamp and the remote control. His coffee table was comprised of three old crates. The side wall sported an old masonry fireplace that probably hadn't exuded warmth in over forty years. In the far corner was a flat-screen TV that sat on a shelf unit. Below that was a DVD player and a stack of movies. The wooden floors were old and battered, with the exception of a few newer boards that stood out.

"I'm going to wait to refinish the floors until the whole place is fixed," Jake said from beside me.

I tried to imagine what kind of story the decades of dust buried deep between the floorboards could tell. I gulped when I realized I was looking at the spot where I gave myself to Kenny almost forty years earlier while Dolly Parton serenaded us from a battered old radio.

I felt a tug on my hand as Jake pulled me back to see his kitchen. He was right. It was raw and outdated. I could see where he'd re-hung some cabinet doors that had fallen off. It was obvious by the shiny new hinges. The huge farm sink that was below the back window was stained with rust, but otherwise clean. "What are we having tonight?"

"I hope you like tacos. I'm not much of a cook," he confessed. He motioned toward the dining room and added, "And as you can see, I don't have a table. We'll have to take our plates to the couch."

"I watched you the night we had Brunswick stew at my place and again the night you scraped your knuckles. You know your way around a kitchen," I reminded him.

"Nah," he said without looking at me. "I'm just a good prepper."

"Tacos sound wonderful, and I normally eat in front of the boob tube. Kitchen tables are overrated. Unless you have a big family."

"Then I'll probably never have a table," he said from beside me.

I gave him a questioning look.

"I don't have children and don't plan on having any. And without any living relatives, it's only me. Has been for a long time."

I felt my heart squeeze in my chest. "I only have Fancy, and honestly, I don't consider her family anymore." I slowly shook my head. "I haven't for a long time. But I have Darlene. If there's one thing I've learned recently, your closest relationships aren't always defined by DNA." I reached out to stroke his arm. "You must have a close friend you consider family."

He'd abandoned the rest of the house tour, turning his attention to the taco preparation. "Not anymore."

"What do you mean, not anymore?" I prodded.

"I had a couple of best friends, but that was years ago. I lost touch with one and the other one died." He shrugged nonchalantly. "I've had acquaintances," he corrected. "But not anybody close. Except for Emmy of course."

And she'd died too. He's known nothing but loss, I sadly realized.

"But don't feel sorry for me, Barbie. I'm a loner. I don't mind the solitude. Not everybody is looking for a gaggle of geese to keep them company."

I laughed at his description and realized we had that in common. "I didn't remember to grab the bottle of wine I was going to bring," I admitted even though I wasn't in the mood for alcohol.

"No worries. I already have some and forgot to offer you a glass. Some host I am, huh?" He held up two bottles, and I was impressed by the choices but asked for a pass. "I think I'd rather have something a little lighter if you don't mind."

"Dr. Pepper or sparkling water?"

We carried our food and drinks to the living room and munched on tacos as we talked. Between mouthfuls, he asked me, "You said something interesting before when I introduced you to Henry."

I swallowed and wiped my mouth with a napkin. "What was that?"

"You said that he would have a lot of room to run with all the acreage that came with the house. Exactly how much property do you think I own?"

I'd been getting ready to take another bite of my taco and stopped. "The Pritchards owned at least forty-five acres."

"Maybe they did back when you lived here as a child, but this house came with only two acres."

"That can't be right." I felt my forehead puckering. "If not you, then who owns the rest of the property?"

He shook his head and looked at me like I'd lost my mind. "I can't believe you don't know this, Barbie. Weren't you involved in the original sale of your grandparents' house? Didn't you know what you bought back from the bank after it was foreclosed on?"

"Of course I knew, Jake. Why are you asking me this?" I set my half-eaten taco on my plate and gave him a serious look.

"When I bought the house and the couple of acres that came with it, I saw a survey of the surrounding land."

"And it showed you who owns the other forty-three acres?" I asked.

"Yeah."

I was getting not only impatient but anxious to know who'd bought ninety-eight percent of the Pritchard land without me knowing it. "So who owns the property, Jake?"

"You do, Barbie. It belongs to you."

CHAPTER 33

DO YOU HAVE ANY OTHER SECRETS?

After some more debating, we both determined that unbeknownst to me, Mr. Pritchard at some point had started selling off his property to my grandfather. I was a kid and had been none the wiser. When my grandmother died, I'd sold the property never knowing it included forty-three acres my granddaddy had purchased over the years from Mr. Pritchard.

"I've hiked the acreage. I'm going to say that most of the old stills and a couple of underground storage bunkers I found belong to you." Jake scooted up to the edge of the couch, and after setting his plate down, rested his elbows on his knees. "Can I ask you something?"

"Sure. Ask away."

"I was surprised when I inquired at the county office about buying the house that it was still in Mr. Pritchard's name. I'd have thought that when he passed, and Jonathan became a ward of the state that South Carolina would transfer the property into some state agency name and sell it off. The lady at the Pickens County Land Assessment and Tax office had no clue as to why that never happened. And she brought up something curious."

I reached down to pet Henry who'd been lying quietly at our feet, tucked in between the couch and Jake's makeshift coffee table. I knew what he was going to say and saved him the breath. "I've been paying the property taxes since I was in college," I explained about my curiosity and the original reason behind my decision.

"But Kenny died, what? Ten years ago?"

"Eight years ago," I corrected.

He shook his head before asking, "Why would you still keep paying it?"

I let out a long breath. "First of all, it barely cost anything. When I was a struggling medical student, yes, it was difficult. But after I became a physician, it was a drop in the bucket. When Kenny died, I thought about stopping the payments and letting the chips fall where they may. But Jonathan was still around…" I shook my head slowly. "I don't know, could be my sentiment has been misplaced all these years. I didn't like the thought of the house being in arrears to the county. It would be a mar on the Pritchard name even though they weren't supposed to still own it, and with Jonathan being the only living Pritchard it didn't feel right." I felt my shoulders sag. "The Pritchards had a bad enough reputation for so many years. Letting some unknown face in the county tax office think they were slackers or loafers didn't sit right with me. I kept up the payments for Jonathan. All the while knowing they could notice their error and sell the house anyway. Dumb, huh?"

"Whew!" He leaned back against the couch. "You are seriously tied to this house. This family. Aren't you?"

"When you say it like that you make it sound like a bad thing."

He shot back up and turned to face me. "No, Barbie. I didn't mean it like that. I only meant that you're the most loyal person I've ever met. And I can believe there was a glitch in the computer system." His tone was sincere. "I had a friend who was pulled over on a random traffic violation. Turned out there was an outstanding warrant for his arrest because he hadn't shown up for a court date when he was seventeen and had been charged with disorderly conduct."

"Seventeen? How old was he when he got stopped?"

"He was forty-something. The county where he'd lived had recently updated their computer system. When it rebooted, it brought up a ton of outstanding warrants that had fallen through the cracks." He laughed and remarked, "I think they got an eighty-year-old man on a twenty-two-year-old 'fishing without a license' charge too."

Henry picked that time to jump up and snatch the last bit of taco from my plate. Jake reprimanded him, but he gobbled it down with satisfaction, and then looked guilty.

We headed into the kitchen where I helped him clean up. Afterward, we went back to the small living room and he called me over to the TV. He pointed to the stack of DVDs and said, "Pick one."

I sifted through some eighties and nineties movies, mostly chick flicks, and asked him, "Where did you get all of these?"

"Sheila let me raid her shelves. See anything you like?"

"I like all of them. Are you in the mood to laugh or cry?" I held up two movies.

"Laugh."

"Then it looks like you're about to meet *Tootsie*."

"Speaking of chocolate…" He bent low and opened the bottom cabinet. He pulled out an expensive box of chocolates and handed it to me. "I wasn't sure what kind you liked so I guessed."

"You can't go wrong with me and chocolate. These are pricey, and you shouldn't have."

"You can always share my favorite." He reached back into the cabinet and snatched a bag of York Peppermint Patties.

"That's your favorite chocolate?" My eyes were wide.

"They're my favorite candy of all time," he admitted while tearing open the bag.

"Mine too!" I exclaimed. "We love the same candy. How cool is that?"

"Very cool, darlin'. Very cool." He put the DVD in, pressed play and led me back to the couch.

I was happy that the movie made him laugh. We only took two quick breaks and that was for him to let Henry out and then back inside. When the credits started rolling, he jumped up and took the DVD out, carefully returning it to its case. "Good choice, Barbie doll." He still had his back to me and I thought it might be the making of an awkward moment when he turned around and said, "There's something else I need to tell you." He stuck his hands in his front pockets and said, "Well, I don't need to, but I want to."

"Okay, go on," I urged.

"I don't know how to say it, so I'm going to just come out with it. Do you remember the first time we had coffee together?"

"Of course I do. It was when you took Darlene's seat at the Crossroads Diner."

"You told me that there was a spike in your utility bills." He blew out a long breath. "That was because of me. I hadn't bought this house yet and was squatting here, trying to figure out if I wanted to buy it. I'd tapped into your electric and was using it to juice the house."

I shifted on the couch, not exactly sure how I should react. Jake had technically stolen from me. Did I care? A nasty thought about his prison record in Texas came to the forefront of my brain, and I quickly stifled it before I said something I would regret. I was glad I did.

"I didn't know how to repay you so I did some odd jobs for you without you knowing." He took a deep breath and gave me a sheepish grin. "I saw a gutter dangling out front that I put back up."

Dustin, I inwardly scoffed. *You let me think you fixed that gutter. You cad.*

"Your new HVAC system was making a loud racket so I tightened a loose bolt." He stared at the floor like he was gearing up for a big reveal. "There's more." I was right about his guilt-ridden body language. "There was a huge surge that knocked out my power, forcing me to reset the breakers. I went to your place to see if your power had been knocked out too. It had." His chin was down but he peered up to meet my eyes. "I wasn't sure if you were back full-time or not and I didn't want your food to spoil so I found the key, let myself in your house and reset your breakers for you." He adjusted his posture and said, "It's how I knew you had an aluminum baseball bat behind your front door. I saw it when I was leaving."

I felt myself squirm. "You were inside my house?" My voice was barely a whisper.

"Yes." He walked over and squatted in front of me. Taking my hand in his, he said, "Only to reset your breaker box in the pantry, Barbie."

"That feels like a violation," I admitted.

Letting go of my hand, he stood back up and gazed down at me. "I did for you what I would've done for any neighbor." When I didn't reply, he brushed his hand through his hair and said, "It's not like I went through your panty drawer, Barbie. Or looked at the balance in your checkbook." He narrowed his eyes at me before adding, "That you'd left on your kitchen table where anybody could've stolen it. And by anybody, I mean any person who could easily find the house key in your lame hiding place on the porch."

I bristled at the rebuke, but realized he was probably right. How many workmen had been at my house over the past few months? How many times had he hinted that I needed to find a new hiding place for my key? I was pondering all these things and more when he said in a gentle voice, "I went straight to where I guessed the breaker box would be in your pantry and back out the front door. I didn't give myself a tour of your house, Barbie. I was only there trying to help."

"Of course," I told him. "And you didn't have to tell me, but you did. Thank you for owning up to it after the fact." I tilted my head to the side and teasingly asked, "Do you have any other secrets?"

He gave me a crooked smile and said, "Sure. Don't you?"

It was a fair question. Of course I had secrets. Don't we all? I shuddered at the thought of playing true confession concerning past regrets. I smiled up at him and with a mock sternness asked, "So, is it true you played baseball when you were a kid or did you make that up when I put you on the spot about my aluminum bat?"

"Little League All-Stars two years in a row," he boasted. I could tell by his wide smile and the relief in his expression that he knew all was forgiven.

CHAPTER 34

YOUR GRANDMOTHER WAS A TOOL

"You're telling me that on one hand, having Jake living so close is giving you pause about having sex with him, and on the other hand, you're wondering why he hasn't tried anything?"

"Shhh, Dar! Somebody might hear you," I whisper-yelled. It was Thanksgiving and we were on dishwashing duty in the kitchen at Hampton House. It was something Darlene volunteered for every year so the people who would typically have to work could have the day off to spend with their families. As soon as we finished, she was heading to Dicey's house for a second dinner. "And yeah, I feel weird having him so close as a neighbor. Especially if we ever do take it to the next level. You know." I paused while I tried to articulate my conflicted feelings. "If it were to go south with him, we'd still be neighbors, and that doesn't sit right with me."

She shrugged and said, "Sounds like your problem is already solved if he's not trying to take things further physically."

"But why? Why isn't he taking things further?" It had been a few weeks since I'd discovered Jake had bought the Pritchards' old homestead. And we'd spent a lot of time together since then. Quality time that never progressed past some spine-tingling lip locks and heavy breathing sessions.

She removed her left hand from the soapy water and swiped her forearm across her face. "Maybe because he feels the same way, Barbie. It's possible that he's one of those men who has truly considered the consequences if you two don't work out. You know, living in the same small town and all." She passed me a pot to dry and added, "Everybody knows Jake is a gentleman. I think we're seeing that he's the real deal."

I nodded my agreement while trying to deny the sinking feeling in my stomach. It was okay for me to have reservations about this part of our relationship, but I couldn't deny that thinking he might feel the same way didn't sit right with me. Changing the subject, Darlene asked, "What have you heard from Fancy?"

"Absolutely nothing." I wrung out my wet towel and reached for a clean one. "I'm a little surprised that she hasn't pursued what she thinks I owe her. She hasn't, and that tells me she's already found someone new. I'm sure she's doing fine."

"And in what kind of condition did she leave your condo?"

I stopped what I was doing and looked at Darlene's profile as she concentrated on scrubbing a particularly nasty casserole dish. With my hand on my hip, I told her, "Here's a shocker. The realtor said she left it in pristine condition. They found her key under the mat."

She gave me a sidelong glance and raised a brow.

"Right?" I swung the towel around, mimicking a helicopter blade. "I expected to have to send in one of those restoration crews after she left. I was certain I'd angered her enough that she would've taken it out on the place. The few pieces of furniture she hadn't sold were untouched, the bathrooms scrubbed clean, the floors mopped. I'm wondering if an alien abducted the real Fancy."

"I guess you should be thankful that it wasn't an ordeal trying to get her to move out," Darlene added before pulling the plug in the sudsy sink.

"I can't believe how much food your boyfriend can eat," came a soft voice from behind us. It was Sheila. She wasn't officially back at work until the following Monday, but didn't want to miss the annual Thanksgiving feast. "I think he went back for a third refill," she informed us.

"Jake can eat," I laughed. "You won't have to worry about packing up leftovers."

Sheila had shared earlier that after he was released from the hospital, her husband showed up at her front door and politely asked her not to call the police while he packed up some of his belongings. We were surprised to hear that he told her how sorry he was for everything and that he was leaving town. He wasn't sure where he would end up but promised to send an address when he had one so she could forward divorce papers. That was weeks ago, and she still hadn't heard from him. He was definitely one missing person I wouldn't miss. After thanking us for helping with the first half of the cleanup, she excused herself to go back to the dining room to supervise dessert.

"I might stop by tomorrow to see how your renovation is going."

Darlene picked up a bottle of hand lotion that was next to the dish soap and wordlessly offered me a squirt.

As we both moisturized, I explained that tomorrow was a big day and I was one step closer to having an upstairs bathroom. Jake would be removing the floor in my old bedroom and the plumber promised he'd get the tub and other fixtures installed on Monday. "It'll be so nice to get that huge bathtub out of my guest room," I confessed. "I'm so glad I haven't put a bed in there yet. I wouldn't have had a place to store the tub."

Darlene smiled at the same moment I felt a warm breath on my neck and familiar arms circling my waist from behind. "I heard a rumor that I'm accused of denying the dinner guests leftovers."

"It's not a rumor if it's true," I teased.

THE NEXT MORNING I heard a familiar scratching at my back door and greeted my visitor with a big smile. I gave Henry the remnants of my toast and said, "I know your daddy doesn't like you getting table scraps but it'll be our secret." I put my hands on my hips and asked with mock offense, "And what? No present for me this morning? Because I have one for you." I reached into my back pocket and bent low to tie a blue bandanna around his neck. "Aren't you a handsome boy?" I stood back and, crossing my arms, smiled at my handiwork. A low chuckle escaped as I considered the many treasures Henry had bestowed on me the last few weeks. Jake and I had surmised that he'd stumbled on a few of the old campsites that gypsy migrant workers had set up in the woods in years past. My new furry friend had a nice pile of goodies stored in the corner of my pantry.

"I knew there was a reason he takes off every morning after he gets his breakfast. He's coming down here for seconds," Jake teased as he turned the corner and nudged Henry past me and into the kitchen. "And presents from my lady."

I uncrossed my arms. "Where did you come from? You weren't supposed to be here until ten."

His right hand reached for the back of my head as he steered my lips to his. My arms looped around his neck and I pulled him closer, reveling in the heat from his muscular form. "Good morning, beautiful," his mouth whispered against mine. "I missed you, baby."

I stood on my tippy-toes and pressed my forehead against his. "I saw you last night," I reminded him as I raked my hands through his hair.

"Even an hour away from you is too long, Barbie." His kiss was gentle, teasing at first, but I found myself sighing and leaning back against the kitchen wall as it intensified. I almost asked him why he didn't stay the night and quickly reminded myself that I hadn't invited him, nor would I. If there was going to be a move toward the bedroom, Jake would have to make it first. And since I still wasn't where I needed to be emotionally in this relationship, it was just as well. A gust of cool air broke the spell, and after closing the kitchen door, he answered the question I asked only moments earlier.

"I finished up early at my house and thought I'd get started on your bathroom floor. Didn't you hear my truck?"

I shook my head as he asked, "Are you helping or watching?"

I glanced at the rooster clock perched above the window over my kitchen sink. "I ordered a specialty fixture the plumber will need for Monday and because it's so big, the post office is holding it. I wanted to pick it up sooner rather than later."

"Go!" He shooed me away as he reached for a mug and helped himself to coffee. I watched as Henry padded his way to the heat vent, found his favorite spot on a tattered throw rug, and curled up into an oversized fur ball. My insides warmed at how comfortable they were in my home. *Feels like a real family,* I thought and immediately dissolved the notion. I wouldn't allow myself to bask in it for too long in case it wasn't real.

"What was Henry's latest present?" Jake asked as he lifted the steaming cup to his lips. "He brought me a disgusting toothbrush and an old turtle shell yesterday," he added before taking a sip.

I laughed and waved toward my pantry. "I got a man's work boot. It's old so I knew it wasn't yours. I was grateful it didn't have a foot in it."

I asked Jake if he needed anything in town, and after assuring me he didn't, I grabbed my purse and keys. "I won't be long," I promised as I snatched my coat from a hook near the kitchen and headed for the front door.

The drive to the post office was uneventful and I was pleased to see the vintage fixture I ordered was exactly as advertised. I arrived home and let myself in the house, the noise echoing down the stairs a clear indication that Jake was hard at work overhead. It wasn't until I reached the top step that I wondered if he'd come across the old flashlight.

When I got to my childhood bedroom, I paused in the doorway and watched him work. He must've felt my presence because he turned around and winked at me. I walked in and took notice of where he'd removed some of the flooring. I cleared my throat and asked, "Did you happen to find anything while ripping up the old wood?"

He stood up and brushed his hands down his jeans. "I did." His tone was mildly curious as he pointed to a corner of the room. "Did you make a habit of hiding your lunchbox under your bedroom floor?"

I followed his gaze and my eyes settled on a Holly Hobbie lunchbox. As my brain scrambled to make sense of the find, he added, "There was a corroded old flashlight down there too. Looks like someone wrote initials on it."

"KP," I whispered as I gravitated to the corner of the room where Jake had placed the buried treasures. Shaking my head, I wondered out loud, "Why would Fancy's lunchbox be beneath my old bedroom floor?"

I could practically feel the shrug of his shoulders from behind me. "I can't help you with that one."

Ignoring the ringing that had started in my ears, I bent over and retrieved them both from the floor. I whirled around to face Jake. "I remember this lunchbox even though I never laid eyes on it," I said as I weighed it in my hand.

He gave me a questioning look.

"It was the first and only summer I went to camp. The summer Kenny ran away," I reminded him. I stared over his shoulder at a spot on the wall and tried to resurrect a memory. "While I was gone, my grandmother bought it for Fancy. She was starting kindergarten, I think." I could feel the crease in my forehead as I grappled with the recollection. "Anyway, when I got home from camp, Fancy had been fussing because it got lost somewhere and they couldn't find another one. I guess Holly Hobbie was all the rage that year." I broke my stare to give him my full attention. "Of course none of this explains how it ended up under my floor."

He motioned with his hand and added, "It looks like it's in good condition. Like it's never been used. Why don't you open it? Maybe you'll find an explanation inside."

I knew he was right but felt overcome by emotional as well as physical paralysis. I wrestled with the fear of having a glimmer of hope that might solve a forty-year-old mystery, only to be let down by the possibility that my witch of a grandmother had deliberately put it there to let me know she'd known about my secret flashlight.

Jake's voice interrupted my internal reflections. "Why the hesitancy, Barbie?"

I blew out a breath. "Because I'm seriously considering the likelihood that my grandmother knew about my hiding place and I'll find a nasty note inside." I bit the inside of my cheek as I shook my head. "Who knows? More than likely she was ticked at Fancy for something and it was a psychological punishment of some sort. The woman was crazy. It could be anything."

"It could be from Kenny."

"No way," I scoffed. "I never told Kenny where I kept the flashlight."

"He could've figured it out." Jake paused and looked around the small room. "There could only be so many places to hide something in a room this size. From what you've told me about Kenny, he was a resourceful kid and your best friend. You may not have told him directly, but he could've deduced it from things you might've said."

I held up the flashlight and squinted to see the faded initials. *Oh, Kenny.* Nodding my head in reluctant agreement, I left the room. I wanted to sit down before I opened it. When I got to the stairs, I turned around and yelled, "Are you coming?"

Jake peeked his head outside the door and asked, "Am I invited?"

"Of course you are."

I sat on the couch and felt the comforting shift of weight on the cushion as Jake took his place next to me. I set the flashlight on the coffee table and placed the lunchbox on my knees. I looked at Jake and smiled when he gave me a reassuring wink. Turning back to Holly Hobbie, I opened the latch and slowly lifted the lid. I gasped out loud as I touched my hand to my heart. "He left if for me. All this time, it was right under my nose."

I reached in and slowly lifted out my grandfather's pocket watch. The pocket watch I'd left with Kenny as a testament and reflection of my love for him the night before I left for camp. The watch that was supposed to have been a good luck talisman in my absence.

"Oh, Jake." My voice was hoarse as I coped with my emotions. "You were right. Kenny must've figured out my hiding place." I swallowed, my throat thick, when I realized the enormity of this find and what my extra week at summer camp had cost me—decades of doubt, pain, loss, and uncertainty.

He listened patiently as I tried to explain through heaping sobs of emotion how upon my return from camp I'd been thrust into a panic when I realized how long Kenny had been gone. I briefly described our communication system and explained my urgency to get the flashlight to signal him from my window. I described my frustration at not being able to find my nail file to pry up the floor and how I grabbed the flashlight from the pantry instead.

"I never lifted the board up again," I admitted as I laid the lunchbox next to the flashlight with shaky hands and wept into Jake's chest while tightly clutching the pocket watch. I don't know how long I cried, but it was long enough to leave a wet stain on his shirt. I felt a warm hand on my back and realized Darlene must've shown up. I hadn't even noticed her arrival. She retrieved a box of tissues, and once I calmed down, I listened as Jake explained the find to Darlene.

"So now you know, honey," came her soothing voice.

"There's something else in there."

Darlene and I both looked at Jake. I was getting ready to state that I'd seen the thermos and didn't think it meant anything, when he reached in and pulled out something wrapped in a yellowed paper towel. He handed it to me. I removed the paper towel and looked at Darlene.

Her expression was one of total bewilderment. "Why would Kenny leave you an old change purse?"

My chest began to tighten as I realized the significance of the gift. "Because it was his most prized possession and all he had left of her," I managed to choke out. "And if I'm right, you'll find exactly four dollars and thirty-two cents inside."

"Barbie?" The question in Jake's voice prompted me to elaborate.

I sucked in a healthy dose of air as a wave of past emotions were brought back by that one inhalation. "Kenny's mother left a year or so before I moved here. He was around ten years old and Jonathan couldn't have been more than three. Kenny remembered hearing his parents quarreling the night before. It wasn't an especially bad fight so he fell asleep without giving it a second thought. When he got up the next morning, his father told him that she'd left and wouldn't be back. He said that she took everything she owned, but she didn't want a reminder of them so she told him he could keep the family pictures. He'd been up all night drinking and tossing them in the fireplace. Kenny was devastated and more so when he ran to her bedroom and confirmed that her closet and dresser drawers had been emptied. She took every single piece of clothing she owned. Every possession. Except for two." I reached for a new tissue. "Kenny said she always wore an apron and she was never without her change purse that she kept in the pocket." I blew my nose before continuing. "She kept the apron on a hook on the inside of the kitchen pantry door. It was the only thing she left. Maybe she left it on purpose or forgot it. Kenny found it and hid it because he was afraid his father would throw it away. The apron and purse were the only things he had left of her. He held on to them because he was certain she'd be back."

"You never told me this," came Darlene's whisper from beside me. I reached over and grabbed her hand, squeezing it too tightly.

"It wasn't my story to tell," I replied.

With her free hand, Darlene picked up the thermos. "Do you think there's something inside?"

Jake reached for it, and taking it from her, said, "Only one way to find out." He unscrewed the cup and the cap that sealed the thermos. He turned it upside down over the table and a rolled-up piece of paper fell out. I seized the yellowed note with my free hand, and let go of Darlene's. I stood and walked toward the fireplace. With my back to them, I slowly read the note that had been neatly printed in pencil. I recognized Kenny's handwriting immediately, and unlike the hastily scribbled initials on my flashlight, I could see that he took his time giving deliberate care to each word.

Dear Barbie,
I know it's Friday night and you're finding this because you're back from camp and you said you would signal me as soon as you got home. I won't be in the tree house to answer you. I have to leave to find my great-aunt. I've never met her but I think she's the only one that might know the truth about something my daddy told me after he caught us the other night. I know your grandma keeps money in a soap tin behind her pickling jars. I'm going to steal it and I'm sorry 'cause I know she'll blame you. I don't have the heart to spend my momma's money. I'm giving you her change purse and your granddaddy's watch for safe keeping.
I don't know how long I'll be gone but I promise to write to you. I know it's safe because you're the only one who checks the mail. I don't know if I'll have an address for you to write back, but at least you'll hear from me. I'll try to call when I think you'll be alone in the house. I'll be back as soon as I can. I love you, Barbie doll.
Kenny
P.S. You can make up a story to tell Jonathan why I'm gone. Just make sure he knows I'm coming back.

I couldn't contain the pain that bubbled up from my chest and lodged in my throat. I stifled a sob as both Darlene and Jake jumped up and came toward me. I handed him the note as Darlene pulled me tight against her. I heard her ask, "Is it okay if we read it?" I nodded my head against her shoulder and listened as Jake read the note for her to hear.

"He loved you, Barbie. Kenny loved you and was coming back to you." Darlene pulled back and cradled my cheeks in both of her hands. With tears in her eyes and a smile on her face, she repeated, "Kenny didn't leave *you*. He *loved* you, and he left for a reason and planned on coming back."

"But why didn't he?" I wailed.

"Probably for the same reason I couldn't face my parents after I got out of prison."

We both looked at Jake and his face bore traces of his pain. "I was ashamed at what I'd done. Ashamed that I'd caused them so much heartache. Mine's a long story that I haven't shared completely, Barbie, but I will one day. I guess Kenny got into something he hadn't planned and it sealed his fate."

"But I never got any letters." My tears were subsiding and I was grateful they hadn't morphed into hiccups. I wrinkled my brow in concentration and the memory that surfaced caused an explosion of anger.

"My grandmother!" I screamed. "That witch!!"

I clenched my fists at my sides and tried to take a calming breath as I filled Darlene and Jake in on a detail from the summer of '79 that I'd long forgotten. As a child, it had always been my job to retrieve the mail, which entailed a mile-and-a-half walk from our house to where our dirt road intersected with the main street. It wasn't bad on school days because that's where the bus dropped us. But during the summer it was a chore I didn't appreciate. Especially after my grandmother entered some stupid recipe contest from one of her magazines. While she was waiting to see if her recipe had been selected there were days she made me run down to the mailbox more than once. One day in particular, she'd taken the car to go into town and got the mail on her way home. It was something she normally wouldn't have done, but she was waiting for good news. I remembered the day clearly. She came in the house with a bundle of mail clutched in her hand and said I'd been relieved of mail duty. She sternly informed me that she'd received notice on a late bill that she never got. She blamed me and said I must've dropped it on the way home. I was never to check the mail again.

I looked over at Darlene whose eyes were wide as recognition seeped in. "You got a letter from Kenny and it had the lousy luck to be on a day when she picked up the mail because she wanted to hear from Good Housekeeping!"

"I'd bet my right arm that's exactly what happened. She never let me check the mail again. She always made it a point to drive up and get it before we got off the bus. She never even waited around to give us a ride back."

"Your grandmother was a tool," was Jake's only comment.

Darlene's eyes were brimming with unshed tears. "That would explain so much, Barbie. You told me how Kenny never responded to the couple of letters you sent him while he was in prison. Did you ever ask him in those letters why he ran off and never returned your granddaddy's pocket watch?"

I stared at the ground in concentration and gave my head a slow shake.

"No. I don't think I ever confronted him about leaving and not telling me why. It was pride on my part. I didn't want him to know how much he'd hurt me. I made the letters very casual because I didn't want him to know I cared. I wrote about nonsense stuff like I was just an old friend trying to catch up. Not like I was the girl whose heart he'd shattered."

"So he never knew you didn't find the lunchbox filled with treasure," she surmised. "Or his note."

Like two lovers tightly woven into each other's arms, my anger and grief melded together and formed an animalistic fury like I'd never experienced. I grabbed the thermos from the coffee table and threw it with all my might against the brick fireplace. The hard plastic cracked, scattering pieces on the hearth and across the floor. I picked up a fireplace poker and brought it down hard against the metal lunchbox. The years of Juanita Anderson's abuse had caused me to finally reach a breaking point. The healer, the doctor had suddenly become the destroyer. And a child's lunchbox had become the hapless victim. I felt Jake and Darlene watching me, both stunned into silence as I took out my pent-up rage on an inanimate object. When the damage was done, I stood back and felt my breathing and heartbeat returning to normal. I tossed the poker on the hearth where it echoed with a resounding metallic ping. "That was for letting Kenny Pritchard die in prison thinking I stopped loving him," I said to the ghost of my grandmother. "And be glad you're not here, Juanita Anderson, because if you were…" I let the words die off as vain imaginations of what I might be capable of swirled around my brain.

"How long have you been holding that back?" Darlene's eyes met mine. They weren't accusatory, but compassionate.

"A long time," I admitted. "Even before I found this," I said, pointing to the unrecognizable lump of metal, "and discovered the true extent of her evil. Her intercepting a letter is the only thing that makes sense because if Kenny said he was going to send a letter, he would've sent a letter."

Darlene bent over and started to pick up the pieces of broken plastic. "I have to agree."

"Are you okay, Barbie?" Jake asked.

"Never felt better in my life," I told him as I headed for the stairs. "Let's get the rest of the bathroom floor up."

CHAPTER 35

TIME DOESN'T HEAL ALL WOUNDS.
SOMETIMES THEY JUST SCAB OVER.

I wish I could say that my mind stayed in a good place after the lunchbox discovery. I marched up the stairs that day feeling like I'd conquered the world. I'd been so grateful to discover that Kenny hadn't run off without attempting to leave an explanation. And as angry as I was at my grandmother, I was happy to know that he'd loved me and had planned on coming back. Sadly, it was short-lived because the unanswered question as to why he'd left was still hanging around like an unwelcome bully in a schoolyard. What had his father said that instigated an immediate and impromptu trip to find an aunt he'd never met?

After months of politely refusing Darlene's invitations to church, I found myself looking for comfort and peace from a Higher Power. One that I'd given up on as a child. My best friend convinced me that not all the answers we seek might be found in this lifetime and perhaps it was time for me to return to the God whom I'd loved and believed in before Kenny's abandonment. She reminded me that I was the queen of second chances, and if anybody deserved one, it was the Creator of the universe. She'd been right.

As I sat in the pew with Darlene's family and listened to a sermon on forgiveness and the freedom that came with it, I felt a different kind of freedom. It was a sense of peace in knowing I was right back where I belonged. I was thinking about inviting Jake to the upcoming Christmas Eve service when a familiar cough caught my attention. I'd been treating an elderly patient at the clinic for bronchial pneumonia and had confined him to bed rest. I peeked over my left shoulder to seek out the man who'd defied doctor's orders when I spotted Jake. He was standing at the back of the church near the doors that opened out into the vestibule. He was watching the preacher, and when he felt my eyes on him, he looked at me with an unreadable expression.

I turned back to face the pulpit and whispered to Darlene, "Jake's here."

She leaned my way and whispered back, "He's always here."

I looked over at her, and when she felt my stare, she quietly said, "He started coming after the first day you met him at Hampton House. He never sits down, just stands in the back. He gets here after the service starts and leaves right before it's over. He's only missed once."

"The morning after he got cut at The Lonesome Keg," I concluded. "Why have you never told me? Why has *he* never told me?" I wanted to know.

"You never asked."

When the service was over, there was no sign of Jake in the church foyer or the parking lot. Like we'd planned, I caught up with him later that morning as we headed off to an indoor flea market a few towns away. We'd recently discovered our mutual love of all things vintage, and as nutty as it sounded, I was on a quest to prevent him from buying a stereo system. I'd discovered a pile of old record albums at his house, and when I asked about them, he told me he'd been on the hunt for a certain type of old-fashioned hi-fi stereo. I found one online and hid it away to give him for Christmas. But now I was faced with the challenge of preventing him from buying one. Every time he came across one he thought he liked, I found something wrong with it to the chagrin of the prospective sellers.

During the forty-five-minute drive, we talked about some of the history of Pumpkin Rest and the large families that lived there. Jake was impressed and a little awed by the size of Darlene's brood and their commitment to one another. That segued into a discussion about church, and I asked why he stood in the back instead of sitting with the rest of the congregation. He casually explained that he was still feeling things out. He turned the tables on me by initiating a conversation as to what prompted me to return to my faith since my move back to Pumpkin Rest. It was a healthy chat where we both confessed to some soul searching that went beyond the physical boundary of an earthly plane. We eventually circled back to family, and he inquired about Fancy and the status of the sale of my condominium in Greenville.

I explained that she'd left the place in surprisingly good condition, and how it was pretty typical for me not to have heard from her. I asked him what it was like growing up as an only child.

"I told you I was a late-in-life baby?" It was a statement but presented in the form of a question.

"Yes, you did."

"Did I tell you I had an older brother? Did I ever mention Phillip?" He shot me a sideways glance, and after a quick shake of my head, returned his eyes to the road.

"You told me you were an only child and that your parents didn't think they could have children. That's why you were a surprise," I reminded him.

"I guess I wasn't an only child. I was raised alone, but my parents adopted Phillip years before they had me."

I turned in the seat and rested my back against the passenger door. The seat belt was awkward but I found Jake's profile and story more interesting than the scenery. "What's he like? Where is he now?"

"I never met him. He died when he was eight and it was years before I was born. So I was raised as an only child, but there were reminders of Phillip everywhere." I suddenly felt the weight of grief he was experiencing and something told me it was a story he needed to tell so I remained quiet and let him talk. "It wasn't until Phillip turned two that my parents discovered he had epilepsy. They did everything they could to make sure he received the best care. My mom admitted to being a little too overprotective with him, but he never gave her a hard time. He was a good kid."

"He died from epilepsy?"

He didn't give me a direct answer, but instead launched into a story. "My parents had a fountain in the middle of their landscape nursery. You should've seen it. It was the most ridiculous ostentatious thing you've ever laid eyes on." He cracked a partial smile at the memory. "Then again, that was Miami in the fifties. It was the first thing people would see when they pulled up to buy plants and flowers, and my parents wanted to make an impression. Mom stocked it with goldfish and it was Phillip's job to feed the fish."

I knew what was coming. What Jake was about to tell me wasn't uncommon with people who suffered from seizures.

"Mom never let Phillip near that fountain unless she could see him. And he knew not to go near it. One day the bus dropped him off like it had hundreds of times, and for whatever reason, he strayed from the norm. Mom always kept an eye out for him and she could see him walking toward the house. She remembered looking away for less than sixty seconds and when she looked back, she thought he'd made it to the house and let himself in. But he must've gone back to the fountain." He paused, took a deep breath, and continued. "She always had milk and cookies laid out for him at the kitchen table, so he usually wouldn't go outside until after he ate his snack."

"She found him in the fountain?" My voice was barely a whisper as my eyes started to mist over.

"No, she didn't find him." He turned to look at me as we stopped at a red light. "A couple who'd pulled in to buy flowers found him. He drowned in less than twelve inches of water."

I reached across the seat and touched his arm. "I'm so sorry, Jake."

"They didn't deserve that, and it's why I carry the guilt of disappointing them even more. As I got older I turned into a smart-mouthed, unappreciative teenager who did nothing but cause them trouble."

"Like ninety percent of teenagers in the world," I chided. "You're being too hard on yourself." It was almost as if he hadn't heard me. The light turned green and he pressed on the accelerator.

"It all started when I became embarrassed by them. They were getting up in age and it showed. During my Little League baseball years, my father never missed one game. He's the reason I pushed myself to make All-Stars." He turned his head my way and asked, "Have you ever noticed the baseball I keep in a glass case on my nightstand?"

We were in Jake's bedroom to select a paint color for the walls and I had noticed the case. I thought it was one of his flea market finds and assumed it boasted a familiar signature. However, I never looked close enough to see whose. "I've seen it. I figured it's signed by some famous player."

He stared out over the steering wheel, his knuckles white as he gripped it tightly with his right hand. "My father gave it to me. When I was striking out and missing catches and generally failing at baseball, my father saw the potential that I couldn't see. So he went out and bought a baseball and asked me to sign it for him. He made a big deal out of it and told me that if I was going to play baseball like the star he knew I could be, I had to feel the part. He asked me for my autograph and displayed it in our living room. He was right. It made me a better player, and like I already told you, I made the All-Stars two years in a row." I could see the pain in his profile, the regret in the slight sag of his jaw. "Other than some faded pictures, that baseball is the only thing I have left of them. It's my most prized possession."

I could only assume that seeing the treasures unearthed in Fancy's lunchbox had brought on a bout of nostalgia, and our earlier discussion about Darlene's close-knit family had exacerbated those feelings. "So what happened?" I softly inquired.

He gave a noncommittal shrug and said, "Like I said before, I was embarrassed by them. I was more concerned with what my friends thought. It only took one kid to ask me why my grandpa came to all my games instead of my father. It was like a switch was flipped. I started comparing them to the other kids' younger and cooler parents. I resented the station wagons filled with families who went on summer vacations that included everything from water skiing to beach volleyball, and the younger dads who were in good enough shape to coach the team and play catch with their boys. Looking back, I was ridiculous and how I treated them is still the biggest regret of my life. That's when I stopped playing baseball, turned into a punk, and started getting in trouble."

Stretching the seat belt tight, I leaned toward him and placed my hand on his right knee. "We all have regrets, Jake. We're all ashamed of things we did when we were children. Things we wish we could take back. From the little bit you've told me, I'm certain your parents forgave you. They sound like they were incredible and caring people. And time heals all wounds. Maybe it's time you let it heal yours."

His voice sounded rusty when he replied, "Time doesn't heal all wounds. Sometimes they just scab over."

"And scabs dry up and fall off if you don't pick at them. Perhaps you need to let this one fall off, Jake."

He grabbed my hand that had been resting on his knee and brought it to his lips. "You are such an amazing woman, Barbie. Even with your painful past you've managed to comfort me about mine." He kissed my wrist, and after letting go of my hand, popped in a CD and turned it up. His favorite country artist's voice filled the cab of the truck.

An old familiar song begins to play
Reminding me and her of the day we first met
And time stood still
A little kiss on the neck and it heats up
So I find a place to park my truck
I let go and let passion take the wheel
It doesn't get better than this

Without warning, he took a sharp right onto a dirt road and pulled over.

I looked around at the secluded area. "What are you doing?"

After putting the truck in park, he reached over me and unlatched my seat belt. He roughly tugged me into his arms and said, "I'm finding a place to park my truck so I can make out with my lady."

And that's what we did. I took the opportunity to climb onto his lap and straddle him. I could feel his arousal through the thickness of his denim jeans, and I moaned into his mouth as I moved against him.

I jumped when there was a loud tap on the glass. Our heads whipped around to find a toothless old man yelling into the slightly cracked window, "This is a private road. Y'all need to be taking your personal business elsewhere. I don't want my grand young-uns interruptin' something they shouldn't be a seein'."

We both tried to conceal our smiles as I climbed back over to my side of the cab. Jake apologized and turned the truck around.

We laughed about it and I secretly wondered how far we might've gone. How far I'd been willing to go. Did I want my first time with Jake to be in the front seat of an old pickup truck? Did he?

His voice interrupted my contemplation. "What are you thinking about?"

"My property," I lied. "I've been told my soil is fertile. I'm wondering if I should consider planting something." I tucked my hair behind my ear. "You know. Other than my crummy little vegetable garden that I've neglected."

"You do have a lot of land. And you also own the stills that used to belong to the Pritchards. Have you ever considered going into the legal moonshine business?"

I was startled by his question. It's one I hadn't pondered. My delayed response brought an apology. "I'm sorry, Barbie. I forgot it's a touchy subject." There was an awkward pause to which he added, "I mean, you told me after the incident at The Lonesome Keg how Dustin and his friends had confronted you about the Pritchard family recipe. And you told them you didn't know it. I'm sorry for bringing it up."

I looked down at my knee and rubbed my hand against a worn spot on my jeans. A few more washings and it would be a hole. His assumptions and apology hung in the air like a floating feather that refused to fall.

We'd arrived at our destination and he parked and turned off the truck. "Barbie?" I wasn't purposely ignoring him. Just stalling. "You don't know the Pritchards' secret recipe, right?"

I unsnapped my seat belt, grabbed my purse and tote bag, and opened the truck door. I got out and turned back to face him. He was still sitting in the driver's seat waiting for my answer.

"Of course I know it, Jake."

CHAPTER 36

SOMETHING HAS BEEN BOTHERING ME

I lay in bed that night and quietly contemplated the events of the day. I smiled when I remembered warding off an aggressive stereo salesman. He wanted the sale so badly he was practically salivating. I felt so guilty for steering Jake away from him, I later made an excuse to use the restroom and circled back to buy some records from the man. He was nice about it and carefully wrapped the LPs before I hid them in my oversized canvas tote bag.

The only part of the day I found mildly irritating was when I quizzed Jake on his favorite vintage bargain and he mentioned an authentic English tea set he'd found for Emmy. I hated to admit it, but his revelation caused a tinge of jealousy.

I stared at the ceiling. The smell of fresh paint and varnish reminded me that my renovation was almost finished. A few more days of tile work and my new bathroom would be ready. I was expecting the cabinets and new appliances the week before Christmas, and if all went well, my new furniture would be delivered the week after. I was torn as to whether or not I should offer Jake some of my used furniture which was slightly nicer than his. I knew he didn't make a lot of money at Hampton House. But I didn't want to offend him either. There was nothing wrong with his stuff. It was just a little more broken-in than mine.

Which brought to mind another concern. I knew he would buy me a Christmas gift and I didn't want him to think he had to spend too much, if anything, on me. I wasn't Fancy who would insist on diamonds and designer purses. I asked Darlene if he'd approached her for ideas, but she brushed me off and said Jake was a big boy and I didn't need to micromanage his shopping trips. Darlene always told it like it was. Blunt to a fault, but in a loving way.

As sleep eluded me, I found myself reliving the conversation we'd had the night Jake made tacos. Some leftover remnant of that evening had been nagging at me, but I couldn't place it. There was a pothole in my memory, and I couldn't grab hold of the details needed to fill it in. And then it came to me. I looked at the clock. It was 2:14 a.m. I knew he was an insomniac and hoped this wasn't one of the rare nights he fell asleep early. I reached for my phone and texted him: R u up?

The sudden ringing startled me and I fumbled to answer my phone. His voice was booming when he asked, "Are you okay?"

"Of course I'm okay. Why wouldn't I be okay?"

"You've never texted me in the middle of the night, sweetheart. I had to make sure nothing's wrong." He sounded relieved and a little bewildered as to why I would even ask. "What's up?"

"Something has been bothering me and I wanted to ask you if you knew. I suppose I could ask Sheila next time I see her, but I thought you might know since you're so close with Jonathan."

"Sure, babe. What do you wanna know?"

I got out of bed and headed downstairs for some water while we talked. "I was wondering if you know how Jonathan, who is a ward of the state of South Carolina, can afford to live at Hampton House? I know it's privately owned and expensive."

There was a pause on the other end of the phone. I used the time to fill my water bottle. "Jake? Are you there?"

"Yeah, I'm here. I don't know much. Only that he's been there for a couple of years now and it's due to the generosity of someone who wants to remain anonymous."

I was ready to take a sip of water, but I set the bottle down on the counter instead. "An anonymous donor? Who could that possibly be?"

Another pause on his end. "Someone who wants to remain anonymous?"

"I know that, Jake. I'm thinking out loud."

I could hear him chuckle. "Look. Don't tell Sheila I said anything, but I think it's connected to Cindy. At least that's what some of the others at Hampton House have guessed." His voice was low and serious.

Before I could ask him to elaborate, he explained, "It's my understanding that when Cindy was placed in Jonathan's group home on the other side of the state, it was supposed to be temporary until a private facility was found for her. It took almost six months before something opened up at Hampton House, and she and Jonathan had become so close there was concern about separating them. Whoever this anonymous donor is, he or she is also paying for Cindy to live there."

"So it's more likely that someone who knows Cindy is responsible," I speculated. I turned off the kitchen light and made my way back upstairs. "That makes sense since I can't think of anyone in the world from around here who could pay for both of them to live at Hampton House."

"I have to agree with you on that one."

After a few more minutes of small talk, we said goodnight. I turned off my phone and pulled the covers up to my chin.

There had been one more thing on my mind since taco night. But I would never ask him about it. That was our first official date and the same evening he confessed to knowing where I kept my key hidden. It brought me back to the night he'd been at my house and we'd shared a jar of moonshine. I'd gotten totally wasted and assumed I'd let him out the front door and numbly made my way up to bed by myself. What if he had carried me upstairs and tucked me in? What if I hadn't imagined the kisses? What if he'd let himself out the door and locked it behind him before returning the key to its hiding place on my porch? It would make so much sense with the exception of one thing. I was certain before leaving he whispered, "I've loved you for as long as I can remember, Barbie doll." I'd barely known Jake at that point so I had to have imagined it.

I was disappointed. About what, I didn't know.

I rolled over and hugged my pillow as I recalled the highlights of my afternoon. They made me extremely happy and were intoxicating in their simplicity. Walking hand in hand with Jake through the throng of flea market sellers. Haggling over dusty reminders of someone else's past. Finding the perfect toys for Henry's Christmas stocking.

I'd offered to split a Philly cheesesteak sub with Jake which he'd refused because half a sandwich wasn't enough for him. And he drank two cans of Dr. Pepper before I could even ask for a sip. When he realized I hadn't had a drink, he jumped up and ran to get me one—such a gentleman. And that was another thing that baffled me. Jake had the appearance and self-assuredness of a criminal, but the manners of a gentleman. He was an enigma, a puzzle. And I'd yet to find the missing piece. The question was, would that piece complete us or destroy us?

CHAPTER 37

HOW'S THE ILLEGAL MOONSHINE BUSINESS?

Christmas and New Year's had come and gone, and the month of January brought some sporadic and unusually balmy weather with it. I sat on my front porch and couldn't hide my grin at my recent house-warming present from Jake. Even though I'd been in the house full-time for almost a year, he'd still insisted on giving me a gift. He called it the renovation-is-finally-done housewarming gift. We'd been spending so much time together I wondered how he'd managed to hide it from me.

"You know that by giving me another Adirondack chair, you're rescinding your offer for me to sit on your lap because I only had the one?" I'd teased.

He'd grown serious before answering. "Your lonely red chair needed a friend, Barbie. Besides, I needed something to do with my hands," he replied to lighten his tone.

I can think of something you can do with your hands. Not allowing my thoughts to follow that road, I asked, "You *made* this chair?" My tone was incredulous.

"Yes, I made it." He didn't say it, but I knew he thought the solitary chair on my porch screamed that a single woman lived here alone. I didn't have the same concern that he did because I felt safe in Pumpkin Rest. Despite that, I'd still let him talk me into buying a handgun and taking a course that made me an official concealed weapons permit holder. The biggest advantage to owning a gun that I could see were the lazy Sunday afternoons I spent out back with Jake's arms wrapped around me as he taught me to shoot at old tin cans. To our surprise, I was a natural when it came to aiming a gun, and as I got better, my targets became smaller.

The position of the sun allowed some rays to sneak beneath the porch overhang, so I lay back against the chair and let myself enjoy memories along with the warm and fresh air. I'd been on the brink of falling asleep when the tinkling of a collar brought me out of my daydream state. I sat up and smiled at one of my Christmas presents from Jake. Lady, a black pit bull puppy who'd been rescued by one of the employees at Hampton House, made her way up the front steps, gave my dangling hand a quick lick, and headed for her water bowl.

"Where's Henry?" I asked as she made her way back to me. They were almost inseparable, and I could only surmise that he didn't feel like playing and was beneath a shade tree somewhere between here and Jake's place. I sat up and placed both elbows on my knees as I took her little face in my hands and let her bestow puppy kisses all over my chin. It wouldn't be too long before she would be too heavy to hold, so I scooped her up and sat back in the chair, cradling her like a baby. "Who's a good girl?" I cooed as I rubbed her smooth belly.

And she was. I'd never seen a dog pick up on training so quickly. Jake had a theory that rescued animals made the best pets because they were more appreciative of their new homes. Plus, it helped to have an older dog like Henry around for her to learn from. I couldn't comment on Jake's dog training theories, but if Lady was the basis for his observations, he was pretty spot-on. She was an angel.

I continued to stroke her tummy. It wasn't too long before she was snoring. "Henry wore you out, huh, my little lady?" The sun glinted off my wrist and I smiled to myself at my other Christmas present from Jake. It was a beautiful charm bracelet and held only two charms. A heart and an orchid. He'd presented it in a small brown box wrapped in Christmas paper. It wasn't until days later that I'd looked closer at the bracelet and discovered it was from Tiffany & Co. I loved that he downplayed the gift by putting it in a nondescript box. But I didn't like that he'd spent so much money. After all, I wasn't Fancy. I absentmindedly fiddled with one of Lady's silky ears and allowed myself the luxury of reliving my first Christmas with Jake.

Jake and I had spent Christmas morning at Hampton House, and the rest of the day at Darlene's with her unending flow of relatives who showed up at various times to visit, help themselves to eggnog and food, eventually going on their merry ways.

Darlene had scrunched up her face before asking, "Why do you care how much it might've cost him?"

"Because he can't make that much working as a caregiver at Hampton House," I countered.

Darlene pulled two more pies out of the oven and placed them on the table to cool. She tossed the potholders on the counter and leaned a hip against it. "He could've robbed a bank before he moved here," she quipped sarcastically.

I rolled my eyes. "I know he has secrets, things he's holding back, but I can't see that as one of them. Besides, I don't think a bank robber would spend his money on the Pritchard farm or drive an old truck."

"Dicey wants to know if you brought any moonshine with you, Aunt Barbie?"

Darlene's oldest daughter had peeked her head in the kitchen. Danielle was in her early thirties and a sheriff's deputy in Pickens County. I loved how upon meeting them last year, all of Darlene's children had started calling me Aunt Barbie. I hadn't been a physical part of their lives while they were growing up, but Darlene made sure they knew about her best friend who'd moved away and finally returned home for good. I was welcomed into their family as if I'd been there all along.

"Check with Jake," I told her. "We brought some, but he may have left it in the truck."

Darlene motioned for me to whip up another batch of lemonade while she started beating some helpless potatoes into mush. "How's the illegal moonshine business?"

"It's not a business or illegal," I emphasized, "if we're not selling it. It's just something we're doing for fun, and we've only made one batch. Which turned out pretty good if I do say so myself."

"Not true," she quickly corrected me. "You need to have a permit. It doesn't matter if the alcohol is for personal use only, not for sale, whatever." She swiped at her forehead.

"If we decide to keep making it and Danielle doesn't turn us in for this batch, I'll remember that." I took a sip of the lemonade and made a face. "Needs more sugar."

"And you're okay with it? The moonshine?" she quickly clarified. "No sad memories of making it with Kenny are resurfacing?" I could hear the concern in her voice and turned to look at her.

I wouldn't tell Darlene, but making the moonshine had always been a chore, a responsibility thrust upon Kenny by his rotten father. And the only thing that made it bearable was that we did it together. "No. Like I said, it's fun with Jake. I'm okay now, Dar. I promise. And Jake is a natural. I remembered the ingredients like they were tattooed on my brain, but I had to work out the steps. He's been great at helping me experiment." I measured out some more sugar and added, "And getting back to my bracelet. I don't want him thinking I'm my sister. He's met her and she's all about the money."

"Jake would never think that about you, Barbie. He knows you're not Fancy."

A thought occurred to me and I stopped mid-stir. "Do you think it's why he hasn't tried to take our relationship any further? Is it possible he's one of those guys that thinks he has to provide for me before we can be a couple?"

I felt Darlene walk up beside me. She pulled at a stray hair that had stuck to my cheek. "You said yourself that you think there might be something he's not telling you. If that turns out to be true, he might think that's a game changer for you. But instead of all this wondering, you could ask him, Barbie."

I shook my head and refused to look at her.

"Why not?"

"Because I like this too much. We haven't gone beyond kissing and feeling each other up, but I don't want it to end. I want to savor it, Dar. Because what if he does have something to tell me and what if it is a game changer?"

"Is there anything you can think of that would be a game changer for you?" she wanted to know.

I didn't answer at first, giving myself time to sift through possible scenarios. This time I did turn to look at her. "Other than him being married or a serial killer, there's nothing."

"Then ask him."

"Who's him and what do you need to ask?"

We both turned at the familiar voice. I could tell by Jake's expression he hadn't heard much, if anything, of our conversation. Besides, he wasn't one to lurk behind corners eavesdropping.

"Darlene said I needed to ask my man why he hasn't kissed me under the mistletoe yet."

I lifted Lady a little higher and nuzzled the top of her head with my nose. I let myself revel in the memory of that kiss beneath the mistletoe. It was long, lingering, and ended with Dicey raising her jar of moonshine and announcing, "That's a kiss deservin' of a good toast. The kind that sets a woman's unmentionables afire and turns into a baby makin' event."

I chuckled at the recollection of Dicey's offhanded comment and the applause that followed. Lady jerked awake when my cell phone and laptop simultaneously pinged. I sat up and placed my fur baby on the porch. I reached for my phone first. I'd been hoping to get a text or message from Sheila. It had been months since her husband had left and she'd hired a private detective to find him. She'd been anxious to get the divorce proceedings started, and was getting nervous when the man had come up empty. It appeared her husband had vanished.

I squinted at the text, not recognizing the number or making sense of the message. It was from someone who must know me and they were apologizing in advance for giving my email address to a casting associate. It seemed that someone from Los Angeles was trying to get in touch with me. I replied with "Who is this?" and was answered with a name. I remembered her from the hospital in Greenville. I didn't remember exchanging numbers with her, but I did have colleagues there who might have given it to her. I wasn't sure what to make of her message and was deciding whether or not to reply when my laptop pinged a second time. I had set it on the Adirondack chair Jake had made. I hefted it up and placed it on my lap. The first email was definitely spam. I hesitated before opening the second email because I didn't recognize the address. It was from a woman from a company I'd never heard of before. They were scouting hospitals in the Greenville area for a reality show. I typed a quick response letting her know that I'd resigned a while ago and didn't understand why she would want to talk to me.

Her reply was almost immediate. While visiting my old place of employment, my name had been brought up several times by previous co-workers. Between my sister running off with my now deceased husband, and my reputation as the Monster of Monteith Medical, they wanted me to consider returning to the hospital. They thought I would make an interesting character in their reality-based hospital series. I replied with a polite but firm, "no, thank you" and closed my laptop.

I watched as Lady ran down the porch steps and sprinted toward Henry, who was trotting his way toward us with something clenched between his jaws. I stood up and used my hand to shield my eyes from the sun. "What are you bringing me now?"

Lady met up with him and tried to wrestle the gift, which looked like a stick, from his mouth, but he held his head high out of her reach as he approached my porch. It was unusual for Henry to bring home an ordinary stick. It wasn't until he got closer that I walked down the steps to meet him. After recognizing what he had in his mouth, I gently removed it, marched back up to my porch and grabbed the phone.

Jake's voice resonated through the speaker, "Hey, baby, what's up?"

"Can you get off work and come over?"

"What's wrong, Barbie? Are you okay?" I could hear the panic in his voice and could've kicked myself for alluding to an emergency.

"No. I'm fine. I didn't mean to scare you. It's just that Henry brought me a bone."

The relief in his voice was evident as he replied with a chuckle, "Isn't that what dogs do? Dig up their bones and rebury them? Or in Henry's case, give them as presents?"

There was a long pause filled with background noise at Hampton House. "It's not one of Henry's bones, Jake. It's a human femur."

CHAPTER 38

WHERE ALL THE EXCITEMENT HAPPENS

J ake asked me not to call the police until he got home and we determined where Henry found the bone. Less than an hour later we found ourselves hiking on the back side of Jake's property where Henry led us to a small clearing in the woods. We could see where he'd started digging, a shredded piece of faded green fabric peeked up from the disturbed earth.

Jake bent down and gently started clearing away the soil, which revealed another bone. "This is a grave, Barbie. I'm not sure if there's a whole body under here or how long it's been buried."

"If the rest of the body belongs to that femur," I motioned to the bone Jake had left on the ground, "it's been here a long time. I'm not a forensic anthropologist, but I do know this person didn't die recently."

Since the grave was found on Jake's property, we returned to his house and contacted the Pickens County Sheriff's Office. We led the county sheriff, Darlene's daughter, Danielle, and a couple of other deputies along with a forensics unit back to the secret grave. They worked all evening and into the night setting up spotlights, and meticulously sifting through dirt. By dawn, they'd recovered a female human skeleton buried with her personal belongings. The most curious find was an empty suitcase. It was almost as if the person who'd buried her had thrown all of her clothes into the grave, placed her on top of them, and threw the suitcase in as an afterthought. It wasn't a cavernous grave, but deep enough that it had kept the forest critters away. She would have probably continued to remain undisturbed if it weren't for Henry.

Scratching his jaw, the sheriff who grew up in Pumpkin Rest before moving to its sister county, commented in a slow Southern drawl, "I was a teenager when it was rumored that Mrs. Pritchard ran off." He placed his hands on his hips and peered at the lonely remains. "I think we might be able to put that rumor to rest."

The state medical examiner would order an autopsy and a DNA test to compare with Jonathan's, but the informal exhumation indicated it was Mrs. Pritchard since her purse and identification were buried with her body. And the damage to the back of her skull was a clear indication that she'd most likely died from blunt force trauma which could only have been inflicted by her husband.

The sad news spread quickly and there was a deep sense of mourning among the local town folk who remembered Missy Pritchard. A quiet and kind woman who moved here from the Midwest when she was a girl, Missy and her parents had been welcomed into the small community and even more so when she married into a local family. Her parents both died within months of each other the year before she had Kenny.

Other than Jonathan, the sheriff's office didn't know of any next of kin to notify. I told them that Kenny had mentioned his mother having an aunt in the letter he'd left me, but other than that, I had nothing else to offer. They did a quick search of the police department records that would've covered Pumpkin Rest back in the early seventies when Missy had left town. It took less than twenty minutes for them to retrieve the paperwork and determine that a wellness check had been requested over four decades ago by a woman claiming to be Missy's aunt.

The sheriff stood in my living room the following day, faded manila folder in hand. I'd just let him read the note from Kenny to which he responded, "You're right. It's vague. It could've had to do with his moth-er's murder, but we'll never know."

I shook my head. "I never even knew that he had an aunt until he left me the note saying he was leaving to find her."

He lazily chewed on a toothpick and opened the folder he was carry-ing. "Says here the aunt, Esther Agnis, called and asked the law back then to check on her niece. She claimed they exchanged letters occasionally and the aunt hadn't received one in a while. The Pritchards didn't have a phone so she couldn't call to check on her."

His eyes left the page long enough to meet mine and quickly returned to scan the decades-old paperwork. "And that lying SOB told them Missy ran off. Says here they verified her belongings were gone and closed the inquiry." He slapped the file shut in an angry huff. "We tried calling the number Miss Agnis left back in 1974, but to no one's surprise, it's been disconnected. And a quick internet search for the woman has come up blank. It appears that Jonathan is her only living relative." Politely raising his hand to his hat, he tipped it toward me and said, "Thanks for your time, Dr. Anderson."

Darlene was the first to offer her family's private cemetery as Missy Pritchard's final resting place, and a memorial service would be held as soon as the state was finished examining her remains.

I had spiraled downward into a mire of melancholy for days after the discovery, my heart not only mourning for the woman I'd never met, but even more so for Kenny and Jonathan. Jonathan was only three when she'd disappeared so he probably didn't have many, if any, memories of her. Especially since nothing had been left for him to remember her by. Not even a photograph. But I knew Kenny had always remained hopeful that she would return. It caused an ache in my chest to know that she'd never left them, and had suffered a terrible fate at the hands of her husband.

Jake, who'd been extremely supportive of my grief, showed up on my doorstep one afternoon and insisted on taking me to his place. I didn't know what he had planned, but I reluctantly allowed him to drive me over. Up until this point, I hadn't left the house, not even to go to work. We walked back to the spot where Mrs. Pritchard's remains were found and I stopped short. I stifled a sob as I stared at the spot where Missy and all her worldly possessions had been so disrespectfully dumped. Jake had been given permission to remove the crime scene tape, and after carefully clearing the area surrounding the grave, he'd created a memorial garden.

I stared in wide-eyed wonder at the stones that outlined the makeshift burial site. They were similar to the ones that he'd used to make a path to his front door. I also noticed a bird bath and a bright garden flag off to the right. I smiled knowing they must've come from his last flea market excursion that I'd missed.

"I can't put in all the plants I want to until the weather gets warmer, but I have plans to fill this whole area, including her original resting place, with as much color as possible."

"Oh, Jake," I cried. "It's beautiful. You didn't even know her and you've created such a lovely spot in her memory. I can't imagine when you were able to do this in such a short amount of time."

"I ordered a bench too," he added. "It'll be perfect over there." He pointed to a large tree that would blossom come spring. "I'm having something etched on the bench, Barbie."

"What's it going to say?"

His voice sounded hoarse when he said, "In loving memory of Melissa Kay Pritchard. Cherished and beloved mother of Kenny and Jonathan."

His eyes started to mist, as he recovered his voice and added, "And it'll have her birthday and the year of her death. Which is obviously the year she disappeared."

I reached for him, wrapping my arms tightly around his back. I buried my nose in his chest and inhaled his scent. Then something occurred to me. I pulled back abruptly and looked up into his face. His eyes were no longer misty but sharp and intent.

"How do you know Melissa Pritchard's birthday?" My voice held a note of skepticism I hadn't intended. "Or her middle name?" I didn't even know her middle name.

He frowned at me in a way that said I should already know the answer. "I asked Darlene's daughter. It was on the driver's license they found in her purse."

"Of course it was," I said with a laugh. "I should've guessed that."

Two nights later, Jake and I were on our way to The Lonesome Keg. His favorite country artist was playing and he didn't want to miss him despite my concerns about running into the two bikers he'd knocked out.

"Stop worrying, sweetheart," he said as he brushed off my apprehension and pulled me toward him. One of the benefits of his old truck was that it didn't have a console separating us. After snapping the lap belt around my lower abdomen, I pressed myself against him and appreciated the weight of his muscular arm lying heavy across my shoulders. "Besides," he'd told me while planting a kiss on my forehead, "you need to get out of your slump. It'll do both of us some good to get back to normal."

I thought he would find it amusing when I told him about the offer to return to my old job and be the star of a hospital reality series based on my reputation as a monster in the medical field. I detected a change in his demeanor, and when I looked up at his face, I thought I noticed a slight tightening of his jaw. I watched him swallow before asking, "Are you considering it?" I pulled back and he peered over at me before returning his eyes to the road. "Well, are you?" I couldn't tell if he was worried or agitated.

"Not even a little," I laughed.

He tugged me closer and whispered against my temple, "I'm glad."

Jake slowed down as we spotted an older gentleman wrestling a tire out of the trunk of his car that was parked on the shoulder of the road. His wife stood off to the side, her lined face compressed with worry. After passing them, Jake pulled over and put the truck in park. I didn't have to ask to know that Jake would insist on helping. I followed him and engaged the man's wife in conversation while Jake made quick work of getting the tire changed and returning the jack and flat to their trunk.

Once we were back on the road, it sparked a conversation about getting older. I told him about Fancy's comment to me the first and only time she'd come to the farmhouse to inquire about our father's coin collection.

"I never thought about it like that, but yeah, I guess we are approaching the fourth quarter." He laughed. "I'm even closer to it than you are, Barbie."

"Doesn't it bother you?" I wanted to know. It certainly had gotten under my skin. Or maybe it wasn't the comment so much as that it came from Fancy.

"Of course it doesn't bother me." He sounded happy as he tapped out an imaginary tune on the steering wheel with his left hand.

I fidgeted in my seat and reached for the radio dial. "Why not?"

"I've never been a big fan of football, but even I know the fourth quarter is where all the excitement happens."

WE ARRIVED at The Lonesome Keg and Jake parked in the same spot as before.

"Please tell me you're not anticipating a quick getaway this time," I begged half-heartedly.

He got out and came around to open my door. "I'm always prepared for a quick getaway, beautiful. But don't worry. Tonight will be fine."

I was surprised to see that Jake had called ahead and asked Mike to reserve the booth we'd shared the night of the fight.

"I didn't know The Lonesome Keg took reservations," I teased.

"They don't," he said as he ushered me into our booth and sat next to me so we could both face the stage.

We enjoyed a night of Dr. Pepper and an array of appetizers that was highlighted with live country music served up by Jake's favorite artist, Jay Drummonds. Though neither one of us were especially skilled in the dancing department, we braved the dance floor for a few of the slower tunes. And as the evening wound down, I couldn't help but smile at the grin that broke out on Jake's face when Mike introduced us to Jay during the break before his last set.

Jay had saved what I now considered our song— "Better Than This"— for this last set. I was happily drowning in the melody and lyrics when I detected a subtle mood change in the crowd. I looked to my left and couldn't stop the "Oh no!" that escaped my lips. "Jake…"

"I see them, Barbie. It's fine."

And to my complete and utter surprise, it was. The two rough-looking bikers who'd engaged Jake in a physical altercation mere months ago were politely paying their respects to us before setting up camp by the bar.

Was I in an alternate universe? What had just happened? I caught sight of Mike who was stationed across the room in his wheelchair. He'd watched and gave Jake a brisk nod before returning his attention back to the stage.

And just like that, I felt a shift in my universe as the last piece of the puzzle finally found its place and Jake's secret was secret no more. I could've been upset. Maybe I should've been, but I wasn't. And there was only one explanation for it. I was completely, hopelessly, and irreversibly in love with Jake Chambers.

I wouldn't ask him because I knew he would tell me when he was ready. And there was nothing like the sense of relief in knowing that when he did find the courage to fess up, it wouldn't be a game changer.

THE NEXT MORNING I met Darlene for breakfast before her shift at the gas station and told her my theory. Before she could comment, I asked, "How long have you known?"

She pierced a piece of country ham with her fork, and before bringing it to her mouth, confessed, "The morning I showed up at your house after you sewed him up. It was something he said at the breakfast table."

"Your tiddlywink moment?" I asked.

She nodded as she chewed. After washing her food down with a healthy swig of coffee, she asked, "Are you going to ask me what I know?"

"Nope," I assured her. "I'll wait for him to tell me."

"Good." She picked up and began to fumble with a jelly packet. "Because I don't like gossip and I already told you at Christmas you should ask him. Plus, I promised him I wouldn't tell you as long as he told you himself. I was about ready to give up on him but seeing how he's so in love with you"—she paused long enough to give me a dramatic stare—"and you're in love with him, I didn't want to interfere."

I grabbed the jelly packet out of her hand and easily pulled the plastic off. I handed it back to her. "I wonder how much Sheila knows," I pondered.

"You can always ask her." She spread her toast with grape jelly. "And you're not denying you're in love with him? Not going to accuse me of starting a rumor?" The sides of her mouth tugged upward in a mischievous grin.

"To quote the man I'm in love with, 'it's not a rumor if it's true.'"

CHAPTER 39

WHAT YOU SEE IS WHAT YOU GET

J ake and Henry showed up at my front door the next morning. Henry rushed past me to seek out Lady who was in his favorite spot chewing on a toy in the kitchen.

I was still in my pajamas, my hair was a mess and I had coffee breath. "To what do I owe the pleasure of this early morning visit?"

He planted a kiss on my lips before I could object. He held up a hammer with one hand. "I wanted to hang that picture in your bedroom before I left for Cleveland." He held up a neatly wrapped gift with his other hand. "And give you this since I won't be here for your birthday. I'm so sorry, Barbie. When I told the Leavitts I'd drive them to Cleveland for their family reunion, I didn't know it would end up being on your birthday."

Closing the door behind him, I took the present and held it up to my nose. "Smells yummy. Like bath bombs for my new tub," I guessed.

He laughed and said, "You can open it now, or on your birthday…"

"Or when you get back," I interrupted.

"Yeah," he said with a grin. "I was hoping you'd say that. We can go out and celebrate. I only brought it over this morning because I didn't want you to think I forgot. I'm leaving tomorrow afternoon but should be back sometime on Friday. Do you want to drive down to Greenville? Or maybe up to Asheville? To a high-end, upscale restaurant? I clean up real nice when I want to. I'll take you anywhere you want to go, sweetheart."

I set the gift on the mantel over the fireplace, and forgetting my coffee breath, leaned against him and looked up. "Greenville or Asheville? Like for the weekend?"

He kissed me on the lips, and ignoring my question, said, "I keep forgetting to hang that picture for you, but I can do it now before I go to work." He held up the hammer, smiled, and headed for the stairs.

I stood with my hands on my hips, watching him take two stairs at a time. "My coffee breath must be worse than I thought," I muttered to myself before following him. When I arrived at my bedroom door, I found Jake standing in the middle of my room, hammer in one hand and glaring. He pointed to my nightstand and said, "What is that?"

Puzzled, I looked past him and answered matter-of-factly, "My gun."

"What is it doing on your nightstand, Barbie?"

"I have it there in case I need it in the middle of the night. I thought you wanted me to protect myself."

I watched him take a deep breath, like I was trying his patience. "Honey, do you realize that if an intruder made it up the stairs without you hearing him, he could get to that gun before you? Someone could use it on you." Before I could answer him, he continued, "Or, if someone were to break into your house while you're not here, it'd be the first thing they'd steal."

"Oh, right," I agreed. Swiping my hand through my unruly morning locks, I admitted, "You're right. I should've put it in the nightstand."

"No!" he practically shouted. "I thought I told you to keep it attached to the back of your headboard. I even put the Velcro back there for you. This way you can easily reach behind you in a dark room without fumbling through a nightstand. Which would be the second place a thief would look. We went over this, Barbie."

He had told me and I'd forgotten. My first instinct was to apologize for not heeding his advice. My second instinct was to lash out in all kinds of ways.

For an assisted living facility caregiver you sure do know a lot about guns and thieving.

If you had any interest in being in my bedroom, you'd have already known I didn't remember about the Velcro behind my headboard.

If you had any interest in **me**, *you'd know that the last thing I wanted to hear when I asked you about your favorite flea market find was about the authentic lady's tea set you bought for your dead girlfriend, Emmy!*

"You know what?" I spat. "I'm not perfect. What you see is what you get. And what you see is a woman who has spent her adult life pulling bullets out of people. I was willing to accept your advice about being responsible for my safety. But you have no right to come into my bedroom and get angry with me for not doing it according to your standards." I narrowed my eyes at him, and his stance and expression appeared to soften.

Unfortunately, and without warning, a squelched insecurity I didn't want to face suddenly rose to the surface. I was slapped with the reality that the reason he hadn't taken our relationship into the bedroom was because he was still grieving a woman he'd been in love with. Jealousy was an ugly emotion, one that I'd not allowed myself to feel since I was a child when I'd begged for any scrap of kindness that had eluded me and was instead bestowed upon my ungrateful sister by our hateful grandmother.

The words were out before I could stop them. "I'm sorry I don't measure up to Emmaline, Jake. I don't know that I'll ever be worthy in your eyes of an authentic English Lord and Lady tea set with provenance. Or a tattoo above your heart for that matter. But I'm not trying to prove anything to you either. I don't have to." He looked perplexed, but I held my chin high and continued. "You know what? I take that back. I'm not sorry. I'll never be sorry for being me."

He threw his hammer on my bed and scratched the back of his head. "What does an English tea set and my tattoo have to do with anything? How did we go from gun safety to Emmy?"

I put my hands on my hips and very snarkily asked, "Seriously? You're going to ask me what Emmy, the perfect lady, has to do with this?" A thought occurred to me, and I smacked my hand against my forehead. "Oh. My. Gosh. I just realized you named my dog after your perfect lady, Emmaline!"

"Emmy *was* a lady, Barbie. What I can't figure out is why it bothers you so much."

I couldn't bring myself to accuse him of still being in love with her so I went with the next best thing. "I can only guess that you haven't tried to take anything further with me because I don't live up to a standard that she set."

He frowned and asked, "Why would I care what kind of standard Emmy would set?"

I waved my hand over the bed, and realizing my defeat and humiliation, evenly said, "Because you've never once tried to get me in bed."

It was his turn to get angry as his brows creased and he slowly walked toward me. "Is that what this is all about? That I haven't tried to sleep with you?"

I gnawed on the inside of my cheek, embarrassed to admit that what he said was true. I shook my head and looked away. "Forget it. Just forget it."

"No, I'm not going to forget it. What is it, Barbie? Do you think that I don't want you? Is that it?"

I kicked at the area rug. "It certainly appears that way."

"I haven't tried to get you in the sack and that's what you're basing this on?"

I looked at him and quirked my head to one side, giving him an imaginary eye roll that I was glad he couldn't see. "We've been together for months now."

"And you would've jumped into bed with me if I'd made the first move?"

This would be tough to answer, but I figured honesty was best. "Not at first," I admitted. "I wouldn't have. But enough time has passed that I'm beginning to think there's a problem."

His jaw was rigid and his eyes were blazing when he said, "You would have turned me down, but now you're mad because I'm respecting you?"

"Respecting me?" I huffed.

"Yeah, Barbie. That's what I've been doing—respecting you. Giving you time to mourn the loss of your marriage and Richard's death, the resurrected memories of Kenny's abandonment, finding out you're not an Anderson." He swiped his hand through the air. "Not to mention your crappy sister and her shenanigans. Not once did you give me any indication that I was invited up here."

I wouldn't look at him.

"Stubborn woman!" he yelled before stomping out of the room.

I closed my eyes. *What have you done, Barbie? You turned a small spat about gun safety into a blow-up about carnal desires.* I plopped down on the edge of the bed, and I put my head in my hands. *And you had to drag his dead girlfriend into it.* Just imagining a pretty Emmaline with a British accent to boot made me nauseous. I stood up when I heard him pounding back up the stairs. He flew into the room and grabbed me hard, pulling me tight against him. His mouth came crashing down on mine in a desperate fury I'd never felt from him.

He pulled back, breathless, his blue eyes startling in their intensity. "You know why I haven't tried to go further with you?"

I was shocked and dumbfounded and could only shake my head.

"Because when we make love, there is no going back for me, Barbie. I could give you a test run if that's what you want." He motioned toward the bed. "But I'm not about that. I've only ever had test runs. I want more. I want it to be permanent. And you're right about Emmy. I wanted to do it in a way she would've approved of."

I was right. Emmy was stuck somewhere in between us.

He reached behind him and pulled something out of his back pocket. "I've been carrying this around forever waiting for the right time. With it being so close to Valentine's Day I thought I'd wait a little longer. But I think we've both waited long enough."

He got down on one knee and opened a small box. A huge amethyst stone, which happened to be my birthstone and favorite color, encircled with dazzling diamonds winked up at me. "Marry me, Barbie. I'm in love with you, and I'm sorry I haven't told you before today. I want to make it permanent and forever. I don't need a test run. Say yes to spending the rest of your life with me."

If I could've made a list of possible reactions Jake could have to our first fight, a marriage proposal would not have been on it. I was stunned into silence as my eyes roamed between the sparkling purple stone and back to the icy blue eyes that held me prisoner as they begged for an answer.

"Marriage doesn't mean you'll spend the rest of your life together," I whispered, remnants of my failed union with Richard threatening to ruin the moment.

"It does to me, Barbie doll. It does to me." He slowly stood up and said, "I'm sorry for not telling you sooner that I'm in love with you." He looked a bit unsettled when he added, "I don't even know how you feel about me, Barbie."

"Really?" I cried as I flung myself into his arms. "You don't know how I feel about you? My outburst of jealousy didn't give you a hint?" I laughed as I stepped back to peer up at him. "I love you too, Jake. I love you with an intensity that frightens me. In a way that I never loved Richard." It wasn't easy for me to be this honest, considering he may never admit to loving me more than Emmy. But I wasn't going to let a ghost keep me from my future. "Yes. I'll marry you."

If this were a scene in a romantic chick flick, Jake would've slowly undressed me, carried me to the bed, and we would've made wild passionate love until dusk and then again until dawn. But, this was reality. I hadn't brushed my teeth, and he was late for work. He put the ring on my finger. It fit perfectly.

He stood back, looking slightly uncomfortable. "I have things to tell you."

I remembered his words the day I found Kenny's note beneath the floorboards of my new bathroom. *Mine's a long story that I haven't shared completely, Barbie, but I will one day.*

I smiled and said, "I know you do. But it can wait until you get back from Cleveland."

He shook his head. "No. It can't wait. I'm working a double shift so I can't come by tonight. I'll need to get some sleep because I'll be driving, but I'll come by here tomorrow before I leave to meet up with the Leavitts. We'll talk before I go."

We wanted to walk hand in hand down the stairs, but Jake was too wide for both of us to fit. So, being the gentleman that he was, he waved me in front of him and followed me down.

We stopped at the front door and he turned to face me. "I still don't see what Emmy has to do with us, Barbie. I told you before, you would've liked her. She was special, and you two would've had a lot in common."

I crossed my arms in front of me and gave him the benefit of looking him in the eyes. It's an honest person who can confess their humiliation, I told myself.

"This is hard for me to say, but I was jealous. Her name on your chest, the special tea set that you went out of the way to buy for her. I know I'm being ridiculous." I chewed on my bottom lip, and earlier moments of bravery were lost as I cast my eyes downward. "Being threatened by someone who's no longer here. But knowing you were in love with another woman…" I paused and looked up at him sheepishly. "Knowing that you'd still be with her if she hadn't died brought out an ugly green monster and I'm ashamed."

I expected him to understand. I expected him to tell me he forgave me and that he would never let Emmaline come between us. What I didn't expect was for him to burst out in a roaring belly laugh.

I took a step back, offended. "I don't see what's so funny, Jake. I'm admitting to being jealous of Emmaline, and you're making sport of it."

"Oh, baby. My sweet Barbie doll. You're so wrong about Emmy and me."

"You have her name on your chest, Jake!"

He stopped laughing and grabbed me by my upper arms. "Barbie, Emmy was special to me, but not in the way you think."

I tried to raise an eyebrow, but couldn't manage it.

"Emmy was a resident at the nursing home where I worked in Georgia. She was ninety-two years old, Barbie. She was a snooty old broad, but I loved her. I worked my way into her life and she wormed her way into my heart."

My mouth fell open, words lost in the silliness of my misunderstanding.

"She's the one who encouraged me to take the road less traveled. The road that led to you. And you're right. Her name is above my heart because she believed in me when I didn't believe in myself." He took a step toward me. "But the spot *over* my heart has been reserved for someone else."

Our eyes locked, mine blinking back tears of relief as he tapped his chest with his right hand.

"It's been reserved for you, Barbie. It's always been reserved for you."

CHAPTER 40

IS THIS SOMETHING YOU DO REGULARLY?

I slept like a baby that night. I could only pray Jake was getting a restful sleep as well, considering he'd be on the road soon. I'd already agreed to care for Henry in his absence so I would've been seeing him anyway before he left, but I knew the marriage proposal and my acceptance prompted an urgency for him to come clean with me before his trip to Cleveland.

I wasn't surprised when Henry showed up without him the next morning. He dropped his latest find on the floor and it landed with a thunk, prompting Lady to scramble toward him so she could smell it. I picked up the rusted canteen, and turning it over in my hands marveled, "I think you may have something old here, boy." I set it on the counter. "Looks like it could be Civil War era." I made a mental note to search the internet later to see if I was right.

I spent the rest of the morning cleaning, and well past lunchtime working on my latest project. I'd started gathering the few items of memorabilia I had from my father and grandfather. I was going to have the treasures mounted in a shadow box that I planned to hang over the fireplace. I heard Jake's truck and went outside to greet him.

He marched up the porch steps carrying Henry's food and favorite toys.

I leaned against the jamb of my front door, "You know I keep a supply of Henry's food. You didn't need to bring more."

"Just wanna make sure you have enough." He gave me a quick peck on the lips and I moved aside to let him in the house. I was following him into the kitchen when he called over his shoulder, "Are you going to keep Anderson or change your name to Chambers after we get married?"

The question was unexpected, one I hadn't considered.

He set Henry's things on the table and turned to face me. "You don't have to change your name if you don't want to, Barbie."

"I've already decided I want to spend the fourth quarter as your wife. So yes, I'll take your name, Jake."

His smile was instant and dazzling but quickly faded.

"What's wrong?" I moved toward him and watched as he bent low to scratch Lady under her chin.

He avoided my eyes, peering around my kitchen like he was looking for something. "We need to talk before I leave." He looked at his watch. "I overslept and didn't save a whole lot of time."

I grabbed his hand and pulled him into the living room, where I plopped onto my new couch. "I don't think this is going to be as horrible as you think it's going to be." I peered up at him and patted the seat beside me. He sat down, and leaning forward, rested his elbows on his knees.

"I told you I had things I hadn't shared with you."

I reached for one of his hands and held it tightly between both of mine. "Before you start, will you answer a question for me?" I scooted up closer to the edge of the couch so he wouldn't have to crane his neck to look back at me. "If you can answer this question honestly, I promise what you have to tell me won't be as awful as you think."

I saw the bob of his Adam's apple as he swallowed and said, "Okay, honey. Ask me."

I raised my chin slightly and locked eyes with him. "Did you have anything to do with what happened to Sheila's husband? The beating he took and his disappearance? I was your alibi that night, but something tells me you know more." I took a deep breath. "It couldn't have been a coincidence that I made an offhanded remark questioning whether or not abusers would continue to do so if they felt the kind of pain they inflicted." I licked my lips. "And Sheila's husband suffered the same fate she suffered at the end of his fist."

He disengaged my hands from his and stood up. He locked both hands behind his head as he paced back and forth. Blowing out a long breath, he confessed. "Yes, it was me. I did that to him." Before I could respond, he added, "And I'm the reason he left town. I told him if he ever went near her again, I wouldn't be so nice the next time."

"But you couldn't have done it!" I jumped up. "You were with me when witnesses said he left the bar. And you'd been at work for hours when they found him." I'd expected him to tell me he had someone, most likely the bikers at The Lonesome Keg, beat up Sheila's husband. Hearing him admit he was the actual perpetrator caught me by surprise. My forehead puckered in concentration as I tried to figure out how he could've been in two places at once.

He stopped pacing and stood with his fists clenched at his sides. After all this time and he couldn't conceal his anger toward the man. "I don't think one beating was enough payback for the physical and emotional agony he'd inflicted on Sheila for years, and I don't regret doing it."

"I abhor violence of any kind, but I get it," I reluctantly admitted. I was afraid to ask if my comment had influenced his decision to retaliate. "She was too scared to ask for help. He could've killed her that night."

Jake agreed then explained how the timing had been perfect. He'd already had something planned and my dinner invitation served up the perfect excuse to use the cheese grater so he could purposely injure his knuckles.

"Because you knew you'd do damage to your hand when you beat him," I'd interjected. "It was the perfect cover-up for when the detectives talked to us at Hampton House." He gave me an affirmative nod and continued with his explanation.

The two bikers had been waiting outside the bar for the man and had him in the trunk of their car before anyone knew he was gone. Jake hadn't left my house to go home and change before going to work like he'd told me. He'd already had his scrubs with him. Instead, he used the extra time to meet them at an abandoned house where he inflicted the same injuries on the abusive bully that Sheila had received. Plus a few more.

"They kept him at the house until I went to work and punched the clock. They dumped him behind the bar where they knew someone would find him after closing."

I tilted my head to one side and gave him an appraising look. "Thank you for your honesty."

He maintained a solid stance and crossed his arms. I could see the defiance behind his eyes as he prepared himself to share the rest of his story. I didn't give him a chance when I asked, "Is this something you do regularly? Mete out vigilante justice?" It was my turn to look worried. "Are you a violent person, Jake?"

He walked toward me shaking his head, "No, Barbie. Not at all. I'm not a bully and I don't look for a reason to hurt people." He took both my hands in his. "But, you should know right now that I will never stand on the sidelines and watch somebody I care about get hurt."

"You're lucky he didn't tell them it was you, Jake." I let go of his hands and walked to the front window. With my back to him I said, "You have a record. It could land you back in jail."

He walked up behind me and encircled my waist with his arms. Pulling my back against his chest, he caressed the nape of my neck with his nose, then his lips. "I wasn't stupid enough to let him see my face, Barbie."

I leaned back into him, the heat from his mouth spreading fire over my skin and burning its way down my spine. I repressed the urge to moan because I knew he had other things to get off his chest and didn't have much time to do it. There was so much I wanted to ask him, but it could all wait until his return from Cleveland.

"Barbie, I need to tell you what I came here to tell you," he whispered against my neck. A moan did escape my lips, but it wasn't one that inspired passion, but rather dread.

Fancy had just pulled into my driveway.

CHAPTER 41

I SHOULD'VE FIGURED IT OUT SOONER

I asked Jake to wait inside while I handled my sister. I let him know I had no intention of inviting her in and would get rid of her as quickly as possible so we could finish talking before he had to leave. I opened the door and walked out to meet her. She got out of her white BMW and was looking much better than the last time I saw her.

Before I could ask her why she was here, she held up a hand to stop me. "Please don't say anything, Barbie. I don't deserve one second of your time, but please hear me out."

This surprised me. "I'm not sure there's anything left for us to say to each other, Fancy."

"Barbara Jean, at least let me get the words out. You don't have to say a thing." Her tone held a note of sincerity that was foreign to me. I noticed she was holding a note or piece of paper of some sort. *Probably something from an attorney,* I silently mused. "Please, just let me talk so I can clear my conscience and I'll leave and you'll never have to hear from me again."

I was standing with my arms crossed over my chest. I lifted my right hand and waved it in the air. "Fine, but please make it quick. I have company."

"Is it Jake?" I was caught off guard by the question and her smile. It was one I'd never seen before. It was a smile that said she was happy for me. *Nah, you're imagining it.*

I approached her and paused on the top step of my porch, maintaining a stance that made sure she understood she wasn't welcome here.

She brushed a dyed blonde lock off her cheek and said, "I have no right to ask that after the way I treated you in front of him in the parking lot that day. I've come to apologize for that." She paused and pressed her lips together. After clearing her throat, she continued. "And so much more. The things I've done to you, the way I've treated you…it's unforgivable, Barbie."

I half-believed her. She must've been taking acting classes the past few months. I refused to ask where she was living. I didn't even want to know how she was doing. She sensed my reluctance to give her the benefit of the doubt. She wobbled toward me on her clunky heels. She had the piece of paper pressed firmly between her perfectly manicured nails. *You found a new man.*

Holding the piece of paper out to me, she said, "This doesn't even begin to come close to what I owe you, but I hope you'll accept it as the first of many payments and as an offer to repair the bridge I've burned. I hope you'll forgive me, Barbie."

I was hesitant to accept the proffered white flag, but my curiosity got the better of me. I unceremoniously took the piece of paper and unfolding it, realized it was a check made out to me.

She rubbed her hands together and looked around, deliberately avoiding my gaze. "Like I said, Barbara Jean, it's not close to what I owe you for what I did at the condo or the doctor's office, but I hope you'll see it as my genuine effort to repair things between us." Her eyes circled back to my feet. She slowly looked up to meet my shocked gaze. "If you ever have an occasion to come to Greenville, please call me. My new number is on the check." Her eyes glistened with unshed tears. "And Richard was never going to have his vasectomy reversed for me, Barbie. Not only did I never want children, but what would the chances be at my age that I'd be able to conceive?"

I could've rattled off the statistics but was still too stunned to respond to what appeared to be a sincere and heartfelt apology.

Seeking the comfort of escape from my possible rejection, she turned around and hastily walked to her car. I wasn't sure if she was for real, and therefore didn't know how to respond. I would have to wait this out to see if and where it might go. She was right about one thing. The check didn't come close to covering the items she'd sold from the condominium. But I had to admit, it was the first time I'd ever known her to not only offer what appeared to be a sincere request for forgiveness, but monetary compensation as well. *Would I get another check next month?* Only time would tell.

"Oh, Barbie, about calling you a snob." She had her car door open and was getting ready to slide behind the wheel. "I'm sorry for that." She gave a little laugh and said, "If you were a snob you wouldn't be dating Jake. That is his truck, isn't it?" She motioned toward Jake's pickup.

I re-crossed my arms, immediately on the defensive. "What is *that* supposed to mean?"

Her expression changed to instant regret as she held up one hand and said, "No! No, please don't take it that way. It came out wrong. It's just that I assumed when I saw him that day that he was a doctor. He was wearing scrubs and driving a Jaguar. And I did a little snooping, you know? Because I was curious about him. And it wasn't easy, but I found a Jake Chambers. And when I dug a little deeper, I found. Well, you know what I found."

I gritted my teeth, aggravated that she'd found it necessary to Google my man, my future husband. I hadn't even done that. I despised the lack of privacy the internet ushered into this age. "Yeah, I'm pretty sure I know what you found, Fancy."

"What I'm saying is, I admire you, Barbie. To think a bigwig surgeon like you would even consider dating a man who's spent almost half his life in prison says a lot about the person you are. And I'm sorry for never having seen that in you."

She gave me a halfhearted smile before closing her door and driving away.

"Barbie?"

I didn't turn around when I asked him, "How much did you hear?"

"The door was cracked. I heard it all." His voice was even, no hint of trepidation.

I swung around and offered a lopsided grin.

His expression was reserved. "You don't seem upset. How long have you known?"

I made my way across the porch and he held the door as I walked inside. "I figured it out at The Lonesome Keg. I should've detected it sooner, but I missed so many signs." We were now standing in my living room, the brilliant sun illuminating dust motes that danced between us. "It all started to come together when I saw the respect the bikers had for you that night. Especially after I noticed a prison tattoo on the back of one of their necks. I've seen plenty of them in the operating room. Were you in prison with them?"

My revelation didn't seem to put him at ease. He wasn't upset, but something was still on his mind. "No, I didn't know those guys in prison, and before you ask me, I wasn't part of the motorcycle gang that Mike mentioned before. But I worked for their leader. I eventually got caught and went to prison."

"Where you met Kenny Pritchard." It wasn't a question.

He didn't answer immediately. "Yes, where I met Kenny Pritchard."

"I don't know what kind of relationship you had with Kenny, but you were close enough that he told you about Pumpkin Rest. And a lot about his life here. About his mother leaving him. About his little brother, who is neurodiverse." I tucked a hair behind my ear. "About me. It wasn't a coincidence the night we watched Tootsie at your place that you pulled out my favorite candy, Peppermint Patties."

He inclined his head.

"Was your original plan to come here and pretend to be the long-dead Kenny Pritchard? Let's face it, I wasn't crazy. You looked like him, didn't you?"

"Honestly? I thought about it." He scrubbed his hands down his face and ran them back through his hair. "And yes, we looked almost identical in prison. Same build, same hair, same eyes." He motioned to his neck. "He even got a tattoo in prison that matched mine. We were always messing with the guards, even the other prisoners. They couldn't tell us apart after he got the tattoo."

"I've seen prison tattoos. I never realized you could get one as elaborate and detailed as yours."

He grabbed the back of his neck with his right hand. "You'd be surprised what you can get in prison, sweetheart."

I walked toward him. "There is so much I want to ask you."

He brought his arm down and gave me a curious look. "You're not mad?"

"No. I'm relieved. I don't blame you for not blazing into town and telling everybody you were in prison with Kenny. If we're being honest now, I'll tell you that it wouldn't have sat right with me. I would've avoided you like the plague." I made a rolling motion with my right hand. "You know, avoiding you would've been avoiding the reason behind Kenny's humiliating abandonment. I wouldn't have been prepared to face it, especially after what happened with Fancy and Richard. I probably would've run as far away as possible so I didn't have to."

Jake stood stone still, his expression closed up.

"You know the reason he left, don't you? Just like you knew he'd left the lunchbox beneath the floor. It's why you suggested I put in a whirlpool tub. It was the only way I'd ever take up those boards."

"Yes," came his tight-lipped reply.

I smiled. "Jake, I don't understand why you seem so tense. I'm telling you it's okay. I understand why you hid it from everyone. From me." A thought occurred to me. "How did you keep it from Sheila? She knew about your stint in Texas, but how did you hide your Florida prison record?"

He gave a slight shrug of his shoulders. "I didn't. She knew about it, because I told her up front. It helped that I wasn't applying for a certified position and came highly recommended from two other facilities. She ran it by the board and I was given a probationary period. The reason for my incarceration wasn't violent, and Jonathan had taken to me immediately. That also helped my cause. She told me she had her back to you when she pulled out my file to show you the day you fainted. She slipped it out without you noticing. She didn't want you to see it because she knew you disapproved of me and would've made a stink."

"I had no right to ask to see your file. It was a breach of ethics on my part." I swallowed my guilt and added, "Like sewing you up without reporting it." It was difficult for me, the rule follower, to admit that I'd had more than one lapse in judgment when it came to Jake. "And Sheila was right. I would've had you run off in a heartbeat." I looked up at him, embarrassed by my admission. "I'm not the same person I was when I first moved back here."

"I'm not the same person I used to be either."

"I know, Jake. That's why, when I figured it out, I didn't care." I looked up at the ceiling. "So much makes sense now. How you hadn't seen or even known about certain movies or pop culture. You missed out on so much."

He scratched at his jaw. "Yeah, that's for sure. I have a lot to make up for."

I reached for his hands and squeezed them tightly. "This isn't for today, but I hope you'll tell me about Kenny. Not for any other reason than to put some things to rest. Did you know Kenny well? I mean, you must have if he told you why he ran away and where he put the note he'd left me."

"Yes, Barbie. I knew Kenny well. I shared a cell with him for nineteen of the twenty-three years I spent in prison."

I stepped back and tilted my head to one side. "Something is wrong, Jake. You don't seem relieved at all to know that I don't care about any of this. I thought you would've been happy to know that there's nothing you can tell me that will come between us. I understand why you hid it from me. I'm telling you that from my heart." I let go of his hands and clasped mine together tightly. "The secret that you've been keeping is out. And it's okay."

He looked crestfallen. Not the expression I was expecting.

"Being in prison with Kenny is part of it, but what I need to tell you is much worse, Barbie." I watched him swallow and look away before bringing his eyes back to meet mine.

I tried to make light of the moment for his sake, knowing that no matter what he told me, it wouldn't matter. The corners of my mouth tugged upward forming a smile to let him know everything would be okay. "What is it then? What do you need to tell me, Jake?"

"Kenny was killed in a yard riot."

I laughed. "I already knew that! See, that wasn't so bad."

I'm sure the color drained out of my face when I heard his next words. "Yeah, but what you don't know is that I'm the one who killed him."

CHAPTER 42

DID YOU OR DID YOU NOT KILL KENNY?

To say my world, my entire universe, tilted to one side would've been an understatement. I wasn't sure I'd heard Jake right, but the pained expression on his face told me I had. I took a few steps back from him, pressing my shoulders against the front door. I closed my eyes and shook my head in denial. "No. Please tell me you're lying. Why you'd be lying, I can't imagine, but you have to be."

He walked toward me and softly grabbed me by my forearms. I opened my eyes and violently shook him off as I stepped away from the door, away from him. "Don't, Jake. Please don't. I need some space."

He took a few steps back and said, "Now that you know, I can explain."

"Explain? Explain what?" I was trying to keep my voice from rising. "That you shared a cell with Kenny Pritchard for nineteen years, sucked up every detail of his life, killed him, and then came rolling into town like you owned the place?"

He started to say something, but I interrupted. "Did cozying up to Jonathan lessen the guilt for killing his brother?" Another thought occurred to me as my anger increased. "The secret Pritchard recipe." I looked at the ceiling and threw up my hands in frustration. "How could I have been so stupid?" My eyes cut to his and I narrowed them. "That's the one thing he never told you. How to make the moonshine. But I told you. That's why you came here, isn't it? For a stupid recipe!"

"Barbie, no. You don't underst—"

I held up a hand and interrupted him. "Did you or did you not kill Kenny?"

There was a moment of hesitation before he lowered his eyes and confessed, "Yes. I did, Barbie. But—"

"You don't get a *but*, Jake. You've told me everything I need to hear." I crossed my arms and turned my back to him. "You should leave." There was an immediate and intense roaring in my ears as black dots bounced around the edges of my vision. I had to get rid of them and Jake before I could digest anymore. Before he could object, a loud banging on my door startled us both.

I hadn't heard a car pull up. I was shocked to see a local man, Travis Webb, standing on my porch. He was nervously rocking from side to side.

"I'm sorry to bother you at home, Doc, but you gotta come quick," he anxiously announced as I stepped out onto the porch.

In a haze of intense panic, he explained that there was a horrific accident at Pumpkin Rest's only intersection. I was closer than an ambulance and they needed me while they waited for help to arrive. They'd tried calling my phone but I hadn't picked up. I was still reeling from Jake's confession and couldn't remember where I'd left it. Thankfully, medical emergencies were my specialty and I was able to segue into trauma mode smoothly. I was grateful for the distraction of having something to do, but not the reason for it. An accident that couldn't wait for an ambulance was bad.

"I need to get my bag," I told Travis. "And I'll ride with you." He responded with a relieved sigh. I turned to go inside and practically bumped into Jake. He'd already retrieved my bag and handed it to me. I took it from him without comment, ran down the porch steps, jumped into the passenger side of Travis's truck, and didn't look back.

It was a nightmarish crash, and would sadly become the first one in Pumpkin Rest's crossroads history remembered for having two fatalities. It involved a semi-tractor trailer hauling heavy farm equipment that lost its brakes and t-boned an out-of-state SUV carrying a family of five. The mother and oldest son were killed immediately, while the rest of the family suffered life-threatening injuries. The youngest child's wounds were so serious, I offered to ride in the ambulance with him. Hours later, I found myself stranded at the hospital in the city with no way to get home. Grateful that I'd memorized her number, I used a landline at the nurses' station to call Darlene's cell phone and got her voicemail. I borrowed a computer to look up her house number and spoke to her husband. Darlene had been planning to fly out to Arkansas to be with their youngest when she had her first baby. The new grandbaby decided to come three weeks early. Darlene's son-in-law had called her right before the accident, prompting her to leave work early and get a ride to the airport. Her husband told me she'd left me a message on my cell phone while they were on their way. He offered to come get me, but knowing he'd already driven down to Greenville and back, I politely refused.

I could've put a down payment on another car with what I ended up paying a taxi to drive me home. I was just grateful to get a driver that didn't mind going so far off the beaten path. Even if I'd had my phone to request an Uber, I doubted they would've driven me all the way out to Pumpkin Rest. I compensated my driver well and dragged myself up to the front door. It was a good thing I kept an emergency credit card and a house key in my medical bag because I'd left my purse and keys at home. Jake must've anticipated how long I'd be gone because I found my porch lights and a few house lights on. I couldn't bring myself to appreciate the gesture.

Like a heavy cloud pregnant with rain, exhaustion like I'd never felt before descended, the weight of it threatening to topple me. After letting myself in, both dogs greeted me, in desperate need to go out. They followed me to the kitchen, where I opened the back door and told them, "You two come right back, okay?"

I finished changing out their water bowl and was about to set their food dishes down when I heard Henry scratching at the back door. After letting them in, I noticed my cell phone on the kitchen table, but avoided it. I'd snacked at the hospital while waiting for the taxi so, instead of food, I opted for a long hot shower. I refused to let myself think about Jake and his bombshell. After putting on my most comfortable pajamas, I headed for the kitchen and popped open a bottle of wine. I was getting ready to pour myself a glass, but I stopped to get something stronger. I headed for the pantry and came out with a jar of moonshine. I picked up my phone and headed for the couch.

I thought about calling Darlene but immediately dismissed the idea. The last thing she needed while welcoming a new grandbaby was my drama to ruin it.

I saw that I had a few missed calls from Jake. He'd left one message saying how sorry he was and that none of the things I'd accused him of were true. He also said if he hadn't already committed, he would've canceled his trip to drive the Leavitts to Cleveland, but he couldn't bring himself to disappoint them at the last minute. It was the one thing he said that I believed, and was secretly happy the Leavitts gave me a respite from the man who'd stolen my heart and then crushed it. Just like my father and grandfather had. Just like Kenny had. Just like Richard had. I was wrong when I'd told Darlene the only game changers would be if Jake turned out to be a serial killer or married. It turned out there was a third one. A man who murdered my first love, and then had the nerve to come masquerading into town as a good guy.

I woke up the next morning with the monster of all headaches. I spent the day on the couch, avoiding my cell phone and only got up to care for the dogs and relieve myself. I even stayed away from the kitchen, the thought of food making my stomach roil. I basked in my misery, letting the disappointments in my life morph into an endless pity party that failed to satisfy. I stayed like this for almost three days, even avoiding two calls from Darlene. She was none the wiser about my current predicament, and after hearing two joy-filled messages about her grandchild, I made the conscious decision to keep it that way. *Thank goodness I never had the chance to tell her about my acceptance of Jake's marriage proposal.*

By the end of the third day, my bloodshot eyes glared at the remote on the coffee table. I raised my arm in its direction in a feeble attempt to Jedi mind-trick it into leaping into my outstretched hand. When that failed, I decided it was time to switch tactics and rescind my invitation to my self-imposed pity party. I hauled my unwashed and ripe body to the kitchen and started pulling things out of my refrigerator. I whipped up breakfast for dinner and realizing I was famished, I barely stopped short of licking my plate clean. I took a shower, got dressed, and opened my laptop. I had a ton of emails to read through, including three more from the casting associate about the reality show. I deleted those without even opening them.

I tried to not think about Jake, but found it impossible. He was in my head, and no matter how much anger I dredged up, I couldn't seem to evict him. I turned my thoughts to Kenny instead and tried to remember how much I'd heard about his death. I knew he'd died in a prison yard fight, but couldn't remember if I'd known how. It would seem to be a detail I would've easily recollected had I known. The physician in me couldn't let it go. I had to see the official document that would provide the cause of Kenneth Pritchard's death. Deep down inside, I hoped Jake was lying to me, even though I couldn't fathom a reason why he would. I wasn't sure how I would go about requesting a 2010 autopsy report from a state penitentiary in Florida. I didn't have a clue how that would work or if there would even be an autopsy for a prisoner who'd died while in custody. I could've called in some favors, but that would mean dealing with professionals from my past. I preferred not to do that. I decided to enlist the help of family. Without needing to know why, Darlene's daughter, Danielle, told me she'd see what she could find out and get back to me.

I wish I could say I slept like a baby that night, but I didn't. However, I did get up the next morning with a plan. Jake would be home day after tomorrow and I didn't want to be here when he came for Henry. I enlisted one of Darlene's nieces to come stay at my house while I took a little trip out of town. She was more than grateful to get away for a few days, as she had college midterms coming up and needed a quiet place to study. My house was perfect.

I was packed and ready to leave when she arrived. After introducing her to Henry and Lady, and explaining their needs and Henry's peculiarity for bringing home presents, I showed her around the house. I told her that Jake would pick up Henry day after tomorrow and he would probably offer to take Lady home. I told her to let him know it wouldn't be necessary since she was staying to care for Lady until I got back.

"What if he asks me when that'll be?" she wondered.

"Tell him you don't know. You have my number and I've left you cash in case you need anything. If for any reason you can't stay longer, let me know and I'll get someone else to stay here."

She waved me off and said, "I can stay here as long as you need me to. It's only ten more minutes from here than my house to get to school. It won't be a problem."

I thanked her and bent low to hug the dogs goodbye, mourning the relationship dynamic that would be shifting thanks to Jake's revelation. I was walking out the front door when I spotted something on the fireplace mantel. I retrieved my birthday gift from Jake and handed it to Darlene's niece.

"I'm almost positive these are bath bombs. You can have them. I'm sure you'll want to use the tub upstairs."

She lifted it to her nose and smiled. "Smells amazing. You sure you don't mind?"

I shook my head and headed out the front door. I stood on the porch and inhaled the first breath of fresh air I'd had in days. I looked to my right, and my fury resurrected itself when my eyes landed on the housewarming gift from Jake. I dropped my bags on the deck and walked toward it. With a sudden strength I didn't know I possessed I picked up the bulky chair and threw it off the side of the porch and out of my sight. I heard it land with a crack. *Good, at least something else besides my heart is broken. Take that, Jake Chambers!*

I got into my Jeep and left Pumpkin Rest.

CHAPTER 43

I DON'T WANT TO BE RICH OR FAMOUS

I drove toward Greenville, not having a specific destination in mind, just an urgency to get as far away from Pumpkin Rest as possible. The irony of doing the exact opposite almost two years ago wasn't lost on me as I drove down familiar streets. I continued to avoid Jake's calls but knew that if I didn't answer when Darlene called, she'd know something was wrong.

After checking into a nice hotel, I walked around downtown Greenville and discovered a new restaurant. I treated myself to an early dinner, which was a waste of money since my lack of appetite had returned. I looked at my watch and wondered if I had enough time to retrieve my car from the hotel and drop in at my realtor's office to check on the status of my condominium sale.

To a stranger, I probably looked like a woman enjoying an afternoon to herself. It's funny how most of us make assumptions based on external appearances. It had been a deliberate effort on my part to climb out of bed and pull myself together this morning. I'd put on makeup and picked a favorite outfit to wear. Nobody I met in passing would know that inside I was crumbling. That I'd been devastated by one blow too many. That it was a tremendous effort to make myself do something that resembled normal.

After another glance at my watch, I deduced there wasn't enough time to walk back to the hotel for my car and get to the realtor who was closing in twenty minutes, so I hit the shops.

Two hours later, I walked out of the last boutique with three sweaters, two scarfs, gloves, earrings, and two sets of pajamas.

As I approached my hotel, I passed a woman pushing a grocery cart filled with her possessions. I stopped her and piled my bags on top of her cart. I pulled out my wallet and yanked out a couple of hundreds and handed them to her. "You can have what's in the bags and this too," I said while pressing the bills into her hand. Her mouth was still hanging open as she watched me walk away.

After closing the hotel door behind me, I fell face-first on the bed and thought about how life had tricked me. Again.

I must've dozed off because the next thing I remembered was automatically reaching for my phone. I saw that it was Dar, and took a deep breath, preparing myself to act as if nothing was wrong.

I was greeted with, "Finally, you answered! I was afraid I wouldn't get to say Happy Birthday."

Oh, that's right. Today was my birthday. I'd lost track of the days and hadn't even remembered it when I handed off my birthday gift from Jake to her niece.

I was glad to let Darlene ramble on excitedly about her new grandchild. She also touched on the accident in Pumpkin Rest, and as heartbreaking as it was, I was relieved to have something to talk about besides Jake. Unfortunately, my best friend knew me too well and it wasn't long before she asked me what was wrong. I tried to brush her off, but she wouldn't have it.

"Spill it, Barbara Jean Anderson. If you don't, I'll cut my trip short and come home tomorrow."

I knew she'd do exactly that, and like a dam on the brink of bursting, the events of the past week came flooding out. She didn't say a word as I told her everything that had transpired between Jake and me since I'd met her for breakfast. Our first fight, his proposal on one knee, my acceptance, Fancy's visit that prompted the conversation leading up to him knowing Kenny in prison. And finally, the coup de gras that delivered a death blow to my and Jake's relationship. I even admitted to asking her daughter to help me obtain Kenny's autopsy report.

"I can see why you ran away, Barbie. It's all too much. But I don't peg Jake as a murderer. I can't even imagine it. There has to be more to his story."

Even though she couldn't see me, I shook my head. "I don't know what else there could be to know, Dar. I flat-out asked him if what he said was true and he said yes."

"You must have some hope or you wouldn't have asked Danielle to track down Kenny's death records."

"Don't read too much into that. That's just me. I'm a stickler for detail, especially when it comes to this kind of stuff." I was sitting cross-legged on the bed and assumed a haughty posture before adding, "You know me, the Monster of Monteith Medical who has to cross every 't' and dot every 'i.'"

"Stop making fun of yourself, Barbie," she snapped.

"You know, when I was dealing with that accident, I wasn't thinking about Jake or Kenny or anybody. I'm wondering if a move back to Greenville might be something I should consider. If I immerse myself back into my work, it'll help me get over this."

"No, it won't!" she roared. "It'll only help you bury it. You have to deal with it now. Not run away from it, Barbie."

I felt my shoulders slump. I wasn't sure how much fight I had left in me, and certainly didn't feel like arguing with Darlene. So I changed the subject.

"Did *you* know about Jake killing Kenny, Dar?"

"Heavens, no!" she screamed through the phone. "He never shared that part of his story. I'm hearing it for the first time from you."

I started drawing patterns on the hotel bedspread. "Then tell me what you did know. What was your tiddlywink moment when you knew there was more to Jake than he was telling us?"

"It was when you told me the morning after you sewed him up that his nickname had been Doc." She excused herself to sneeze and then came back on the phone. "I didn't immediately remember what seemed familiar about that nickname, but then it came to me. You know that early on Kenny and I exchanged a few letters."

"Yeah."

"Kenny had mentioned in one that he'd been thinking of taking some college courses. He mentioned that another prisoner, Doc, was working on his degree. I didn't even know convicts could get college degrees but they can."

"Jake told me he had a college degree," I huffed. "At least that's something he hasn't lied about."

"I don't think he's lied about anything, Barbie. It's the exact opposite. Sounds to me like he's told you everything and probably even more than you need to know."

"He still hasn't told me why Kenny left, and I'm not sure now if I even want to hear it," I lied.

"From everything you've said, you didn't give him a chance to tell you." She snorted. "And you're a horrible liar, Barbie. Of course you want to know. You just don't want to face Jake to ask him."

After almost two hours, I insisted that Darlene go back to fussing over her new grandbaby. I ordered some snacks from room service that sat untouched, and fell asleep while watching one of those ridiculous medical shows that are way more exciting than real life.

I spent the next two days in Greenville, visiting some of my old haunts and reconnecting with a few friends. I was welcomed with open arms and felt a slight stab of guilt for fleeing town without so much as a backward glance. I'd checked in with Darlene's niece every day and wasn't surprised to hear that Jake had returned and done exactly what I'd thought he'd do. He offered to take Lady and asked when I would be back. After relaying to him what I'd told her to say, she hadn't seen him since. I asked if Henry showed up and she said no. That was curious, but I figured Jake was keeping him at home as a way to respect the space I needed.

I knew I couldn't stay gone forever, but prolonged my absence from Pumpkin Rest to coincide with Darlene's return. I didn't want to admit it, but I wanted her close by once I got back and faced reality.

It was my last day in Greenville and I found myself digging for the check that had been tucked away in my wallet. I still had reservations, but wanted to find out for sure. Before I knew it, I was yanking the phone away from my ear as Fancy's squeals of excitement blasted through the speaker. She thanked me profusely and agreed to meet me for lunch before I drove home.

I found myself staring slack-jawed at the woman sitting in front of me as we picked at our lunch at a quaint sidewalk café. It was my sister, but it wasn't my sister. Fancy was different. She'd changed. She babbled on about finally finding something she loved. Not someone, but something.

"You know I've never had a passion before, Barbara Jean."

Actually, I hadn't known that. I never knew my sister well enough to become acquainted with her interests beyond other women's husbands and their bank accounts.

Fancy had a glint in her eyes when she leaned over the table and said, "I've been told I have a presence."

"What kind of presence?" She had my curiosity piqued.

She sat back and took a sip of her wine. "In front of the camera."

I could see that. Fancy was attractive enough to be a model. "Modeling?" I asked.

"Well, yeah, that too, but I'd like to try out for local commercials. Like a spokeswoman for a car dealership or an insurance firm." She reached in her purse and removed a compact. "Just to start with."

"That's wonderful, Fancy. I'm glad you found something that makes you happy."

She powdered her nose and reapplied her lipstick. I don't know if it was the way she clicked the compact closed or how she looked at me, but my hackles were immediately raised. I'd seen the look before. She was plotting. I didn't have to wait long for her to vomit out the truth.

The casting associate who'd approached me about the hospital series had found my sister, and after realizing that a character like Fancy would be pure gold in a reality show, enlisted her help in trying to convince me to return to Greenville and my old job. Husband-stealing Fancy would be the perfect contrast to me, the Monster of Monteith Medical, the studious sister with a failed marriage and an ex-con boyfriend. If they dug deep enough, would they discover that Jake was responsible for Kenny's demise? There was no way I was going to let that happen. I would put a stop to this immediately.

I reached into my purse and took out Fancy's check. I knew then that the person trying to persuade me must've given Fancy some compensation for her part in trying to get me on board. Well, it had failed. I placed the check on the table and said, "This stops here. I'm not cashing it because you're going to need it more than me."

"Don't be ridiculous, Barbara Jean. We can both be rich and famous."

I shook my head. "I don't want to be rich or famous, Fancy. And for the record, I've researched the person who keeps hassling me. She's a nobody, a wannabe with some cash in her pockets. Why she would waste it on you, I have no idea. I don't know how many times I have to tell myself I'm done with you, but now I can say with certainty: This is our final goodbye."

If looks could kill I would've been instantaneously vaporized from the face of the planet.

"Tell your contact to stay away from me and my life or I will get an attorney involved and sue for invasion of privacy and harassment." I stood up and scooted in my chair as I repressed the urge to give vent to a few choice words. She stood up too and threw her napkin on the table.

"You ruin everything, Barbara Jean. You always have! I take back my apology because I didn't mean it. You are a snob and I'm glad I trashed your condo before I moved out."

I found her last comment about my condominium confusing, but ignored it as I turned my back on her and walked away. My first instinct was to call Jake and tell him all about it. But I could no longer do that. Because Jake had murdered my Kenny.

CHAPTER 44

LET'S GO GET OUR MEN

This wouldn't be the first time I drove away from Greenville convinced I was finished with my sister, but it would undoubtedly be the last. The queen of second chances had finally run out of free passes. I had none left to give.

I would return home, visit with Jonathan and Cindy on Jake's days off, and possibly increase my hours at the clinic. I no longer had my renovation to keep me busy, but I did have a county full of Darlene's relatives that treated me as one of their own. I'd survived a broken heart before. I would survive this one too. I would find something else to occupy my time. For some odd reason, I'd had Grandma Dicey on my mind recently and wondered if she would let me record her memoirs. She had a fascinating history. One that I was convinced would be a best seller. I had no clue how to write a book, but I could find someone that could.

I showed up at my realtor's office, and after spending only a few moments with her and insisting she come clean, the meaning of Fancy's last comment became increasingly clear. Fancy had moved out of my home but hadn't left it in the pristine condition I'd been led to believe. She'd done the opposite and had gone out of her way to make it as unlivable as possible. I listened in stunned disbelief as the realtor described the lengths the last tenant, my abhorrent sister, had gone to deface my place. Fancy had literally taken an ax or crowbar to every tile, every countertop, every wall. She poured paint on the carpets, hardwood floors, and cabinets. And that was only the visible damage. She didn't even try to hide the empty five-pound bucket of hydraulic cement that she'd poured down my drains and toilets. I was told it was a quick-drying type that ruined all the internal pipes in the condo. It was a miracle it dried quickly enough that it didn't leak into the building's plumbing system.

"How did I not know about this?" I was feeling flushed, but I didn't know if it was from fury or embarrassment.

The realtor leaned across her desk and whispered, "I wasn't supposed to tell you, but you do own the property, and I told him that if you asked, I would have to be honest."

"Who is he?" I needed to ask. But I already knew.

She fidgeted nervously in her seat and said, "Mr. Chambers called me a few months back. He told me that you might have a situation with getting your sister removed from the residence. He anticipated that she might not be so nice about leaving. He asked me to notify him if she left the condo in anything less than perfect condition. And you've obviously found out that she did."

I was speechless and could barely choke out a question. "Jake paid for the repairs?"

"Paid for the repairs is putting it mildly," she informed me. "He shelled out a small fortune. I don't know if you intend to pay him back, but there's no way your profit on a sale will cover his expenses."

I barely heard her as she launched into a professional spiel about having found potential buyers. Afterward, I drifted out to my car in a fog, a state of befuddlement tagging along for the lengthy drive home. I'd given Darlene's niece a heads-up about my return and found her and Lady sitting on the front porch when I pulled up.

We chatted for a few minutes at which time she told me she would dog-sit for me whenever I needed her. I told her I appreciated the gesture. I was almost inside the door when she called out to me.

"Oh, I almost forgot! Aunt Darlene called me and wanted me to tell you she wouldn't be back for another two days. Something about you needing to take care of something on your own."

Of course she did. I felt my insides wilt a little.

"And that gift you told me I could use." She opened the car door and tossed her bag in her car. "Not a bath bomb, but it was in a box that came from a store that sells them so I can see why you thought that. I left it on your dresser." She waved before climbing inside and said, "And I didn't read the note that was with it."

I avoided my bedroom by spending the next thirty minutes sitting on the living room floor, frolicking with Lady. Rolling around with her was good medicine. My mood lifted and I charged up the stairs, squealing as she nipped at the back of my heels.

I picked up the box and sat on my bed. The paper had been torn off, but the box revealed the name of the store. I lifted it to my nose and inhaled. He must've gotten it from one of the many birthday parties they'd had at Hampton House. I began to envy the woman who'd actually received fancy bath soaps before giving the empty box to Jake. It would've been easier for me to dismiss a gift that could be swallowed up by a drain.

I carefully lifted the lid and looked inside. There was something wrapped in tissue paper and a note had been tucked in next to it. I took out the note. It wasn't a birthday card, but a white piece of paper folded in half.

Dear Barbie,
Birthdays should be special. I wanted to celebrate yours by showing you how much you mean to me. The only way I could think to do this was by giving you something that holds the most value to me. Other than you, this is what I cherish most, and because of that, I want you to have it.
Love,
Jake

I willed my eyes to stay dry as I set down the note and pulled out Jake's most cherished possession. A forty-five-year-old baseball with the signature of a boy who filled up his life with more regrets than victories.

I lay back on the bed and screamed at my ceiling. "Why are you doing this to me, Jake? Why did you make me fall in love with you?" I cried.

As if to answer my question, my phone vibrated in my back pocket. I lifted my hip high enough to retrieve it and saw that it was Darlene's daughter, Danielle. I quickly sat up, and after collecting myself, answered.

She explained that thanks to a good friend connected to the prison system in Florida, she was able to have Kenny's records located and sent priority mail. She didn't answer me when I asked if it was legal and whether or not she could get in trouble, but instead got directly to the point.

"I have all of Kenneth's medical records, Aunt Barbie. Not just the autopsy report. They've got everything here from when they dispensed his first aspirin up until he died."

I asked her to please skip to the autopsy findings. After listening to her recite the medical examiner's report word for word, I had to shake my head to clear it. She must not be reading it correctly, I assumed.

"You're sure? He didn't die from a stab wound?"

"No. It says he died from an infection." She went on to read the exact medical terminology. It was definitely an infection.

Jake killed Kenny by giving him an infection in a prison yard fight? That can't be right.

Before I could tell her she was missing something, she said, "Oh, wait. There is something here that says he was admitted for a stab wound a few weeks prior to his death. But it was superficial. Looks like the wound didn't kill him, but the infection did."

"That makes more sense," I told her.

"I'm not an expert, Aunt Barbie, but from reading this, I'd say the prison infirmary was negligent."

Lady jumped on the bed and I absently stroked her with my free hand. "It's impossible to say. He could've resisted the antibiotics. He might not have told them it was bothering him until it was too late. It might not be negligence on the prison's part."

"I don't know if this is important to you or not, but it also says that Kenneth insisted that it was an accident. Sounds like he didn't want whoever did it to get in trouble."

I couldn't get off the phone fast enough. Jake's stab wound hadn't killed Kenny. An infection had, but he was still holding himself responsible. Just like he still carried the grief of being ashamed of his elderly parents when he was a child. *Oh, Jake. We both have so much healing to do. Please forgive me for ignoring your phone calls.*

I realized that I hadn't heard from Jake since before he got back from Cleveland. I only knew he'd returned because Darlene's niece told me when he'd come for Henry.

Tossing my phone aside, I ran down the stairs with Lady at my heels and grabbed my keys off the coffee table. She followed me out to my Jeep and I let her jump in on my side and make her way to the passenger seat. "C'mon, girl. Let's go get our men."

I backed out of the driveway, and as I started to pull away, I glanced over at my house. The solitary red Adirondack chair mocked me. I guiltily chanced a peek at the one I'd left sprawled and broken on the ground beside the porch, but it was gone.

The minute I pulled up to Jake's house, I knew something was wrong. I immediately sensed his absence. I jumped out of my car without shutting the door, Lady following behind me.

"Don't panic. Don't panic," I told myself. "His truck is gone but he's probably at work."

I started calling for Henry, but he didn't come. I ran to the far side of the small house and saw that the used trailer he'd bought to haul his motorcycle was also gone. I stopped dead in my tracks and stiffly turned around to look at the side porch where Jake had built a ramp so he could keep his motorcycle out of the weather. A sliver of fear made its way down my spine. No truck. No trailer. No motorcycle. No Henry. *You're reading too much into it. He's probably taken a few days off and took his motorcycle and Henry on a little getaway.*

I ran up the side porch ramp and around to the front of the house. I peeked in the front bedroom window. No furniture. I ran to the front door to open it, but it was locked. I then looked in the living room window and a brutal reality landed firmly in my stomach. The room was bare. I turned around, pressing my back against the window and slowly sank to the porch. My heaving sobs tapping out a rhythm that could only equate to devastating grief. I felt Lady's wet nose sniffing at my neck and I grabbed her tightly, burying my tears in her fur.

I was too late.

Jake was gone.

CHAPTER 45

WHY CAN'T YOU JUST LOVE HIM?

M y grief was excruciatingly intense. The heaviness in my chest pressed down like a pile of boulders. Not even Lady's gentle nudges and licks could relieve my heartache. I stood on shaky legs and used the sleeve of my blouse to wipe my face. I would go home, collect myself, and call him.

I was halfway to my Jeep when Lady took off down the driveway. When I realized where she was heading, I started to cry again. Jake's truck came into view and was pulling up on the side of his house. The broken Adirondack chair peeked up over the edge of the bed and he was towing an empty trailer. Henry was sitting next to him in the front seat as Lady ran alongside them. Apparently we were both anxious to get back to our men.

Jake smiled at me and instantly noticed I'd been crying. He made quick work of parking and getting out of his truck. He stalked toward me, his expression concerned. I charged toward him and jumped on him, almost knocking him over. I wrapped my legs tight around his waist and showered him with kisses. He managed to keep his balance and held me in place.

"I'm sorry. I'm so sorry, Jake. I didn't give you a chance to explain. And I've been ignoring your calls. Please forgive me. Tell me it's not too late for us. Tell me you didn't take the chair back because you no longer want to be with me." I knew I was babbling, but I didn't care.

"Whoa, whoa, Barbie. It's okay, honey. I took the chair so I could fix it."

I slowly disengaged my legs from around his waist and my arms from around his neck. Looking up at him, I confessed, "I saw that everything was gone, including Henry. And when I looked in the window, I saw your furniture was gone. Why is your furniture gone, Jake?"

He gave me a half grin. "Because I'm sanding the floors and most of it is stacked up in the kitchen and on the back porch." He turned around and motioned toward the empty trailer. "And I just dropped my bike off. It needs some work."

"I was so scared you'd left. I shouldn't have cut you off when you told me what happened. You were trying to tell me you killed Kenny, but that it was an accident and I wouldn't let you get a word in."

He stared down at me, his eyes serious. "It *was* an accident, Barbie. In a prison yard fight, it's every man for himself. I had a shiv and felt someone at my back. I turned around swinging. I didn't know someone had tripped Kenny and he'd fallen against me. I got him right in his thigh as he lost his footing."

"I saw the ME report. The wound didn't kill him, Jake. It wasn't life-threatening. He got an infection that killed him."

"An infection he wouldn't have gotten if I hadn't caught him with my shiv, Barbie." His eyes flickered with regret. "I'm responsible for his death."

"But it wasn't deliberate, Jake. You didn't try to kill Kenny." He looked at the ground and I grabbed his face with my hands, forcing him to meet my eyes. "I understand why you thought you needed to confess this. But it wasn't your fault Kenny died."

His voice was husky. "I didn't want anything to come between us, Barbie."

"And this won't, Jake. I don't hold you responsible, and Kenny didn't either."

"Can you love somebody like me, Barbie doll?" His mouth was set in a hard line as he waited for my answer.

"It's too late, Jake. I already do."

He asked me to wait while he went inside to get something, so I sat on the front porch steps. He returned moments later and took a seat beside me.

"When Kenny died, I got his belongings. There wasn't a whole lot, but the reason why he left you is in here." He held up a worn envelope. Reaching into it, he took something out and pressed it into my hand. It was a Civil War coin.

"Is this the piece from my father's collection?" I asked incredulously. His answer was a nod. "Kenny stole it from my grandparents' house?" He shook his head and launched into a shocking explanation that in the end made so much sense. My father and Kenny's mother had shared a secret.

Missy Pritchard had been a real beauty, and when she moved to Pumpkin Rest, had all the boys' heads turning, including my father's. But Missy had a hankering for older bad boys, and she only had eyes for one. Kenny's dad. My mild-mannered and quiet father had pined after her for years, and handled it stoically when she got married. Missy's announcement that she was pregnant prompted my father to make plans to leave Pumpkin Rest.

About that time, Mr. Pritchard left town to deliver his illegal moonshine, was caught, arrested, and thrown into jail. Missy couldn't come up with the bail so he was stuck in a county lockup two states away. My father wanted to leave but felt bad knowing that Missy was at the end of the road, alone and pregnant. Mr. Pritchard was several years older than my father, so they were never friends, but Dad thought he should do what he could to help Missy out in her husband's absence. He found her one day, crying on her back porch. She'd just discovered that she wasn't pregnant after all. That she'd never been pregnant. It had been a false alarm. It was especially upsetting because she'd lost her mother a few months earlier.

Putting aside his feelings for her, my father decided she needed a friend. He continued to do what he could to help her in the wake of her husband's absence. She was still reeling from the loss of her mother, a husband in jail with no way to communicate with him, and a false pregnancy. My father was mourning the loss of the one girl he'd loved since she moved to Pumpkin Rest. Before they could stop themselves, they turned to each other. Neither one of them ever intended for it to happen, but it did. Then a telegram arrived that said Mr. Pritchard had been released and would be on his way home. My father asked Missy to leave with him, but when she refused, he knew it was time to say goodbye. He saw her one last time before he left, and it was to give her his favorite and most treasured Civil War coin. He let her know how valuable it was and told her to hold on to it in case she ever needed it.

It took Mr. Pritchard longer to get home than he'd anticipated, and during that time, Missy began to suspect another pregnancy. She'd never told anyone but my father that she wasn't pregnant the first time, and in the end, it was a good thing because Missy was carrying my father's child. When Kenny was born after his supposed due date, no one suspected a thing because, for all they knew, Missy had been very newly pregnant when Mr. Pritchard left for that moonshine run. Kenny had been a twelve-pound baby, only making it more believable that Missy had carried him past her due date.

"Are you telling me that Kenny was my half brother?" I practically screamed. "And nobody knew or suspected?" Without giving him a chance to answer, I bombarded him with more questions. "Did Kenny know?" I cried. "And if so, how did he find out?"

"I'm getting to that, Barbie."

We were still sitting on the front porch steps and I started nervously drumming my foot against the wood deck, as Jake continued to reveal the reason behind Kenny's suspicious and abrupt disappearance from my life.

Eventually, the Pritchards' marriage started to deteriorate. Mr. Pritchard was drinking the moonshine faster than he could make it, and he started selling off his land to my grandfather to pay the bills. It got worse after Jonathan was born and they found out he had developmental issues.

He discovered Missy one day, sitting on the edge of their bed crying. She had something pressed between her fingers. It was the Civil War coin my father had given her. She'd kept it hidden from Mr. Pritchard, afraid he would sell it if he discovered its value. He demanded to know where she got it. One thing led to another, and in a moment of hastily exchanged words, Missy Pritchard let it slip that she should've run off with my father.

That was when Mr. Pritchard discovered that he was not Kenny's biological father. He'd never been a warm or caring father, but after discovering Kenny wasn't his child, he became angry and resentful. And as his biological son continued to show signs of being developmentally challenged, Mr. Pritchard became increasingly abusive to Kenny.

"Did Kenny ever tell you what his parents fought about the night she supposedly ran off?" Jake asked me.

I shook my head, finding it hard to believe he hadn't shared. "No."

"He heard his mother crying and asking, 'Why can't you just love him?' Kenny thought she was talking about Jonathan and his handicap. He surmised years later that she must've been talking about Mr. Pritchard's inability to love him, not his little brother. He went to bed that night thinking it was just another fight. But in reality, it was a fight that sparked a rage dark enough for Mr. Pritchard to kill her and make up a story that she'd run off."

"So, he killed her, tossed all of her belongings in a grave—except her apron and change purse—and found and held on to my father's coin. Why?"

"You know why." I looked over at him and saw a vein pop out on his neck.

When I didn't respond, he continued, "He waited until the day he could use it against the boy he'd grown to hate. Why do you think he never gave Kenny a hard time about hanging out with you?"

I was at a loss and shook my head.

"Because he wanted you and Kenny to fall for each other so he could rip any smidgen of happiness out from under him."

I jumped up and looked down at Jake. "It's why he wasn't mad the night he caught us together. All I can remember is that evil, maniacal laugh when he came home. It's because he was glad. Oh, my poor, sweet Kenny."

"After you left he gave Kenny the coin and told him he'd just slept with his sister. It was as if he'd spent all those years, waiting to ambush a kid's heart. And the sad part was, Kenny loved him in spite of his cruelty. Kenny got a punch in the face for calling him a liar. The old man tossed the coin at him and told him he could ask his aunt. Pritchard knew his wife had been exchanging letters with her aunt because he'd found and burned them."

Jake reached into the envelope and took out a picture. It was of a toddler sitting on his mother's lap. Missy and Kenny.

I brushed away a tear and stared at the photo. "He was so little and innocent then. Did he find her, Jake? Did he find his aunt Esther?"

He gave a little chuckle. "Yeah, he found her, and she relayed the story I just told you. She's also the one who gave Kenny this picture because she took it. And her name wasn't Esther Agnis like the police records showed. There is no Esther Agnis."

I turned to look at him, momentarily dumbfounded. "Then who was she?"

One corner of his mouth dipped down wryly. "Sister Agnes. She was a nun and whoever the idiot was that took her call, misheard her and wrote down Esther Agnis."

"A nun? I never knew Kenny had an aunt who was a nun!"

"Neither did he until his father told him. All he got from him was that she liked to take pictures, her name, and the city from the postmark on the last letter she'd sent to Missy. It took Kenny almost two years to find her, but he did. He tracked her to a church in Fort Lauderdale, Florida. She was temporarily assigned there until they could figure out a place for her."

"Why did they need to find a place for her?"

"She was losing her eyesight. It was a shame because after he'd tracked her down, he found out she was a very talented photographer." He motioned to the picture I was still holding. "She took that one. Kenny told me she had a pile of photographs she prayed over. She called them her unanswered prayers."

He stood up and took me by the hand. "If you're wondering, she confirmed what Kenny's father had told him. Missy had written to her and told her about the false pregnancy and then getting pregnant by your father. As the years went by, the letters became sadder. Missy confessed that, in hindsight, she should've left with your father, but she was still in love with her husband back then. Sister Agnes told Kenny how sorry she was that she didn't do more to find out why her niece had stopped writing. It was about the time her eyesight started failing and she had to rearrange her life to deal with that."

"It all seems so surreal, Jake." I blew out a long breath. "Was I right? Had he written to me? Did Kenny ever tell you if he tried to write?"

"Yeah, Barbie, Kenny wrote to you. You were probably right in assuming your grandmother must've come across that first letter and never let you near the mailbox again."

I didn't have the strength to muster up more anger at Juanita Anderson, so I asked a question instead. "Did he learn anything else from his aunt? Anything useful?"

Jake's expression closed up. "Kenny told me that before he left Pumpkin Rest, he went to church every Sunday morning and again on Wednesday night."

"True," I agreed. "We both did."

"He remembered that Abraham was married to his half sister, Sarah. And he asked his aunt if it would be okay with God if someone nowadays wanted to marry their half-sibling."

Oh, Kenny. Even after two years away from me, you still wanted me.

"When he didn't get the answer he wanted, he knew he would never see you again."

CHAPTER 46

WE COULD'VE BEEN TOGETHER

"I need to know everything, Jake. Tell me more."

He took me by the hand and we started walking, Lady and Henry in tow.

"When Kenny left Pumpkin Rest, he headed in the wrong direction. His father, or the man he thought was his father, either deliberately sent him on a wild goose chase, or his aunt had been at a convent somewhere in Alabama before being sent to Fort Lauderdale. The only clue he had was her name, Sister Agnes, and that she always had a camera strung around her neck. She'd visited Missy only once, and that was when she met Kenny's dad and took the picture I showed you."

Jake continued to describe Kenny's long journey and how he eventually found out his aunt was in Florida. He met up with a traveling carnival in Jacksonville and hung with them for a while and checked with every Catholic church along their route. He became friends with a guy about his age, and after discovering the kid was nothing but trouble, he took off and ended up in Fort Lauderdale. He found his aunt and the sad truth about what his father had told him. Kenny didn't know what to do with himself after that. He was torn.

"He knew he couldn't be with you. Which is ironic now that you know you're not an Anderson. And he knew that as cruel as his father was, the rotten SOB loved Jonathan and would never hurt him. So he wandered around, struggled with his future. He stayed in one place long enough and mailed you a few more letters, that time giving you an address to use. But you never did and we both know why."

I swallowed a huge dose of regret and grief. Tucking a stray hair behind my ear, I whispered, "He could've come home. We could've been together."

"Yeah, but he still believed you were his half sister, Barbie."

When I didn't reply, Jake continued with the rest of his story. It turned out that a year or two later, Kenny ran into the guy from the carnival who'd told him he was in a motorcycle club, and if they accepted him, Kenny could earn good money. So, he got himself a used bike, joined up, and before he knew it he was part of something he didn't know how to get out of."

"Did he know Mike from The Lonesome Keg, like you did?" I wanted to know.

"He did. The leader of the motorcycle gang owned the bars where Mike worked. Before you ask, Kenny and I had never crossed paths. Remember, I was in prison in Texas about that time."

"You didn't meet Kenny until you went to prison?"

"Right," he admitted. "But, we'd heard about each other in passing because we looked so much alike. If it weren't for this"—he pointed to his neck tattoo—"some people couldn't tell us apart. When doing her search, if Sheila had brought up our most recent mug shots instead of our original ones, because you know they get periodically updated in prison, you'd think you were looking at brothers. You weren't crazy, Barbie, and I'm sorry for anything that made you think you were."

I waved him off. "It's okay. I knew I wasn't crazy. I know it's scientifically proven that total strangers can pass for twins. Everybody has a doppelgänger out there somewhere." I gave a thoughtful pause, slowly digesting the onslaught of information. "I know Kenny went to prison for murder, but…"

"Kenny didn't murder anyone, Barbie!" Jake barked. "Sorry, didn't mean to yell, but Kenny wasn't a murderer. He was railroaded because he happened to be there when his gang and a rival gang started fighting. Yes, he defended himself, but he didn't kill anyone. Three men died and the law rounded up everyone involved in the fight and the prosecutor threw the book at everyone. His trial was a sham."

I would never know if what Jake said was true or if he was valiantly defending a guilty Kenny. "I was going to ask what you did to land in prison with Kenny in Florida? You told me before that you weren't part of the gang but you worked for their leader."

Jake described how he fell into criminal activity. It turned out that his nickname, Doc, hadn't been because he was a Dr. Pepper addict. That night at The Lonesome Keg, Mike thought fast when he made up that story. All the other things Mike told me were true, except for one. Jake earned the nickname Doc because he was a thief. A safecracker. Jake explained to me that anybody could open a safe with a crowbar. If not a crowbar, they could blast it open. But when they needed the job to be done quietly with no proof that it had been compromised, they asked for Jake. His tool? A stethoscope. Thus the nickname Doc. Back then, everyone had the safes with tumblers and dials that required a stethoscope or other type of sound-magnifying device to crack. Jake would get in and out with the safe's owner being none the wiser.

"Okay. What did you steal and how did you get caught?"

He rolled his eyes. "I had a partner back then. We broke into the home of a guy who'd been laundering money for the criminal elite without any traceable evidence. We'd gotten a tip that he temporarily, and stupidly I might add, transferred the money to the safe in his home. We broke in and took it."

"And got caught?"

"Not right away. My idiot partner was brought in on some other more serious charges and rolled on me as a bargaining tool to have his sentence reduced. The police raided my house."

I felt like I was watching a real-life crime drama. "And found the money?" I asked breathlessly.

"No. They never found the money, Barbie. But they did find a crapload of other things I'd stolen. Jewelry, antiquities, lots of stuff. I was just as stupid as the guy with the safe. I normally unloaded my hauls immediately, but I got caught red-handed."

"Whatever happened to all that…?" I didn't have to finish the thought. "You've kept it hidden for all these years, haven't you?"

His back straightened. He squeezed my hand tighter before answering. "Yes."

"It's how you paid to have my condo restored after Fancy trashed it. You're the reason Jonathan and Cindy are at Hampton House. She doesn't have a benefactor, does she? It's been you all along?"

"I promised Kenny before he died that when I was released I would make sure Jonathan came back to Pumpkin Rest. I made it happen when I was still in Georgia."

I didn't ask but wondered if Sheila knew and if it influenced her to convince the board to let Jake work at Hampton House. "But you were in prison for twenty-three years, Jake. That seems excessive for a jewel thief."

"Barbie, when you're in a hostile environment like prison, you do anything you can to survive. I'm ashamed to admit that I did things while incarcerated that kept getting my sentence extended."

I listened in a state of shock as Jake explained the prison hierarchy and the man who ran the place. It wasn't the warden like I'd assumed, but another inmate. The bar-owning leader of the motorcycle gang was eventually arrested and ended up on death row. He ran the prison until the day he died by lethal injection.

"He was a bad guy, a diabolical guy, but he was also fair, and as much as I didn't want to, I respected him," Jake confessed. "Everyone had jobs. I'd rather not tell you what mine was, but let's just say it relates to how skillfully I messed up Sheila's husband." I cringed, and he quickly added, "I'm sorry, Barbie, but it was a matter of survival."

"It's okay. But tell me how you came to respect this horrible man who made you do those kinds of things."

"I already told you how I'd done some jobs for him before we ended up in the same prison. He'd heard about the heist I'd pulled off and knew a lot of money was unaccounted for."

"How much?" I interjected.

"One point six million."

I'm certain my mouth fell open.

"Anyway, the first thing he did was call a meeting and asked me where I'd hidden the money. You've got to understand, this guy had men everywhere who would do his bidding. He could verify if I was telling him the truth. I had two choices. Tell him the truth and say goodbye to my haul or lie and suffer the consequences when he found out. I told him the truth."

"But he didn't take your money, did he?" Henry chose that moment to interrupt us when he trotted over with an intact jar of moonshine. After fussing over him for a few minutes and trying to discern where he might've dug it up, we went back to our conversation.

Shaking his head, Jake said, "No, he didn't take the money. He rewarded me for my loyalty for telling him the truth. He also told me that there'd been some talk of men who wanted to convince me to give up my stash. He made sure everybody knew that he got to me first and there was no money left."

"He protected your money so you would have it when you got out."

"That's exactly what he did."

"Who was this guy? Did he have a name?"

"He had a name, but you're better off not knowing it. He was a brutal man who instilled a lot of fear, Barbie."

"Pfft…what do I care? You said he's been dead for years. I'm not afraid, but I am curious. What was this name that instilled so much fear and demanded loyalty?"

"He went by Grizz."

CHAPTER 47

I WANT YOU MORE THAN MY LUNGS
WANT AIR

"Grizz, schmizz, I don't care what he went by, I'm glad he's dead!" I announced.

Jake chuckled. "I'm sure there are a lot of people out there who are in agreement with you."

"Tell me more about you and Kenny." Something occurred to me and I had to ask. "He didn't tell you about my aversion to blueberry pancakes, did he?"

"Of course he told me. It's one of the reasons I ate them in front of you. I wanted to know if you were as stubborn as he said."

I laughed. "Did he also tell you that one day when we had our own house he promised he would make them for me every morning?"

Jake grew solemn. "He might've, but I don't remember it."

I couldn't figure out why but I thought I might've somehow hurt Jake's feelings. So I circled back to something that had been nagging at me.

"The night at my house when I got drunk on moonshine. Did you—"

He didn't let me finish the sentence, but stopped walking and pulled me close to face him. He caressed my cheek with the back of his hand and told me, "I carried you up the stairs and put you in bed. And I told you that I'd loved you for as long as I could remember."

I stared into his eyes and asked, "How could that be? You'd only known me at that point for a couple of months at the most. And I know I wasn't very nice to you for a long time before that."

"I've known you for as long as I knew Kenny, Barbie." His expression was guarded, unreadable. "Do you know what it's like to spend almost twenty years with another person in a room no bigger than your new bathroom? Believe me when I say you have a lot of time to talk."

I opened my mouth to answer him but he continued, "I knew every-thing about you, about Jonathan, about Pumpkin Rest. You don't think every chance Kenny got, he didn't talk about the girl he loved? The girl he would never stop loving. The girl he could never be with because she was his half sister. I knew everything about you, Barbie. Even after you moved away and went to college."

I took a step back. "That's impossible. I didn't stay in touch with Kenny after the couple of letters I sent him while he was in prison went unanswered."

"But he kept in touch with the facility where Jonathan had been stay-ing. He knew about your visits to see his little brother and how even after they asked you to stop coming, you always made it a point to stop in once in a while and watch Jonathan from afar without him seeing you. They appreciated that you kept your distance so it didn't upset him."

I looked away and shifted nervously. I'd never have guessed that while in prison Kenny was able to communicate with someone from Jonathan's group home. It was a stupid assumption on my part. Prisoners were allowed to exchange letters. Just because he didn't write to me didn't mean he couldn't write to someone else. Darlene being the obvious example.

"And how you still managed to make the long drive from school to drop off some of Jonathan's favorite things that you regularly bought on a college student's budget. Don't you see? I didn't fall in love with the girl Kenny left behind. I fell in love with the woman you became, Barbie. I mourned right alongside Kenny when Darlene wrote to him that you'd gotten married. When I told you that Emmy encouraged me to take the road less traveled, she wasn't talking about the road to Pumpkin Rest. It was the road to you, Barbie."

"Oh, Jake," I cried while looping my arms around his neck. "I'm so grateful you listened to Emmy."

He kissed me. A long, lingering, tender kiss that shot straight to my heart and weakened my knees. When it ended, we resumed our walk, and before we knew it we were at my house. I waited to see if he was going to suggest that we finally consummate our relationship, but he knew what I was thinking and immediately cut to the chase.

"I've only been able to dream about being inside of you, Barbie. And right now, I want you more than my lungs want air. But I'm gonna stick to my guns about marrying you first. I've waited this long. I can wait a couple more weeks." A look of panic flashed across his face when he asked, "It won't be more than a couple of weeks, right?"

I couldn't help but laugh. "We can get married tomorrow if you want,

Jake. But I'm going to use your chivalrous and gentlemanly insistence on abstinence to plan something intimate. Darlene would never forgive me if she wasn't part of our nuptials. And I'm sure I can pull it together in a week or so."

He blew out a sigh of relief and we turned around and started walking back to his house.

"I have to tell you. I appreciate that you've been so willing to wait, Jake. I can't imagine what it must've been like for you in prison for all those years without sex." I quickly caught myself and said, "Well, I'm sure you had sex. Just not with women. Wait, I wasn't trying to imply you had sex with men, I'm just saying…"

"Stop, Barbie," he said with a laugh. "It's okay. I know you're not implying I had sex with men in prison. And I wasn't completely abstinent behind bars."

I gave him a curious look. "But you couldn't be with a woman in prison, right?"

He looked skyward. "I had sex with women while I was in prison, Barbie. So did Kenny."

"You had conjugal visits with girlfriends?" I was feeling selfish because I didn't like the thought of either of them having women they cared about while they were behind bars.

"Conjugal implies marriage. I didn't marry any of the paid prostitutes that came to the prison. I had sex with them." He said it like it was common.

I stopped walking and looked over at him. "You had sex with prostitutes in prison? How is that possible? And please tell me you used protection."

He tightened his grip on my hand and pulled me along. "About the protection. Always. And with the right connections and a deep purse, you can have anything inside prison that you can have on the outside, except your freedom—everything from women and drugs to liquor and Pop-Tarts. In more recent years, cell phones were even available. There are very few people who won't take a bribe, Barbie. Especially in a facility where the prisoner-to-guard-and-staff ratio is so skewed. And even more so when you're incarcerated in the most corrupt detention facility in the United States."

"Did you have a cell phone?"

He shook his head. "I didn't need one. I didn't have anybody to call."

That was enlightening. And sad. I still had some things I wanted to know about Kenny, but felt I needed to broach the subject delicately.

"Is it okay if I ask you more about Kenny? I promise I won't ask after today. I don't want you to think he'll always be part of us, Jake."

He stopped and gave me a serious look. "Barbie, I'm not threatened by your feelings for Kenny. And I completely understand your curiosity. Don't apologize for wanting to know more. Kenny Pritchard was my best friend. He was closer than a brother. We shared everything. Whether we want it or not, he'll always be part of us. Ask away, sweetheart."

I turned to him, trying to observe his actions nonchalantly. "You said you had a job in prison. Did Kenny have one?"

"Kenny had the hardest job of anyone." He scratched his chin, his expression thoughtful. My mouth hung open of its own volition as I waited for him to tell me. He paused long enough to pick up two sticks. We watched as Henry and Lady raced to get them. "Kenny's job was to be a model prisoner."

I listened, fascinated, as Jake told me that Kenny continued to work for the same man on the inside that he'd worked for on the outside. The man they called Grizz. He explained that Kenny's job was to gain the trust of the facility guards and staff members. And he did an excellent job of it because one of Kenny's prison duties was to empty the garbage cans from their offices at the end of the day.

"That was about the time Kenny and I started matching up our ink. It was part of Grizz's plan to get access to the safe in the warden's office. We started slowly. I had the ball and chain put on my left bicep and it was the same size and shape as Kenny's pocket watch." Jake looked over at me. "He had that pocket watch done to replace the one he'd left under your bedroom floor. He was always thinking about you, Barbie."

My only response was a sad smile.

"Kenny had the skull with flames put on his neck to match mine and it covered that birthmark he had." Jake brushed his fingers where Kenny's birthmark had been. "He eventually filled in the pocket watch so it would look like my ball and chain. As we got older and started filling out in the same places, we looked even more alike and Grizz saw an opportunity there. He tested the waters by having us swap our uniforms and pretend to be each other. When we all realized that we could fool people…" He squeezed my hand. "And let's face it, in prison, nobody cares. You're practically invisible anyway so what we were doing didn't draw any attention. When it was obvious we could get away with it, Grizz used it to his advantage."

"How?"

"When Kenny was emptying garbage cans in the infirmary, he swiped a stethoscope. And the next night, I did his rounds dressed in his uniform. When I emptied the garbage can in the warden's office, I..."

"Emptied his safe too," I finished for him.

"No. Grizz didn't steal from the warden. Someone would've noticed. He liked being one step ahead of him and he knew that the warden kept important papers in the safe. Instead, I would access the safe every few weeks and inform him of what was in there."

"Wow!" I said. "You and Kenny did share everything. Tattoos, jobs, maybe even women." I looked down and kicked at the dirt so I didn't have to see the truth in his eyes about the women.

"Our dreams, our memories, all of it," Jake finished.

"You knew how to make moonshine before you came here, didn't you?" I teased.

"Yes, just like Kenny knew everything there was to know about growing flowers and how to crack a safe. He didn't need me to keep swapping jobs with him. He got into the warden's safe all by himself until it was upgraded to one of those digital types. Kenny knew about my brother, Philip, and my regret at how I'd treated my parents. If I'd died before I was released, Kenny would've gotten my baseball and the story that went with it. We were more than cellmates, Barbie. We were soul brothers."

I knew everything I needed to know, and because the conversation had turned melancholy, I asked him to tell me something funny. I couldn't imagine there being anything to laugh about in prison, but if there was, I wanted to know it. The conversation became lighter when Jake described some of their antics. I was glad to know that as difficult as their lives had been, there were some brighter moments to remember.

Jake's house had come into view. "Kenny was a bit of a prankster. Even in the worst circumstances, he would always find a way to make me smile. And as horrible as his father treated him, I never once remember seeing Kenny shed a tear."

Jake agreed and followed it up with, "I only saw Kenny cry twice."

I stopped short and looked up at him. My heart ached knowing something or someone had hurt him. "What made him cry?"

"The day he got Darlene's letter that said you'd gotten married."

I sucked in my breath and, after letting it out, asked, "And what was the second thing that made him cry?"

"Meeting the daughter he never knew he had."

CHAPTER 48

HE WOULD'VE BEEN HAPPY FOR US

F inding out that Kenny had a daughter could've toppled me over. I latched on to Jake's arm to steady myself.

Grabbing me, he asked, "Are you okay, Barbie? I'm sorry if you find it upsetting. Maybe I shouldn't have told you, but it probably would've come out eventually."

I collected myself. "No apology is necessary, Jake. I'm shocked, not upset." I couldn't help but ask with a lump in my throat, "Who was her mother?"

"It's another long story if you're up for hearing it."

I told him I was, and after feeding the dogs, we returned to the front porch stoop where our conversation originally began. It had been less than thirty minutes since Jake had returned home and we'd set out on our walk to my house and back, but it felt like hours.

Jake described a despicable tale of a gang rape in South Florida. I shivered when I heard the details of how two seasoned motorcycle gang members had tricked Kenny into believing his initiation was to rape a woman.

"It wasn't true, and Kenny refused to participate," Jake explained. "There was no initiation. Just two rogue members who were messing with him."

I cringed. "The guy from prison, was it his motorcycle gang?

"Yes, but it wasn't legit. I told you that guy was bad, and he was. No doubt there. But he never enforced a club initiation that involved rape. Never." Jake leaned forward and rested his elbows on his knees. Staring straight ahead, he described how the two older men had taken Kenny out on a motorcycle run for beer. They stopped at a convenience store and dragged an unsuspecting customer behind it, where they both forced themselves on her. They told Kenny if he didn't do it, they would kill him and the woman.

I sat straight up. "Is that true? Would they have killed Kenny if he didn't rape her?" My heart was pumping wildly and I took deep breaths to calm myself.

Jake looked over at me. "Yes, Barbie. They took turns holding a gun on Kenny, forcing him to watch, while they raped that poor girl. Then they pushed him down on top of her and insisted he do the same." Jake's voice was flat, lifeless. "They had the gun pointed at his head the entire time. Kenny told me he would've rather died than touch her, but they'd threatened to kill her in front of him. So yeah, they would definitely have killed them both."

Jake paused to take a deep breath and slowly exhaled.

"Kenny did what he was told. He told me while he was on top of the girl he whispered in her ear how sorry he was." Raking his hand through his hair, he continued, "When it was over they took the girl's purse with her identification. They told her if she went to the police they knew where to find her. Other than leaving you and Jonathan, it was the biggest regret of his life."

"That is a horrid story. That poor girl." I placed my hand on Jake's back and rubbed it. "Wait a second. If it was a gang rape, how did she know Kenny was the father of her baby?"

"That's where it gets a little bizarre," he told me. "The victim saw the gang patch on the back of their jackets as they rode away. Of course, Kenny wasn't a member yet so he didn't have one. She discretely asked around and found out who they were and where they met up. It was an old motel way out in the middle of nowhere. She started parking at a grocery store she knew they would have to drive past and she started following anybody she saw on a motorcycle. She was particularly interested in finding Kenny because she didn't think he was like the other two. She knew he did what he did against his will and she was going to ask him to get her identification back. It freaked her out knowing that those men had her address, and she saw some compassion in Kenny despite what he'd done to her."

"I can understand why she saw compassion in Kenny," I admitted, my voice gravelly. "And I know with all my heart that Kenny would never deliberately do that to a woman."

"I agree with you, Barbie," came Jake's soft response. "But he did and he carried his guilt to the grave."

I shook my head. "I wish he was here so I could tell him that studies of male physiology suggest that erections are only partially under voluntary control. They're known to happen during times of extreme duress and definitely in the absence of sexual pleasure." I clasped my hands together tightly in front of me and closed my eyes, trying to imagine the guilt Kenny had to live with. "Elevated blood flow and adrenaline can result in an erection for pretty much any man in a stressful situation. Sounds to me like having your life threatened by two individuals who are capable of following through on their threats would be considered more than stressful."

I opened my eyes when Jake cleared his throat and said, "Sounds like a pretty clinical description of what can happen in that type of situation."

I gave a less than enthusiastic nod. "It's not my area of expertise." I shrugged. "I'm just repeating what little I do know about the subject. I only wish he'd known it before he died." I started to chew on the inside of my cheek when a thought occurred to me. "Jake, how old is Kenny's daughter?" I looked over at him and waited for an answer. After he replied, I used my fingers to tick off the years. "Oh, Jake. Kenny was only a teenager when this happened." I shook my head. "He was a teenager!" I shouted, throwing my hands up in the air.

"Yeah, he was young, Barbie. And I believed him when he said there was nothing remotely pleasurable about it. He mentioned that after he left, he had to stop twice so he could puke." His voice was thick with emotion. "Getting back to the story. She wanted to find Kenny, but she hadn't seen his face. They'd dragged her behind the store, it was night and there was very little light. Plus, they insisted she keep her eyes closed. She peeked a few times and she saw the birthmark on Kenny's neck. This was long before he went to prison and we matched up our tattoos. It's the birthmark you were looking for the first morning we had coffee at the diner."

I looked away, embarrassed. "You're right. Even though I knew you couldn't be Kenny, there was something in me that had to be sure." I patted his leg. "Don't worry. I knew it was a ridiculous assumption."

"Anyway, she spotted him one day and followed him. To her surprise, he ended up at a Catholic church. She was so stunned that instead of trying to talk to him she waited until he left and went inside to see if he'd spoken to anyone there. That's where she met Sister Agnes, Kenny's aunt. She befriended the nun and never told her what her nephew had done. I'm not sure why, but she stopped following Kenny and started spending time with his aunt. She found out she was pregnant about the same time Sister Agnes transferred to another church." Jake stopped and scrubbed a hand down his face. "On a side note." He looked over at me. "Kenny told me he never finished what he'd started during the rape."

"You mean he never ejaculated inside her?"

"Yeah, he told me he went soft, which is understandable."

"He didn't have to ejaculate. He wouldn't have known that pre-ejaculate was leaking out. It's why people should never rely on pulling out as a means of birth control." I side-eyed him and said, "Yeah, that's the physician in me again. Sorry for interrupting."

He smiled. "No problem. Anyway, when the baby was born, and without even knowing back then she was carrying Kenny's child, she named the baby after Sister Agnes."

"So, Kenny has a daughter named Agnes."

"No. She named the little girl Bevin. That was Kenny's aunt's name before she became a nun."

"Bevin," I whispered. "Please tell me about Bevin, Jake."

He smiled then. "Bevin's mother, whose name was Celeste, never told her the rape story or who her father was, but somehow, and I don't know how and neither did Kenny, Bevin found out. Celeste had been a law student when she was attacked. She later became a judge and was notorious for throwing the book at convicted rapists. Judge Celeste Marconi earned herself a reputation and became known as Maximum Marconi."

"Good for her!" I shouted before I jumped up from my perch and started pacing. "How did Celeste know Kenny was Bevin's father?"

Jake shook his head. "I guess as time passed, and with her contacts in law enforcement, she had her daughter's DNA run through the system and got a hit. Years later, when Bevin eventually discovered her father's identity, she confronted her mother and demanded the truth. It caused a falling out between mother and daughter at which time Bevin took it upon herself to meet Kenny in prison. That only made it worse. When her mother found out about the visits, she gave Bevin an ultimatum. She had to choose between the woman who'd raised her or the man who'd fathered her."

I sat back down at which time Lady walked over to me and tried to sit on my lap. Even though she was getting big, I managed to settle her comfortably and asked, "How did Bevin's visits with Kenny go?"

"At first, not good," Jake said. "Kenny told me that after he got over the shock of meeting a daughter he never knew existed, and realizing she wanted to get to know him, he tried to scare her away by describing the crowd he used to run with in gruesome detail. He told her that it wasn't safe for someone like her to visit a prison as corrupt as the one where he was incarcerated. He'd hoped it would frighten her into not visiting him because he thought she deserved better than a criminal father who was never getting out of jail."

I could feel the energy slowly draining out of me. How awful it must've been for all of them. For Bevin to learn she was conceived during a brutal rape. For Celeste to be the victim of such a heinous crime. And even for Kenny to come face-to-face with a daughter he never knew about, and to know that she knew the story behind her conception. It was all too awful.

"He died without ever getting to know his daughter." I felt limp.

"Not true." His voice perked up a tad. "Bevin was a persistent young lady and didn't frighten easily. She forced her way back into Kenny's life whether he liked it or not. She wasn't terribly invasive, but she had wanted to know a little bit about the man who'd fathered her so she kept showing up at the prison. He relented. He didn't tell her about you or Jonathan or Pumpkin Rest. The story he shared with her pretty much started after he ran away from home. She was relieved to find out that Kenny wasn't a hardened criminal nor a rapist. At least not a deliberate one. She seemed satisfied with that. When Kenny died, they'd not seen each other for a while, but had been on good terms. I'm not sure if Bevin knew that her mother, the judge, had visited Kenny in prison too."

"Tell me that part," I insisted.

Jake plucked a blade of grass that was growing up between the deck boards. "The judge and Bevin hadn't been on speaking terms because, when Bevin found her father and confronted her mother, Celeste described the attack in a way that didn't cast blame on Kenny. Bevin accused her mother of having feelings for Kenny, which was ridiculous. They had a falling out over it, and like I already said, it only got worse when Celeste found out Bevin had been visiting Kenny. The judge later told Kenny when she went to see him in prison that during the assault she'd peeked a few times and could see that Kenny had a gun held to the back of his head. She'd also heard Kenny pleading not for his life, but for hers. He begged the guys to kill him and just let her go."

I stroked Lady's head. "I could see Kenny doing that."

"The judge had forgiven Kenny, but still didn't want her daughter visiting him in prison. She asked Kenny to convince Bevin to cut ties with him. Bevin had fallen in love and was getting married. She was starting a new life with a criminal prosecutor of all people. She's now Bevin Bear, not Marconi," Jake said with a laugh. "It has a cute ring to it. Anyway, Kenny understood where Celeste was coming from and he agreed that she didn't need ties to a father who was serving out a life sentence. He told Bevin it was okay, that he preferred it if she chose her mother over him."

"He was one of the most unselfish people I ever met," I told Jake. "I feel sad now. I don't want to feel so low, but knowing that Kenny was such a good human being, and how he got dragged into something so awful that he felt he couldn't get out of…" My words died off and Jake reached for my hand. "It makes me want to cry. He didn't deserve it, Jake. He just didn't deserve it."

"I know he didn't, sweetheart." He looked wistful when he added, "And don't think I don't have a streak of guilt for my happy ending with you. But, I knew Kenny better than anyone. Even you, Barbie. And he would be happy for us."

I leaned my head against Jake's shoulder and continued to stroke Lady's fur. "You're right. He would have been happy for us, Jake."

CHAPTER 49

HE NEVER STOPPED BEING THE PERFECT
GENTLEMAN

The next two weeks flew by in a whirlwind of activity. Darlene insisted on taking the helm and planned the perfect small-town wedding. Instead of sending out invitations, we spread the word that everyone was welcome.

We got married on a sunny day at Darlene's church with a reception that started in the parish hall and spilled out onto the lawn due to the number of guests that showed up. I'd asked Darlene to be my matron of honor, but she declined and told me she'd be too busy making sure everything went smoothly. She did offer an alternate suggestion. Since Jake had asked Jonathan to be his best man, it only seemed fitting that Cindy should be my maid of honor. It was a good call on Darlene's part because watching how proud it made Jonathan and Cindy to be up on the altar with me and Jake brought us immeasurable joy.

The preacher pronounced us man and wife and made sure Jake knew he was welcome to sit down during Sunday services. I laughed and promised him that Jake and I would both be sitting together in the future. For our wedding dance, we chose Alabama's "Feels So Right" because it didn't just feel so right, it felt more than right. It felt perfect.

Even with Darlene's help, the rush involved in pulling together a last-minute wedding made it nearly impossible to plan a honeymoon, so we opted to postpone it until we could decide where we wanted to spend it.

My wedding night exceeded my wildest expectations. Especially when I found out Jake had made arrangements with one of Darlene's relatives to keep Lady and Henry at their farm so he could have uninterrupted time with me. He carried me over the threshold of my house, which was now our home, and kicking the door closed behind us, sprinted up the stairs with me in his arms. Not too shabby for a man approaching the fourth quarter. My man.

In hindsight, I might've found myself feeling a bit bashful considering my husband had never seen me without clothes. But making love to Jake was as natural as breathing. There was no shyness, just an intense longing to become one with each other.

That night, as we lay spent in each other's arms trying to regain our breath, I ran my hand over his chest and beamed at my name so prominently displayed over his heart. In addition to him promising me all his tomorrows at the altar just a few hours earlier, I thought his new tattoo was the best wedding present ever.

The next few days were spent making love with breaks only for nutritional sustenance and long soulful talks about our plans for the future. For someone who'd spent almost half his life in prison and had only occasional trysts, Jake was an exceptionally skilled lover and more concerned about my pleasure than his own. He was the perfect combination of tenderness and animalistic need. I'm ashamed to admit that during one of our more passionate moments, I let my mind wander back to my first experience with Kenny. Jake was inside me, and we were in perfect unison. We'd quickly discovered each other's rhythms and he knew how to pace himself so that we would find mutual release. It was during that release that I'd briefly fantasized about what it would've been like to make love to an adult Kenny. He'd only been fifteen when we lost our virginity and our experience, though beautiful, could never have been described as passionate. The thought was only fleeting and I promised myself at that moment that I would never let myself think of Kenny with anything other than a brotherly affection again.

Our honeymoon at home flew by, and before I knew it, we'd seamlessly blended our lives together. We moved Jake's belongings into my home and rented his house to one of Darlene's relatives. Jake and I both continued to work and spent our free time taking care of our property, our dogs, and nurturing our marriage. We found pleasure in simple things. I finally loosened up enough to enjoy motorcycle rides. We spent Friday evenings catching him up on what I considered cinematic masterpieces that he'd missed out on while in prison. The more I grumbled about my hot flashes, the more Jake teased me that they couldn't have been as big a deal as I'd made them out to be. I took it upon myself to introduce him to a hot flash of his own. One brutally hot day I switched the air conditioner in my Jeep to heat and put Jake's seat warmer on without him noticing. He never teased me again. We took Jonathan and Cindy on picnics and fishing trips and spent a lot of time with Darlene and her huge family.

We eventually honeymooned in the Poconos, not even caring that it was peak ski season. We preferred the quietness of our cabin and long nature walks to snow-covered slopes. Besides, neither one of us knew how to ski. I'm pretty sure Jake told me he loved me more in the first few months of our marriage than Richard had in over two decades. And I never tired of hearing it.

The next several months brought triumphs and tragedies. Darlene and her husband welcomed another grandchild but had to say goodbye to Granny Dicey. The niece that dog-sat for me finished her associate degree and got accepted to Clemson University. Sheila's husband was located and signed the divorce papers without complaint. Dolly quit her job at Hampton House to go back to school full-time. She was currently engaged to the man she'd started seeing after Jake's rebuff. Yvonne had found a new beau and was no longer pining after the flea market furniture salesman.

My condo was sold, and we bought and began restorations on an old house in Pumpkin Rest that would serve as a new group home for Jonathan and Cindy. Jake's money couldn't have found a more noble investment. This would be a little different than Hampton House in that the residents would find jobs based on their skill set. Jonathan was already practicing for his new job at Hampton House. He'd followed in his brother's footsteps and was responsible for emptying the wastebaskets and helping with general chores. He thrived as did Cindy, who left each day to work at a fabric shop. We were all excited for the renovation to be complete so the new residents could move in. As soon as it was finished, Jake would resign from Hampton House and work at the new home instead.

I loved being married to Jake. He never stopped being the perfect gentleman and was right when he'd told me, "the fourth quarter is where all the excitement happens."

CHAPTER 50

I FINALLY HAD MY HAPPY ENDING

Before we knew it, we were approaching our first anniversary. I'd just walked out to the porch with iced tea. I set our drinks on a small table and was getting ready to sit on the Adirondack chair Jake had so graciously repaired a year earlier when he grabbed me and pulled me down onto his lap. He made growling sounds while kissing my neck. Lady, who'd been lying in the sun, jumped up thinking it was his invitation to play. An older and wiser Henry didn't bother to lift his head.

I closed my eyes as Jake buried his face in my neck. I sighed and reflected on our first year of marriage.

"What are you thinking about?" he whispered in my ear.

I had a silly grin pasted on my face when I answered. "About how happy I am."

"How happy *we* are," he corrected.

My eyes held a glint of mischief as I daydreamed about the past year with Jake and the marital bliss we'd shared. It was so different from what I'd had with Richard. There was passion with Jake. Lots of passion. But it was more than that. Our marriage was fun. Like the night he blindfolded me and guided me to the backyard where he'd set up a makeshift bedroom. We spent the night talking, drinking moonshine, and making love under the stars. Or when I surprised him with a new motorcycle. He'd had his eye on it and I bought it for him before he had the chance to buy it for himself. Our relationship was built on mutual respect, trust, and friendship. The thing I loved most about our marriage wasn't that he couldn't get enough of me, cellulite and all, but that we never, ever ran out of things to learn about each other. He was my best friend and always would be.

Sometime during our first year together, I'd casually mentioned Richard once when Jake and I were watching a movie called *Baby Boom* with Diane Keaton. There was a part where the characters decide to make love. The scene fades to black and when it resumes four minutes later, they'd finished. I told Jake that I was all for a quickie, but there was something very clinical about the scene portrayed in the movie that reminded me of Richard. He looked over at me and teased, "Nine minutes I could understand, but four minutes isn't long enough."

I remembered hitting him with a pillow and asking, "What's so special about nine minutes?" His answer was a bite on my ear that ended with both of us on the living room floor sans clothes and surrounded by couch pillows.

A gust of wind collided with some wind chimes and their melodic tinkling brought me back to the present and the man who held me.

I pulled back so I could look at him. "You were right about the fourth quarter being where all the excitement happens. Married almost a year and I feel like we're still in the honeymoon stage." I could sense that he detected a hint of worry in my expression when I confided, "I hope that doesn't change."

He threw his head back and laughed. "You're kidding, right? There's no way it'll change, Barbie. Passion is wasted on the young. For anybody who thinks it's all over in their fifties, they're in for a surprise. It's just getting started and we're living proof."

I shifted my weight and could feel the afterglow of that passion between my thighs. I'd woken up that morning to find my husband under the covers, with his face buried between my legs. He said it was his favorite thing to do, and I was more than happy to indulge his preferred hobby.

I could've stayed on his lap all afternoon, but knew it was time to take my seat when he shifted beneath me because my weight was causing his leg to go numb. He slapped me hard on my butt as I walked away to plop in the matching chair.

We sipped our tea and talked about how well Jonathan and Cindy had settled into their new home. We discussed which one of us would have time to take both dogs for their yearly shots and checkups. Jake made an executive decision that we would make the time to take them together. The subject shifted to motorcycles and somehow segued into gang names when I asked him if Kenny had one?

Jake set his tea down and said, "Yeah, he had one, and I bet you can guess what it was."

I shook my head. "How in the world would I be able to guess Kenny's nickname? He never had one when I knew him."

Jake challenged me to think about it, and when I still came up clueless, he rolled his eyes and said, "It was Hooch. Kenny's gang name was Hooch. Before going to prison he'd made a batch or two of moonshine to share with his crew and the nickname stuck."

"Of course." I slapped my thigh with a laugh. I was bringing my glass to my lips when I stopped and looked over at him. A thought had bubbled up from nowhere and refused to be stifled. "I can't help but think that with all the shenanigans you've told me about you and Kenny in prison, and how you fooled people in the prison, that if you'd wanted to, you could've switched places with him."

Jake took a slow swig of his drink and rested the glass on the arm of his chair. He didn't say anything, looking straight ahead.

I tilted my head to one side and narrowed my eyes at him. "If you had switched identities with Kenny, would you tell me?"

"First of all, you're being ridiculous, Barbie."

I bristled at the comment. "Am I, Jake? You're the one who told me that anyone could be bought and we both know you had and still have plenty of money. You and Kenny had everyone at the prison fooled. Why would it be ridiculous to think that for the right price a nobody in the prison infirmary could be convinced to switch out the names on an autopsy report? Huh? What if Jake Chambers is the one who died, and Kenny served out Jake's sentence and was released? I mean if they knew everything about each other, Jake would've told Kenny where he hid the money."

He rubbed the back of his neck. "Yeah, I guess you're right. It could've happened that way if we'd planned it ahead of time. But it didn't. And seriously, sweetheart. Would you honestly want to know?"

I sat up straight, startled by his question. "Why wouldn't I want to know?"

"Think about it, Barbie doll. If I tell you that I'm not Kenny, I'll have to live the rest of my life with the disappointment I'll see in your eyes."

"That's not true, Jake!" I argued.

"I know you think that, but I don't know if I want to take that risk."

I made a face at him, aggravated that he could even think such a thing.

"And let's pretend for just a minute that I am Kenny. Do you think you can live the rest of your life with me knowing I was involved in a sexual assault?"

I knew that Celeste had been the sole victim in that horrific scenario. But I also knew Kenny never would've deliberately participated in something so heinous. "A sexual assault that Kenny was forced into at gunpoint," I corrected.

He ignored me. "Or that I walked away from a potential relationship with Bevin to be with you? I could've told her mother to take a hike."

An unselfish and respectful decision on Kenny's part to abide by her mother's wishes, I thought but didn't voice.

After a long hushed moment, and having made my decision, I sank back in my chair. Not wanting to face any of the scenarios Jake presented and grateful that my husband had the wisdom to show me how some things were better left alone, I nodded my acceptance. All I knew was that I was deeply in love with the man sitting next to me and was excited to spend the fourth quarter waking up in his arms every day for the rest of my life. I got up and walked over to him. He held up his hand and I took it as I lowered myself back into his lap. We stared out over our property and delighted in what spring had delivered almost overnight. We'd finally figured out what to do with all that fertile earth. Rows and rows of brightly colored flowers stretched against a blue sky as far as the eye could see.

"I love you, Barbie doll."

"I love you too, Jake."

His breath was warm against my ear. "It doesn't get much better than this."

"No it doesn't, Jake." I sighed and realized I finally had my happy ending.

EPILOGUE

WHAT ARE YOU IN THE MOOD TO HAVE FOR
BREAKFAST, SWEETHEART?

Spring and summer zipped past us, and before we knew it, an unusually cold autumn dropped in like an unwelcome guest. We were getting ready for church and I was fretting about having to dig out warmer clothes. Jake had already showered and was downstairs with the dogs. I was rummaging through my dresser when I remembered an old box of winter clothes I'd tossed in the guest room more than a year earlier.

I found it stuck in the back of the closet and grimaced when I saw Fancy's scarf on top. I couldn't believe I'd never gotten rid of it. I would rectify that the next time I put together a bag of clothes for charity. I tossed it aside and started wading through some scarves and hats I hadn't seen in a while. I came across a large brown envelope that had been stuffed down in the bottom. It didn't have anything written on it and it wasn't until I undid the metal clasp that I remembered what it contained. Darlene's daughter had given me Kenny's medical file that she'd obtained, but because she'd told me what it said, I'd never felt the need to open it. For a reason I couldn't explain, something prompted me to do so now. I pulled out the stack of papers and took a brief glance at the ones on top. The records reflected what she'd said. Kenny died of an infection.

I don't know why I felt compelled to look through the rest of his medical history. I checked my watch and had plenty of time, so I sat cross-legged on the floor and briefly scanned the papers. Danielle wasn't kidding when she'd told me there was a record of every aspirin and antibiotic ever administered to Kenny. I was getting ready to put the paperwork back in the envelope when a specific word caught my eye. I blinked twice trying to make sense of what I was seeing. I brought my hand to my mouth in dismay when I realized that, while in prison, Kenny had been diagnosed with a malicious form of cancer. Much like the one that took Richard's life, but even more vicious. It was a verdict without hope, and based on what I was reading, if he hadn't died from that infection, he would've passed away soon after. *Oh, Kenny. Life was so unfair to you.*

I kept reading and wasn't shocked to see that he'd refused treatment. Who could blame him for not wanting to extend a life that would never see freedom? I hadn't read through the entire file and didn't feel like it after the morbid discovery. I tried unsuccessfully to stuff all the papers back in the envelope. A few of them kept sticking out, so I removed them while I finagled the larger wad inside. Satisfied that I'd managed it, I picked up the leftovers and was getting ready to fold them in half thinking they'd slide in more easily, when one sentence caught my attention. A single sentence that would define the rest of my life and the man I'd chosen to spend it with.

After shoving the extra papers inside the envelope, I calmly made my way downstairs and found Jake rummaging through the refrigerator. He heard me and without turning around said, "I'm not sure what I want for breakfast. Do you have an inkling for anything, Barbie doll?"

"Blueberry pancakes."

His face was buried in the refrigerator, and I watched his knuckles turn white as he gripped the handle tightly. He straightened up, and after closing the door, slowly turned around to face me.

Giving me a look that said he must not have heard me right, he asked again, "What are you in the mood to have for breakfast, sweetheart?"

"I told you, blueberry pancakes."

His forehead puckered. "And you want me to make them?"

"I do," I told him.

He looked away, his Adam's apple bobbing as he swallowed hard. "You told me once that Kenny had promised he'd make you blueberry pancakes when you were together and had your own house. I'm not sure if this is you messing with me or telling me you're not the stubborn girl you used to be and you're ready for blueberry pancakes a la Jake."

I stared at him. The longest twenty seconds of my life passed before I said, "You never should've told me about the things you got away with in prison. The stories about the way you tricked the guards and other prisoners and how over time they couldn't distinguish between you and Jake."

He laughed. "You mean me and Kenny."

"No. I mean you and Jake." I noticed a tic in his jaw as I held up the envelope. "I almost missed it because I wasn't looking for it. But it's all right here in Kenny's medical records. Except they're not Kenny's. These records belong to Jake Chambers. The real Jake Chambers. Your best friend was dying, wasn't he?"

"Barbie, you got it all wro—"

"Stop it right now. Just stop. I'm not stupid." I tossed the envelope on the kitchen table. "I can only surmise that you and Jake kicked it up a notch after he received his hopeless prognosis. It's when you switched places permanently, and the reason why he refused treatment for his cancer. Because he didn't want you getting chemo and radiation you didn't need. Someone was paid off to swap out the names and dates on every piece of paper in your files and probably in the computer too. It was you who accidentally stabbed Jake in the prison yard. And when you confessed to killing Kenny to me, you were confessing to killing him metaphorically." I waved my hand in the air. "Or maybe you did feel responsible for Jake's death and wanted me to know that you carried that guilt. I can only guess that you felt the need to come clean with me about everything. Everything except your true identity."

He stood still, his fists clenched at his sides.

"All those stories you told me as Jake, about the pain of how you treated your parents. Those were Jake's stories, but you made them yours. And I almost believe you think they were yours to tell."

I saw the defeat in his eyes and a slight sag of his shoulders. "Other than his prized baseball, they were all Jake had, Barbie. If his stories didn't get told, he'd be forgotten, and I couldn't let that happen. He was my best friend." He tucked his hands in his front pockets. "Besides, I couldn't very well tell you stories about my childhood, now could I?"

He had a point. "I should've guessed it. I should've let myself think it out from the beginning. Jonathan wouldn't let a single man near him in over thirty years. Was I supposed to believe that Jake Chambers was the first blue-eyed man who'd ever tried to work with him? It always had to be you, and I don't know how he knew it, but Jonathan recognized you. Didn't he?"

He scratched at his jaw. "I still can't believe you deduced all this because Jake was dying of cancer."

"It wasn't his cancer that made me realize it. I still would've believed you were Jake if I hadn't kept reading."

He cocked his head to the side and squinted his eyes. "What was it?"

"Two words. Renal agenesis. You were born with only one kidney. I remember you telling me about it when we were kids. Of course we didn't know the medical term for it."

"Yeah, so?"

"The medical report I just read states that Kenny Pritchard had been treated for a ruptured kidney while incarcerated. He must've gotten into one heck of a fight. The doctor recorded his treatment and noted that his other kidney had no damage. And since you only have one kidney, it was obvious I was reading Jake's file."

"I always said you were the smartest person I ever knew, Barbie."

"Please don't patronize me. I'm not the smartest person you've ever known. I'm a physician and it was all in the medical report. What I don't understand is why you couldn't tell me!" I cried. "Why couldn't you trust me? Why all the subterfuge and secrets?"

"Because Kenny Pritchard should still be sitting in prison serving out a life sentence," he said through gritted teeth. "If you'd rejected me, turned me away, or worse, turned me in, I would go back to prison, Barbie. I would lose you and Jonathan all over again."

What he said made perfect sense, but I was still operating in the Twilight Zone and wasn't processing all the information. It was like my brain was on overload. "You came back here believing you were my half brother. Were you thinking that we could be together?"

"You can't even imagine the struggle I had with that." His expression was pained. "One day I'd convince myself I could live down the road as your neighbor. The next day I'd tell myself I wanted you more than I wanted air in my lungs and could forget we shared a father. And then I'd have nightmares that you'd find out and be disgusted." He stopped and shook his head slowly. "I know I kissed you the night I carried you up the stairs. And there were a few more times we locked lips before Granny Dicey told you the truth about your father, and you told me. Just so you know, I spent every Sunday standing in the back of church asking God to forgive me and asking for a sign of what I should do."

"Oh, Kenny, I…"

"You can't call me that, Barbie! You can never call me that name!" he snapped. "Everyone accepts that Jonathan calls me Kenny. But I'm Jake Chambers now. Dr. Pepper-drinking, safe-cracking, baseball-loving Jake. I *have* to be him." He looked at the ground and said, "And to be honest, I've been Jake since 2010. I'm not sure if I can remember how to be Kenny anymore."

"Mike from The Lonesome Keg knew you both, but thought you were Jake because of the skull tattoo." It wasn't a question, but a statement.

"You were part of that guy Grizz's motorcycle club. And Jake worked for him, but wasn't part of the club. Am I right?"

His eyes darted up. "Yes. And the respect you saw the bikers giving me the second time we were at The Lonesome Keg was because they believe I'm Jake Chambers. Mike had filled them in after I knocked them out that first night, and they heard what the real Jake did for Grizz while in prison."

"Which was?"

"Like I told you before, Jake cracked safes, but he was also part of Grizz's muscle inside. So much so, that he earned a reputation in and out of the penitentiary for being a pretty scary dude." He gave me an even look when he added, "And I stand by what I told you about myself. I never deliberately hurt a soul, but I did what I had to do to survive while incarcerated. We both did."

It was obvious he knew how to take care of himself based on what he'd done to the bikers that night at The Lonesome Keg, as well as how he'd handled Sheila's husband. Kenny Pritchard was no longer the mild-mannered and innocent boy I remembered and loved.

"When you were sharing Jake's stories of regret with me, you were in so much anguish. It was almost as if—"

"I was sharing my own pain," he finished, and stared at the floor.

I slowly walked toward him but he didn't sense me until I lightly brushed his arm. His eyes shot up as he steadily met my gaze. But there was a dullness, a deadness to the sharp blue eyes that had held my heart captive since I'd tried to put a splint on a terrified bullfrog more than forty years earlier. How was it that I hadn't recognized them? *Who are you kidding, Barbie? You've known. Somewhere deep inside, you've always known.*

I shook off the internal accusation. "Getting a cadaver dog was deliberate. You were looking for your mother, weren't you?"

"Yes." Swallowing, he asked, "Where do we go from here?"

"You asked me a question last spring when I suggested that it was possible for Kenny and Jake to swap places permanently. You asked if I could live the rest of my life knowing you were involved in a sexual assault. Or that you gave up a possible relationship with your daughter to be with me."

It was the first time I'd ever seen fear in his eyes.

I reached for his hand and squeezed it tight. "The answer is yes. Yes, I can."

He pulled me so hard against his chest, it almost knocked the wind from my lungs. Burying his face in my neck, I thought he was laughing and I smiled. Then I realized he wasn't laughing as I bore witness to the third time in his life that Kenny Pritchard cried.

I lightly stroked his back as he pressed his face tighter against my neck. Temporarily ignoring his 'no name' rule, I whispered, "I've missed you so much, Kenny. Welcome home, my love. Welcome home."

THE END

A NOTE FROM THE AUTHOR

Even though the subject of sexual assault is not a central theme of this story and is not mentioned until the last few chapters of the book, I want readers who may be struggling with their own experience to know they are not alone. Reporting sexual assault does not change the past, but for some, a report can help survivors seek justice and begin the healing process. To report criminal sexual assault, call 911, visit the emergency room, or call the National Sexual Assault Hotline at 1-800-656-HOPE to be connected to a local rape crisis center. For those who are unsure if they are ready to report an assault, additional methods of healing and support can be accessed through your local crisis center, or by calling the above hotline. Remember, you have options, and the only person's opinion that matters in how you move forward, is your own.

ACKNOWLEDGMENTS

I once again find myself at the end of a very long journey. And if you're reading this, you've taken this journey with me, and for that I am forever grateful. For all my loyal readers and the new ones who are meeting me for the first time, you have my heartfelt and sincerest love and appreciation. Thank you for giving me and my words your precious time. Thank you for telling someone if you like the story, and thank you too, even if you didn't like it. If that's the case, I hope you'll pass it on to someone who might.

I find that acknowledgments can be the most difficult part of finishing a novel because I can never seem to find the words to adequately describe the level of appreciation I feel for the dear family and friends who contributed to bringing this story to fruition. I hope it's okay to do a general love-filled shout out to everyone who, in their own special way, helped me bring Jake and Barbie's story to life.

Adriana Leiker, Alyson Santos, Amy Donnelly, Angie Longgwood, Beth's Niners, Cheryl Desmidt, Darlene Avery, Dr. Stacy Waltsak Lexow, Ella Fox, Hazel James, James Flynn, Jay Aheer, Judy Zweifel, Katie Flynn, KC Lynn, Kell Donaldson, Kelli Flynn, Kim Holden, Kirstie Fletcher, Natasha Madison, Nicole Sands, Peggy Tran, Scott Dry, Jr., and Tijan.

A very special thank you to my friend and talented country music composer, musician and artist, Jay Drummonds, for allowing me to use the lyrics for his song, Better Than This. I hope you'll check out Jay and his music at:

https://amzn.to/2XAYlaM
http://www.jaydrummonds.com/

"Better Than This"
Words and music by Jay Drummonds and Kurt Thomas Used with Permission

If there are any discrepancies or errors in the healthcare, medical, legal or law enforcement aspects of the story, they are a result of my creative license and do not reflect on the professionals who so patiently provided their knowledge.

P.S. Nisha, I miss you.

About Beth Flynn

Beth Flynn is a fiction writer and USA Today Bestselling Author who lives and works in Sapphire, North Carolina, deep within the southern Blue Ridge Mountains. Raised in South Florida, Beth and her husband, Jim, have spent the last twenty-one years in Sapphire, where they own a construction company. They have been married thirty-five years and have two daughters and a lovable Pit bull mix named Owen.

In her spare time, Beth enjoys studying the Word, writing, reading, gardening, and motorcycles, especially taking rides on the back of her husband's Harley. She is a nine-year breast cancer survivor.

Keep in Touch With Beth

Thank you for reading *Better Than This*. I'd love to hear from you!

Beth Flynn
    P.O. Box 2833
    Cashiers, NC 28717
    USA
    beth@authorbethflynn.com

Website: www.AuthorBethFlynn.com
    Twitter: @AuthorBethFlynn
    Facebook: Author Beth Flynn
    Facebook Group: Beth's Niners
    Instagram: bethflynnauthor
    Pinterest: beth12870
    Goodreads: Beth Flynn

Bonus From Nine Minutes

Prologue, Chapter One and Two

I hope you enjoyed Better Than This If you'd like to start at the beginning, this excerpt will take you back to where it all began.

NINE MINUTES

Book One of the Nine Minutes Trilogy

Prologue

Summer 2000

I'd never attended an execution before. Well, at least not a legal one. My husband sat to my left. A reporter for *Rolling Stone* was on my right.

The reporter, Leslie Cowan, fidgeted nervously, and I looked over at her. I'm pretty sure this was her first execution of any kind. *Rolling Stone* had an upcoming issue dedicated to celebrity bikers. They thought it would be interesting to include a real biker story in that issue. The story of a girl who'd been abducted by a motorcycle gang in 1975.

That girl was me.

The remnants of Leslie's accident three weeks before were still visible. The stitches had been removed from her forehead, but there was a thin red line where the cut had been. Her eyes weren't quite as raccoonish as before, but it was apparent she'd recently suffered two severe black eyes. The swelling of her nose had almost gone down completely, and she'd been to a dental surgeon to replace her broken teeth.

When we'd first started the interview, she'd told me she wanted me to be completely honest about my experience with the man who was about to be executed. I'd spent the last three months with her and held almost nothing back about my relationship with him. Today was supposed to be the culmination of the interview, a chance for her to truly understand the real side of that experience. To see the unpleasant alongside the rest.

Of course, a man's death should be more than just unpleasant.

I knew as well as he did that he deserved what he was getting. It was strange. I thought knowing it and believing it would make it a little easier, but it didn't. I thought I would get through his execution unscathed emotionally. But I was only fooling myself.

Just because I hadn't been with him for almost fifteen years did not mean I didn't have feelings for him. He was my first love. He was a true love. In fact, he was the biological father of my firstborn, though she would never meet him. He wanted it that way. And deep down, so did I.

The curtain opened. I was no longer aware of anyone else in the small viewing room around me. I stared through a large glass window at an empty gurney. I'd read up on what to expect at an execution. He was supposed to be strapped to the gurney when the curtain opened, wasn't he? I'm sure that was procedure. But he was never one for following rules. I wondered how he'd managed to convince law enforcement to forego this important detail.

With a jolt, I realized someone had entered the sterile-looking room. It was him, along with two officers, the warden and a physician. No priest or pastor. He didn't want one.

Him.

His name was Jason William Talbot. Such a normal-sounding name. It's funny. I'd known him almost twenty-five years and it wasn't until his arrest fifteen years earlier that I learned his real middle and last name. That is, if it was his real name. I'm still not certain.

He was always Grizz to me. Short for Grizzly, a nickname he'd earned due to his massive size and brutal behavior. Grizz was a huge and imposing man. Ruggedly handsome. Tattoos from neck to toe covered his enormous body. His large hands could crush a windpipe without effort. I knew this from experience. I'd personally witnessed what those hands could do. I couldn't keep my eyes off them now.

He had no family. Just me. And I was not his family.

I immediately sensed when he spotted me. I looked up from his hands into his mesmerizing bright green eyes. I tried to assess whether those eyes held any emotion, but I couldn't tell. It'd been too long. He'd always been good at hiding his feelings. I used to be able to read him. Not today, though.

As he looked at me, he lifted his handcuffed hands and used the fingers of his right hand to encircle the ring finger on his left hand. He then looked down to my hands, but couldn't see them. They were in my lap and blocked by the person seated in front of me.

Would I give him that last consolation? I didn't want to hurt my husband. But considering I was the reason for Grizz's impending death, I felt the stirrings of an old, old obligation to comfort him in those last moments. At the same time, I felt an uncomfortable thrill in having some control over him. In having the ability to be in charge of something, to be the decision-maker, the empowered one. For once.

Perhaps I was the empowered one all along.

I felt my husband's hand on my left thigh, just above my knee. He gently squeezed. A memory almost twenty-five years old rushed over me of another hand squeezing my leg. A harder, crueler hand. I turned to look at my husband, and even though he was looking straight ahead, he was aware of my glance. He gave an almost imperceptible nod. He'd decided for me. I was okay with that.

I removed my wide wedding band and lifted my left hand so Grizz could see it. He smiled ever so slightly. Then he looked at my husband, nodded once and said, "Let's get this shit over with."

The warden asked if he had any last words. Grizz replied, "I just said 'em."

Leslie had caught the exchange between us and mouthed, "What?"

I ignored her. That was one part of my story that wouldn't make it into her article. Even though I'd vowed to be completely forthcoming, some things, no matter how insignificant, had to remain mine. This was one of them.

Grizz wasn't an easy prisoner, so the guards assigned to him were super-sized, just like him. Much to their surprise, this day he put up no resistance. He lay down and stared at the ceiling as his handcuffs were removed and he was strapped tightly to the gurney. He didn't flinch when the doctor inserted the IV needles, one in each arm. His shirt was unbuttoned and heart monitors were attached to his chest. I wondered why he didn't fight, wondered whether he'd been given a sedative of some sort. But I wouldn't ask.

He didn't glance around. He just closed his eyes and passed away. It took nine minutes. It sounds quick. Less than ten minutes. But for me, it was an eternity.

An elderly woman in the front row started to sob quietly. She said to the woman sitting next to her, "He didn't even say he was sorry."

The woman whispered back to her, "That's because he wasn't."

The doctor officially pronounced Grizz dead at 12:19 p.m. One of the guards walked over to the big window and closed the curtain. Done.

There were about ten of us in the small viewing room, and as soon as the curtain closed, almost everyone stood up and filed out without a word. I could still hear the elderly woman crying as her companion placed her arms around her shoulders and guided her toward the door.

Leslie looked at me and asked just a little too loudly, "You okay, Ginny?"

"I'm fine." I couldn't look at her. "Just no more interviews for the rest of the day."

"Yeah, sure, that's understandable. I have just a few more questions for you before I can wrap this story up. Let's meet tomorrow and talk."

My husband took my hand, stood with me and told Leslie, "It'll have to wait until we get home. You can reach us by phone to finish the interview."

My knees felt wobbly. I sat back down.

Leslie started to object, then noticed the expression on my husband's face and stopped herself from saying more. She managed a smile and said, "Okay then, until Sunday. Have a safe trip home."

She left the room.

My husband and I were the only ones remaining. I stood to leave and couldn't move. I fell into his arms, sobbing. He gently lowered me to the floor and sat down with me, holding me against him. I lay like that in his arms, crying, for a long time. A very long time.

Chapter One

It was May 15, 1975. A typical Thursday. A day just like any other day, nothing extraordinary or even remotely exciting about it.

But it would be the day that changed my life forever.

I'd gotten up a little earlier than usual that morning and done some chores before school. I didn't have to do chores, but I was used to doing for myself, and there were certain things I wanted done. I had a quick breakfast of toast and a glass of orange juice, then loaded up my little backpack. It wasn't really a backpack, more like a baggy cloth purse with strings that I could arrange around my shoulders and wear on my back for easy carrying. It looked small but could hold a lot.

That morning it would hold my wallet with my driver's permit and four dollars. I wasn't old enough to have an official license yet; I'd just turned fifteen three months before. The bag also held my reading glasses, a hairbrush, apple-flavored lip gloss, two tampons, a birth control packet and two schoolbooks: advanced geometry and chemistry. I'd finished my homework the night before, folded the notebook papers in half and stuck them between the pages of my books. Everything else I needed for my classes I kept in my locker at school.

I wore hip-hugger, bell-bottom blue jeans with a macramé belt, a flowery peasant top and sandals. I had on the same jewelry I wore every day: silver hoop earrings and a brown felt choker that had a dangling peace sign. Even though this was South Florida in May, the mornings could still get a little cool, so I wore a red and white poncho Delia had knitted.

That morning my stepfather, Vince, had driven me to the bus stop. I could've walked, but it was far, so I grabbed rides from Vince whenever I could. He would've taken me all the way to school, but he had to drive in the other direction to do that, and I had no problem riding the bus.

I might have asked Matthew for a ride, but something was off with him. Matthew was a senior I was tutoring, and we'd become close. We weren't a couple, but I knew he was interested. I was also becoming close to his family. I actually spent more time with them than my own. Less than a week ago, he'd kissed me goodnight on my front porch. But now he was telling me he wouldn't need my help with tutoring and he didn't have time to be my friend. Before, he was always offering to give me a lift to and from school. Not anymore, I guess. But like I said, I didn't have a problem with the bus.

"See ya later, kiddo," Vince said as I jumped out of his rickety van.

"Later, Vince."

That day was a regular day at school. I was spared the awkwardness of running into Matthew. We didn't take any of the same classes and didn't hang with the same crowd. But still, it would've been nice to ask him the reason behind the abrupt halt to our friendship. I was more curious than hurt. I mean, it was just a simple goodnight kiss.

I'd finished all my homework by the time Study Hall ended, which meant I could allow myself to go to the public library after school. If I'd had homework, I would've gone straight home or to Smitty's. But on days I didn't have homework, I loved to go to the county library and immerse myself in books. I'd been going there since grade school, and I'd made friends with everyone who worked there. I'd just need to take a different bus from school. We weren't supposed to swap buses without a signed permission slip each time, but the bus drivers all knew me, and Delia had given her approval earlier in the year. I did it so often they'd stopped asking for a slip.

"Hey Gin, no homework today, I see," Mrs. Rogers, the librarian, said as I walked through the doors. I just smiled and nodded at her as I headed for the card catalog. For a long time I'd been meaning to look up some books on John Wilkes Booth. We were studying President Lincoln's assassination in school, and I'd already devoured the books from the school library. I wanted to see if the local library had anything else to offer on the subject. I was in luck.

By five o'clock it was time to start packing things up, so I hauled my three books to the desk to check out.

"Need to make a call?" Mrs. Rogers asked.

"Yes, please," I replied. They were used to letting me use the phone to call Delia or Vince for a ride home.

Vince must have been running behind on his delivery schedule and wasn't back at the warehouse yet. I left a message saying I needed a ride home from the library, but that I'd try calling Delia too. Which I did, but there was no answer where she worked. That could've meant a few things: She'd left, or she was talking to a customer and didn't want to pick up the phone, or maybe she was in the back room and didn't hear it. Oh well, this had happened before. No big deal.

"You going to be okay, Ginny?" Mrs. Rogers asked. "I don't want to lock up and leave if you don't have a ride. I'd be glad to take you home."

She was sweet. She offered this every time I didn't have an immediate lift home.

"Oh, no problem, Mrs. Rogers. I'll walk over to the convenience store and get a drink. Vince knows to come by there if the library is closed."

And that's what I did. Like I had done a hundred times in the past. I bought a soda and sat out front with my back against the entrance. I drank my soda and was so engrossed in one of my books I barely noticed when a noisy motorcycle pulled up.

It wasn't until the person driving turned it off and started walking toward me that I realized someone was talking to me. I heard a little chuckle and then, "That must be some good book you got your face buried in. I've been asking you what you're reading since I got off my bike and you didn't even hear me."

I glanced up. He looked like a typical motorcycle guy. Average height. Brown, shaggy hair that just touched his collar. He wore jeans, boots and a white T-shirt under a leather jacket. He smiled then, and I answered with a smile of my own.

"History. Lincoln." That was all I said. I wasn't a flirt and didn't think he required any more than that. I immediately looked back down at the book I had propped up against my knees.

That answer seemed to suit him because he didn't say anything else as he swung the door open and proceeded inside.

He came out a few minutes later with a Coke. He squatted next to me and looked at the book I was reading as he drank his soda. Without any prompting he started to engage me in conversation about Abraham Lincoln and more specifically about Booth. I found what he said interesting so I closed my book and turned to give him my full attention. He was nice and seemed like an okay guy—nothing like what I'd expected a man on a motorcycle to be like.

After a few minutes of discussing John Wilkes Booth the conversation turned personal, but not in a disturbing way. He asked how old I was and seemed genuinely shocked when I told him fifteen. He asked me what grade I was in, where I went to school, my hobbies, stuff like that. He seemed really interested and even teased, "Well, I guess I'll have to come back in three years if I want to take you on a real date or something."

Oh, my goodness. He was flirting with me. I had boys at school flirt with me all the time. They'd say things like, "Gin, how come you're not out there cheering? You're just as pretty as the cheerleaders." They were always offering to give me a ride home or asking if I wanted to hang out after school.

The boy I'd been tutoring, Matthew, had seemed interested, too. At least up until a couple days ago. He was a popular senior and our school's star running back. He went by the nickname Rocket Man. He was cute and sweet and flunking two classes. I was tutoring him in English and math. Truth was, I liked boys, and Matthew was growing on me. I liked the kiss we shared. But I wasn't interested in a serious boyfriend, especially one who would be leaving for college in the fall. I had too much to accomplish before I could get involved in a relationship.

But this was a man flirting with me, not a boy. And I realized I was more than a little flattered that he was taking an interest in me.

Unfortunately, I didn't know how to flirt back, so I reopened my book and just pretended to keep reading while he talked.

After he finished his soda he asked, "So, what are you doing sitting in front of the convenience store? You waitin' on someone?"

"Yeah, my stepdad is supposed to pick me up. He should be here in a minute."

He stood up and looked around. "Well, I can give you a ride home. How far ya live?"

"Oh no, that's okay. I wouldn't want him to show up and me not be here. He would worry."

Actually, that wasn't true. Vince wouldn't see me here and assume Delia picked me up, and he would just go home.

"Can you call him or somethin' and let him know you're gettin' a ride?" Before I could answer he said, "You ever been on a motorcycle before? You'll like it. I'm a safe driver. I'll go real slow and let you wear my helmet."

Again I didn't answer, just looked at him.

He laughed then and said, "It's not like I can do anything to hurt you while you're on the back of my bike. Seriously, it's just a ride home. If you don't want me to know where you live, I can drop you at a corner close to your house. C'mon. Make an old guy's day."

"Why not?" I thought as I tried to mentally guess his age. He was older than me, but I didn't think he was an old guy. I closed my book and stood up.

"Well, I guess it'd be okay. I live off Davie Boulevard, just west of I-95. Is that out of your way?"

"No problem at all."

He tossed his Coke in a garbage can, came back over to me and held my bag open while I stowed my library book away. He made some comment about how my satchel was probably heavier than I was. He walked toward his motorcycle and grabbed his helmet, which had been hanging on the handlebar, and gave it to me. I put my bag on my back, took the helmet from him and put it on. It was loose, so he tightened the strap under my chin.

He swung a leg over the bike, started it up and then stood. I realized he was standing to make it easy for me to get on behind him, which I did with no problem. He revved the engine and I felt a little thrill at being on the back of a motorcycle with an older guy. I wasn't the type to care, but for a second or two I actually hoped someone I knew might see me. How prophetic that thought seemed much later. I yelled that I was going to have him drop me at Smitty's Bar and asked if he knew where it was on Davie Boulevard. He nodded yes.

I guess that was the moment I was officially abducted.

We started out in the direction I'd told him. At a red light he turned and asked if I was enjoying the ride. I nodded yes and he said very loudly that he was going to take a different route to give me a little longer ride. Not to worry though, he would get me safely to Smitty's. I didn't worry. Not even for a second. I was enjoying myself too much.

It wasn't until we were on State Road 84 heading west and missed the right turn onto U.S. 441 that I felt my first stirring of fear. It was then I realized I didn't even know his name, and that with all the small talk and questions he had for me at the 7-Eleven, he'd never even asked mine. That suddenly struck me as very weird.

I leaned up so my mouth was near his ear and shouted, "Hey, this is the really long way around. I have to be home soon or my parents will be worried."

He never acknowledged that he heard me.

I leaned back against the backrest on the motorcycle. *Don't panic, don't panic, don't panic.* My bag was still on my back, and I could feel the library books digging into me through the thin fabric. It was then that I noticed his jacket for the first time.

It was a skull with a sinister smile and what appeared to be some kind of horns. A naked woman, somehow tastefully covered, was draped seductively across the top of the skull. She had dark brown hair with bangs and big brown eyes. As I peered closer, I saw she was wearing a brown peace choker. I raised my hand to my neck. It looked just like mine. Before I could ponder that strange coincidence I looked lower. To my horror, I noticed the name embossed beneath the morbid design.

Satan's Army.

Chapter Two

I'd soon find out I was nothing more than a thank-you gift after a long initiation ritual.

I sat in the rickety lawn chair and surveyed my surroundings. I clutched my bag to my chest as I tried to adjust my eyes to the dimming light. There was a campfire and a hodgepodge circle of people surrounding it. I can't remember now if I couldn't make out their faces in the waning light or if I was too frightened to notice. I knew where I was but wasn't exactly sure what to do about it. I'd started praying as soon as I realized the seriousness of my predicament. I should've taken my chances when there were more people and cars around. I should've risked jumping off a moving motorcycle. It would have been better than what I faced now.

I remember starting to physically shake when the reality hit me as we'd made our way west on State Road 84.

These days 84 is updated and modernized, but in 1975 it was an under-developed two-way road. Today it runs parallel to a super highway, I-595, that takes you from the Everglades to the beach in a matter of minutes with all kinds of development in between—houses, schools, shopping centers and gas stations. In '75, it was the highway to hell, famous for its head-on collisions. It had little to no turnoffs with the exception of a little bar called Pete's.

When we passed Pete's I felt the nausea rising in my stomach. I knew there was nothing beyond it except the entrance to the deathtrap highway called Alligator Alley that connected the two Florida coasts. I thought the Miccosukee Indian Reservation was out there somewhere, but I didn't have a clue where.

It was getting dark and there were no other headlights in sight. About ten minutes after passing Pete's, we slowed and made a right onto a dirt road. I noticed some dim lights for the first time. Just a little way off the road, and barely visible due to the growing brush, was an old motel.

It was one of those little fifteen- or twenty-unit motels with old jalousie windows. It had an unlit sign identifying it as the Glades Motel. I hoped maybe it was still in business. A working motel might be good. Someone had to be running it. This might be my chance to explain I had made a mistake and ask to use the phone.

I guess it was originally built with the intention of giving travelers a place to stop in the middle of nowhere, but for whatever reason, it couldn't stay in business. As we pulled into the pitted and worn-down parking lot, I saw old gas pumps off to the right. It was obvious they were no longer in use. A couple of rooms had lights on, but what looked like the office showed no signs of life.

As we passed the old gas pumps I looked to my left and noticed a group of people between the motel and us. They were sitting around a dying campfire among the rusty old swings, slide and an antiquated carousel. It looked like a picnic and playground area that had seen better days. On the other side of the playground looked like a pool area. I couldn't tell for sure, but I thought it looked like it didn't have any water in it.

We circled to our left, and I noticed about six or seven motorcycles scattered in front of the units. He pulled up next to one and cut the engine. That's when I heard them.

It was a mixture of laughter, cursing and what sounded like two women arguing. I thought I heard Steppenwolf's "Magic Carpet Ride" coming from somewhere.

He stood up and said, "Get off."

I stood on the foot pegs and swung my leg over. My legs almost buckled, probably from a combination of the ride and fear, but I caught myself. I adjusted my backpack and stood straight. I figured the best way to deal with this was with confidence. I was scared to death, but darn if I was going to show it. He put the kickstand down and got off the bike.

"So, how long before you can give me a ride back?" I asked. I sounded a little too perky even to my own ears.

He didn't reply. He looked straight at me and gave me a smile that was born from pure evil. Was that the smile I'd seen at the 7-Eleven? I couldn't remember. How could I have not noticed it then? The realization of my situation hit me like a lead bullet.

I remembered once when Delia and Vince weren't home and one of his supposed friends stopped by. He'd convinced me to let him in the house to use the phone.

"You can trust me, sweetheart. I'm a friend of Vinny, your stepdaddy."

That should've been a red flag. Nobody called Vince by the nickname Vinny. I'd released the deadbolt and as I was leading him toward the kitchen, where our only phone was mounted to the wall, he grabbed me by the back of my hair and threw me on the cracked linoleum floor. That's when I knew true fear. I'd felt a heat slowly work its way up my spine.

Before anything could happen there was a loud pounding on the front door. It was our neighbor, Guido. That was his real name. Well, that was the name he told us. Vince was convinced Guido was some Mafia guy in the Witness Protection Program. He didn't fit into our neighborhood at all. He was a total bully, and now he was loudly complaining because Vince's friend had parked on his lawn.

That's what Guido did. He sat on his front porch and waited for someone to do something wrong so he could assert himself. Normally I disliked Guido, but at that moment, his big mouth and heavy New York accent were music to my ears.

The mystery man, who never mentioned his name, had flipped me on my back and was sitting on my stomach with one hand over my mouth and the other holding both of my hands over my head. He was yelling for Guido to go away and that he'd move his truck when he damn well pleased. It wasn't until Guido threatened to call the police that the man let go of my hands and jumped off me in one swift movement.

He told me if I ever told anyone what happened he would come back and finish what he'd started. I told him it would just be our secret. I wouldn't say a word. I wasn't hurt. No harm done. I would never tell. He could trust me.

I told. The minute Delia and Vince got home I told, and they called the police. After I described him and Guido described his truck, Vince knew who he was. Some low-life drifter named Johnny Tillman, who'd been hanging out at my parents' local haunt, Smitty's Bar on Davie Boulevard. He wasn't a friend of Vince's, but he'd had enough conversations with him to learn his name. How he'd known about me, I had an idea. I'd never seen him before, but he may have seen me. When I couldn't get a ride from my friends, sometimes I'd walk from the school bus stop to Smitty's to wait for Delia or Vince to give me a ride home. They could be counted on to stop in for a beer most days. The owner was a real nice lady. I'd sit in the corner and do homework, and she'd give me an orange soda and French fries on the house.

Now, standing in the middle of nowhere, Steppenwolf playing and motorcycle guy still smiling evilly, I was so paralyzed with fear I couldn't even remember her name. But one thing I wish I could forget was Delia's remark after that incident: "How can someone as smart as you do something so ridiculously dumb?"

Back then, I'd tried to reason my way out of it: "But Delia, he knew

Vince." I'd even tried to convince myself the man seemed familiar. But that was a lie. She was right. It was the stupidest thing I'd ever done.

Until an hour ago.

Now all I could think was, "You're on your own, girlie. No Guido here this time."

Motorcycle guy grabbed me roughly by the arm and pulled me forward. "C'mon, time to meet your new family."

Family? I was in too much shock to try to decipher that remark. We walked toward the group of people sitting around a campfire, the noise from earlier slowly fading. As we approached, I heard a long, low whistle and comments coming from all directions.

"Oooh, look what Monster brought us."

"Hey Monster, thought you liked blondes and gigantic titties."

"That one'll bring in a pretty penny. Help pay the bills."

Then a shrill female voice hissed, "Don't know what you think you're doin' bringing that piece of trash here."

A very articulate male voice retorted, "What's the matter, Willow? Afraid Grizz might be interested? Everyone knows he likes brunettes, and I'm pretty sure he's had his fill of you."

"Fuck you, Fess, and your momma and your daddy. She's too scrawny for Grizz and ugly, too."

Good, let them think I'm scrawny, ugly. Anything to get me out of here.

A gravelly male voice added, "No, she ain't none of that, Willow. But don't you worry, honey. You've been with Grizz going on two years now. He ain't ever lasted that long with one woman. I guess it's really love with you guys."

That seemed to placate Willow. The exchanges were so quick and the campfire so dim I couldn't put a face to a voice. My captor roughly plopped me down in a scratchy lawn chair within the group, then took the one beside me. I leaned forward, took my backpack off and placed it in my lap. I realized I wasn't wearing my poncho and the most ridiculous thought popped into my head that at least my poncho was safe and sound at the library. I wrapped my arms around my bag and started to look around, assessing my surroundings.

That's when my captor spoke. "Where's Grizz?"

Monster. I think that's what someone called him. Monster. God help me.

"He's here somewhere. Just went in to make a call, I think," someone answered.

"Why? What you need Grizz for?" snapped Willow.

Monster leaned forward in his chair as if to emphasize his point. "Well, bitch," he spat, "I want to show Grizz my gratitude for letting me be a member. You know, like with a thank-you gift. And this here is it," he said, waving his hand in front of my face.

I felt like a prize on some cheesy game show, and Monster was the model showing off the goods. Of course, I couldn't have been any further away from a soundstage somewhere in California than I was at that moment.

"It being what? Her?" Willow snarled.

My eyes had somewhat adjusted to the dim light, and I finally saw the source of the irritatingly shrill voice. Willow picked this moment to stand up and point at me, the campfire illuminating her. She was small. I couldn't guess her age, but she was probably younger than she looked. She had mousy blonde hair that hung limply around her face. There was nothing really special about that face, although I thought maybe she'd been really pretty at one time. She had smudged dark makeup under each eye. Her eyebrows were pencil-thin and overly arched, which added to her sinister look. She probably didn't need expressive eyebrows to achieve that, though. Hard living, probably including some serious drug use, had aged her. Even in the dim light I could see traces of slight acne scars, and her cheekbones were almost too prominent. They stuck out in sharp contrast to the hollowness that had likely been full cheeks at one time. She was wearing a purple tube top and ratty jeans that rested on her bony hips. And she called me scrawny? She had an assortment of dirty macramé and beaded bracelets on both arms. Almost every part of her skin that was showing was covered in tattoos with the exception of her face and hands. I looked down and saw she wasn't wearing any shoes. Her feet and toenails were filthy.

This was Grizz's woman? Whoever this Grizz was, I wondered if he was into dirty feet.

"Yeah her, Willow. I saw her sitting at the 7-Eleven and thought she looked like the girl on our jacket. Then I saw the damn choker and knew I had to get her for Grizz. Got a problem with that?"

"Damn right I do. He ain't gonna want her and you and your stupid ass should know better than to bring her here."

"Well why don't we let Grizz decide."

"Let Grizz decide what?"

I was so busy watching the exchange between Willow and Monster I didn't notice the large man walk up. Startled, I turned my head to the left and was eye level with the zipper of a pair of blue jeans. I slowly raised my eyes and my breath actually caught in my throat.

I thought Monster and his evil smile were something to fear. The man who stood next to me was not only large and impressive in appearance, but I could feel his raw energy and aggression radiating like a beacon. This was a person of authority. This was a person you didn't mess with.

This was Grizz.

He was the reason I was abducted, and I feared I now belonged to him.

At that moment my mind went in a million directions. I remember hearing snippets of conversation as to why I was there. Apparently Monster, the newest member of this group or gang or whatever they were, had just finished an initiation ritual. This final part wasn't required, and from what I later learned rarely, if ever, carried out: Kidnapping someone to be presented to the leader as a thank-you gift to do with whatever they wanted.

That was me. The thank-you gift. Now that I thought about it, Monster's leather jacket looked brand-spanking new. He couldn't have been part of this group for very long.

Just then my eyes reached Grizz's, and he was looking down at me. I couldn't read his expression. He wasn't classically handsome, but he wasn't ugly either. He was rugged, hard. Even in the semidarkness I could see he had compelling eyes. He was wearing a T-shirt that had the sleeves ripped off. He was muscular and covered in tattoos. His hair looked dirty blonde or maybe light brown, a little long and unkempt. I couldn't guess his age. For someone with such authority, he seemed like he should have been older than he looked. But I couldn't tell.

The dim light and my own fear caused all reason and clarity to leave my brain. I suddenly couldn't think or feel. I was numb.

He didn't smile. He didn't frown. He just continued to stare down at me with those eyes. Willow's voice broke the spell.

"Stupid asshole here thinks you're gonna want this little scrawny piece of shit, Grizz. I told him you wouldn't like her. Right, baby? You don't want her, do ya? The guys can have her, huh? If she's a gift to you, you can do whatever you want with her, like give her away. Right, baby? And he should know better than to bring someone here. Gonna kick his ass, aren't ya babe?"

He looked up then and stared at Willow without saying anything. I could see her face, and it had a pleading look. She wouldn't take her eyes off of him. Just stared with that look of someone who knows they've just lost.

She then turned her anger on me. She lunged at me with her hands outstretched. She was going for my neck.

Before she reached me, Grizz grabbed her by the throat and lifted her off the ground with one hand. He had her suspended, and she was kicking her feet. She had both her hands wrapped around his one hand and was trying to pry his fingers loose. Gurgling sounds came from her throat. Without saying a word, he tossed her, and she fell onto one of the flimsy lawn chairs, crushing it beneath her.

A figure rose from the group and went to her. I recognized the gravelly voice from earlier.

"It'll be okay Willow, honey. He'll play with her a couple of days and be back in your bed before the weekend is over." The man tried to help her up but she brushed him off.

"Shut the fuck up, Froggy," Willow barked. "You don't know nothin'. I'm supposed to feel better knowing my man is sleeping with that white-trash piece of shit? You just leave me alone. Stop touching me! I can get myself up."

She stood up and brushed herself off. She stuck her nose in the air like a queen and started to walk toward the motel.

"I'll be in our room, Grizz darlin', waitin' for ya, honey. Just come on home when you're done and I'll show you how a real woman feels underneath ya."

I watched her walk to the motel, open one of the doors and walk in. I looked back up and he was staring down at me. Without taking his eyes off mine he said, "Moe, take her to number four. Settle her in. Stay with her."

Take who? Me?

A tiny person rose from the ground. She'd been sitting close to the fire and had been staring into it during the whole scene. At first I'd thought she was a young boy. I remember thinking they had kids here so it couldn't be too bad. Now that hope was gone. She had short, jet-black hair. She was wearing a Black Sabbath T-shirt, black jeans and combat boots. As she rose and walked toward us, I could see her face was done up with black eye makeup to the extreme. She probably had a pretty face under all that paint. As an adult I would see young girls made up during the Goth craze, and I would think none of them held a candle to Moe. The original Goth girl.

Without saying a word she walked over to me and just stood there. She didn't meet my eyes, but looked at the ground. I looked to my right where Monster was sitting. He wasn't even looking at me. Sometime during the last ten minutes (or had it been an hour?) he'd gotten a beer and was sitting there with his head thrown back, chugging it. To his right was the man called Froggy, the one who tried to help Willow. He was looking down at the broken lawn chair. Maybe he was trying to see if he could fix it. I don't remember anyone else, although I know they were all there that night. Sitting around the campfire, watching, waiting, obeying.

I stood up and Moe slowly walked toward the motel. I clutched my bag to my chest and looked straight ahead as I followed her. Without turning around I knew with certainty that those mesmerizing eyes would watch me until I was behind the closed door of room number four.

Made in the USA
Middletown, DE
22 September 2019